THE MAGICIAN'S DIARY

GLASS AND STEELE, #4

C.J. ARCHER

WWW.CJARCHER.COM

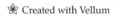

CHAPTER 1

LONDON, SPRING 1890

*I*mpatience was a disease that infected us all. The air in the entrance hall of number sixteen Park Street, Mayfair, thickened as Matt, Cyclops, Willie and I stared at Chronos, who stood just inside the threshold.

My grandfather.

I felt as though I ran a fever, with my trembling hands and skin alternately hot and cold. My head may as well have been suffering from the fog of a fever for all its sudden lack of clarity. I'd had questions moments before. So many questions. But they'd fled, and only two clear thoughts remained.

Chronos was my grandfather.

And we'd found the man who could fix Matt's magic watch.

Willie recovered from her shock first. She patted Matt's waistcoat at his chest and muttered, "Where is it? Show it to him."

Matt closed his hand over his cousin's. "We have a guest, Willie. There'll be time for that later."

"We ain't got time to play tea parties, Matt!"

He plucked her hand away and kept it enclosed in his. She winced. "Mr. Steele?" Matt said with a tone that fell just shy of

1

being pleasant thanks to the strain in his voice. "We dine in a little over an hour. Will you join us?"

Chronos looked over his shoulder at the formidable figure of Cyclops standing with his arms crossed over an enormous chest. His good eye drilled into Chronos, and the scar dripping from beneath the patch over the other eye would make most men think twice about attempting escape.

Chronos cleared his throat. "I would be delighted."

"You English and your goddamned manners," Willie scoffed.

"Matt's not English," I said automatically.

"He's been around you too long, India. It's brought out the English half of him. Come on then, Matt. Let's go to the drawing room so Chronos can look at your watch before dinner."

I had a quick word with Bristow to set another place for dinner and to inform Miss Glass. Ever the unruffled butler, he moved silently toward the service stairs at the back of the house.

Matt waited for me at the door to the drawing room, the others having gone in ahead of him. His eyes were bright and his breathing a little fast as he held his hand out to me.

"Are you all right, India?" he asked as I took his hand.

"Somewhat overwhelmed, but I'll recover. And you?"

He placed my hand in the crook of his arm and covered it with his own. "I had no idea until now that it was possible to feel both numb and thrilled at the same time."

We entered the drawing room together to face the man with the power to bring Matt back to full health. I had no idea where or how to start, but it was Chronos himself who broke the silence.

"I didn't get to finish my ale at the Cross Keys before your man accosted me."

Matt tugged on the bell pull and Peter the footman

appeared a moment later. "A brandy for Mr. Steele," he said and the footman left again.

Willie slid a round occasional table next to a winged chair and moved the vase of flowers from its surface to another table. She slapped the chair's back rest. "Sit, Mr. Steele. You've got work to do."

Chronos tensed. His gaze flicked to Matt.

"Sit!" Willie grabbed Chronos's arm and forced him down onto the chair. "Have you got your tools? If not, India can lend you hers."

"Willie," Matt chided. "Give him a few minutes to settle. Mr. Steele, I'm sorry for the inconvenience. I hope Cyclops wasn't too forceful."

Chronos rubbed his shoulder. "He was insistent."

Cyclops apologized. "I asked nicely," he added. "The first two times."

"Why didn't you want to come?" Willie asked.

Chronos sank into the chair. He looked small within its bulk, but not frail. I calculated dates quickly in my head—he was seventy-one, and he looked it with the multitude of wrinkles and a cloud of wispy white hair. Considering his age, having Cyclops order him into a carriage must have been frightening. So why resist?

"Your servant is certainly loyal to you, Mr. Glass," Chronos said.

"Cyclops is a friend, not a servant. As is Duke," Matt added when Duke entered behind Peter. "Willie is my cousin."

The footman deposited a tray on the table then bowed out. He shut the door behind him.

"Why isn't he working on your watch yet?" Duke asked Matt. He smelled of horse and leather after driving the carriage to the coach house. Until Matt hired a new coachman, Duke would share the role with Cyclops.

Matt poured from the decanter and handed the tumbler to Chronos. Chronos sipped, nodded his approval, and drank the entire contents. Willie crossed her arms in a pose that matched Cyclops's and mouthed, "Drunk."

Chronos held the empty glass out for more. Duke snatched it before Matt could. "After you've looked at Matt's watch," Duke grumbled.

"We are sorry about this." I forced myself to speak. I would have liked to sit quietly and observe before saying anything, but that would serve no purpose. I agreed with Willie and Duke—the sooner he looked at Matt's watch, the better. Answers to my other questions could wait. "Cyclops probably told you that Matt's magic watch is slowing down. It needs fixing, and Dr. Parsons suggested that only you know the spell. Would you mind, Mr.—" I cut myself off. "What should I call you? Mr. Steele doesn't seem right considering…"

"I'm your grandfather." He studied me, his light gray eyes scanning my face twice before sweeping down my length and back up again. "You look like your mother." He gave no indication whether that was a good or bad thing.

"It doesn't feel right to call you Grandpapa either."

He grunted. In approval? With laughter? I couldn't tell. "Chronos will do."

Willie tapped a finger on the tabletop. "Matt. Your watch."

Matt pulled his magic watch out from the inside pocket of his waistcoat where he kept it safe from thieving fingers. There'd already been one attempt to take it, most likely coordinated by Sheriff Payne, the man who wanted to destroy Matt in any way possible.

"The magic is not as effective," Matt said as he handed the watch to Chronos. "I need to use it every few hours rather than every few weeks. Nor does it bring me back to full strength when I do use it."

"That's hardly surprising." Chronos turned the watch over and pried open the back to reveal the ordinary inner workings of the device. "Magic never lasts. How long has it been?

Five years? That's longer than I expected." He sounded pleased with himself.

My chest tightened. I didn't dare look at Matt but I could feel the effect Chronos's words had on everyone. It was as if the air had been sucked out of the room and no one could breathe.

"But you *can* fix it?" Willie prompted in a thin voice.

Chronos plucked a small cloth wallet from his inside jacket pocket and set it down beside the watch on the table. He unbuttoned the cloth and opened it out to reveal an eyeglass, tweezers, a screwdriver and vials containing spare gears of various sizes. He removed the eyeglass but paused when I leaned in to get a better look.

"I have depthing and gear rounding tools upstairs if you need them," I said, leaning away again.

"I don't need tools. The problem is with magic, not the watch. I just need a spell."

He inspected the mechanisms through the glass then placed the watch to his ear. He said something in a foreign language. The watch glowed purple, the soft light the same color that infused Matt's veins when he used it to heal himself. Chronos spoke a few more words of the spell then closed the watch's back. The light extinguished. He returned it to Matt.

"Try it now," he said.

"Try?" Duke echoed, his head cocked to the side. "You don't know if it's fixed?"

Chronos concentrated on putting the eyeglass away and folding the cloth kit. "That's the same spell I used to infuse the watch with magic the day I extended your life, Mr. Glass."

It wasn't a direct answer to the question, but no one else seemed to notice. Duke nodded, satisfied, and Willie and Cyclops only had eyes for Matt. He opened the case, closed his fist around the watch, and breathed deeply as the magic seeped through his skin to join his blood. The web of light disappeared into his cuffs and re-emerged above his collar. It quickly spread over his face to the tips of his ears.

With a deep breath, he snapped the case shut and the light extinguished. His skin was normal again.

"How do you feel?" Willie asked on a breath.

"Fine," he said without taking his gaze off Chronos.

Chronos slapped his hands down on the chair arms. "Then I'll be off. Thank you for the dinner invitation—"

"Wait," Matt said. "India will have some questions for you."

I blinked hard, smarting from the sting of Chronos's rejection. Did he not have questions for *me*? He'd not seen me since I was a baby. Didn't he at least want to know how my father—his son—had died?

Chronos turned his back to me.

"Mrs. Potter is cooking a leg of lamb," Cyclops said hopefully.

Chronos strode to the window and peered out. He looked up and down the street, twice. "I can afford another hour or so, I suppose."

"Are you looking for someone?" Duke asked.

Chronos returned to the chair. He glanced at me, sitting on the sofa. "You will want to know why I didn't contact you all these years."

I nodded. "Before you answer my questions, I think someone should tell you that you're not going anywhere until we know if Matt's watch is fixed. It'll be a few hours before we're certain."

The wrinkles around Chronos's mouth flattened. "I am a prisoner?"

"No," Matt said at the same time Duke, Cyclops and Willie said, "Yes."

"We are requesting your help in this matter," Matt said with a hard edge directed at his friends.

"The matter of saving his life," Willie added.

"A life that should have ended five years ago," Chronos shot back.

That silenced her like nothing ever had.

I watched Chronos, but he did not look my way. I wanted to get his measure, but he wasn't making it easy. All I knew was that his eyes were clear and his hands had moved quickly and with confidence when he handled Matt's watch. Despite his age, he was able bodied and had his wits about him.

"How many people have you saved by combining your magic with a doctor's?" I asked.

Matt's chin jutted forward and he frowned. He'd probably expected a more personal question. From the way Chronos's brows arched, he had too.

"Just the one," Chronos said, studying his hand as it gripped the chair arm. "Magical doctors don't grow on trees. They aren't born every year, and Dr. Parsons refused to try again after that time in Broken Creek." He clicked his tongue and shook his head.

"He's dead," Matt told him.

"I know."

"Have you ever met another magical doctor?"

"No."

"Are you searching for one?" Cyclops asked.

Chronos gave him a flat smile. "Yes."

I cleared my throat to get his attention. "If you haven't combined your magic with another doctor's since you saved Matt's life, you won't know if the spell you just spoke has fixed his watch."

"You are correct, India."

"But Dr. Parsons said you could fix it!" Willie cried.

"How would he know?" Chronos said. "He was guessing. I'm guessing. Everyone is guessing, Miss Glass."

"It's Miss Johnson, but everyone just calls me Willie," she muttered, once again deflated. "The Glasses are Matt's English relatives, and the Johnsons are American, on his mother's side. You must remember me from Broken Creek."

"Why? Did you have a magic watch? Are you a magical doctor or other type of magician?"

"Well…no."

I bristled at his tone. It was almost impossible to offend Willie and yet he'd done it without batting an eyelid. Was he truly so selfish that he only noticed people of interest to him? Was he so obsessed with magic that those without it were inconsequential?

"Did you try to fix it?" It took me a moment to realize he spoke to me since he didn't quite look at me. "The watch? Did you try to fix it, India?"

"I took it apart," I said. "As a simple watch, it works perfectly. When I discovered its importance to Matt, I knew it required magic and that I was out of my depth."

"Are you a magician?"

"Yes."

He grunted. "He didn't teach you about your magic, did he?"

"Do you mean my father?" I asked. "No. He wasn't a magician."

"He was."

"No, he—"

"He *was*. But he denied that part of himself. Denied that part of you too, it seems. How did you discover your magic?"

"Slowly, through a series of events, almost two months ago."

"Two months!" That finally made him look directly at me. "You've only just learned about your talent?"

"I've only just learned about the existence of magic at all. I was as unaware as the artless," I said, using the word magicians used to describe someone without magic. "I don't know any spells."

The pattern of wrinkles on Chronos's brow drew together.

"Elliot did you a disservice. He should not have denied you the knowledge. To be an adult and not know your power! How old are you?"

"Twenty-seven."

"An old maid."

My back stiffened. "I had a fiancé." I don't know why I needed to defend my spinsterhood to him. Perhaps because I felt incomplete, somehow, as if I lacked a certain quality that other women—married women—did.

"He turned out to be as crooked as a dog's hind legs," Willie said. "As her kin, you ought to call him out. I can tell you where he lives, if you like, and lend you my Colt."

"India's marital status is none of your affair," Matt said to Chronos. "If you're worried about her, then I can assure you she has a home here for as long as she wishes." His voice softened. "Her company is most welcome."

The papers for my Willesden cottage, bought with the reward money after I helped the police catch the Dark Rider, sat in my dressing table drawer along with papers from Matt's lawyer to lease it out. I had not signed them, as I intended to move to the cottage and commute to Mayfair when required. Matt didn't like the idea and tried to convince me to stay, only relenting earlier today when I insisted.

Except it wasn't what I *wanted*, but what I *needed*.

"You live here?" Chronos's face clouded. "With Mr. Glass?"

My spine stiffened even more. "And other people, including his elderly aunt. You'll meet her at dinner." No doubt she was changing into something more appropriate for dining with a guest.

"Your parents would not approve. They were very…moral."

"You make it sound as if that is a fault."

"Merely an inconvenience."

"Is that why you avoided them after I was born? Is that why you have not sought me out all this time? Is that why you never came to my father's funeral?" I heard the pitch of my voice rise, felt my face heat, yet I couldn't control my anger. I didn't want to control it. This man deserved my ire—and more. "He was your son! Your only child! I am your only living relative and you...you abandoned me!"

He shot up from the chair again. "I didn't ask for this." He strode to the door, only to be blocked by both Duke and Cyclops. He did not turn around but stood with his back to me, hands fisted at his sides.

"What did you expect me to say to you?" I pushed on. "You expect me to welcome you with open arms and forgive you? You haven't even tried to explain why you didn't contact me all these years."

"You misunderstand, India. I expected your anger. What I meant was I didn't ask for a granddaughter, or a son, or marriage. I didn't ask for any of it! Yet here I am, countless years later, burdened by my past. And by the knowledge that you exist."

Every word was like a punch, knocking the breath out of me. Matt moved to my side and placed a hand on my shoulder, but it didn't stop my trembling. With his touch came the brutal reminder of why Chronos was here, and that we needed him on-side. I sucked in several breaths to dampen my anger.

"I thought you were dead," I choked out, in the hope it would justify my outburst.

Matt's hand moved from my shoulder to the back of my neck, cooling my hot skin. Chronos took that moment to face us. He noted the position of Matt's hand and huffed out a breath through his nose. I couldn't determine what he thought, however, and I didn't care.

"I'm afraid India is correct," Matt said. "We can't let you go until we know if your spell worked and the watch is fixed. I'm sorry, Chronos, but it's necessary. We'll know in a few hours."

"And if it didn't work?" Chronos asked.

"You try again," Willie bit back. "You try again and again and again until you make it work. Understood?"

Chronos's nostrils flared and he glanced at the window again.

Matt moved to the window and looked out. "Are you expecting anyone?"

"Just checking that no one followed me." Chronos sat again and eyed the empty glass. Duke poured him another drink then one for himself.

"Who would follow you?" Matt asked.

Chronos shrugged one shoulder and sipped.

Matt strode up to him and leaned down, his hands on the chair arms, his nose an inch from Chronos's. "I hope you haven't brought danger to my friends and family," he growled.

"It won't be me who has brought danger to your door, Glass. It will have been you, since I had no say in coming here." Chronos lifted the glass in salute and drank.

Matt returned to the window where he stood watch, arms crossed, his gaze sweeping the darkening street outside.

I ought to have taken the opportunity to ask Chronos about my magic, but I couldn't bring myself to speak to him. For his part, he'd taken to not looking at me again. Perhaps that meant he was ashamed of his words. Good. He deserved to be embarrassed, at the very least. Remorse was perhaps too much to ask.

Willie had no such qualms. "If India's father was also a magician, why didn't he teach her how to use her magic?" she asked.

"To keep me safe," I said.

"To spite me," Chronos said.

"That's absurd and self-centered."

"And yet true. Elliot hated me."

"Considering you have just told me you regret being a

husband and father, is it any wonder?" I had never aired my dirty laundry in public before, except for that one time I berated Eddie Hardacre in the shop after he ended our engagement. But I felt no shame speaking to Chronos like this in front of my friends. Their presence gave me the confidence to allow my anger free reign, because I knew they were on my side. "My father was a good man. He didn't deserve your disapproval."

"I never said I disapproved of him. You're not listening, India." Chronos spoke mildly, as if I were a child in need of guidance. I disliked him even more because of it. "I said I regretted being his father. I'm not the sort of man who ought to marry and father children. I'm selfish—"

"Clearly."

My muttered comment earned a grunt from Chronos. "I'm selfish and arrogant. I prefer to be alone, accompanied only by my ambitions."

"That ambition being to extend life by combining your magic with a doctor's?"

He nodded. "I've made it my life's work, my *raison d'être*. Mr. Glass wouldn't be here if I had not. Ironic, isn't it? My granddaughter discovers she detests me because my ambition overrides my familial attachment, and yet it's that ambition which saved the man she's dependent upon."

"I am not dependent on him. On anyone! I have a cottage in Willesden. I'm going to move into it soon."

I glanced toward Duke as his head jerked to look at me and caught sight of Cyclops's face too. His jaw hardened and he focused that single eye on me with unwavering intensity.

"You can't leave!" Willie declared. "Not now!"

"I'll visit almost every day," I said. "Anyway, I thought you would be pleased. You never wanted me here in the first place."

She sniffed. "Changed my mind. Got to have someone to

teach poker to. Letty ain't no fun. Did you know about this, Matt?"

"I did," he said quietly from the window. "If India wants to leave, she can. We can't keep her here."

She folded her arms and slumped back into the chair. "It ain't right."

Chronos ambled over to the clock beneath the glass dome on the mantelpiece. "Very nice. Very expensive." He touched the glass and recoiled. "It's hot. Magic heat." He eyed me over his shoulder, a deep line connected his eyebrows. "Have you worked on this?"

"I've worked on all the clocks and watches in this house."

"Because you need to," he finished for me, turning back to the clock.

I didn't confirm it. He must know the restlessness that came with *not* working with timepieces.

"You lied." His words dropped like stones into the silence.

"I beg your pardon," Matt growled before I could think of a retort. "India is not a liar."

"She is. The magic here is so warm it almost burns and yet she tells me she has only just learned of her magic and doesn't know any spells. Unless another watchmaker magician has worked on this, she's lying."

Matt's stance relaxed. I even heard a grudging laugh escape his lips.

Chronos's eyes narrowed. "What aren't you telling me?"

"That's not your business," Matt said.

"India?"

"You have your secrets," I told Chronos. "And I have mine."

He smirked and nodded slowly. In approval of my retort? "I'll tell you who I suspect is following me and why if you tell me why this clock is warm yet you did not work a spell on it."

"Very well."

"India," Matt said quietly. "I don't think that's wise."

"I disagree. Chronos is precisely the man who should be told what I can do. If anyone can guide me, he can."

"Guide you?" Chronos rolled his eyes to the ceiling rose and shook his head. "Just because I'm old doesn't mean I would make a good teacher. Besides, I can't stay here simply to teach a raw magician, so don't expect that of me."

"Oh?" I said sweetly. "So you don't wish to know why my magic incapacitates people?"

His eyes became huge. "Incapacitates them? What are you talking about?"

I sighed. It was odd to him too, which meant he'd never heard of such a thing and probably couldn't help me after all. "Never mind."

"Tell me. I'm intrigued." He touched the dome again and this time let his hand linger. "And tell me how you used magic without a spell. It should be impossible."

"Not for India," Matt said with a hint of pride.

"Do we have an agreement, Chronos?" I asked. "My information in exchange for yours?" He nodded, so I went on. "When my life is in danger, any clocks nearby that I've touched save me. My watch too."

His crackling laugh faded when he saw that no one laughed with him.

I told him how my watch chain wrapped around the wrist of my attackers and sent shocks through them, and how a clock I'd thrown had diverted its course to hit my assailant. Chronos's face grew graver, all hint of mockery gone. He did not offer comment when I finished.

"Have you experienced such a thing?" I asked him. "Or heard of other magicians whose creations save their lives?"

He shook his head. "Remarkable. All that and without a spell. Your magic is incredibly strong."

"Why?" I blurted out. "Why am I like this?"

There was a knock on the door and Bristow entered upon Matt's word. "Dinner will be served in fifteen minutes, sir."

"Thank you, Bristow."

"And Miss Glass wishes to meet Mr. Steele. I've managed to delay her so far."

"I'll be out to speak to her in a moment, but she'll have to wait to meet Mr. Steele. Our guest wishes to freshen up for dinner."

Chronos looked surprised to be allowed out of the drawing room until he noticed Matt's nod at Cyclops.

"Come with me," Cyclops said to Chronos.

"We'll finish our conversation later," Matt said. "You owe us an explanation."

Chronos followed Cyclops out. Willie watched him leave with a scowl. "It ain't a good idea to let him out of your sight, Matt."

"Cyclops has it in hand."

I rose to leave too, wanting to change my outfit for dinner. Matt walked with me up the stairs.

"How do you feel?" I asked him.

He paused then said, "It's too soon to tell."

"Nonsense. You feel no different, do you? If you did, you would say so."

The corner of his mouth kicked up but there was no humor in his crooked smile. "I cannot hide anything from you, India. You're right. I don't feel as healed as I used to when the watch worked perfectly."

I swore under my breath and Matt stopped mid-step to stare at me.

"My apologies," I said. "But I'm upset."

He opened his mouth to speak but shouts from the depths of the house had us both spinning around to find the source. Below us, Bristow rushed into the entrance hall.

"Mr. Duke! Mr. Duke!" he cried between gasping breaths.

Duke and Willie appeared at the drawing room door. "What is it?" Duke said.

"Mr. Cyclops requests your urgent assistance." He waved Duke toward the back of the house. "Go!"

Duke ran off, Willie on his heels.

Matt hurried down the stairs. The butler looked startled to see him there. "What is it, Bristow? What's happened?"

Bristow breathed deeply and pressed a hand to his chest. "Mr. Steele has run away, sir."

CHAPTER 2

*M*att sprinted past Bristow, not a hint of ill health in his strides. I could not keep up but followed the echo of his footsteps down the service stairs to the kitchen. The housekeeper, Mrs. Bristow, pointed wordlessly at the scullery. I raced into the scullery only to back track when I heard Willie's angry shouts coming from outside.

I joined her and the others in the courtyard, halting at the sight of Chronos lying face down on the cobbles, his arm twisted at his back by Cyclops. "Don't hurt him!" I cried.

Cyclops let go and assisted Chronos to stand. He held him until the older man regained his balance. Chronos's hair stood on end, floating above his head like reeds swaying in the breeze. He dusted off his hands, but there were no grazes. He appeared to be unharmed.

"Are you all right?" I asked, taking his hand and patting it.

He snatched it away and straightened his neckerchief. "Of course."

"Cyclops was rough with you."

"I said I'm all right. Don't fuss."

I linked my fingers behind my back, trying not to let Chronos's words sting. My grandfather didn't like to be reminded of his age, that's all. Pushing me away wasn't personal.

Cyclops looked down at his feet. "I didn't want him to get away, India. I'm sorry."

I was about to tell him that he ought to apologize to Chronos, not me, when Chronos said, "I got past you though, eh? There's life in these legs yet."

Cyclops grunted. "I underestimated you. You've got vigor for a man of your age."

"I may be old but I'm not pathetic. Perhaps you're just slow because of your size. And your face must scare women and children wherever you go, eh?"

I turned on my heel and stalked back to the house. Cyclops didn't have to apologize to that rude old codger.

* * *

I WAS LATE TO DINNER, joining the others well after the gong sounded.

"Finally!" Miss Glass announced upon seeing me descend the staircase. "We're all half starved, India. Let's proceed without delay before we expire."

I apologized for my tardiness and headed into the dining room behind her. Chronos was flanked by both Duke and Cyclops, with Willie ahead and Matt behind. They seated him on the opposite side of the table from the exit.

Introductions must have been made in my absence because Miss Glass spoke freely to Chronos. Indeed, she carried almost the entire conversation throughout the three courses. If she noticed that Chronos was practically a prisoner, she did not let on. Nor did she seem to notice his disinterest in the dull yet safe topics. He even appealed to me on one occasion by asking why the family shop had been sold.

"That's not a conversation for the dinner table," I said. I was already angry with him, and discussing how Eddie had stolen my shop from me would only make me angrier. It was better than being upset by it, as I used to be, but it was still not appropriate for dinner.

Finally the meal ended, and Matt managed to convince his aunt to retire for the evening. I suspected she knew something was afoot and that Chronos wasn't merely my long-lost grandfather returned to London to be with his granddaughter. Her good manners were far too ingrained to let on, however.

Ordinarily, after a dinner party, the men would retreat to the smoking room and the women would wait for them in the drawing room. But this was no ordinary dinner party and we all filed into the drawing room together. Bristow served drinks then retreated, closing the door behind him.

Duke and Cyclops took up positions by the door without being asked. Willie sat in the seat by the window, perhaps thinking to block it too. I doubted Chronos was sprightly enough to make his exit through the window, however, but I didn't say so.

He eyed his captors with a narrowed gaze and tight lips. "Lucky you have good brandy," he said to Matt. "Or I might not be so willing to spend time in your company."

I gripped my glass harder. Clearly spending time with *me* was not something he considered worthwhile either.

"We have unfinished business," Matt said, taking a seat beside me on the sofa. "India kept her side of the bargain, now it's your turn. Tell us who you're hiding from and why."

Chronos studied the glass he cradled in both hands. "The Watchmaker's Guild, among others, would like to punish me."

My heart thundered once in my chest then stilled. It would seem getting into trouble with the Watchmaker's Guild was a family trait.

"As to why, that's a long story."

"It's because you're a magician," I said.

"In part. I'm a magician who is not content to grow old in his workshop tinkering with timepieces belonging to the artless. They would put up with me if I hid my magic like your father. But that's not something I could do."

"Not even for the sake of your family's safety," Matt said darkly.

"How have my family been affected? Elliot was a member of the guild."

"Because they thought him artless. They learned that India inherited magic and banned her."

"If she wanted membership, she ought to have kept her mouth shut as her father did. It's not my fault they guessed she had magic tendencies. I didn't tell anyone."

"They didn't guess," I said. "My father told my fiancé, Eddie Hardacre, and he told the guild."

"Hardacre." Chronos peered at me over the rim of his glass. "The man who now owns my shop."

"My father's shop," I corrected. "Father bequeathed Eddie the shop in his will, assuming Eddie would marry me. Eddie betrayed his trust. He betrayed me."

Chronos grunted. "Never trust the artless with your secret, India." His gaze slid to Matt. "They don't understand."

"*I* will not betray India's secret," Matt snapped. "Nor will anyone else in this room."

Chronos set his glass down on the table beside him with a slow, deliberate move. "Then you are truly a unique individual."

Matt's jaw set, and I thought he might grasp Chronos by his jacket lapels and threaten him. Instead, he spoke with remarkable calm. "You said that the Watchmaker's Guild is after you only *partly* because you are a magician."

"Not just the Watchmaker's Guild. Every bloody guild in London would like to see me exiled from the city. I have had entanglements with almost all of them, at one time or another, before I fled. It was unavoidable. Where else to begin looking for a magician? Most hide in plain sight, like your father. It's simply a matter of finding the best craftsman in the respective guilds and he, or she, will be the magician."

I knew that from our investigations into the murders of the apothecary and the apprentice mapmaker. "You were not discreet?"

"Discretion does not get the right results. It was bluntness or nothing."

"You're a goddamned fool," Willie said. "You left them with no choice but to banish you."

Chronos smirked. "Ah, but I found what I wanted."

"Dr. Parsons," Matt murmured.

Chronos plucked his glass off the table and drank half the contents.

"You're not telling us everything," I said. "You have not answered Matt's question fully—what is the other reason the guild is chasing you? It's not simply because you're a magician, is it?"

That knowing smile appeared again. "You are more my kin than Elliot's."

He was avoiding answering the question by distracting us, but I did not fall for his tactic this time. "Why, Chronos?"

He finished his brandy and held his glass out for more. "My magic killed a man."

Everyone either sat or leaned forward. Matt stopped pouring.

"It was around the time you were born, India," Chronos went on. "I'd already spent years searching for other magicians to combine my magic with and thereby extend their magic. I'd been moderately successful, and sometimes the magic lasted for years. One gown made by a dressmaker magician did not tear or fray for two decades, and an entire barn held together with nothing more than the builder's magic for nigh on five years."

"No nails?" Duke asked, impressed.

"No nails." Chronos took a sip. "I'd practiced whenever I could, so I was ready to experiment on a human, if only I could find a doctor magician. It took years, but when we did finally meet, he was as keen as me to combine our magic. After careful consideration, we found a suitable subject. You were not my first attempt, Mr. Glass. A man named Wilson was. I don't know his first name. We found him dying in a Bethnal Green alley one winter. He had no home, no family. No one cared whether he lived or died."

"What was he dying of?" I asked.

"The cold, old age, a combination of things. I don't know. We took him back to the doctor's rooms and got to work immediately."

"Without seeing if he got well first?" I said. "What if giving him medicine, warmth and food saved him? At least with Matt there was no doubt he would die, but this man had hope."

Matt poured himself another drink. Chronos tracked his progress and I watched Chronos. He showed no signs of remorse. Matt drank the contents of his glass in a single gulp and poured himself another. He rarely drank more than one glass of an evening. He'd once let slip that he used to indulge his vices to excess before his grandfather shot him in Broken Creek. Drinking had been one of those vices. Almost dying had led him to change his ways. While he could drink a glass on occasion without needing more, he preferred not to gamble at all. I sometimes wondered what other vices tortured him in his more hedonistic days.

"According to the doctor, there was no hope of a natural recovery, even with his superior medical skills," Chronos said. "Have you finished judging me, India? Would you like to hear what happened next?"

I bit the inside of my lip until it hurt.

"We combined our magic, weaving our spells together, but the patient's heart rate sped up too much. He died of heart failure. The doctor refused to try again but somehow his guild, and mine, got wind of it. I don't know how. I think he told someone who told someone...you know how rumor spreads. The Surgeon's Guild ostracized him and wanted to report him to the police. He became frightened, so I think he blamed me and told them I coerced him. I did not. It was a mutual interest. But he had a family to protect." He shrugged.

"You had a family too," Matt pointed out. "Weren't you frightened for them?"

"My wife was quite capable of taking care of herself," Chronos bit off. "Indeed, she was probably glad the blame shifted to me because it meant I had to flee the country. She was rid of me, finally, and could operate the shop her own way. Our marriage was not a good one, India. I offer no apologies for it. Your grandmother and I were opposites in every way."

"Then why did you marry at all?"

"We had no choice. Our parents arranged it. They wanted a union between two great horology magicians. The magical lineage of both families was strong and pure, with every marital pairing going back generations possessing magic. I'm a strong magician, your grandmother was too, and Elliot..." He spread his arms wide. "I don't know how powerful he was. His mother begged him to hide his magic from an early age. He could have been more powerful than either her or me, but he was secretive. He refused to answer my questions when I asked. You, however... You..." He chuckled into his glass. "If only our parents were alive to hear you tell of your magic working without spells, and in such a dramatic fashion too. They would rejoice. Of course, you did have four magician grandparents."

"Four!" I blurted out.

"Your maternal grandfather was a magical confectioner and your maternal grandmother was a magical baker before they married. Her specialty was cakes. Your mother inherited the baking magic. Didn't Elliot tell you?"

I stared at him, open-mouthed, until Willie clicked her fingers in my ear. "You still with us, India?"

I nodded. A magical confectioner explained why I liked sweets so much. I was drawn to bonbons almost as much as I felt compelled to touch clocks and watches. "I thought I merely had a sweet tooth," I said.

Matt laughed softly.

"So back to the story," Willie prompted like an eager child. "The guilds chased you out of England."

Chronos nodded. "They would have called the police on me had I stayed."

"And now you're back, and they're still after you."

"Even years later, they have not forgotten," he said. "Abercrombie, the guild master, is the son of the last guild master, the one who wanted to catch and punish me."

"He knows you're in London?" I asked. This was why Chronos hadn't come to my father's funeral. This was why he'd not tried to find me. He was a hunted man. I watched him through half closed lashes. It could also be because he was selfish and uncaring.

"I'm not sure," Chronos said. "I thought you were his people when I saw you at Worthey's factory. I panicked and fled. Cyclops says you found me through that imbecile, Dr. Hale. He was only an apothecary magician, not a doctor. Did you know?"

Matt nodded. "We made the same mistake you did, thinking his magic was in healing. But at least he led us to you."

"How ironic," Chronos said tightly.

"Why did you come back to London?" Matt asked.

"Wait." Willie held up her hand. "You're jumping ahead, Matt. To Chronos, she said, "You left England and went to America after your experiment on the vagrant failed."

24

"Not straight away. You see, the doctor magician told me about his cousin, who was also a magician. The two had not seen each other in years and lost contact. The cousin traveled to France and Italy, that's all I knew. I followed his trail across the entire bloody continent. He rarely stayed anywhere long. Then I lost him altogether. He'd left Prussia in the early eighties, with no forwarding address. It took some time and considerable money to learn he'd gone to America." His gaze turned wistful. "A pretty Prussian widow finally gave up that piece of information, but it took effort on my part to get it."

"Dr. Parsons is the cousin," Duke guessed. "The man you chased all over Europe."

Chronos nodded. "I found him in that stinking hole, Broken Creek. Took some convincing before he would try combining our magic. In the end, it was you who convinced him, Glass."

"Me? How? I never spoke to either of you before I was shot."

"You were young and in good health, and your death came at another man's hand, not a disease or act of god, as that pious fool put it. You had people who cared about you too." The sweep of his arm took in Willie, Duke and Cyclops. They exchanged grim glances with one another. "I pointed all this out to Parsons and he agreed to try. If you'd been an aged vagrant with no family, I doubt he would have."

"Why did the spell work on me but not the first time on Mr. Wilson?" Matt asked.

"That doctor spoke one of the words incorrectly. The accent was difficult and he pronounced it wrong. Dr. Parsons made no such mistake with you."

"Thank you for convincing Dr. Parsons to try." My quiet voice cut through the silence. No matter what I thought of this man or his experiments, without him, Matt wouldn't be here at all.

Chronos's jaw worked as he stared at me then at Matt.

"Afterward, Parsons wouldn't stop muttering about it not being right. I wasted too much time trying to change his stubborn mind. If I hadn't lingered in America, I could be further along in my search now."

"Your search?" Matt echoed. "For the original doctor magician?"

"No. He's dead. But I'm quite sure another exists."

"How do you know?"

Chronos drank then wiped his beard with his thumb and forefinger. "You see, Parsons's cousin, Dr. Millroy, my original co-magician here in London, had a son."

Matt shot to his feet and paced the floor. "He shouldn't be too hard to trace. Have you tried?"

"Sit down, Matt," Willie said. "Why are you restless all of a sudden?"

I swallowed and waited for Matt to answer but he didn't. He merely glared so hard at Chronos I thought his gaze would drill holes through him.

"Where did Dr. Millroy live?" Matt pressed. "His wife and son may still be there. If not, the new residents might know where to find them."

Chronos shook his head. "Millroy didn't have any children with his wife. He had a son with his mistress."

"Hell," Matt muttered.

"Do you know the mistress's name or where she lived?" I asked.

"No," Chronos said.

I pressed my hand to my stomach. I felt sick. The task of finding her all these years later would be near impossible.

Chronos hadn't fixed Matt's watch and it was now clear why—he needed to combine his magic with a doctor magician's again. It was so obvious that I couldn't believe we hadn't realized. We'd blindly believed the dying Dr. Parsons when he had claimed only the original watchmaker was required. Had he deliberately lied? Or simply not known?

"Why do you need the son?" From Willie's high voice, I suspected she knew the answer to her question. "Well?" She stomped across the carpet to Matt and thumped him hard in the shoulder. "Why didn't you tell us his magic didn't fix it? Huh? Answer me, Matt." She went to punch him again but he caught her fist.

She burst into tears and wrenched free. She kicked the side of the sofa then kicked it again and again until Matt put his arm around her. Duke took a step forward and Matt steered her into his arms. She went with surprising meekness.

"Tears aren't going to find the illegitimate son," I told her, my own tears of frustration welling. "If you think about it, we're actually closer to fixing Matt's watch than we were yesterday."

"How do you figure that?" Willie wailed.

"Yesterday we had neither a doctor magician nor Chronos. Now we have one as well as solid information to find the other. We just need to locate Dr. Millroy's mistress. Someone somewhere will know what happened to her and her son."

"We gotta hope he ain't dead too."

Matt sat next to me and took my hand. He wrung it a little too hard, but I didn't have the heart to tell him to stop. He seemed to need the contact. "You're right, India. You always manage to put things in perspective."

"India's got a positive outlook," Duke told Chronos over Willie's head, which was still buried in his chest.

"As do I," Chronos said, as if he were keeping tally of our similarities and differences. "You find the bastard son and you'll most likely have yourselves a doctor magician, *if* he inherited the power from his father."

"Millroy taught him the spell?" Matt asked.

Chronos shook his head. "The boy was just a baby when his father died." He held up a finger to silence our barrage of questions. "There's a diary. Dr. Millroy wrote everything in it,

27

including the spell. I know that for a fact because I saw it written in there."

I placed my other hand over Matt's, hardly daring to look at him. I only did when he withdrew his hand and stood. He leaned an elbow on the mantelpiece and dug his fingers through his hair.

"The diary could be anywhere now," he said heavily. "It could have been destroyed."

I stood to go to him but sat again. It wasn't my place to comfort him, and I didn't dare give him a sign that I cared for him. He might act on the sign, and I was afraid my willpower would crumble if he did.

I picked up my glass and sipped. Chronos watched me, a brow lifted in curiosity. Then he grunted a half laugh and nodded slowly. He missed nothing.

"So we start looking for the diary at the widow's house," Duke said. "Any idea where she lives?"

Chronos shook his head. "The diary's not with her. I made inquiries. She said it was not with his things when the police found him, something she thought odd. He always carried the diary." He patted his waistcoat pocket. "Right here."

"So it's gone." Willie sniffed. "Probably burned to keep some old hag warm."

"Or it's with his murderer."

"Murderer!" several voices, including mine, chimed.

"Millroy was killed." Chronos made a slashing motion with his hand across his throat. "According to the police, a witness saw a cloaked man leave the scene with Dr. Millroy's possessions."

It's not often we were all left speechless, but that did it.

"Before you ask," Chronos said, "I don't know who the murderer is. It's impossible to get anything out of the police but no one was arrested."

Matt had contacts at Scotland Yard. It may not be impossible for us to learn more about the investigation. Perhaps their records contained a list of suspects. "Then we will help you find Dr. Millroy's killer." I looked to Matt. "This is something you and I are quite good at."

Matt seemed unconvinced. Indeed, he seemed distracted. "I have a proposal for you, Chronos," he finally announced. "You're in hiding. This is as good a place to hide as any, particularly since my friends and I can offer some protection. Stay here and we'll help you find the diary and Dr. Millroy's son. Agreed?"

"And in return?" Chronos asked.

"In return, you help India understand her magic."

Chronos hesitated for the barest moment then held out his hand. "Agreed."

"Get him to sign something," Willie whispered loudly as Matt shook his hand. "I don't trust him."

"You can trust me," Chronos said. "India has me intrigued enough to want to learn more about her magic."

My magic, not *me*. A small kernel of disappointment lodged in my chest.

"We'll seal it with a drink," Matt said, pouring another for Chronos and one for himself. "India?"

"No, thank you," I said. "I think I'll retire."

Matt intercepted me at the door, a frown marring his handsome brow. "Are you all right?" he murmured. "Do your injuries from the accident still hurt?"

I'd almost forgotten about the bruises obtained when our carriage overturned, costing our coachman his life. It seemed like it happened months ago, not mere days. "I'm simply tired," I assured him.

His fingers touched mine. Tingling warmth washed up my arm. I pulled away and would have walked off if he hadn't spoken.

"Stay." The word was as soft as a breath. No one but me could have heard it. The plea in his eyes pinched my heart and had me wondering if he was referring to staying for a drink or staying at his house.

"I can't."

Those chocolate brown eyes searched mine and my skin tingled again. I couldn't move. I was hypnotized by his intense gaze; I felt myself falling into it, unable to stop. That one look, both vulnerable yet strong, had me wanting to put my resolve aside and stay where I could see him whenever I wished, could imagine myself lady of the house and his wife.

"Matt," Willie barked. She did not need to add "she ain't for you" for me to hear it in her tone.

I picked up my skirts and rushed out of the room, my heart pounding in my throat.

I'D BEEN a fool to think I could sleep. I strained to hear footsteps in the corridor outside, but no one passed and Matt's bedroom was located further along than mine. He could not sneak that quietly, not with the creaky floorboards. It was almost midnight, and Matt must be exhausted. Even if he'd drawn on his watch's magic again, he still required regular sleep. Perhaps I ought to see that he was taking care of himself.

I threw a wrap around my shoulders and stepped into a pair of slippers. The corridor was quiet but voices drifted up to me from downstairs. I knew my way in the dark and required no candle to navigate the stairs. A lamp glowed softly in the entrance hall where I paused to listen. The voices came from the drawing room not the service area. I put my ear to the door.

"Are you sure?" I heard Willie say. "That's a lot."

"You can match it," Matt said in a somewhat irritated tone. "You've been winning all night."

"That's what worries me. I never beat you."

"I'm rusty."

"That ain't rust. It's just plain bad luck."

"My luck has deserted me of late." I had to strain to hear his words.

"Don't, Matt," came Cyclops's voice. "End this now. You know you shouldn't be playing." Matt had only played poker once for money since I'd known him, and only then to win back something of value to Willie. Why hadn't his friends stopped him tonight if it was so bad for him to play?

"You know you don't like it when you drink this much either," Duke added.

"Don't play nursemaid," Matt growled.

"Let the man drink!" Chronos's voice was clear as a hot summer's day. "A fellow's got to have some vices or what's the point of living?"

"Shut it," Willie snapped. "You don't understand nothing about Matt."

"I have eyes. I can see."

"See what?" Matt asked. I imagined him glaring at Chronos, and Chronos weighing up whether it was a good idea to answer or not.

I put my hand on the door handle to interrupt them and diffuse the tension. Then Chronos spoke and I found I wanted to hear what he had to say.

"I can see that you're angry and frustrated, and that my granddaughter is foolish."

How dare he call me that? He hardly knew me!

"India is no fool," Matt said.

"Then why is she going to live in a cottage on the edge of the city when she can live in luxury here? This is Mayfair, for God's sake. The only way a woman like her can live in a house like this is if her wealthy lover puts her up in it, and even then—"

Muffled sounds of a scuffle followed.

31

"Christ!" Chronos cried. "I didn't say she was *your* mistress, Glass. Let me go."

I should have entered then. I should have pretended to have just woken and come in search of my friends. But I didn't, and so Matt caught me eavesdropping.

He suddenly filled my vision. The flush on his cheeks heightened as he looked down at me. I swallowed my gasp as I took in the signs of exhaustion etched into every crease bracketing his mouth, every shadow under haunted eyes. It wasn't just tiredness I saw, however. Misery dogged him too.

CHAPTER 3

*M*att's brow plunged into a frown. "How long have you been here?" he demanded.

I drew in a fortifying breath. He was angry but not necessarily with me. I hoped. "Long enough to hear you defending my honor. Thank you."

The muscles in his face relaxed. "Your grandfather has poor manners."

"That's a small price to pay for what he can do for you."

He shifted closer and bent to whisper in my ear. He smelled of expensive brandy and cologne. "If he disparages you again, report it to me."

"I can manage him on my own."

He slowly straightened. "I know you don't need me, India, but you could pretend to once in a while for the sake of my masculine pride."

"I *do* need you." The words were out of my mouth before I could stop them. I bit the inside of my cheek hard lest I repeat them.

Matt stared at me. His breathing quickened. I wished he'd say *something* to break the charged silence, but he seemed at a loss.

"Your money," Willie said from behind him.

"Keep it," Matt said without turning around.

I stepped aside to let him pass then studied his stiff back as he headed up the stairs. A numbness seeped into my bones. I wasn't sure what to think or how to react. Could he read my thoughts? Did he know *why* I had to move out of the house?

"Leaving now ain't a good idea, India." It would seem Willie could read them.

She sat with Chronos at the card table they'd brought in, Duke and Cyclops nearby but not playing. All four of them looked at me with varying degrees of interest. Only Willie had a fiercely determined set to her jaw, however. I braced myself. She was not one to hold back her opinions. She and my grandfather ought to get along well.

"Ordinarily I would want you to move away," she went on. "On account of him going back home to America when his watch is fixed and you being a temptation to stay in London. But not anymore. Now I want you to stay in this house a while longer."

"What changed your mind?" I asked.

"Before tonight, it was seeing how well you and Matt solve puzzles together. Puzzles like who has that diary and where to find the doctor's bastard son."

"I can help him solve those puzzles while living elsewhere and visiting every day."

"It ain't the same. Sometimes urgent business comes up and you'll be too far away."

I acknowledged the point with a nod. "And after tonight? Why do you want me to stay now?"

"Because of this." She indicated the table, the empty crystal decanter and glasses.

A weight settled into my chest.

"Well?" Duke prompted. "You going to stay, India?"

Cyclops gathered up the glasses in one big hand. "It'll only be until this is over and Matt's watch is fixed," he said, depositing the glasses on the tray. "Then we'll go home and you can do as you like."

I folded my arms against the chill but it inched up my spine anyway. "I'll think about it."

* * *

I DIDN'T HAVE a chance to speak to Matt in the morning. He left directly after breakfast to call upon Police Commissioner Munro at New Scotland Yard. Before he departed, he suggested Chronos and I work in his study, away from prying eyes and ears.

I saw to Miss Glass's comfort first and after Cyclops promised to keep her company, I made my way to the bedroom Mrs. Bristow had assigned to Chronos. He followed me from there to Matt's study, where he sat on Matt's chair behind the desk, leaving the other chair for me.

His gaze brushed over the contents of the desk and, seeing nothing of interest, said, "Show me your watch."

"Why?"

He sighed. "So I can see what magic you put into it."

"I told you, I didn't *put* magic into it. Magic simply found its way in. Somehow." It sounded absurd but neither of us laughed.

He stretched his arm across the desk. "Show me the watch, India. I need to see what you're capable of before I can teach you what you don't know."

"I don't know anything. That's the point. Anything I have done is entirely by accident." Nevertheless, I placed my watch in his palm.

He dropped it on the desk surface and shook out his hand. "Blimey!"

"Careful!" I snatched up the watch and inspected the silver

case for dents. "My parents gave me that watch. It's my most valued item."

"It's a relatively inexpensive hunter," he said absently as he inspected his palm.

"It may be relatively inexpensive to you but it's priceless to me. Not that I expect you to understand. It would seem you only see value as a monetary thing."

"Not quite." He looked up from his hand. It was red. My watch had done that. Or, rather, my magic in the watch. Of all the times I'd touched an object that had been handled by a magician, I'd only ever felt warmth, not a burning sensation that left a mark. Chronos must be more sensitive to it.

"You're angry with me," he said.

"How astute of you."

He sighed. "I didn't ask for this."

"So you said last night. You didn't ask to be a husband, father or grandfather. I know you expect that to absolve you from blame for leaving the family when you did, but I won't forgive you."

"I left because my life was in danger. I didn't seek you out when I returned because my life is still in danger. Do you want me killed?"

"I haven't yet decided."

He chuckled. "You have a lot of your grandmother in you. She was a fire cracker. We clashed terribly."

I hadn't always been a fire cracker. I used to be meek and mild, and sometimes I still was. That was the woman Eddie had liked, and so I didn't particularly like her anymore. Still, that side of me often surfaced. Chronos, however, brought out my inner shrew.

I held my watch by its chain. "Do you want me to open it for you?"

He pulled out a handkerchief from his waistcoat pocket and used it as a barrier between his skin and my watch then he retrieved his portable cloth case of tools. With his magnifier in place, he opened my watch's casing and used tweezers to remove a spring. "How many times have you worked on this?"

"A hundred or more. It's something I do to calm myself when I'm upset. Working on it soothes my nerves. That sounds silly," I added.

He made no comment, merely continuing to extract parts with his tweezers. I was not concerned. It was easy enough to put them back again.

"That explains why it's so hot," he said.

I leaned forward, thinking he'd found the explanation among the watch's workings. But there was nothing unusual among the innards laid out beside the device. They were ordinary parts of an ordinary watch. "What do you mean?"

He returned a spring to the housing. "Each time you've worked on this, you've added another layer of heat. The clock in the drawing room was also hot to touch, but not as hot as this."

"I've worked on that perhaps three or four times."

"Because it was slow?"

"No."

He smirked. "Because you needed to work on a timepiece."

"It's a compulsion." I rubbed my hands together in my lap and told myself I did not need to help him put the parts back.

"That's normal. Any magician, no matter his or her discipline, will tell you their craft calls to them."

I nodded, remembering Oscar Barratt the journalist and ink magician saying the same thing.

"What I don't understand," Chronos went on, "is why there is heat in this watch and the clock when you didn't use a spell. In my experience, magic heat should only be present after a spell casting."

"Could the watch's heat be from my father's magic? He gave it to me, along with my mother, who you say was also a magician." A rawness opened up inside me like a wound. I rarely thought about my parents, thanks to being so busy helping Matt lately, but when I did, I felt their loss keenly. My mother had been gone for years yet I still missed her, still cherished the memory of her gentle hands arranging my hair, her comforting arms around me, her smile. And her delicious baked goods. Father's death was more recent and my memories of him fresher and sometimes so painful I could burst into tears. I closed my fist around my watch and drew in a deep, steadying breath.

"It doesn't explain that much heat," Chronos said. "Not unless he worked on it hundreds of times too. And it doesn't explain the clock downstairs." He stood and moved to the mantelpiece where a crystal regulator clock ticked quietly. He touched one of its gilt feet only to quickly let go again.

I joined him and touched the clock too. "It's warm," I admitted.

"Hot," he corrected. "It's likely you can't feel the strength because it's your magic causing it." He shook his head at me. "Remarkable," he said softly. "You're powerful indeed."

I stared down at my hands. It was somewhat thrilling to be called powerful, until I remembered what it meant— almost nothing. Granted, my watch and some clocks had helped me, and for that I was grateful, but if I didn't own a shop or factory, what use was the magic? Even if I did own a shop and sold timepieces, what would my magic's purpose be?

"A goldsmith magician once told me—"

"Goldsmith!" he said, sitting in Matt's chair again. "How fortunate for him."

"He's dead and was likely the last of his kind. Besides, he couldn't *make* gold, only detect magic in gold that had been worked by a magician in years past. It was he who told me that magicians use magic to achieve the thing they want most from their craft. For a doctor, it's to save lives, for a builder, it's to have their structures stay up, for a mapmaker it's to locate things, timepiece magicians want our devices to run efficiently."

He held up a hand for me to stop. "Your point?"

"Magicians only have a single trick."

"Not all. I have two, for instance. Making a timepiece run efficiently, and extending the length of others' magic."

I leaned forward. "Go on." Finally, I might understand the purpose of magic.

"Let me clarify. I've met quite a few magicians in my endeavors, and most believe, as you do, that magic is pointless. But listening to the tales from other magical cultures older than ours, more remote and untouched than ours, I think it used to serve a greater purpose."

"I did hear one story about maps coming to life and rivers bleeding off the edge and flooding villages." I shook my head. "Fairytales."

"Are you sure?"

I snorted in a most unladylike manner. "Have you ever heard of a village drowned by a line drawn on a piece of paper?"

His lips twitched with another supercilious smile. "Do you read the bible?"

"I go to church regularly. More than you, I'm sure."

"That's highly probable, but wasn't my question. If you read the bible, you'd recall the stories of plagues, floods and miraculous events."

"Are you saying those events were all caused by magic?"

"There are other legends and myths too. Flying carpets, hair made of snakes, beautiful gardens that require no water, or water that flows upstream."

"I ask again—do you think magic explains them?"

"Why not? It makes sense to credit them to magic. Some of them are seemingly impossible and yet we have evidence of them today. Ancient structures, for example. Pyramids, aqueducts, tunnels, viaducts... Many still stand after thousands of years. How, if not for magic?"

"You're mad."

"You wouldn't be the first to call me that. Not even the first of my relatives." He picked up his handkerchief and returned it to his pocket. "But I've lain my hands on the stones of an Egyptian pyramid and I can swear to you, they were warm."

"Egypt is a hot place."

"Magical warmth feels different than heat from the sun. Even you know that. Stop trying to be deliberately provocative, India."

"I am not!"

"You are. You're like me in that regard," he said with a wry twist of his mouth.

"I wish you'd stop saying that," I mumbled. "I'm not like you at all."

"You don't know that yet. You hardly even know yourself."

"Of course I know myself, and better than you do. What an absurd thing to say."

"Learning who you are and your place in the world doesn't come to one fully until one is about forty."

I rolled my eyes and crossed my arms. "For you, perhaps. Anyway, I am not going to make watches or clocks, or use my magic in any way other than to occasionally tinker. All of those myths you talk about are just stories now. If spells once made a carpet fly then the spell is lost. Perhaps it's for the best. Anyway, magic is not allowed to be practiced. Perhaps that is for the best too."

"You've never considered what the world would be like if we magicians could use our magic freely? If the artless accepted us? Even came to us to fix their imperfect artless creations?"

I kept my focus on the watch still in my hand. "The artless

tradesmen and women would lose their customers, their livelihoods."

"And magicians would have a better one. So?"

I looked up sharply. "Are you so heartless that you would wish thousands upon thousands of people out of employment? You would want their children to starve?"

"They would find other work."

I clicked my tongue but didn't bother to argue with him. I would not change his mind with a few words.

"Now you sound like your father," he said with a shake of his head. "And your mother, your grandmother—"

"Stop it! Stop talking about them as if they were merely mutual acquaintances. They may have meant nothing to you—"

"I never said that!" He shot to his feet and strode to the door but he did not leave. The clock on the mantel chimed the hour, its high, delicate tune loud in the dense silence. "I'm not sure I can teach you."

"Pardon?"

"I'm not sure I can teach you anything, India. You already seem to know how to fix watches and clocks."

"Not all. There were two in my father's shop that eluded me. One ran slow and the other fast."

He turned to look at me, white eyebrow raised high. "You tried fixing them?"

"Once, yes, when I was young. Father didn't want me touching them after that. He said their faults made them interesting, unique. He never did try to sell them."

He sighed. "I never understood Elliot."

He plucked the clock off the mantel and signaled for me to join him on the other side of the desk. He pulled my chair around too and we both sat, the clock on the desk in front of us.

"Teach me the accuracy spell," I said in case he had a mind to talk about something else.

He did. It was rather simple, just a few lines in a foreign tongue that sounded quite musical.

"What language is that?"

"Magic."

"That's not a real language."

"If you can find it in a book with a neat label to describe its origins, then by all means, call it that if you like. But I will call it the language of magic as I have always done, and how every magician I've ever met has called it."

If he wasn't so arrogant I'd be glad to call it the language of magic. It sounded rather romantic. I wouldn't tell him that. I doubted he had a romantic bone in his body. He would only mock.

"Now the other spell," I said. "The one that extends the length of other magic when joined. The one you used on Matt's watch. Teach me that."

He fidgeted with the clock, taking his time closing the housing at the back.

"Go on," I prompted, sliding the clock to my side of the desk, out of his reach.

"It's a more complex spell."

"Teach it to me."

"I was going to, India," he said with an exasperated sigh. "Some patience wouldn't go astray. You've got as much of it as —" He cleared his throat. "Never mind."

There were many more words in the extending spell and I had trouble remembering them all. Chronos wouldn't let me write them down, however, saying it was too dangerous to have them lying around. Few magicians wrote down their spells, preferring to pass them on orally. It explained why so many spells had been lost, and I wasn't sure it was a good way to insure the longevity of magic, but I did understand the need for secrecy. Dr. Millroy seemed to be the exception, having written the spell in his diary.

Even after I remembered the words in the correct order,

Chronos said I hadn't got the spell quite right. There were nuances, some words were meant to be spoken softly and others harsher. I also needed to get the accent exactly right.

"I think you have it," he said after half an hour of repetition. "You picked it up quickly. Of course, we won't know if it worked until you try combining it with another magician's spell, and even then you must wait to see if the other magic wears off or stays."

I repeated both spells again, paying particular care with the extending one.

"Very good." Chronos dragged his hands through his wisps of hair, making them dance above his head.

"Now I just have to remember it."

"You will, with practice. We'll say the words every day, several times a day, until you do." He tapped his temple. "It'll sink in, soon enough. For now, we should stop and rest. My head aches."

I followed him to the door. "How did you learn the extending spell?" I asked.

"My grandfather taught my father, who taught me. My grandfather was a powerful magician. There wasn't a watch he couldn't fix, a clock he couldn't make run on time. Quite a feat with the rudimentary scientific knowledge of his day."

"Did he ever use it to extend someone's life as you have done?"

"I don't know. I never asked him, and he never mentioned it. It wasn't until after his death that I began my experiments, and it was years after that when it occurred to me that the spell might work to save a life when combined with a doctor's magic. I sometimes wonder what he would have thought."

"Was he a good man, or was his moral compass as skewed as your own?"

His gaze narrowed. "For someone who needs my help, you've got sass, as the Americans say."

"Ah, but I don't need your help anymore. You've given me

the spells." His face fell and a bubble of satisfaction rose within me. "Don't worry, *Grandpapa*, I won't ask Matt to throw you out. We are family, after all, and family must look after one another, no matter how cantankerous."

I strode down the corridor ahead of him, wishing I had eyes in the back of my head to see his face. I refused to turn around and look. Let him think I had no interest in him.

I wish I did have no interest in him. But that was very far from the truth.

* * *

IT BECAME apparent as the morning wore on that Chronos was a man who preferred action to sitting with ladies in drawing rooms. Hardly five minutes had passed in Miss Glass's company when he suggested going for a walk. Cyclops, standing by the door, shook his head.

"That's not a good idea," he intoned.

Chronos threw his hands in the air. "I won't try to escape. I have an agreement with Mr. Glass."

"Escape?" Miss Glass said, setting aside her correspondence.

Chronos looked trapped. I'd told him not to discuss magic in the presence of Matt's aunt for the sake of her fragile mind. As far as she knew, he was my long lost grandfather come home to see his granddaughter.

"A figure of speech," he said. "I don't like to be cooped up inside for long."

She folded her letter and returned it to the portable writing desk on her lap. "I'll amuse you with conversation."

His gaze darted to Cyclops, as if he had a mind to tackle him and run out.

I smiled and settled into the sofa. "An excellent notion, Miss Glass. What shall we discuss? Your friends? The new fashion for puffed sleeves? Oh, I know. Tell Chronos all about your nieces. I'm sure tales of the Glass women will quickly banish thoughts of escape from his mind."

If looks could kill, Chronos would have had me hung, drawn and quartered.

Miss Glass made a disgusted sound in her throat. "Nobody wants to hear about those silly girls, India. You are in an odd humor today." To Chronos she said, "Tell me about your travels. My brother, Matthew's father, traveled extensively. Matthew did too when he was young. I always wanted to see the Continent but my father and eldest brother would not allow it."

"A pity," Chronos said. "Travel improves the mind and broadens one's view. I find the thinking of people who've never traveled to be narrow and staid."

Miss Glass smiled but I did not. "I've never traveled," I told him. "Am I staid and narrow-minded?"

"I hardly know you well enough, but in my experience, you probably are." He lifted one shoulder, as if a shrug could soften the blow.

How rude! He may be my grandfather but he had no right to speak to me like that.

"Have you never been out of London?" he asked me.

"Rarely. We were always too busy with the shop. Of course, if my grandfather had been present he could have assisted while my parents took me to the seaside on holiday."

Miss Glass muttered, "Oh dear," and studied the wood grain on the writing desk.

"The shop hardly brought in enough money for frivolous extras like holidays," Chronos shot back. "Perhaps if your father and grandmother had used their—" He cut himself off when I shook my head furiously. "Perhaps if they'd had better business sense they would have made more money," he said instead.

"It was hard for them, particularly for my grandmother," I said. "By all accounts, even when you were in London, you rarely helped. You were always chasing...your other interests."

"Your grandmother preferred that arrangement. She liked things done a certain way—her way. She disliked my interference in the running of the shop. Your father was not much different. If the truth be told, I wasn't a very good shopkeeper. My other interests, as you call them, were far more important."

"Only to you."

He sighed and rolled his eyes to the ceiling. "Everyone was better off with me leaving."

"And severing contact altogether?"

"It was for the best."

"How can you know how everyone felt when you never saw them again?"

"Stop it!" Miss Glass snapped. "Stop your arguing. It makes my head ache. India, I expect better from you. You've never behaved as childishly as this."

Her rebuke rendered me speechless. I wasn't sure whether to be offended or to defend myself. But a few moments of silence cooled my temper, and I had to agree that she had a point. I didn't like the person I became when Chronos riled me. It was too late to change what had happened, or make him understand the effect his absence had on our family, and I was better off saving my energy helping Matt find Dr. Millroy's diary and illegitimate son.

Matt himself took that moment to enter. He hesitated in the doorway, a small frown on his brow. "Has something happened?" he asked carefully.

"Everyone is a little tense," Miss Glass said, putting out her hand. "Help me up, Cyclops. I'll take my correspondence to my room."

Cyclops left with her but before he shut the door, he spoke quietly to Matt. Whatever he said, Matt didn't like it. He scowled at Cyclops and turned his back to him. Cyclops shook his head then signaled to me that Matt needed to rest.

Matt did indeed look terrible. Despite his well groomed appearance, the rims of his eyes were red and the skin beneath them as dark as fresh bruises. I did not order him to rest, however. Sometimes it was best to handle him delicately.

"What drove my aunt away?" he asked as he settled beside me on the sofa.

"Petty arguments between Chronos and me," I said. "It won't happen again."

Chronos grunted. "So what did the police say?"

"Commissioner Munro was reluctant to open up an old case at first," Matt said.

"Why?" I asked. "The murderer was never discovered. Wouldn't they welcome new evidence?"

"We don't have new evidence. He considered it a waste of police resources."

"But you convinced him to change his mind?" Chronos prompted.

Matt nodded. "Eventually, yes. That's why it took so long. After seeing Munro, I sought out Brockwell, a detective inspector of our acquaintance."

"Brockwell!" I made a face. "I haven't made up my mind whether I like him or not. He was rather plodding in the murder case of Dr. Hale."

"Methodical," Matt countered. "He got the job done in the end and made sure there was no room for error or misinterpretation by his superiors."

"I don't think he had much to do with that," I said. "Besides, he's not aware of magic. How can we share information with him without mentioning it?"

"With care."

"I agree with India," Chronos said. "This Brockwell seems like he could be a thorn in our side."

"He was my only option," Matt snapped. He squeezed the bridge of his nose with his thumb and forefinger. I resisted the urge to lay a hand on his arm. "Brockwell had a word with Munro and the commissioner agreed that Brockwell can help us until something more pressing comes across his desk."

"You bribed him," Chronos said flatly.

Matt shook his head. "Brockwell cannot be bought."

"That makes him unique among the constabulary."

"He doesn't like loose ends," Matt added. "This is an open case and he wants to find the murderer. I think unfinished business bothers him just as much as an unfinished book bothers an avid reader."

"So what did Brockwell find out about Dr. Millroy's murder?" I asked.

"We spent some time in the archives reading reports from the detective inspector in charge of the case. He's deceased now, but his records were thorough. Millroy's throat had been cut with a sharp blade that was never found. There was a lot of blood at the scene." He stretched out his legs and crossed them at the ankles. "A child witness saw a tall man walk away from the body, but he couldn't see the man's face."

"Is that it?" Chronos asked. "I knew all of that from reading the newspapers."

"That was all the physical evidence from the scene," Matt went on. "After interviewing the widow, the investigating detective discovered that Dr. Millroy had been confronted by members of both the Surgeon's Guild and the Watchmaker's Guild before his death."

"Watchmaker's!" I said. "Why them when he didn't belong to that guild?"

"Because they'd learned about our experiment on Mr. Wilson," Chronos said heavily. He rubbed his beard absently, his gaze distant. "Abercrombie confronted me too. That's the previous Abercrombie, not the current one, his son. I'd like to know how the guilds found out about the experiment."

"Are you sure you never told anyone?" Matt asked. "Not even your wife?"

"Especially not my wife. Doesn't mean Millroy had the same good sense."

"He could have written it down in his diary," I said. "Someone may have read it and passed on the information to both guilds. But who? And why?"

"His killer?" Matt said. "Perhaps he hoped to get Millroy into trouble with the guilds out of revenge for killing Wilson, but when that didn't happen, he took more drastic action."

Chronos shook his head. "That points the finger at someone who cared for Wilson, and no one did. The vagrant we experimented on had no family, no home, no friends."

"A moral crusader?" I suggested.

"The problem with that theory," Matt said, "is that the killer should have come after Chronos too."

We both looked to my grandfather. "Perhaps he tried," Chronos said. "I left London the day after I read about Millroy's murder in the papers. Abercrombie from the Watchmaker's Guild called on me, accusing me of using my magic to murder people. He told me he would notify the police and inform them of my role in the vagrant's death, and he even accused me of being involved in Dr. Millroy's death. I fled that afternoon."

"Did the reports say how the police learned of the guilds' confrontation with Dr. Millroy?" I asked.

"His widow told the inspector," Matt said.

I wagged a finger at him in thought. "She might have a reason to kill her husband. We know he had a mistress and even fathered a child with that mistress. Perhaps she killed him out of jealousy or anger. Perhaps his murder had nothing to do with the guilds or the experiment. You could have been running in fear all this time for no reason," I said to Chronos.

"The guilds still want me blamed for the vagrant's death."

"Scotland Yard is not aware of your involvement," Matt

said. "I asked Brockwell if the police are looking for you in relation to any crimes. He checked and said they are not."

"They're not?" Chronos said weakly. "So...Abercrombie never followed through on his threat?"

"You still need to remain in hiding. I don't trust the Watchmaker's Guild and they don't trust you. They might still approach the police if they know you're alive and here."

Chronos nodded slowly. "You're right. It's a weight off my shoulders nevertheless."

"If Mrs. Millroy is involved in her husband's death," Matt said, "she got someone else to commit the actual murder. A man was seen leaving the scene, not a woman." He suppressed a yawn while avoiding looking at me. "I'll visit Abercrombie this afternoon and see what he remembers about his father's visit to Dr. Millroy before his murder."

"Good luck getting him to tell you anything," I said.

"If he's like his father he's a slippery little weasel," Chronos added.

"Then he's exactly like his father."

Matt pushed up from the sofa and stifled another yawn. He headed for the door only to stop and spin on his heel. He frowned at me. "Ordinarily you would ask to come along on an investigation, India. But you didn't this time. Why?"

Damnation. I'd wanted to avoid mentioning Oscar Barratt until after I'd seen the journalist. But I couldn't lie to Matt. "May we speak alone?"

His gaze flicked to Chronos.

"I'm going, I'm going." Chronos sidled past me but paused before leaving. "The spell, India. The second one I taught you." He nodded at Matt. "You ought to try it."

My eyes widened. I stared at him. He thought *I* could fix Matt's watch, when he couldn't?

It was worth a try, I suppose. I raced to Matt and unbuttoned his jacket. Chronos stepped closer too, a curious light in his eyes.

Matt put up his hands in surrender as I took to unbuttoning his waistcoat. The heat coming off him warmed me, sent a thrill through me. My fingers fumbled. There was only his shirt between his skin and mine, but that held no interest for me now. I only wanted his watch.

What if I could succeed where Chronos failed? What if my magic was strong enough to fix the magic watch without a doctor?

I withdrew the watch from its pocket with trembling hands and closed my fist around it. I spoke the words Chronos had taught me, careful to get the cadence and accent right. It took three attempts then the watch glowed purple, brighter than it had glowed for Chronos. Matt's white shirt became purple too and my fingernails. Beside me, I felt Chronos shift his weight and move closer to see. Matt's swallow was audible but I did not look up at him until I handed him back his watch.

"Try now," I said, unable to keep the smile from my voice.

I watched, not daring to breathe, as he closed his eyes and drew the magic into his body.

CHAPTER 4

"*W*ell?" I prompted when Matt shut the watch's case.

"Is there an improvement?" Chronos pressed. He sounded excited too, and for the first time, I felt a connection to him.

Matt blinked down at the watch in his hand, the chain dangling through his fingers. "Something's different."

I sucked in a deep, shuddery breath then clamped a shaking hand over his. "Matt..." I couldn't speak, couldn't form the words needed to ask.

He lifted his head to meet my gaze and folded his other hand over mine. "I feel stronger, India, healthier. Healthier than I have in weeks."

"As good as the first time you used it in Broken Creek?"

"No." Matt pulled my hand to his lips and kissed it gently, never taking his gaze off me. "But it's a positive development."

"Yes," I said, somewhat numb. "It is."

"Thank you," he murmured, his lips against my hand.

I caught Chronos backing from the room out of the corner of my eye. He shut the door, leaving Matt and me alone in the drawing room.

Matt quickly lowered my hand. "I need to apologize for last night."

The rapid change of topic caught me by surprise. I wanted to discuss his health more, and I thought he wanted to talk about me not visiting Abercrombie with him.

"You have nothing to apologize for," I said.

"I do. I was a boor."

"If you think you behaved poorly, you should apologize to Willie and the others. Anyway, you were upset about the watch not working after Chronos cast his spell. Your hopes had built up only to be dashed." I squeezed his arm. "It's understandable you wanted to forget for a few hours."

He cringed and I noticed the lines at the corners of his eyes looked smaller, the shadows mere smudges not bruises. It was no different to how he always looked after using the watch. "Don't be so forgiving," he said quietly. "I don't deserve it."

I smiled. "Do you need to rest?"

"Not quite as badly as I have of late." He sounded surprised.

"That's something."

"I'll rest before I see Abercrombie. Speaking of which, why aren't you insisting on coming with me this afternoon?"

"I want to call on Oscar Barratt," I said. "I ought to see how he is."

"Ah." He gave me a flat smile. "Wish him well in his recovery from me. Will you take him up on his offer to go to the theater?"

"But...*you* promised to take me." Good lord, I sounded pathetic.

"I haven't forgotten my promise, but there's no reason you can't go with him too."

I regarded him from beneath my lashes. "Why?"

"Why not? He likes you. He's a good man, although a little

eager. About magic," he added then cleared his throat. "Give him my regards," he said, turning to go.

It took me several seconds to recover from my disappointment at his changed attitude toward my friendship with Barratt. But without seeing his face, I couldn't begin to determine what it meant.

"One other thing," he said over his shoulder. "About your intention to move out...is that decision final?"

"I'm still considering what to do. I thought my mind was made up but now I'm not sure."

The corners of his mouth lifted ever so slightly. "Take your time. There's no need to rush."

* * *

OSCAR BARRATT HAD GIVEN me his home address some time ago so that I could visit him, day or night, if I had any questions about magic. I assumed he was there recuperating, but I was wrong. His landlady said he'd gone back to work and I found him at *The Weekly Gazette's* office on Lower Mire Lane, the insignificant little street off the more industrious Fleet Street. *The Weekly Gazette* wasn't one of the city's pre-eminent papers but it had a solid following among the middle classes who preferred its sensationalist stories over the political and financial slant of the better known dailies.

I found Mr. Barratt at his desk out the back, his arm in a sling, writing furiously. Another journalist in the adjoining office tapped at a mechanical typewriter. Its rhythmic *clack clack* was more soothing than I expected, and I hadn't realized my nerves were jangly until I drew in a deep breath.

"Not even a bullet wound can slow you down," I said to the dark head bent over the desk.

Mr. Barratt looked up. "India! What a pleasant surprise." He got to his feet quickly, only to wince and touch his arm.

"Are you all right?" I edged around the desk but stopped before getting too close. I offered a sympathetic smile.

"I'll be fine. Just got up too suddenly." He indicated I should sit on the chair opposite. "I'm glad you're here. I wanted to call upon you but I wasn't sure if I should. Inspector Brockwell said you had quite a scare the day I was shot."

"At least I wasn't injured."

"How did you escape from Mr. Pitt? Brockwell was vague on the particulars."

"Matt was there."

"If he saved your life, Brockwell would have said so." He leaned forward. "Was it your watch?"

I glanced over my shoulder at the door. Even though no one stood there, I whispered. "It did, along with Matt's distraction."

He threw the pen down on his paper. Ink splattered but he didn't care. "I knew it!" He beamed. "Excellent." He reached forward to pat my hand but knocked his arm on the edge of the desk and winced.

"You look like you're in pain, Mr. Barratt. Can I get you anything?"

He hesitated. "A new shoulder without a hole in it." He smiled crookedly, turning his handsome features into something quite extraordinary. "It actually doesn't hurt as badly as you might think. The bullet didn't go right through, merely grazed me. It's still lodged in the wall in the printing room."

"You were very lucky. I am so glad you're all right, as is Matt. We feel terribly responsible for involving you. None of this would have happened if we hadn't sought you out after reading your article."

"I'll forgive you on one condition."

Oh dear. What did he want from me? More than a ticket to the theater?

He laughed softly, making him even more dashing.

"There's no need to worry. My condition is that you call me Oscar, since I've taken to calling you India.

I smiled, more in relief than with humor. "I can do that."

"And anyway, it wasn't your fault. *I* wrote that article about Dr. Hale, drawing attention to myself and to magic. I probably should take a leaf out of your book and be more discreet."

"You have drawn the notice of some people. Speaking of which, did you know Mr. Pitt took me to Lord Coyle's house when he kidnapped me from here?"

"Brockwell informed me but claimed Pitt had overreached his acquaintance with Coyle." He adjusted the sling and gingerly rested his arm on the desk. His face brightened, as if he could sense an intriguing story in the air. "Was Coyle behind Hale's murder, somehow urging Pitt to act on his behalf?"

"We don't know, but I just wanted to warn you to be careful. If Lord Coyle asks you about magic again, it may be best to be as vague as possible until we know why he collects magical objects. He's rich and influential, and he knows how to get what he wants. Fortunately, Inspector Brockwell cannot be bought."

He huffed softly. "Or perhaps the right currency hasn't been tabled."

I ought to defend Brockwell's integrity, but he'd made things difficult for us during the investigation into Hale's death. Matt may like him, but I wasn't as willing to be his friend. "I want to discuss something with you, Oscar. Something that you've mentioned before but Matt and I dismissed. I think it's worth exploring again."

"This sounds intriguing. I'm all ears."

"Let's talk about writing an article revealing magic to the public."

CHAPTER 5

Oscar sat back heavily, which must have jolted his shoulder, yet he didn't so much as wince. He stared at me. Then slowly, slowly, his lips curved into a smile. "You want me to write an article exposing magicians?"

"I want to discuss the implications of it, that's all."

"With a view to publishing it."

"Perhaps."

He removed a notepad and pencil from his top drawer then flipped to a blank page. He rested his sling-bound forearm on the little book and drew a line down the center of the page, dividing it into two columns. He labeled one PRO and the other CON.

"Is this why you came without Mr. Glass?" he asked as he finished writing. "Because his cautious nature only sees the negatives?"

"He's not cautious regarding most things," I said. "Indeed, he can be rather reckless. But on the topic of magic, he doesn't think the world needs to know about us. He thinks such knowledge will only lead to danger for magicians. While I do agree, to an extent, I also have more faith in my fellow man. I don't think it would cause the chaos he predicts, although there will be an unsettled phase until the artless and magicians can learn to live and work together. Put that down in the CON column."

He wrote *unrest* beneath CON and *enlightenment* in the PRO column. I thought that over-selling my point. "Like you, I have faith that there are more good people than bad in the world, India. Mr. Glass must have had some misfortune with his friends to give him such a cynical view."

"It's not his friends." I regretted saying it as soon as it left my mouth. He would guess that it was Matt's family who'd betrayed him. Matt wouldn't want him to know. "Note down that artless businesses will suffer in the CON column."

He did and countered it with *better products* and services in the PRO list and added *freedom for magicians* and *no more fear*.

I nodded at that. Freedom to live in the open meant a doctor magician would be easy to find. Writing articles about magic could be the fastest way to flush out a medical magician. Perhaps Dr. Millroy's illegitimate son would even reveal himself.

It could also send the desperate and ill to his door hoping he could cure them. Of course he could only extend their life briefly, if at all—without me or Chronos, that is. "False hope," I said quietly.

Oscar looked up, pencil poised. "What do you mean?"

"Magic is temporary. Any object infused with it will not keep its magical quality for long. False hope could lead to anger from those ignorant of the limitations."

"Perhaps there are spells to extend magic's usage. Drawing out magicians may also draw out some of the older spells thought lost." He looked very pleased with himself at the suggestion.

I held my breath, weighing up my own list of pros and cons for telling him about Chronos and the extending spell. Oscar's enthusiasm to share magic with the world might override any caution. On the other hand, he'd agreed not to write openly about magic. I could trust him to keep this a secret. I *wanted* to trust him.

I glanced over my shoulder at the door again. Not quite satisfied that we couldn't be overheard, I got up and closed it. Oscar sat very still, his eyes huge as he waited for me to tell him more. I had certainly piqued his curiosity.

"What I'm about to tell you cannot be mentioned to anyone else," I began. "You cannot write about it or even allude to it with veiled references. Do you understand, Oscar?"

He nodded. "What is it, India? What have you discovered?"

"There is a spell to extend the life of another magician's magic."

His brows almost disappeared into his hairline. "A time magician," he said on a breath. "You can do it, can't you?" He slapped the desktop and beamed at me. "I have wondered. Ever since meeting you, the thought entered my head, but I've not heard of magic being combined with another's before and dismissed it. Tell me, how did you discover it was even possible?"

"First of all, promise you won't tell a soul about this."

"I promise."

I breathed out a pent-up breath. "I found someone to advise me on my magic."

"Another timepiece magician? Who is it?"

"He'd rather no one knows about him. He's very secretive."

"Sounds intriguing." The light in his eyes shone brighter and he sat forward. Oscar would have enjoyed being a detective as much as Brockwell.

"He taught me a spell that makes a watch or clock run on time," I said. "I wasn't able to fix all beforehand, only most."

He waved this off with a flap of his hand. "An admirable

spell, and I suppose it's representative of what watch and clockmakers want to achieve most in their craft. Good for you. I'm pleased you found someone to help you. But the extension spell?"

"His forebears taught it to him, and he spent years experimenting with other magicians, combining his magic with theirs using the spell. He has had some success."

"What types of other magic?"

"Builders, dressmakers, ironworkers. All of the magic has held for longer than it usually would."

"A doctor?" he asked without missing a beat. He was fast. Almost too fast for me to match him. It was not a connection most would immediately make.

"He's searching for a medical magician." It was more a lie by omission than an outright lie. My conscience was quite comfortable with it.

He studied the lists in his notebook then drew a line beneath them. "A pity he hasn't been able to find one. Imagine the possibilities. The lives that could be saved, the—"

"No. Stop." I took his notebook and closed it. He blinked at me, surprised by my response.

"What is the matter, India?" He reminded me of Chronos with his enthusiasm and blinkered outlook. Like Chronos, he did not seem to see the dangers.

"There are consequences to combining the two spells. Extending the life of someone who ought to have died is wrong; it's playing God. It could create all manner of havoc, some of which we could not even anticipate in a discussion such as this."

"What if the person should not have died? What if the victim of a murderous madman lies dying but there is enough time to save them using magic?"

It was so close to Matt's own situation to be chilling. I rubbed my arms but it did nothing to warm me. "You cannot use the spell on some people and not others," I said, changing the subject. "Nobody has the right to make that decision."

"So you would deny a mother life-saving magic to prolong her dying child's life? Even if she begged you?"

"Don't, Oscar."

"Very well, here's another thought. You clearly know the extending spell, as does your mentor. You don't know where to find a doctor magician now, but what if you do locate one? Should you and your mentor be the only ones to take advantage of the spell? Isn't that unfair?"

"We won't take advantage of it. We know the ethics." It was an outright lie, and he detected it.

"*You* may, but does he? Besides, can you honestly say you would not employ the spell if someone you loved lay dying and you knew of a way to save him or her?" He threw down his pencil and it rolled across the desk, hitting the inkstand.

"You cannot tell anyone, Oscar. You can't write about this."

"Then why are you here, India?" His raised voice filled the small office. "Why tell me at all if you want to keep it quiet?"

I swallowed hard. I would not let him turn me into the villain. Enthusiasm was one thing, but outrage was another. "Because I wanted to discuss the viability of a general article to bring us into the open." And because I hadn't expected him to make the leap to medical magic so quickly. "I know so few magicians, and you're the only one I wanted to share this with. I thought I could trust you, Oscar. I thought your common sense would override your desire to expose magic. I was wrong." I gathered up my reticule and with my heart beating a loud yet stoic rhythm, I stood. "Good day. I'll see myself out."

"Wait." He came around the side of the desk and caught my elbow.

I kept my face averted so he couldn't see the tears welling there. I felt utterly foolish. It had been stupid of me to come here and trust a journalist. Matt would not have made such a miss-step.

"Wait, please, India." The plea in his voice was soft and gave me hope. "I need to apologize. You are right. Extension magic needs to be kept quiet. We know so little about it, and it does have potential to create problems. I tend to get excited about the possibilities and dismiss the negatives. Do you forgive me?

I swept my gaze up to his. He looked sincere, but I couldn't trust my instincts on this score. "Only if you promise not to tell anyone about combining time magic with other magic. That includes writing about it, or alluding to it too."

"I already promised."

"Promise again."

His thumb stroked my arm before letting go. "I promise, India. For you."

Me?

"Shall we try combining my ink magic with yours to extend its use? Do I require a different spell to make it work?"

"I do but you don't."

"How many spells did your mentor know?"

"Only two. He believes all magicians used to know more but they've been forgotten over the years when magicians were forced into hiding."

He slid a piece of paper toward him and reached for the inkstand.

I stayed his hand. "Not today."

He looked disappointed. "Very well. You know where to find me if you change your mind."

He walked with me through the outer office where the editor nodded a greeting. In the front reception room, Oscar touched the door handle but did not open the door. "Have you put any more thought into what show you'd like me to take you to?" he asked.

So he hadn't forgotten. "I...I think we ought to wait until your shoulder is better."

He hesitated then smiled. "Then I hope my recovery is swift. Good day, India."

* * *

MATT ARRIVED BACK at Park Street shortly after me. He looked exhausted again, all benefits from using the watch after my spell having vanished. My heart sank to see it. He threw himself into a chair in the library and scrubbed a hand across his forehead. His deep sigh resonated around the book-lined walls. He must feel as unwell as he looked.

I poured him a cup of tea and cleared my throat. Matt looked up, smiled weakly, and accepted the cup.

"You're no better, are you?" I almost didn't want to hear his answer, although I suspected what it would be before he gave it. His ill-health was written into every tired groove on his face.

"The magic lasted longer this time," he said with more cheerfulness in his voice than I expected. "You did well, India."

"Not well enough." I sighed. "I hoped there'd be significant improvement."

"I didn't rest after using it this time. I told you I would but I wanted to see how long I could stay focused without resting. So there you go. Your magic *has* helped."

"That is something," I added, trying to match his cheerfulness. If he could do it for my sake, I could do it for his.

"Is my aunt home?" he asked.

"Bristow said she went out with Lady Rycroft."

"Aunt Beatrice? Where?" His confusion was understandable. The sisters-in-law could not abide one another.

"I believe they went shopping."

"I hope they don't kill each another in the process."

"I should have gone with her," I said, picking up my teacup. "I am supposed to be her companion."

"She knew you were going out to see Barratt. If she had other plans and wanted you there, she would have told you so."

Still, I'd become lax in my duties lately. I must change that. But for now, I had work with Matt to accomplish. "I see Abercrombie didn't set the police, vigilantes or dogs on you."

"You haven't seen the teeth marks." He flashed me a grin and I relaxed. No matter how tired, he could almost always manage a smile for me. "I'll discuss what Abercrombie said when the others arrive. I've sent Bristow to fetch them, and Cyclops is taking the carriage to the coach house." He concentrated on sipping his tea slowly, eyeing me over the rim of the cup. "What about you? How is Barratt?"

"Oscar's not too badly injured."

His cup hit the saucer with a china-chipping *clink*. "Oscar?"

My face heated so I kept it lowered. "I mean Mr. Barratt." I cleared my throat. "The bullet merely grazed him. He's back at work already and was interested in the facts surrounding Dr. Hale's murder case. Brockwell didn't divulge much."

"Nor should he. Barratt can't be trusted to keep the particulars out of his newspaper."

"Surely he has a right to know how events played out. He was as much a victim as you or me."

"First of all, I am not a victim." His manner had switched from friendly to growling in an instant. "Second of all, he doesn't have a right to know anything. Brockwell clearly didn't trust him. Knowing the irresponsible articles Barratt has written on magic in the past, I can only agree with his assessment."

If he knew why I'd really gone to see Oscar, he'd be even angrier. I kept my face averted. "Then why were you amenable to me visiting him? You even said he was a good man. Why have you changed your mind so quickly?"

He paused for so long that I was compelled to look at him. "I...I don't know." He shook his head and passed a hand over his face. "You're right, India. Perhaps I'm not being fair on him. He is probably a trustworthy fellow, just over-eager about magic. I do see why you like him. You two have a lot in common."

I set my teacup and saucer down. "You're doing it again. Being inconsistent. And what do you mean we have a lot in common? Aside from magic, I don't see anything."

He tapped his finger on the side of the teacup then suddenly pointed at me. He clicked his fingers. "His family is in a craft trade too, like yours. There's a similarity."

"Thank you for pointing out my inferior roots."

He frowned. "I said they're similar, not inferior."

"Not to his, to yours." I stood and stalked to the door, not entirely sure where I would go. I just knew I couldn't be near Matt if he was going to push me in Oscar's direction.

Unfortunately, Matt wouldn't allow me to leave. He somehow managed to beat me to the door. His impressive frame blocked my exit, the severe frown emphasizing the lines of exhaustion. "That's not what I meant," he said.

"I don't know anything anymore, Matt!"

He placed his hands behind his back. "You're right. I'm difficult of late. My temper is getting the better of me too often. I'll try harder."

"No, Matt." I closed my eyes, wishing I could take back my outburst. "It's not that. I'm also feeling out of sorts. So much has happened these last few weeks, and I'm trying to gather my scattered wits together. It's like running behind an omnibus that I need to get on, only I can't catch it."

"I'm running alongside you," he murmured.

Heated voices came from the stairs outside the library, but I wasn't finished with Matt. I suddenly wanted him to understand something. "I have no interest in Oscar Barratt in the way you...in any way other than friendship. I do think he can be trusted, but that's a separate point. In regard to my feelings for him, I have no romantic ones."

His gaze searched my face but he did not have time to respond before Willie, not watching where she was going, bumped into his back. She barely paused to apologize before returning to her discussion with Duke and Chronos.

"You take that back, Duke!" she shouted.

Duke held up his hands. "I'm not saying nothing that ain't true."

"You are! Not all us Johnsons are bad seeds. You tell him, Matt."

Matt tore his gaze away from me. "What?" he asked, some-what absently.

"Duke's been telling Chronos about our family. He's been saying all us Johnsons are bad."

Duke held up a finger. "I said mad, not bad. And I didn't say *all*. I excluded Matt."

Willie thrust her hands on her hips. "You're calling me mad?"

"You're the maddest."

"Ha!"

Duke indicated her attire. "I ain't ever seen another woman dress like a man."

"That ain't mad," she shot back. "That's just plain good sense. This is a man's world, and if some people mistake me for a male for a minute or two, then good. Makes it even. Ain't that right, India?"

As much as I didn't want to get between them in an argu-ment, I had to agree with her. "I'm not sure that wearing trousers levels the playing field for long, but I do see your point, Willie. Sorry, Duke."

He grunted. "That ain't the only reason you're mad, Willie. There's carrying a revolver around London, for one thing."

"My Colt's saved me a time or two," she said with triumph. "Got any other reasons, Duke, or is that it?"

"That's enough," Matt snapped, striding to the fireplace. "The next person to start bickering will be sleeping in the stables."

Chronos winked at me as he passed. "Better keep your mouth shut, India."

Matt glared at him. I found it a little amusing but bit my lip to stop myself smiling. Matt was in no mood to appreciate the humor.

"Tea?" I said to the newcomers.

"Got anything stronger?" Chronos asked.

Willie made for the sideboard where Matt kept a decanter of brandy and glasses. Duke caught her wrist, halting her. He shook his head and jutted his chin in Matt's direction. Awareness dawned slowly across Willie's face.

"We'll all have tea, India," she declared. "Bristow don't like it when we drink before dinner. He says it ain't the done thing here in London."

"Perhaps not *this* part of London." But Chronos didn't press the issue and accepted the teacup I passed to him.

Cyclops joined us a few minutes later. "What have I missed?"

"I was about to tell everyone what Abercrombie told me," Matt said, remaining standing while the rest of us sat. "He admitted that his father flushed magicians out of the guild in his time as master. He was proud of it, in fact, and it took no convincing on my part for him to open up."

"More's the pity," Willie muttered. "If anyone deserves to be *convinced* by you, it's him."

Chronos looked from Matt to Willie and back again. "Him?"

"Matt may seem all gentlemanly and English but he's got the American Wild West running through his veins. Ain't no one can stay silent once he sets his mind to getting information from 'em."

Chronos eyed Matt like he was seeing him in a new light. "My kind of fellow."

"Can I continue now, Willie?" Matt said drily.

She gestured for him to go on.

"Abercrombie called it his father's legacy," Matt went on. "He forced two magicians out of the guild after learning of their secret. The present Abercrombie knew about you, Chronos."

"Abercrombie senior would have passed on as much information as he could to his son before he joined his maker," Chronos said. "Does he know I'm alive and in London?"

"I couldn't gauge whether he did or not."

"Why didn't you ask outright?"

"Because that might alert him to the fact that you *are* alive, and here, and I know it."

"A good point," Duke said.

Chronos agreed with a grudging nod.

"Abercrombie thinks you inherited your magic from Chronos," Matt said to me. "He seems to think your father was artless, and he did not mention your other grandparents."

"He wouldn't know about them," Chronos said. "My wife's family kept their magic a secret. As to India's maternal grandparents, their magic was in another craft, and they also kept it a secret."

"So Abercrombie doesn't know how strong she is," Duke said. "I wonder what he'd do if he did."

No one had an answer to that, and the room fell into silence until Matt broke it. "I told Abercrombie you want to know more about your grandfather, India. I asked him specifically about the controversy surrounding the last years of Chronos's life. I mentioned the stories you'd heard and wanted verified. He was pleased to tell me all about your experiments in extending magic, Chronos, and the death you caused."

"It wasn't entirely my fault," Chronos said with a pout in his voice.

"Abercrombie recalled the sensation the experiment caused within the Watchmaker's and Surgeon's Guilds. His father and the master of the Surgeon's Guild at the time met and vowed to bring justice for the victim."

"How?" Chronos cried. "They couldn't even know his name!"

"The only reason they didn't get far is because Dr. Millroy died a short time later—as did you, apparently. I couldn't tell from his expression whether he knew your death had been falsified, however."

A cold lump formed in my chest. I set down my teacup to not draw attention to my trembling hands. I found myself agreeing with Abercrombie on this matter. My grandfather may have believed he was doing the right thing, a good thing, but he was still a murderer. He'd ended a man's life before his time. It sickened me.

"India?" Matt asked gently.

I signaled for him to continue. I couldn't look at Chronos, but I felt his gaze drilling into the top of my head as I stared down at my lap.

"I questioned Abercrombie about Dr. Millroy's murder," Matt said. "He was in his twenties then, and his father was at the height of his powers in the guild. He admitted to knowing only what was reported in the newspapers and suggested Millroy's murderer was probably an opportunistic thief looking for valuables."

Chronos made a scoffing noise into his teacup.

"Do you know if any valuables were found on the body?" Cyclops asked.

"The police file said there was only a pencil," Matt said.

"It may have been opportunistic," Chronos said. "But there

are unanswered questions. For one thing, why was Dr. Millroy even in that area? His patients were a better sort, not slum dwellers."

"Looking for another subject for an experiment?" I bit off.

"I told you, he was set against another experiment after Wilson died on us."

"Perhaps he changed his mind."

Chronos grunted but looked unconvinced. "Didn't Abercrombie want to know why you were questioning him about Dr. Millroy?" he asked Matt.

"I told him India wanted as broad a picture of her dead grandfather as possible."

Chronos gave another grunt.

"If he suspects you're here, it's not because of me." Matt glanced at the decanter and glasses then refilled his cup with tea. He resumed his stance by the mantelpiece. In the masculine environment of the library, surrounded by leather-bound books and solid furniture, he looked strong and healthy. It clawed at my heart to know he was not.

"I went to the Surgeon's Guild hall after leaving Abercrombie's shop," he went on. "I wanted to know who the master was at the time, so I could question him." His lips curved into a smooth smile. "You've met him, India."

I thought quickly. There were only two doctors I knew of the right age. "Either Dr. Ritter or Wiley."

"Ritter."

"Who?" asked Chronos.

"The principal surgeon at the London Hospital," Matt said. "We met him while investigating Hale's death."

"Do you think it's a coincidence?"

Matt lifted one shoulder. "Hard to say for certain."

"Did you question him?" I asked.

He shook his head. "He wasn't at the hospital, and I didn't want to drive all over London looking for him. I was running out of time."

There was no need to ask why. We all knew he needed to use his watch and rest. Matt no longer liked using it outside of the house for fear that someone would see. Sheriff Payne had already spotted him using it in the coach. Not that the house was always safe either. His cousin Hope had also seen him use it after bursting into the drawing room one day.

"We'll go tomorrow," I said. "This time I'll join you."

"To keep an eye on me?" he asked with a tilt of his lips.

"To protect you from Dr. Ritter." I winked at him. "He struck me as rather fierce."

He laughed softly into his teacup.

Willie rolled her eyes and shook her head but thankfully made no comment. Chronos sported a smile that was far too smug for my liking. What did he have to be smug about?

"Want me to speak to the nurse I met at the hospital last time?" Willie asked. "She was mighty helpful."

"No need," Matt said. "But thanks."

The door suddenly opened and Bristow entered. He looked hot and his tie sat askew. It was the most disheveled I'd ever seen the butler. "I'm sorry to interrupt, sir," he said, smoothing back his hair. "You are required in the drawing room. Miss Glass is here and she's in quite a state."

Matt strode past him before he even finished speaking. The rest of us had to race to catch up. My mind raced too, thinking of all the things that could have happened to Miss Glass. Neither her mind nor her body were particularly strong.

I should have gone with her.

CHAPTER 6

"They want to lock me away, Harry." Miss Glass clung to Matt's arm. Her face was flushed, her eyes wide as she appealed to him. "You mustn't let them take me."

"I won't," he assured her. "You're home now, Aunt Letitia. You're safe."

"Take me with you, Harry. I've changed my mind. I want to go to the Continent too."

"Who's Harry?" Chronos whispered.

"Matt's father, her brother," Willie said. "She sometimes thinks Matt is him."

"You mean she's barking?"

I shot him a withering glare but he was intent on the scene playing out before him on the sofa and didn't notice. I crouched in front of Miss Glass, took her hand in both of mine, and spoke quietly yet firmly to her. "It's me, Miss Glass. It's all right."

"Veronica?" She glanced around the room. "What are you doing at Harry's place?"

"And who's Veronica?" came Chronos question.

"A maid she once knew," Willie told him.

72

I turned and gave Chronos the benefit of my fiercest glare. "This is a private matter. Do you mind?"

"Private?" he said. "But you're not family."

"I am her companion." I turned back to Miss Glass, and although I did not see him leave, I heard his retreating footsteps. "Would you like to lie down?" I asked Miss Glass. "Or sit here and have a nice cup of tea to calm your nerves."

"I need an ice." She flapped her hand in front of her face. "It's quite hot in here."

She did look flushed and her breathing was elevated. I frowned at Matt. "Shouldn't she be with Lady Rycroft?"

"With Mama?" Miss Glass shook her head over and over. "You do say the oddest things, Veronica. Mama passed away some years ago."

Matt and I both glanced at the door. "Bristow!" he bellowed.

Miss Glass covered her ears and I gently chastised him. He apologized before asking Bristow how Miss Glass arrived home.

"I don't know," the butler said. "She knocked on the door and was on her own."

"Aunt?" Matt said. "Letitia? Did you walk here?"

"Of course." Miss Glass patted her hair at the back of her head. The carefully arranged curls had dropped and some strands hung loose down her back. "I have no money for an omnibus or hackney. I wouldn't know how to direct one to pick me up anyway. Well, Harry? What do you say? Can I come with you after all?"

She thought she was back in the time before her brother left England, some forty years ago. Apparently he'd offered to take her with him on his travels, but she'd refused, somewhat reluctantly, and had lived a stifled life ever since under the guardianship of her father and then her brother. Even in her advanced years she'd been under the domain of her brother and sister-in-law, Lord and Lady Rycroft, and had rarely been allowed out on her own. It would seem she was re-living those long ago days, perhaps even playing out a different outcome where she did go with Harry to the Continent. It was sad to think she regretted making the decision to stay.

"You can come with me," Matt said gently, holding her hand. "We'll have adventures together."

She smiled at him, her lower lip quivering. "Veronica shall come too."

Peter brought in a tray with tea things and I poured her a cup. She took it with shaking hands and sipped slowly. The familiar ritual seemed to soothe her. No one interrupted as she quietly drank the entire cup and set it down again.

"Aunt Letitia?" Matt asked carefully. "How do you feel?"

She touched the back of her hand to her cheek. "It's very warm in here. Have you got the fire going, Matthew?"

I exchanged a small smile with Matt. He was her nephew again, not her brother. How quickly she changed.

Willie flounced into a chair and expelled a measured breath. "Nice to have you back, Letty."

"Do not put your feet on the table," Miss Glass snapped at her. "This is not a saloon."

"I weren't going to!" Willie grinned.

Miss Glass frowned. "What's got into you? Why are you smiling like a madwoman, Willemina?"

"Guess I'm just happy."

"Well stop it. It's not English to smile like that."

"I ain't English, and we Americans smile like this all the time."

"Where's Aunt Beatrice?" Matt said.

"At home, I expect." Miss Glass frowned at her teacup as if she wasn't sure how it got there. "She took me out."

"Where did you go?"

"Shopping, and then we called on a friend of hers. She used to be a friend of mine too, years ago." She sniffed and turned away to stare into the fireplace. "I cannot abide the woman now. All silly ruffles on her sleeves and a pink flower in her hair. The ruffles and flowers were pretty when she was young, but now they're an embarrassment. She thinks she's still a girl of seventeen having her first season." She tapped her temple. "She's gone quite mad."

The booming voice out in the hall announced the arrival of Lady Rycroft. Bristow tried to inform us but he hadn't even finished saying her name before she barged past him with a click of her tongue. Her three daughters filed in behind her in height order.

"There you are!" Lady Rycroft marched up to her sister-in-law and for one horrid moment I thought she would slap her. She kept her hands by her sides, however, and merely stood like a towering chimney spewing out anger with every huffing breath. "You stupid, ridiculous old woman! How dare you humiliate me like that!"

Patience Glass, the eldest daughter, gasped in horror at her mother's tirade. The middle one, Charity, snickered behind her hand, and the youngest and prettiest, Hope, reddened but remained otherwise unaffected. Her clever gaze hardly lingered on her aunt or mother, however, but took in Matt twice over as if she were drinking in the sight of him after a long absence.

Miss Glass remained surprisingly unaffected by her sister-in-law's outburst. "Whatever do you mean, Beatrice? If anyone is ridiculous it's Penelope. Did you see that flower in her hair? At her age? I couldn't abide her company for another moment."

"So you took it upon yourself to leave?" Beatrice screeched. "Without informing anyone and leaving me wondering where you'd gone? Are you inconsiderate as well as mad?"

"Aunt Beatrice," Matt warned. "Compose yourself."

He didn't need to concern himself on behalf of his Aunt Letitia. Miss Glass was quite capable of standing up for herself these days. Living with him and not her brother had given her confidence. She and I were alike in that regard. "Don't pretend to care about my wellbeing, Beatrice."

"Of course I care!" Lady Rycroft snapped. "Rycroft would blame me for your disappearance."

"Well, it *was* you who dragged me to see Penelope when you know what she did to me." Miss Glass's voice faded into a choke that had me frowning at her. What had this Penelope done to her to not only make her want to walk home alone but also given her a turn?

"What did she do to you?" Hope asked. As the most brazen of the three, I wasn't surprised she spoke up. Patience was far too shy, and Charity had lost interest in the discussion already and was busy trying to catch Cyclops's attention.

Cyclops edged further away. He might flee altogether if she dared to do anything more than stare.

"Aunt Letitia should not have had to make her own way home," Matt said. "Why was she unaccompanied?"

Lady Rycroft straightened, emphasizing her height. "That is entirely the point, Matthew. Why was she unaccompanied when she has a companion?" She looked pointedly at me.

It was difficult to put on a defiant face when I felt guilty.

"India had work to do for me today." Matt's lie rolled easily off his tongue.

"India is not my full-time companion," Miss Glass added. "I share her with Matthew." She clasped my hand as I'd clasped hers earlier. "As to whose fault it was, it was mine alone. I decided to leave. The blame rests with no one else."

Of all the people in that room who could have responded, it was Willie who got in first. "You weren't in your right mind when you got back, Letty. You sure you even knew where you were?" No one got to the heart of a matter like Willie.

"Of course I knew," Miss Glass retorted. "We were visiting Penelope. I don't like her so I left."

"You thought someone was chasing you, wanting to lock you up."

"She ought to be locked up," Lady Rycroft muttered.

The three Glass girls repeated their responses of before—Patience gasped, Charity snickered, and Hope's cheeks reddened. Hope glanced at her mother, one of the few times she'd looked away from Matt.

"Would you like to stay for tea?" Matt asked.

Sometimes I could throttle him.

Hope smiled. "That would be—"

"No," Lady Rycroft said. The room itself seemed to heave with the collective sighs of relief. "The day has been long enough. Letitia, the girls and I leave soon for Rycroft House to prepare for Patience's wedding. You will come with us. Pack all of your things. It has been decided that you will not return to London. The best place for you—"

"I beg your pardon!" Miss Glass said. Her voice may be frail but she managed to instill as much majesty into it as the queen. "I am not going to travel with you, and I am not staying at that moldy old place. I am staying right here and will only travel with Matthew when the time comes."

"Don't be absurd. You love the estate. You're just being difficult to vex me."

"My aunt is not going with you unless she wants to," Matt said. "If my uncle is unhappy with that arrangement, he can speak to me. Is that clear?"

Lady Rycroft's nostrils flared. She was settling in for battle. "She will do as her brother sees fit."

"No." There was a solidness to that single word; an immovability that could not be swept aside. Matt had no intention of giving in.

"I beg your pardon?"

"I said no." He stood and held out his hand in the direction of the exit. "Now, if you don't mind, I'm a busy man. Please pass on my regards to my uncle."

Lady Rycroft quivered with anger, making her double chins shake. "You are as stubborn as your father."

"Thank you."

She narrowed her eyes at him. "Consider your family, Matthew. Consider the damage her embarrassing turns can do to our reputation. I was humiliated today in front of my friend. What if Penelope tattles? What if Letitia has another turn?"

"Then do not take her out again. The solution is quite simple."

"She needs to be somewhere she will be well cared for, to stop her running off and saying things to our friends."

"She does not run off when she's here. Don't," he added in a low tone when she opened her mouth again. "Do not say another word on this subject. Is that clear?"

Her jaw tensed, and if her eyes narrowed any further they'd close altogether. "Come, girls."

Hope and Charity followed their mother out, but Patience remained. She was the last of the three I expected to defy her mother. She bent down to Miss Glass and kissed her cheek.

"Thank you for the wedding gift," she said softly. "It's lovely."

"That's quite all right, dear," Miss Glass said. "Run along now or your mother will explode."

Patience turned to go but did an extraordinary thing. She caught my hand and dragged me alongside her. "I need to tell you something," she whispered.

I looked at her but she kept her gaze directly ahead. She walked slowly so as not to catch up to her mother, now waiting at the front door.

"Do you remember that ill-mannered fellow who burst into our dinner party here that night?" she asked.

"Sheriff Payne?" I said. "Yes, why?"

"Hope spoke with him yesterday."

I stopped and stared at her. We were alone, Matt having

gone ahead to speak to his Aunt Beatrice, and I was grateful. Patience could not have said anything more shocking. "Why? How did she even know where to find him?"

"My sisters and I were out walking and spotted him loitering outside our house upon our return. Charity and I wanted nothing to do with him, but Hope confronted him. They spoke for several minutes and her expression changed from irate to curious. When she rejoined us, I asked what he wanted and she claimed it was nothing. I didn't believe her."

"Patience!" Lady Rycroft called. "What are you talking about?"

I squeezed her hand and whispered, "Thank you."

She gave me a smile and joined her mother and sisters. Lady Rycroft clicked her tongue at the delay. If Hope suspected her sister had spoken to me about her she did not let on. The girls followed their mother out like sheep.

Matt shut the door after they left. "I tried to distract my aunt for you as you spoke to Patience. It didn't work for long."

"Never mind," I said. "She managed to say what she needed to. Matt, she told me something quite unnerving." I glanced into the drawing room. Miss Glass was still there with Willie, Duke and Cyclops. I couldn't say this in front of her. We were quite alone in the entrance hall, however, so I sidled closer to him. "Patience told me that Hope spoke with Sheriff Payne yesterday."

"What?" His explosive whisper was loud enough to draw Duke's attention. He frowned at us but did not join us.

I took Matt's arm and directed him to the staircase, out of sight of the drawing room altogether. I did not want Miss Glass suspecting a thing. "Patience said they saw him outside their house and Hope confronted him." I filled him in on the rest, brief as it was.

He leaned an arm on the newel post and raked his hand

through his hair. He needed to rest now, not worry about this. I wish I hadn't told him.

"We'll discuss it later," I said, giving him a little shove. "It can wait."

"I'd rather discuss it now."

"But—"

"Don't, India." It was the same stern tone he'd used with Lady Rycroft. He must have realized because his face softened and he touched the tips of my fingers. "I'm fine, and I want to talk about it now."

"What's going on?" Duke asked from the drawing room doorway.

Matt let go of my fingers and told Duke what Patience had said.

"Payne!" Duke swore. "What's that snake up to now?"

"Fishing for information about me," Matt suggested. "He wrongly suspects that my family will know my weaknesses and perhaps my movements."

It sounded plausible but I wasn't convinced. An observant person would know he rarely visited his titled relations. Perhaps that's what Payne was doing—observing. Perhaps he'd learned that the Rycrofts could tell him nothing.

"Then why did Hope talk to him for so long when she knows nothing?" I asked. "Why did she talk to him at all? She saw the way he barged into our dinner party, and how you threw him out, Matt. She must know you despise him. And yet she did not send Payne on his way. Instead, she conversed with him and sported a curious look on her face, according to Patience. To me, that means one thing—he told her something about you, not the other way around. Something that intrigued her."

Duke sat on the second lowest step and swore again. "This ain't good, Matt. What lies is he spreading now?"

"She did look at you rather oddly today," I said. "Very

intensely, as if she were trying to gauge something about you."

"I noticed too," Duke said. "I thought it was because she liked him and her mother's trying to marry them off."

"That was my first thought too," I admitted.

Matt looked at me through his lashes.

"He must have told her about the crimes he reckons you committed," Duke said with a shake of his head. "He wants to cause a rift between you and your family. Too bad for him there already is one."

Matt nodded slowly, deep in thought. I sat beside Duke on the step, a little awkwardly thanks to my corset and bustle, and considered the possibilities and whether we should confront Hope. It might work. Perhaps Matt could charm answers from her.

"Why would Patience betray her sister?" *That* was Matt's question?

"Because I suspect Hope is awful to her," I said with a shrug. "Perhaps this is her way of evening the score after a lifetime of living in the shadow of her prettier, more vivacious younger sister."

He lifted his brows. "It's hardly Hope's fault that she's prettier."

"Lady Rycroft makes sure Hope's sisters know she is the favored daughter. Hope isn't the sort of girl who lets them forget it. I know you think I'm doing her a disservice, but I don't think I am. Patience's reasons for tattling don't concern me, anyway. What does concern me is that Hope has seen you use your watch, Matt. She knows your secret."

He signaled for me to move along the step. I made space for him and he sat, sandwiching me between both men.

"She can't possibly know what it means," he said. "Not even her wildest guesses would come close to the truth."

"Payne also knows that watch is important to you," Duke said. "He tried to steal it."

"Again, he doesn't know its true function."

"He saw the glow in the coach once," I said. "If he knows about magic, he might guess."

Matt shook his head. "You're both scaremongering. Hope is my cousin. She won't betray me." He stood and headed up the stairs, taking two at a time. He quickly disappeared from sight.

Duke sighed and leaned back on his elbows. "He's not doing so good, India."

"I know," I said quietly. "His health is one problem, but the state of his mind is another. He's under enormous strain, and now he has to worry about Payne getting to his family. He may not like them, but he would feel responsible if something happened to one of them."

"Aye."

I had a thought and turned to Duke. His friendly, blocky face looked back expectantly. "What if we're wrong and Payne isn't looking for information about Matt or trying to spread nasty rumors? What if he's trying to seduce Hope?"

He sat up suddenly. Then he burst out laughing. "Good luck to him."

"Duke! I'm serious. Matt would feel responsible for her wellbeing."

"That girl can take care of herself. Imagine if they wed. It'd solve all our problems. Payne would be saddled with a sneaky little miss, and Hope'll be tied to a man who'll wind up in jail sooner or later. They deserve each other."

"You forget one thing. The daughter of a British aristocrat won't marry an American sheriff. But he can ruin her."

* * *

DR. RITTER WAS as happy to see us as I expected. That is, not at all. A nurse at the London Hospital escorted us to his office, unaware that we knew our way, and announced us when the principal doctor invited her in.

His heavy brow descended into a thunderous scowl. "What do you two want?"

The nurse wisely scuttled away before Dr. Ritter could admonish her.

"You were once the master of the Worshipful Company of Surgeons," Matt said, using the guild's formal title.

"So?" Dr. Ritter was as old as Chronos but, like my grandfather, he was hale and hardy. He wasn't a big man, but he had a strong presence with his thick gray beard and a verdant set of eyebrows that commanded attention.

"So Miss Steele and I are undertaking a new investigation into an old murder. The victim was a member of the guild at the time you were master."

He sat back in his chair, all the bluster knocked out of him.

"I'm referring to Dr. Millroy," Matt added.

Dr. Ritter did not look surprised. "Why are you making inquiries now? What has it got to do with you?"

"Police Commissioner Munro is pleased with the number of murder cases we've solved. He asked us to re-open this one in the hope of finding the killer." Mentioning a name and rank was designed to impress Dr. Ritter and make our visit seem more official. It was impossible to tell if the tactic worked. Dr. Ritter still looked stunned.

"There must be dozens of unsolved murders in the city," he said. "Why this one?"

Matt merely shrugged one shoulder. "Why don't you ask Commissioner Munro?"

Matt approached the desk and pulled out a chair for me. Dr. Ritter blinked stupidly at us, as if he couldn't quite believe this was happening to him again. He had every reason to be wary of us. While he hadn't been involved in Dr. Hale's murder, our investigation had uncovered his attempts to profit from the illegal sale of Hale's medicines. It would seem the hospital's board had not yet removed him as principal. Another scandal could force their hand.

"I can see from your reaction that you recall Dr. Millroy," Matt said as he settled into the chair. He took a few moments to look around the office at the bookshelves crammed with medical texts, the framed degree from Cambridge, sketches and documents stacked loosely on the desk surface. He seemed comfortable in his role of interrogator, and completely in command. "Tell me what you know about Dr. Millroy's death," he went on.

"Nothing," Dr. Ritter spat. "It was so long ago...I can hardly recall the particulars."

"Tell me what you do recall."

Dr. Ritter's gaze slipped to me. "In front of a lady? I think not."

"Don't mind me," I said, removing my notepad and pencil from my reticule. "I'm used to gruesome details. As Mr. Glass said, we've worked together to solve a number of murders for the police. Nothing you say will shock me, but I appreciate your concern."

Dr. Ritter sighed, perhaps seeing no way out. Yet another mention of the police seemed to do the trick, too. "I didn't find out about Dr. Millroy's death until I read about it in the newspaper like everyone else. Naturally I was shocked and saddened. He was an excellent doctor, by all accounts, and a member of the guild when I was its master."

"An active member?" Matt asked.

"Not particularly, but few are. There are only so many Court of Assistants positions to fill."

"You say he was an excellent doctor," I said. "How do you know?"

"Certain members get certain reputations. I hear about them, both good and bad. The medical field is a small one, Miss Steele, particularly at my level. Dr. Millroy was highly sought after by some very elite patients."

As were many magicians in their respective trades. Mr. Pitt the magician apothecary also had customers from the upper classes. Of course, he'd lost them all now and was in danger of losing his life if a jury found him guilty of killing Dr. Hale.

"That's why it's odd that he was killed in a slum." Dr. Ritter wrinkled his nose as if he could smell the unwashed in the poorest areas of London. "He couldn't have been seeing a patient there."

"Perhaps he offered his services *gratis*," Matt said.

Dr. Ritter snorted. "Not Millroy. It's more likely he was simply lost and a local criminal took advantage."

"Do you know anything about a diary he kept on him?" Matt asked.

"No. I told you, I didn't know him well."

"But you did know that he experimented on a sick man who subsequently died."

Dr. Ritter's throat worked but no words came out.

"You confronted Dr. Millroy over his part in the vagrant's death," Matt went on.

"How did you find out about that?" Dr. Ritter finally asked.

"The police told me."

Dr. Ritter thumped his fist on the desk, making my nerves jump. My pencil drew a crooked line across the page. "This is absurd. I had nothing to do with Dr. Millroy's death."

"How did you learn about the experiment on the vagrant? I doubt Dr. Millroy admitted it to you or to anyone in your guild."

Dr. Ritter smoothed his hand over the leather cover of a large medical text on the desk. "His wife came to see me. She told me as much as she knew about the experiment."

It wasn't clear whether she mentioned magic to him, or if he knew of its existence and involvement in the case. I doubted Matt would ask directly, although I thought it a good idea. A direct question drew more direct answers. But his thoughts on the matter were very different to mine.

At least we had the source of the information now. "Why would she betray her husband?" I said to Matt.

It was Dr. Ritter who answered, however. "Women tend to tattle. He was foolish to entrust her with the information."

"I beg to differ. Women are as capable of keeping secrets as men. She had a reason for coming to you, Dr. Ritter. Do you know what it is?"

"Of course not. A woman's mind is unfathomable."

"For some men, certainly." I wanted to ask him if he was married and whether his wife would ever take harmful information about him to his superiors but decided against it.

"Do you know who might have benefited from Dr. Millroy's death?" Matt asked. "A rival, perhaps, or an heir?"

"He had no rivals that I knew of, but he was an excellent doctor with a list of wealthy and influential patients. That sort of success breeds envy. As to an heir, I believe he had no children. I assume his wife is his beneficiary." Dr. Ritter got to his feet and indicated the door. "Do you mind? You're keeping me from my sick patients."

I led the way out but Matt paused in the doorway. "One other thing. Did Mrs. Millroy happen to mention Dr. Millroy kept a mistress who bore him an illegitimate son?"

"What?" Dr. Ritter said on a laugh. "Is this a joke?"

"No."

"Of course she never mentioned it, and no, I did not know. How could I?"

Matt walked beside me back through the hospital's warren of corridors and wards. We did not speak until we breathed the cloying air outside.

"Are we going to visit Mrs. Millroy now?" I asked as we descended the front steps.

"After we make a diversion," Matt said.

"Where to?"

"I want to see where Dr. Millroy died." He opened the carriage door for me and folded the step down. "Do you think you can manage it, India? It's not in a good area."

"Of course. I'm hardly a snowflake that'll melt at the first sign of heat." I gathered up my skirts and took his offered hand.

Matt smiled and gave Duke directions to the crime scene. It was in Whitechapel, not far from where the Ripper murders had taken place a mere twenty months ago. I clutched my reticule to my chest. The solid shape of my watch inside was a comfort. We might need it.

CHAPTER 7

*C*oaches were a rare sight in Whitechapel. We drew
attention on our slow drive through the labyrinth of
gloomy streets but it wasn't from curiosity. Not even the children looked upon us with wonder in their eyes, but rather
with calculating assessment. If we wanted to keep our possessions, we had to keep our wits about us and our valuables
hidden from light fingers.

We pulled to a stop outside a brick archway too narrow
for the coach to fit through. The faded sign painted above the
arch announced Bright Court waited beyond. The singularly
unsuitable name was a joke played on the miserable stranger
in search of safety. There was no beautiful sun-drenched land
beyond the sooty bricks. It was all gray, in every direction.
Even at mid-morning, the soupy air made it feel like dusk.

My only possession of value was my watch. I'd hung it
around my neck, tucking it out of sight beneath my jacket. It
would chime a warning if danger came near. Even so, I took
Matt's offered arm and kept close to him. Duke remained
with the coach and horse. I wished we'd brought either
Cyclops or Willie with us, but Cyclops had volunteered to
stay at home and keep an eye on Chronos, as he didn't yet

trust him not to leave. Willie had announced she was going out for the day. I suspected she would regret not coming with us, only because the opportunity to wave her gun around was likely to present itself at some point.

"Shall we split up and question twice as many people?" I asked, counting the number of tenements edging the square court. There appeared to be eight, but it was impossible to tell if the old buildings, some made of wood and others brick, were split into even more tenements inside. How many families did each one house?

"Only you could joke about that," Matt said.

We crossed the slippery cobbled courtyard with care, heading for a stooped woman struggling with a pail at the pump. Water sloshed over the sides with every jerky step and splashed over her skirt.

"Allow me," Matt said, taking it from her.

She swatted his arm. "You give that back, you prick! It's mine!"

"I don't want it," Matt explained with a hint of humor in his voice. "I merely want to help you carry it to your destination." He nodded at the nearest door. "In there?"

The woman stretched her back and rubbed her hip with red, chafed hands. She wasn't as old as I originally thought. Her face was clear of deep lines and none of the strands of hair that escaped from beneath her cap sported any gray. Her eyes, however, were as tired and hollow as Matt's when he needed to use his watch. I guessed her to be about forty.

"What do you want from me?" she said carefully. "I ain't got nothing for the likes of you." She eyed me. "I ain't *that* kind of woman. You want to go round the corner for your pleasure."

"That's not why we're here," I assured her, not wanting to think too carefully about her assumption. "We simply need to ask if you remember a crime that happened here years ago."

She hunched her shoulders, drawing her ragged shawl

further up the back of her neck as if warding off a chill. "You don't look like the pigs."

"We're not," I said. "We're relatives of a man who died here and simply wish to find out more about his death for our own peace of mind." That was the explanation we'd rehearsed in the coach, and I thought I did an admirable job at lying. Matt probably would have done better, but we'd agreed that if we spoke to a woman, I ought to question her and he the men. Women tended to trust their own gender more, particularly women in this part of the city who were often mistreated by their menfolk.

"You got to be sp'ific," the woman said. "There's been a lot of crime here, a lot of death."

"This was a murder," I said. "It happened years ago. Did you live here then?"

"I've lived in Bright Court my whole life." The woman sucked air between her gapped teeth. "I remember it. I were only a child then." She pointed to the corner at the back of the court, not far from a door. "They found him there one morning. Toff, he was. Like you, sir. That's why I remember that one."

How many murders occurred in Bright Court that she would struggle to remember them all?

"Did you see the body?" I asked.

The woman held out her hand. Matt took a coin from his pocket and placed it on her palm. She squirreled it away among the folds of her skirt. "Aye. We all saw it before the police showed up."

"What do you remember about it?"

"Not much. His clothes were covered in blood, here." She indicated her upper chest and throat.

Raised children's voices came from inside the nearest tenement. Our informer didn't blink an eye or move to check on them. Behind us, someone coughed. I looked around to see a woman watching us from where she stood over a steaming copper. She prodded the contents of the copper with a staff, but her gaze never left us. She was the only other person in sight, yet I sensed a dozen eyes. I felt conspicuous in the courtyard, despite my simple gray dress, and very exposed. With only one exit, we would be trapped in here if anyone chose to attack.

Like Dr. Millroy.

"A child claimed to have seen the killer leave the scene," I said. "Were you that child?"

"My brother," our informant said. "He liked to come out here at night when our Ma was working and Pa slept."

"Where can we find him now?"

"Pauper's grave in Kensal Green." She laughed at her joke, a brittle sound that ended in a dry cough.

"Did your brother tell you anything of note about the killer?" Matt asked.

"He said he were a man, but he couldn't see his face. Said he just walked away, all calm like, wiping the blood off his knife on his coat. He weren't in no hurry to get away." She adjusted her shawl at her neck again. "Who kills someone then don't run off? That's what got me."

"Did your brother see the killer steal anything from the body?"

"He thought so. The killer was at the body's side for a bit after, so he prob'ly did. I would of. The dead don't need chattels no more."

"You said you saw the victim's face," I said. "Had you, or anyone living here, seen him before?"

"No. They told us he were a doctor." She shrugged thin shoulders, dislodging her shawl again. "He were a stranger. He didn't do his doctoring round here." She snorted a laugh.

"Any thoughts on why he might have been in Bright Court at all then?" Matt asked.

Another shrug of her shoulders. "He got lost after visiting

a whorehouse." She flashed a grin at me. "That shock you, miss?"

"Not at all," I said. "I don't suppose there was a whorehouse operating within Bright Court at the time?"

Her grin slipped. "We're respectable women here!"

"I'm sure you are. But what about then?"

She wiped her nose with the back of her hand. The movement did not distract from the direction of her gaze. It slid to where the body of Dr. Millroy had been found. Then it shifted to the door.

"Is there something you want to tell us?" I prompted.

"May be, but gawd, I'm starving." At that moment, two children burst out of the nearby door, cursing one another at the top of their lungs. "My little uns be starving too. I got to go see what I can scrape together for 'em." She did not move off.

Matt took the hint and handed her two more coins. They vanished like magic into her skirt.

"Old Nell had men call on her sometimes," she said. "There was always enough food on the table for her and her baby, her brother too. We children guessed why, partic'ly because our mothers never liked her."

"They didn't like her because she was a prostitute?" I asked.

"Aye, but because Old Nell thought she were better than them too. She were hoity toity then and is even worse now, on account of her son doing all right for himself."

"What sort of clients came and went from her lodgings?" I asked. "Were they men like Dr. Millroy?"

She mused on that for a moment before finally nodding. "Makes sense, but she never said nothing about him being known to her at the time."

Why would she if she had something to do with his murder? Even if she didn't, she wouldn't want to attract the attention of the police or more hostility from her neighbors.

"Anyways, her customers weren't gentlemen like him," the woman said as her children ran past again, still shouting at one another. "But they weren't the worst sort, neither. Laborers with a bit of ready to spend, mostly. Her brother found 'em for her. He used to live with her but he's long gone."

"And her baby?" Matt asked. "Is that the son you spoke of, now doing well for himself?"

The question took her by surprise. "Aye. Jack no longer lives there but he visits reg'lar. But he can't tell you nothing from those days. He were a mere babe."

"She still lives in that tenement?" Matt asked, nodding at the door near where Dr. Millroy's body had been found.

"Aye." She shifted her weight. "If you got more questions, then I got to ask for more coin. It's the children, see. They're starving."

Matt handed her another coin. "Where do you want this pail?"

She stared at him with round eyes, as if she'd expected him to drop the pail now that he'd got what he wanted from her. "Inside."

"India, come with me."

I followed the woman and Matt in, passing by the two children, a boy and a girl, who stopped arguing long enough to watch us. The tenement was clean, although a damp odor came from the walls and the floorboards were uneven. We bypassed a staircase leading up to another family's residence and headed along the short corridor. The tenement comprised of two rooms downstairs, one a bedroom with two sagging beds in it and mattresses on the floor, and the other a kitchen and sitting room all in one. Matt set the pail down on the floor by the table, thanked the woman, then headed back outside.

"You ask Old Nell the delicate questions," Matt said, offering me his arm without looking at me. His eyes were fixed on the door near where Dr. Millroy's body was found. "You're better at that than I am."

"I don't necessarily agree," I said, taking his arm. "We'll see what sort of woman she is. She might respond to your charms better than my direct questions."

He laughed softly, and I was pleased that he was in a good mood. I wondered how much it had to do with the fact we were about to speak to the woman who might have been Dr. Millroy's mistress and their son—we could be on the brink of finding a medical magician.

Matt rapped firmly on the door and a voice from the depths ordered us to leave her alone. Matt knocked again.

"Go away you filthy little devils before I set my Jack onto you!"

"Just go in," said the woman sweating over the boiling copper. "She don't get out of bed no more, and the children sometimes play nick-knocking to set her off. And sir?"

"Yes?"

"Don't believe everything Maisie tells you." She nodded at the neighbor's house where we'd just been. "She'll say anything for a bit o' ready. That information's for free." She grabbed the staff with both hands and stirred the laundry. Behind her, a shirt hanging over a line dripped into the muddy puddle.

"Do you know anything about the murder of Dr. Millroy, some twenty-seven years ago?" Matt asked her.

She shook her head. "Before my time."

"We're back at the beginning if we can't believe Maisie," I said to Matt as we studied the door.

"Perhaps. Or perhaps we have to untangle the truths from the lies. Most lies incorporate some of the truth for authenticity."

I squeezed his arm. "Let's see what Old Nell has to say."

He opened the door and headed into the gloom. It took my eyes several moments to adjust to the dark. When they did, I realized the layout was similar to Maisie's place, with a narrow staircase leading up to our left and an equally narrow hall on the right. Straight ahead, at the end of the hallway, was the kitchen. Someone moved around back there, chopping. Cooking smells wafted up to us. It was a pleasant change to the damp odor of Maisie's rooms and the smoke from the fire beneath the copper.

We headed toward the kitchen but stopped at a door behind the staircase. It was open and led to a bedroom. A woman sat up in bed, propped against a pillow, her eyes closed. She wasn't as old as Chronos, but she was past middle age, and only the ghosts of her beauty remained in the high cheekbones and full lips. A thick blanket covered most of the bedspread and another was folded on the chair tucked into the dressing table by the wardrobe. On the dressing table was a white enamel hand mirror and matching brush, and on the table beside the bed, a lamp glowed softly. A tin of sugared sweets sat open, half empty. This was not the bedroom of a woman struggling to make ends meet. It was simple, but not filthy, damp or sparse. Someone took good care of Old Nell.

Matt nudged me.

I cleared my throat. "Nell?" I said, wishing I'd learned her last name from the neighbors.

Her eyes opened and her mouth worked furiously. I thought she was struggling to speak but then she made a sucking sound, and I realized she had one of the sweets in her mouth. "Who're you?" Her voice was another thing I wasn't expecting. It was strong and deep for a woman, and not at all thin or frail like the figure in the bed.

"My name is Mrs. Wright and this is my husband," I said, using the false names we'd decided upon on the way.

Nell's gaze flicked over me but lingered on Matt. She arranged her long white hair over her shoulder and picked up the tin. She smiled, revealing a patchwork of teeth. "Sweet?"

It took me a moment to realize she was offering him one of the confections from the tin but not me.

He popped a sweet in his mouth. "Mmmm. My favorites. I buy them from Oxford Street." He inspected the label on the side of the tin. "Where's this shop?"

"I don't know. My son buys them. He's very good to me."

If her son was the source of the sweets, blankets and trinkets, then he was indeed doing well. He had more money at his disposal than most East Enders. Because he was a doctor? Or, if not a university trained doctor, at least some sort of healer?

I was about to question Nell when she said to Matt, "You're not an Englishman."

"I'm lately from America."

"How exotic."

He complimented her on the smells coming from the kitchen. "Is it cake?"

She sniffed. "I don't know. Mary will know. Mary! She's deaf," she added, quieter. "If I don't shout, she won't hear me. Mary!"

A young woman entered but stopped inside the doorway when she saw us and gasped. She must indeed be hard of hearing if she hadn't heard us enter.

"Mary, this is Mr. Wright and his wife," Nell said. "Are you baking?"

"A cake for Jack." Mary blushed. "He seemed a mite unhappy last time he were here so I wanted to cheer him up."

"Jack is fine. He's always fine. Fetch cake and tea, Mary. I have guests."

"We can't stay," I said. "We have a few questions we need to ask you and then we'll be on our way."

Nell's face fell. "Pity. I get so few visitors now. Not like the old days." She chuckled into her chin. "Such a time I used to have when I was younger. I was real pretty. My hair was blonde and it curled real nice too."

"It's still beautiful hair," Matt said gently.

Nell smiled. "Off with you, Mary."

"Yes, Miss Sweet." The woman bobbed a curtsy and left.

"She's not good company," Nell said. "And she's rather plain to look at, but she don't cost my son much, on account of no one else wants her. She's had it hard too. Hard like me. But Mary and me, we're soldiers. We fall down, then get back up again."

"Mary's very lucky to have you and your son," Matt said. "Not everyone is so fortunate."

"Aye, true."

"Did she call you Miss Sweet?" Matt asked with an arch of his brow and a smile on his lips. He indicated the tin. "Sweets for Sweet?"

Nell giggled. "Does your wife know you're a flirt?"

"Actually, I do," I said.

Nell's smile faded, and I decided to stay quiet. Matt would do better without me where Nell Sweet was concerned, *if* he ever got around to asking her questions about the murder. He seemed to want to talk to her about everything else except that.

"Your son must be an excellent fellow," Matt said. "I find gentlemen who take care of their mothers usually are." I thought calling the son of a fallen woman a gentleman was a stretch but bit my tongue.

Nell smiled. "Do you have children, Mr. Wright?"

"Not yet."

"Well, don't leave it too long." She looked at me. "She's not getting any younger."

I bit my tongue harder.

"Where does Jack work?" Matt asked.

"In a shop in a good part of London, that's what he said."

"In what trade?"

"Fixing things. That's my Jack, always fixing things."

"What sort of things?"

People, I willed her to say.

"I don't know." She leaned forward and lowered her voice. "I'm right glad he got himself a reg'lar job, out of Whitechapel. The people round here, they'll lie to your face and sell their own mother for a bob. But my son is a good boy. He cares about his old mum."

"And his father?"

"Dead." She lowered her gaze to her lap. "God rest his useless soul."

"When did he die?"

"A long time ago. Years and years."

"What was his name?"

She blinked hard at him and tilted her head to the side. "Why do you want to know?"

Matt put up his hands. "I'm merely curious."

Nell replaced the lid on the tin of sweets. "What do you want?" It would seem she'd suddenly woken up to his charming tactic. Perhaps questions about Jack's father made her close up.

"One of your neighbors suggested we speak to you," I said. "We have questions about an old crime that was committed here. Do you remember the murder of Dr. Millroy? His body was found just outside your door."

"I know that. Course I remember. I'm old, not daft."

"Did you see the body?"

"No."

"Do you know why he was in Bright Court?"

"Course not. Why would I?"

"So he didn't come to see you?"

She crooked her finger, beckoning me. I cautiously stepped closer. "Look here, Mrs. Wright," she sneered in my ear, "I didn't need no doctor then. You prob'ly heard how I got by in those days, how I put food on the table for my brother and son."

I felt my face redden despite my efforts not to be embarrassed. It was one thing to discuss prostitution, but quite another to discuss it with the prostitute herself.

Nell poked me in the shoulder with more strength in her bony finger than I expected from a frail old woman. "That Maisie's got a vicious tongue on her and likes to spread lies about me whenever she can. Well, let me tell you, I was clean. That doctor never came here. He died outside my door, but that ain't my fault."

"What about someone else visiting you that night?" Matt asked. "Could one of your...guests have known him?"

"I don't remember if I had any callers that night. It were too long ago."

"What about your brother?"

She sighed and shook her head. "It weren't him," she said with no anger in her tone. "He was gone by then. Ask anyone."

"Gone?"

Her big blue eyes filled with tears. "I don't know where he went." She sniffed and dabbed at the corner of her eye.

Matt patted Nell's hand. "Thank you," he said. "Can we come back if we have more questions?"

"No. You can come back if you want to sit with me and share my sweets, but not if you've got questions. I don't like talking about the past. Unless it's about Jack. You can come and talk about Jack any time."

I thanked her too and we left, seeing ourselves out. We crossed the yard, and my spine tingled with a chill. Nell's neighbors watched us, I was sure of it, although the yard was entirely deserted. Only the unattended copper boiled away over the fire, and two shirts now hung on the line. I couldn't even hear the sounds of Maisie's children fighting with one another.

"Everything all right, Duke?" Matt asked as we reached the coach.

Duke stood by the horse, his hand on its nose. "Aye. Just some stares and a cheeky lad climbed in."

Matt chuckled. "Thought one would try."

"He enjoyed his few minutes playing lord of the manor with his friends guffawing from the pavement."

"We'll proceed to Mrs. Millroy's house," Matt said, opening the door for me. "Then return home for lunch."

And a rest, I knew, but didn't say.

"I was thinking of something else," Duke said. "I got bored while I waited so I asked some of the folk if they knew about a society offering shelter for the homeless near here. You see, I started wondering if the vagrant what Chronos and Dr. Millroy experimented on was really homeless, or if he'd tried to get into one of them charitable establishments or maybe a workhouse. I don't see a reason for any man to live on the street if he don't have to. There's one in Bethnal Green, not far from here, and Chronos said he and Millroy picked up Mr. Wilson in Bethnal Green. I reckon we should go now since we're close."

"It might be worth trying," I said to Matt. "Someone may remember him."

"It was so long ago," Matt said. "It's unlikely any of the staff who were there then are still there now."

"They might keep records. We know he was named Wilson. Lets visit this one then leave it at that if it's a waste of time."

Matt stroked the horse's flank. "You're right. We'll see what we can unearth, but there's no way we can get to all the shelters and workhouses. I suppose if Wilson did try to find shelter that night, he would likely have gone to the one in Bethnal Green."

I climbed into the carriage and Matt followed. Duke folded up the step and the carriage dipped as he climbed up to the driver's seat. Matt removed his hat and scrubbed his hand through his hair and down the back of his neck. He stretched out his legs, angling them to the side for maximum space. I did not ask how he felt. He looked in no mood to tell me the truth anyway.

"Do you think Nell could have been Dr. Millroy's mistress?" I asked, deciding it was best to keep his mind occupied. "She claims she was beautiful back then, and I believe her."

"I'm not sure beauty is enough."

"It is for some men. Indeed, for many, it's the only thing that matters."

He huffed softly as he watched Whitechapel slip past in an endless stream of gray. "Any man who says that is an utter fool who does not appreciate good conversation and wit. Anyway." He finally turned to me. There was no sign of the charmer who'd made Old Nell blush. "For one thing, it seems she was still...being attended upon by other clients then. I would expect a well-to-do doctor to demand exclusivity."

I pulled a face. "I can't believe we're discussing this as if she were a box at the opera. It's so sordid."

"It's a sordid business, but make no mistake, her profession is a business. However, I still don't think she was his mistress." He turned back to the window. "For a few minutes I thought we'd found Dr. Millroy's bastard son. I thought she was his mistress and her son, Jack, the illegitimate child. Then it fell apart somehow. I'm not even sure when."

"I don't agree."

He turned sharply. "Go on."

"She said Jack fixes things. A doctor fixes people, in a way. Could that be what she meant? Could the shop where he works be a surgery or center for patients who aren't too discerning about university degrees?"

"Perhaps. It's a tenuous connection but it is still a connection. We have so little else linking Dr. Millroy to her. All we know for certain is that he was murdered outside her building. The location could be mere coincidence."

When he put it like that, our evidence was sparse. I was beginning to think he was right and we'd learned almost nothing today. Perhaps we should have questioned more of the Bright Court residences.

"Did you notice how Mary called her Miss Sweet?" I said. "A slip of the tongue, or do you think Nell never married?"

"The latter, but it seems she did remember the boy's father."

"She called him useless. And what do you think about her brother?"

He shrugged. "He either left or died before the murder, so he's not a suspect."

"Unless he came back and she's protecting him."

"Good point." A small smile crept across his lips. "I like that theory."

I smiled back and allowed the rocking coach to lull me into contemplative silence. Matt did too, his handsome features schooled in thought.

"Nell's life must have been hard," he said to the window's reflection. "She brought up her son alone. It's not easy for a woman on her own."

"Only for those without independent means." I had independent means, thanks to the reward money. With it invested in the cottage, I shouldn't need to worry about marrying.

The thought opened up a hole in my chest. I may not need to marry, but I wanted to. To the right man, of course. I turned away from Matt and studied my own reflection in the other window. I wasn't young anymore, and if I wanted children, I had to marry within a few years. Since marrying Matt was out of the question, if I wanted to do the right thing by him and his aunt, I must turn my attention elsewhere.

I wasn't sure I could stomach it.

"Have you put any more thought into whether you'll stay or go?" Matt asked softly.

My gaze connected with his in the window's reflection. It

was as searing as looking at him directly. "When this is over, I'll make my decision. For now, I'll stay in your house." And keep an eye on his drinking and gambling habits.

"When this is over, everything will be different," he said. "In a good way."

I finally turned back to face him and smiled, even though it hurt to do so. I didn't want him thinking I hoped he wouldn't be healthy again. Of course I did, and yet it meant a difficult discussion would need to be made, hard truths brought to the surface, and he would most likely leave England angry with me.

But I was getting ahead of myself. He had to get healthy first. That was our priority. It was also possible the feelings he alluded to having for me would dampen by the time we found a doctor magician.

It was a short drive to the Society for Affording Shelter to the Homeless in Bethnal Green. Like Whitechapel, Bethnal Green crammed London's poor into as many of its nooks and crannies as it could. Duke drove right past the non-descript entrance to the shelter and had to turn back after Matt thumped on the cabin ceiling to alert him. The shelter looked to be part of a long building with a plain brick façade and regularly spaced windows. There was nothing striking about the building at all, but it looked solid, and that was perhaps its single most redeeming feature for the homeless in search of shelter.

It was quieter than I expected inside. Female voices drifted to us from the back of the building but there were no signs of the miserable poor coming and going through the door. Matt opened the next door to see where the voices came from. Beyond was a large room filled with row upon row of rectangular boxes laid out on the floor, each lined with a flat hessian sack. There must have been hundreds. It took me a moment to realize the boxes were the so-called beds and the hessian sacks used as pallets to sleep on. The beds weren't long enough to fit a man of Matt's size, that was for certain.

The left part of the room was sectioned off with faded old curtains. A woman flipped a curtain back, and I caught a glimpse of a wash stand. Cleanliness was valued here, but comfort was not, it seemed.

Another woman broke away from two companions rearranging the beds. "May I help you?" she asked, pushing a pair of spectacles up her Roman nose.

"Are you in charge here?" Matt said.

"Mr. Woolley is." She pointed at a closed door to the left. "I'm one of the volunteers who comes in each morning to set the place to rights again."

"Before tonight's batch of men come looking for shelter?" I asked.

"Not just men, madam. We have women and children too, on the other side of Mr. Woolley's office."

"How many each night?"

"That depends on the weather. On a fine evening, only a quarter of these beds will be filled. In winter, we simply don't have enough room."

"Do you turn people away?"

She nodded, causing her glasses to slip. She pushed them up her nose again. "If you're here to make a donation, it will be greatly appreciated. We're always in need of clean linen, carbolic soap and food."

"You feed them too?" Matt asked.

She nodded and smiled. She had a pleasant face, if unremarkable, and I was glad there were people like her willing to do such work here. London needed her.

"Are there any staff members who've been here for twenty-seven years?" Matt asked.

She blinked at him, surprised by the question. "Mr. Woolley may have, but no one else. May I ask why?"

"We're trying to trace the movements of a homeless

man who died twenty-seven years ago. We hoped he may have spent a night or two here at the time and someone would remember him. We want to learn more about him."

She pressed her hand to her stomach. "I see. This used to be a doss house in those days."

"Doss house?" Matt asked.

"Poor unfortunates with nowhere to go paid a small fee for a bed. Times have changed though, and a charity took over. No fee is required now, but the beds only go to the *deserving*."

"Wastrels need not apply?" I mocked.

"Definitely not," she said, all seriousness. "Perhaps Mr. Woolley will remember the victim or he can look him up in the records for you."

"There are records that far back?" Matt asked.

She smiled again. "Most likely. He's a meticulous record-keeper. Our benefactors require it, you see, so that they can tally the numbers. I believe the government pays a stipend for each person who seeks shelter here."

That sounded like a system rife for corruption but I didn't say so.

"Nor does Mr. Woolley like to throw anything out," she went on. "It makes the cellar quite crowded, but despite our requests for more storage space, he won't destroy anything. He says the benefactors or government may require the information one day and it isn't his place to destroy it. Come with me. I'll introduce you."

Mr. Woolley welcomed us into his office with an enthusiastic greeting. The office was as uninspiring as the building itself. Other than a large portrait of the shelter's founding benefactor, the walls were barren. Paperwork and ledgers decorated most of his desk's surface, and I suspected the filing cabinets off to one side were filled with records of those who'd sought shelter recently. My hopes swelled as I anticipated rummaging through the records in the cellar and finding our Mr. Wilson.

"How may I help you?" Mr. Woolley asked, steepling his fingers. He was rather nondescript too, with his balding pate and trimmed beard. The faint smell of carbolic soap drifted from him, or perhaps it came from the dormitory room. It gave the impression the entire building, as well as its occupants, had been scrubbed clean.

Matt introduced us and repeated the reason behind our visit. He finished with, "Since you have been here longest, perhaps you remember him."

"I wasn't here twenty-seven years ago, although it does feel like it sometimes." Mr. Woolley laughed. "Besides, we have so many people come through our doors that it's impossible to remember all their names. Some spend only one night here and we never see them again. We've housed thousands over the years if you include the days of the doss house."

"Perhaps your records are more revealing."

"They may be, but I cannot let just anyone look through them." He parted his hands and shrugged. "I am sorry, but that's my rule."

"Then why keep the names at all?" Tension edged Matt's voice. He gripped the chair arms so hard his knuckles whitened. I resisted the urge to lay my hand over his to show my support.

"To know if those who come here are truly worthy of assistance or are simply lazy." At our blank looks, he added, "Too many requests for assistance usually mean the resident is taking advantage of our charity, and not trying hard enough to find employment and permanent lodgings."

"Or it means there is no employment or affordable housing available," Matt countered.

Mr. Woolley pressed his lips together. "In my experience, which is extensive, these people will take something for nothing if they can. Hence the records. I write their names in the ledger then at the end of the week, I transfer the dates of their stay to their individual file. One must keep score or suffer the return of the undeserving night after night. They must be forced to help themselves, sir, or they become their own worst enemy."

"You turn people away even if you have available beds?" Matt said, incredulous.

"Of course."

"Widows with children too?"

"Naturally."

"How many nights do you deem enough?" Matt said hotly. "Is there a number that separates the deserving from the so-called undeserving?"

Mr. Woolley paused. "With respect, sir, you do not know these people. You don't know how readily they'll take advantage of charity. I do."

"We're here on police business," I said before Matt forgot his manners altogether and ruined our chances. "Commissioner Munro has asked us to investigate the murder of a Mr. Wilson in sixty-three."

"As I already said, I cannot just let anyone see the records." He opened his hands again then flattened them together as if in prayer. "Do you have a letter of introduction from the commissioner stating that you're assisting with his investigation?"

"You don't believe us?" Matt growled.

Mr. Woolley's lips pinched. "I hope you understand that I cannot give away private—"

"You made your point." Matt stood abruptly.

I rose too. "Thank you for your time, Mr. Woolley. We'll return with the letter from the commissioner."

"Thank you for your understanding, Miss Steele. I look forward to seeing you again." He gave my hand a weak shake. Matt didn't offer his, and I admonished him for it on the way out.

"He went out of his way to be difficult," he said as he opened the front door for me. "He could have let us into his cellar today. Now he has a chance to remove any record of Wilson."

"You think he lied about being here back then and knowing Mr. Wilson? You think he has reason to destroy Wilson's records?"

"It was the impression I got."

I'd got no such impression, but I wasn't the best at recognizing when people lied to me. "Should we go to Commissioner Munro now and return immediately?" It grew late and Matt needed to use his watch again before too long.

Duke thought the same as me. When Matt ordered him to drive to New Scotland Yard, he refused at first. "You need to go home."

"Don't tell me what to do," Matt snapped.

I bit my tongue and did not make the same mistake as Duke. I remained quiet on the journey to New Scotland Yard and did not enter the building with Matt. I sat with Duke on the driver's seat and watched the passersby on the Victoria Embankment until Matt rejoined us, in a blacker mood than when he went in.

"He's out all day," Matt said before we could question him. He assisted me down from the driver's seat and back into the cabin. "We'll return home for luncheon. We've wasted enough time. After lunch we'll visit Mrs. Millroy."

"What about returning to the shelter?" I said. "Do you think it's not worth it after all? It's not a certainty that Mr. Wilson spent the night there or that his records will reveal personal information about him that will be of any use to us."

"I will return." He stretched his arm along the window sill and drummed his fingers on the frame. "You're staying home, India."

"Why?"

"Because I plan on going back tonight."

I gasped. "You're going to break in?"

"I'm going to seek shelter there and locate the cellar."

I stared at him and waited for him to tell me he was joking. He did not. "Don't be absurd, Matt. Mr. Woolley knows your face as does at least one member of the staff. They'll recognize you."

"Then I'll go in disguise."

He was mad. There was no other explanation for it. Mad and desperate. "Alone?"

"Yes."

"No."

He turned to me. "Pardon?"

"I said no. I'll go with you."

He huffed out a laugh, as if I'd said a pathetic joke. I arched my brow at him. "You don't think I'm capable of disguising myself as a woman in need of shelter? Perhaps I ought to remind you that I was very close to sleeping in a place like that the day I had tea with you at Brown's. If you hadn't taken me in, the only roof over my head would have been a charitable one."

Matt drew in a breath and held it. His gaze lowered to his lap. "You're not coming."

We would see about that. His idea was wild and his mood foul. He needed someone to accompany him and insure he kept his wits about him. Cyclops, Willie and Duke were all too conspicuous with their accents, and I didn't trust Willie to be discreet anyway. Matt needed a steadying influence. A pocket watch that chimed when danger neared was a good alarm to have on side, too.

We drove home in strained silence but Matt was all gentlemanly again as he assisted me from the coach outside number sixteen Park Street.

"I'm sorry for snapping at you, India."

"It's all right. You're under enormous pressure."

"There's no excuse for it." He folded his other hand over

mine. "I'm glad you snap right back at me. I deserve nothing less." He lifted my hand to his lips and kissed the back of my glove. He raised his gaze to mine and watched me through his long lashes. It nearly broke my heart to see the misery in the depths of his eyes and for a moment I couldn't speak through my tight throat. "Do not let me get away with that kind of behavior," he murmured.

I was saved from attempting a response by the front door opening. It was not Bristow who greeted us, however, but my friend Catherine Mason, wringing her hands and looking wretched. What was she doing here? And where was everyone else?

"Catherine?" I raced up the steps, Matt at my side. "What's the matter?"

"Oh India," she moaned. "It's all my fault."

"What's happened?"

"He's gone! Your guest—Chronos—is gone! And it's all my fault."

CHAPTER 8

*M*att grasped Catherine's shoulders. "What do you mean, gone? Cyclops was supposed to keep an eye on him."

Catherine's face paled and her lips trembled. "He and I were talking in the sitting room," she wailed. "We had tea and cake and were deep in conversation. And I'm afraid Chronos slipped out."

"Didn't Bristow or one of the other servants see?"

Catherine shook her head, sending the tear hovering on her eyelid sliding down her cheek. "Bristow and the footman are helping Nate search now."

It took me a moment to remember Nate was Cyclops's real name and how he preferred Catherine refer to him.

"It's not your fault," Matt said, scanning the street. "Cyclops should have been paying more attention."

"Matt!" I scolded. "That's not fair. Chronos could have gotten away from Cyclops at any time if he chose to do so."

"Cyclops does not get easily distracted, India. He wouldn't have if not for…" He shook his head and headed back down the steps. He climbed up beside Duke and after a few curt words, they drove off at speed.

"It's not your fault, Catherine," I said, steering her back inside.

"Matt seems to think it is, despite what he said." She sniffed and wiped away her tears with her handkerchief. "And now he's going to be angry with Nate. I wish I hadn't come today."

"And miss out on a chat with Cyclops?" I put my arm around her slender shoulders and directed her into the drawing room. "They'll find Chronos soon, I'm sure. But even if they don't, it no longer matters. I know his spells."

She blinked watery eyes at me. "Pardon?"

"Cyclops didn't tell you all about him?"

"No. He said you had a houseguest but that was all. Who is he?"

"My grandfather."

She clutched her handkerchief to her throat. "But both of your grandfathers are dead."

"My parents lied to me." I told her how Chronos had disappeared after getting into trouble with the guilds and authorities but did not mention the death of Mr. Wilson the vagrant or Dr. Millroy, his co-conspirator. "We wanted him to stay here to teach me his spells. He has done that so it's not such a great disaster if he leaves."

In my opinion, Matt had overreacted and made Catherine feel awful for no good reason. He may be ill, but his behavior had gone too far.

She asked a dozen questions, many of which I couldn't answer or didn't want to. So I asked her some questions about her conversation with Cyclops instead. She blushed and told me they'd hardly noticed the passing of time.

Miss Glass joined us, inquiring about lunch. Mrs. Bristow brought in a tray of sandwiches that we three nibbled. Miss Glass didn't have a big appetite, and neither Catherine nor I felt like eating. We continuously glanced at the door and jumped at every sound.

Fortunately Miss Glass didn't seem to notice. "Where is Willie?" she asked.

"Out," I said. "She didn't say where she was going."

"I thought you were with Matthew this morning, India."

"I was, but he brought me back and had to go out again with Cyclops and Duke."

"Ah yes, to search for Chronos. I heard the servants talking," she added. "So he truly is our prisoner?"

I choked on a crumb. "No, of course not. Matt is just concerned about him. He hasn't been back in London long and he may get lost."

"Why? Because he's old and we old folk can't remember where we live?"

In her case, sometimes she could not, but I didn't say as much, just gave her a reassuring smile which seemed to satisfy her.

The clock on the mantel chimed gently, drawing Catherine's attention. "Goodness, I have to go. Goodbye, Miss Glass."

"Goodbye, dear. Do come back. I'll be sure to tell Cyclops that you're breathless with anticipation at seeing him again."

Catherine's eyes rounded and her pale skin turned spectacularly pink. I ushered her out before she recovered her wits. I liked that Miss Glass had something to keep her mind busy, and matchmaking was an innocent enough endeavor when it didn't involve Matt or me. Besides, I agreed with her and thought Cyclops and Catherine would be a good match. He was the perfect man to show her the world while bringing her home again when she needed to see her family.

"Please tell Nate I'm sorry," she said to me in the entrance hall. "I do hope he doesn't get into too much trouble."

"I'll see that Matt keeps his head. So did you enjoy yourself until that point?"

She smiled. "I did." She leaned closer. "He's very charming, in his own way. It's sort of an innocent way, like he doesn't know he's being charming. I suppose that's what makes him…well, charming."

I laughed and was glad to see her laugh too. "He enjoys your company, Catherine. He told me so after your last visit."

"Oh?" She bit her lip but couldn't stop her smile.

"Perhaps he can take you to the theater or out for an ice now that the weather is warming up."

"That would be lovely, but…" She sighed. "I dropped enough hints about wanting to see this show or that and going for walks, but he didn't take any of them. I *think* he likes me." She toyed with her gloves, smoothing the wrinkles out of the leather and tugging on the cuff. "So why doesn't he want to see me outside this house?"

I'd already discussed the matter with Cyclops, but I wasn't sure it was my place to tell her everything he'd said. She was right, however, and Cyclops did like her. But he was worried about what her family would say if she, a respectable middle class English girl, went out with a dark skinned man with a price on his head in his own country. While he was no longer in trouble with the law, he had angered a powerful man who would pay good money to see him hanged. Cyclops wouldn't drag Catherine into that.

"I know we'll get stared at, India," she went on. "I'm not so naive to think everyone will accept us. I know my parents will lecture me at first, and try to persuade me not to associate with him, but I also know that's because they're worried about the effect the stares and whispers will have on me. But I don't care about that, and I don't want them to care either. I just want to find out if I like Nate enough to allow him to court me."

"It will probably be more than stares and whispers, Catherine." As much as I wanted to tell her about Cyclops's past, I would not. He had to do that himself to gain her trust.

She kissed my cheek and I let her out. I watched her walk up the street, and searched both directions after she disappeared. There was no sign of Chronos or any of his pursuers.

It wasn't the fact that they hadn't found Chronos that worried me. It was the fact Matt would desperately need to use his watch now, and with him sitting conspicuously on the driver's seat, he would not get the opportunity.

I returned to the drawing room and Miss Glass. We chatted about her friends, shopping and Patience's wedding. She dozed off after a while, but woke up when Bristow entered and I greeted him enthusiastically.

"You're back!" I straightened his tie, allowing myself to get close enough to whisper, "Did you find him?"

"He returned of his own accord," he said. "He's been eating bread and honey in the kitchen these last fifteen minutes."

"And no one thought to tell me?"

"I chastised Mrs. Bristow for her oversight. But she did say that you did not seem worried about his absence."

I couldn't admonish her for thinking that since it was true. "And Matt? Cyclops?"

"I don't know. I only just learned they'd gone out looking for Chronos too."

"What are you two conspiring about?" Miss Glass called out. "Bristow, send in some tea please. I'm parched. India, will you join me?"

"In a moment. I'll see if Chronos would like to join us."

I found Chronos in the kitchen, mopping up honey on a plate with a piece of bread. "India," he declared, waving the bread at me. "Glad to see you."

"Where have you been?" I snapped.

He shoved the bread into his mouth and offered a shrug. That answer would not suffice. I grasped him by the arm and marched him out of the kitchen. I pushed him into Bristow's office and slammed the door.

"Where have you been?" I said again.

He rolled his eyes. "I've had enough of this from the bloody butler."

"The entire household has been looking for you."

"Don't exaggerate, India."

"Matt is still looking for you, and he ought to be using his watch. He's going to be in a terrible state when he gets back." I poked my finger into his shoulder. "Not only that, but he'll berate Cyclops for not watching you, and that's not fair."

"It is somewhat fair. He was too busy flirting with that pretty girl to notice me."

I smacked his arm. "That girl is Catherine Mason."

"Mason has a daughter? Well, isn't she a sweet little thing. Does Mason know she's having a liaison with a pirate?"

"He's not a pirate, and they're not having a liaison. Where did you go, anyway?"

"For a walk. I was tired of being cooped up inside all day. Wish I hadn't come back now, if this is the way my own granddaughter is going to treat me. What did you think would happen? That I'd run away? Why would I? I'm being fed for free and the roof over my head is very nice. A man could do a lot worse. So could you, India. You need to set aside your notions of independence and open your eyes to what you have in your grasp."

"Me leaving here has nothing to do with my independence. And do not change the subject. The fact is, you deliberately ran away while Cyclops was distracted without telling anyone where you were going."

"What does it matter? You have my spells. Why do you even need me?"

"That's a good question. I'm not sure we do. Perhaps I'll write to Mr. Abercrombie directly and tell him we have you. Or, better yet, I'll notify the police. They might be interested in what you can tell them about both Dr. Millroy's murder and the untimely death of a homeless man in sixty-three."

He put his finger to his lips and hushed me. "The servants might hear you."

I threw my hands in the air. I gave up. There wasn't a shred of remorse in his tone. I opened the door and ran smack into Matt about to enter.

He caught me by the shoulders as he'd done with Catherine on the porch and held me in a grip so hard his fingers dug into my flesh. He glared at Chronos over my head, his eyes flashing with anger, the muscles in his jaw bunching. The signs of exhaustion were there in the lines and pallor of his skin, but the signs of fury overshadowed them. I could feel him shaking.

"I've been looking for you," he said in a low, ominous tone. He ushered me inside and shut the door with the heel of his shoe.

I heard Chronos gulp behind me. "I went for a walk. Now I'm back. No cause for alarm. I was quite safe."

"It's not your damned safety I'm worried about."

"Then what?"

I glanced at Chronos over my shoulder. He looked pale but some of the color was returning to his face. He shook his head, confused as to why Matt was angry. As was I.

"You're India's grandfather, and you promised to stay and help her," Matt snarled.

"I have helped her. She knows my spells. There are only two. Ask her if you don't believe me."

"Teaching her a few spells is not the only way you should be helping her. You are the last member of her family. She thought she was alone after her father died, even more so when her fiancé betrayed her. When she needed a guiding hand the most, you weren't there. When she needed someone to stand with her, you weren't there. You chose not to be there twenty-seven years ago. You ran away from your family once, Chronos. You're not running away again. I won't let you."

I stood there, utterly stunned, unable to move my feet. I

felt as if I'd sprouted roots into the flagstones. Was Matt truly so upset and angry on my behalf? He wouldn't look at me yet he still gripped my shoulders. We stood so close that his breath ruffled my hair and I could feel the blood thrumming through him.

"She doesn't need *me*," Chronos said. "Not when she has you."

Matt suddenly let me go and placed his hands behind his back. I missed his strength and stumbled a little when Chronos pushed past us. He opened the door and almost ran into a scowling Cyclops.

Cyclops grabbed his arms, pulling the older man up onto his toes. He shook him.

"I've been looking everywhere for you." Cyclops may be a gentle giant, but he was capable of putting a great deal of menace into his voice. "I thought I'd have to return and tell Matt you'd disappeared. Believe me, I was *not* looking forward to it."

Chronos jerked out of Cyclops's grip and rearranged his jacket. "You're safe. He took all his frustrations out on me."

"Not all," Matt growled.

Cyclops swallowed heavily.

Chronos rushed off, and Cyclops was about to follow when Matt swayed. I caught him by the arms and tried to steady him. Fortunately he didn't collapse entirely and Cyclops was quick, because I wouldn't have been able to hold him up on my own. We directed him to a chair and I helped him remove his watch from his inside waistcoat pocket.

I tugged off his glove and opened the watch case. His fingers folded around it and magic immediately flowed into his body. He closed his eyes until the colorful glow crept up to his hairline, then he snapped the case shut.

"You were supposed to be watching him," he said to Cyclops.

"It won't happen again, Matt," Cyclops said to his boots.

"Be sure it doesn't."

"It's not Cyclops's fault," I said. "Chronos would have got away at some point if he truly wanted to."

Matt merely grunted, but I wasn't sure if he agreed with me or not. "It's not like you to let someone out of your sight, Cyclops," he said. "What happened?"

Cyclops cleared his throat. He suddenly looked young and innocent, and it was easy to ignore his size and the fierce scar. "Miss Mason came, but with India out, I took it upon myself to keep her company."

"Where was my aunt?"

"She joined us after a while, and that's when I noticed Chronos gone. I raised the alarm and sent Peter and Bristow out searching for him, then I went too."

"Catherine is blaming herself," I told him.

Cyclops winced. "That ain't fair. It wasn't her fault."

Matt narrowed his gaze at his friend but his anger seemed to have dissolved. "You should tell her that to her face."

"Next time she comes here, I will."

"Why not visit her? You could go this afternoon since Chronos has proven that he'll return if he goes out."

"Don't, Matt. You know why I can't do that." Cyclops turned and strode out of the office.

"I know why you *think* you can't," Matt called after him. "But your reasoning is thin, Cyclops. So thin that I can see right through it."

"And yours has got a large gaping hole in it, Matt, but I ain't calling you out."

He disappeared from sight and Matt expelled a breath. He lowered his head, and I was tempted to place my hand on the back of his neck. He muttered something I couldn't quite make out then, with a deep sigh, pushed himself out of the chair. I half expected him to stagger again and I prepared to steady him. He caught a hold of the desk, however, and took a moment to compose himself.

"Will you be all right getting up the stairs or should I get Peter?" I asked.

He glared at me but said nothing.

I met his glare with my own. "I asked you a question."

"I have a slight headache, that's all. I can walk on my own."

"Good, because your mood is far too ferocious for me. I'd rather be talking to Miss Glass than seeing if you made it to your room in one piece." I left before he saw that every word was a lie.

* * *

BY THE TIME Matt woke up, it was too late to call on Mrs. Millroy. He seemed better, not only in terms of the rejuvenation that a nap after using his watch provides, but also in his general mood. He entered the sitting room where we played cards and apologized to Cyclops for berating him over Chronos's disappearance.

"Where's Willie?" he finished, taking up a position by the fireplace.

"She came home about an hour ago," I said, studying my cards. "She changed and went out again."

"Where to?"

"She wouldn't say."

Duke tapped the top of his cards with his fingertip. "She's too secretive for my liking. Whenever she's secretive it means she's up to no good, and Willie up to no good is dangerous."

Cyclops nodded solemnly. "She'll either come back having lost her gun at cards or with gold cufflinks she won't even want but is over the moon to have won off a poor milksop."

"That's our Willie for you, Chronos," Miss Glass said from the sofa where she was reading a book by the lamplight. "She's either ecstatic or miserable. There is no in between."

She lowered the book to her lap. "Although I'm not so certain that she's gone to play cards. She left smelling like rosewater."

That got everyone's attention, except for Chronos, who didn't look up from his poker hand. "If your friend wants to attract a gentleman, she should wear a dress and comb her hair," he said. "A sprinkle of rosewater won't be enough. It's like adding a vase of flowers to a pig sty."

He did not seem to notice the heavy silence that followed, too intent on his cards was he.

Duke fidgeted with his collar and loosened his neckerchief. He concentrated on his hand for a long time then threw the cards on the table. "I'm out." He crouched in front of the fireplace and stabbed at the coals with the fire iron.

Matt and I exchanged glances. Cyclops half rose from his chair then sat again at my signal. It was probably wise not to talk to Duke about his feelings for Willie in front of the rest of us. Besides, Miss Glass might be wrong and Willie hadn't smelled of rosewater when she left. Even if she did, it could have been for a number of reasons. I just couldn't think of them at that moment.

"Someone remind me," Chronos said. "What's it called when you have five cards all of the same suit?"

Cyclops and I threw in our cards. Chronos smiled and raked in his winnings.

Matt looked at the discarded cards and chuckled. "He was bluffing."

"He's a fast learner," Cyclops said, gathering up the pack.

It was some time before we could speak in private. Miss Glass retired early and Chronos looked like he wouldn't be far behind her. He stifled a yawn behind his hand.

"Gallivanting around the city tiring, is it?" Cyclops asked with a wry smile. He was still bitter that Chronos had got the better of him and escaped.

"I did a lot of walking," Chronos said. "What about you

two?" he asked Matt and me. "Are you any closer to finding the diary and Millroy's son?"

Matt and I told them what we'd learned at Bright Court and the homeless shelter, and finished with his plan to return tonight and search the old records.

"Blimey," Chronos muttered. "That's a risk."

"It'll be fine," Matt said. "I've done this sort of thing before."

"I'm going with him," I told them before Matt could say otherwise. He merely frowned but did not overrule me.

"No." Chronos shook his head. "No, you're not."

"Yes, I am," I said hotly.

"I'm still your grandfather and I forbid it. It's much too dangerous."

"I beg your pardon." Both Cyclops and Duke shrank back from my icy tone. "You have not been a grandfather to me my entire life, so don't presume you can waltz in one day and tell me what to do the next. I am going tonight, and that is the end of it. Kindly keep out of my business." There. That got my point across.

Chronos folded his arms over his chest. "I cannot believe you allow her to do this sort of thing, Glass."

"I know better than to try and stop her," Matt said. "The women in my life have always been strong willed. India is no exception."

I wasn't quite sure how to take that. Had he just counted me among his women-folk? It was both pleasing and alarming.

"She won't come to any harm," he went on. "It should be a simple enough exercise if she keeps her wits about her, and India has more than enough wits to fool the staff at the shelter."

Chronos snorted. "No gentleman wants a difficult woman, India. You ought to remember that."

I rolled my eyes and caught Matt smirking. I resisted the urge to throw a cushion at him.

"I'll come too," Duke announced.

"No." Matt gathered up the cards and shuffled them. "Just India and me."

"I can drive. You'll need to get away fast before you're seen. I'll be a better choice than Cyclops."

"I know, I know," Cyclops muttered. "I'm too conspicuous."

Duke agreed with an apologetic shrug.

"I am good for lurking in shadows," Cyclops went on, warming to the idea. "If you won't let me come inside, at least let me linger outside in case there's trouble."

"There won't be any trouble," Matt said, dealing. "Duke, are you playing?"

"Aye." Duke sat in the seat Chronos vacated.

"I'm retiring," Chronos said. "You all enjoy your nocturnal investigation. And Glass? I'm warning you. If India is harmed—"

"She won't be, and I don't appreciate the insinuation that I can't take care of her."

"You should be fine if you use your watch before you go, but if you don't, you won't be able to protect yourself let alone her."

Matt stood, rising to his full height, and glared at Chronos.

Chronos stepped back beneath the force of it. "Right. Well. I've said my piece. Goodnight, all." He hurried from the room.

"Are you finished frightening old men?" I asked Matt. "Because if you are, I'd like a stiff drink, please, and some cards. Make them good ones. I need to end my losing streak."

He finished dealing while Duke poured drinks at the sideboard. He rejoined us at the card table, but he wasn't concentrating and lost badly. I lost as well. It was difficult to focus on each round with Matt quietly simmering opposite me. He lost too, so perhaps there was some justice. Cyclops thrashed us all and collected his matchsticks with a gleeful smile before returning the matches to the box for the next time we played.

When the clock chimed nine, Matt told us to prepare our disguises.

"Shouldn't you rest again?" I said as Cyclops and Duke filed out.

"I'll have a few minutes of shuteye in here while you change," he said.

"Not with all the distractions." I plucked the glass from his hand. It was his second brandy for the evening.

His jaw slackened but his eyes hardened. "You think I can't control my drinking?"

"I wasn't referring to the drinking." I nodded at the clock. "Its chiming will wake you on the hour."

He took back the glass. "In that case…" He downed the remaining contents. "I'll have another."

I picked up my skirts and rushed past him. I got to the sideboard first and put my arms out, protecting the decanter behind me. "You will not."

"India," he purred in a silky voice that brushed my skin. "I've picked you up and moved you out of the way before, and I can do it again."

I lifted my chin. "Go ahead." He wouldn't do it. I knew he wouldn't. Not this time. Not when being so close affected us both in ways we had to deny.

After a moment, he laughed softly. "You win. I didn't want another anyway, I simply wanted to see what lengths you'd go to."

"You think I'm going to a great length now?" I shot back. "Hardly. I can withstand the force of your ire, Matt. It doesn't frighten me."

I thought he was going to walk away but he hesitated. Then a strange smile crept across his lips. "Is that so?" He leaned closer until his chest was mere inches from my face. He reached his arms around me, trapping me.

I dared a glance up, only to see him looking down at me, his smile gone. His inky black gaze warmed me from head to toe.

"What about now?" he murmured. Behind me, crystal tinkled as he removed the stopper from the decanter. "Can you withstand the force of what's between us, India? Because I don't know if I can for much longer, despite…" He closed his eyes and sucked in a breath.

I pushed him in the chest and he stepped back without resisting, his gaze lowered. "You've had too much to drink, Matt. You don't know what you're saying."

"I've had two brandies. I'm in complete control of my faculties." He rubbed his forehead, as if trying to scrub away an ache. "But I am sorry." Finally, he lifted his gaze to mine. His eyes were clear with not a hint of desire in their depths. I hoped mine were clear too. "I'm sorry for being too familiar with you," he added.

I forced my shoulders back and my spine to straighten. "This is when you're frightening, Matt. When you allow your emotions to override your common sense. You are correct. You should not be familiar. It's not right."

"No. But it feels good." He smiled tentatively, boyishly, and my heart lurched.

"Stop it." I managed to put a believable measure of irritation into my voice then gathered my wits and my skirts and rushed out of the room. I didn't look back to see if he stared after me. I didn't want to see the confused expression I knew I'd see there. The best thing I could do was dissuade him from any tender feelings he'd developed for me. After another dismissal or two he would take the hint and stop seeing me in *that* way altogether.

* * *

THE DAMP EVENING air in Bethnal Green didn't come from rain

but from the miasma that clung to the slum's decaying buildings and settled into the dark corners of its wretched lanes. It brought with it the reek of the sewers and misery that seemed to be present wherever London's poorest lay their heads.

It wasn't a cold night, so the Society for Affording Shelter to the Homeless had beds available for a man and woman newly arrived in the city looking for work. With no employment to be had anywhere, and their last coin spent on bread the day before, they'd decided to seek accommodation at a charitable institution rather than risk another night sleeping rough. The slum streets were no place for a woman, even one with a husband to protect her. So Matt explained to the thickset man at the door when we arrived.

The man opened the door to the dormitory and the scent of carbolic soap hit me like a wave. I wrinkled my nose and tried not to breathe too deeply. Only half of the rectangular wooden boxes were filled with men, some sleeping, some watching us with curious eyes. Whispered voices came from somewhere but I couldn't determine if it was the men or the staff taking jugs of water to and from the curtained area. A woman wearing a crisp white apron over a plain brown dress sat at a small desk near the door. It wasn't the same woman from earlier in the day, thank goodness. Although our disguises had changed our appearances, I didn't want to put them to the test. Matt should be safe in his bushy whiskers and false beard, but I merely wore a black wig. I'd left it unarranged to hide as much of my face as possible. If I kept my head lowered, I ought to get by if we met with Mr. Woolley or the kind volunteer from this morning.

"You've missed mealtime," the woman said when we approached. She did not stand but pulled a clipboard toward her and picked up a pencil. She didn't have a friendly face like the volunteer we'd met earlier. Rather, her mouth was pinched and her heavy brow looked like it had never been raised above the level of a scowl. "We dine at six at this time of year. The men sleep in here, the women through there." She did not lower her voice in deference to the men already asleep in their wooden boxes, but none shushed her. Perhaps none dared.

"And the married couples?" Matt asked in a faultless working class drawl. He'd lost his American accent completely.

"Married or unmarried, it makes no difference," the woman said. "Men in here, women through there. We can't have fraternizing. It wouldn't be proper and this is a respectable institution." She sniffed and peered down her flat nose at me. "If you don't like our rules, you can leave."

Matt held up his hands in surrender. I kept my hands tucked inside the coat I carried close to my chest. Bound up with the coat was the smallest lamp we could find and a box of safety matches.

"That is our first rule," the woman said. "No fraternizing. Our second is you must be clean. There are soap and water behind those curtains. Our third rule is that you must respect your fellow unfortunates and in no way harm anyone. Our fourth rule is a requirement that you give us your details. Are these rules acceptable to you both?"

Matt and I nodded.

"Good. You may call me Matron." She held a pencil to a clipboard with crooked columns drawn on the page. Each column was half filled. "Your names?"

"Mrs. Anne McTavish," Matt said for me. I didn't trust my accent and we'd decided he would do all the talking. "I'm William McTavish."

"Last known place of residence?"

"Wraysbury."

"Can you be more specific?"

"Baker Street," he said. I didn't know if there was a Baker Street in Wraysbury and I doubted Matt had been there, but it was a good guess and it was unlikely Matron had ever been to the village.

"Did you apply for work today?"

"Why?"

"We only provide shelter to those trying to find employment, not lazy ne'er do wells. If you return again and again, we'll check to see if you have indeed looked for work where you say you have."

"Right you are, Matron. Let's see. I asked at the docks and a timber yard on Glower Street."

Matron wrote that down and signaled to the staff. A man and woman approached, neither of whom I recognized.

"May I kiss my wife goodnight?" Matt asked.

"No," Matron said. "You may shake hands."

Matt's beard twitched. Was he trying not to laugh? I didn't see how any of this was amusing. My nerves jangled so much it was a miracle no one heard them.

Matt clasped my elbows rather awkwardly. "Goodnight, my love."

"Goodnight, William," I said.

"Don't let the bed bugs bite."

"Our beds are clean," Matron said snippily. "Any lice in our linen have come from the dirty bodies of those seeking shelter here. That's why we urge you to wash thoroughly. Unfortunately some don't wash as thoroughly as others."

The man led Matt to the curtained area and I was led separately to the other end of the bank of curtains.

"I'll give you two minutes," the woman said, passing me a towel. It was already damp and the water in the basin a muddy color. How many had washed in it before me?

"Thank you," I said, keeping my voice and head low. Hopefully she would think me shy, not deceitful.

She deposited a lamp on the floor and left. I set down my coat and hidden lamp then washed my hands with the soap. If I didn't smell like carbolic, she would grow suspicious and make me wash again. The towel was somewhat useless so I finished drying my hands on my skirt. It felt like an age since I'd worn the dress I used to wear almost every day when I worked in the shop. It was a simple style with a high collar and by unpicking the hem after dinner, I'd managed to make it look worn.

I touched my watch beneath my bodice, ignoring the strong urge to pull it out and check the time. I didn't need to. I knew when two minutes was up as well as I knew my name.

The woman returned a minute late and led me to the female dormitory. Unlike the men's quarters, it was almost full, with each wooden rectangular box occupied by a woman or child. The smaller children slept in the same bed as their mothers. It was noisier in here. Babies cried, mothers whispered soothing words or scolded their children. Someone near the back snored.

I followed my guide to an empty bed. I did not look at the faces of the women we passed but at the exits. I spotted two doors at the back of the room. Beyond would be the kitchen, scullery and other service rooms, as well as the stairs down to the cellar.

My guide stopped in front of an empty bed. A thin mattress didn't even cover the entire rectangle of floor within the confines of the box. A blanket had been folded neatly at the foot.

"This is yours for the night," she said. "We strongly discourage moving about, but if you need to relieve yourself there are pans back there." She pointed to a shelf running between the doors where several porcelain bedpans were set out. "Are you hungry? I might be able to find some bread left over from dinner."

"No, thank you." I offered her a smile. "You've been very kind."

She gave me a curt nod then walked off, taking her lamp with her. Lamps on each wall still illuminated the edges of the room for another hour, then all but two were extinguished. One remained lit near the bedpans, and another glowed by the door leading to the men's dormitory where my guide sat on a chair, her head rolling forward in sleep. Around me, the children had settled and several soft snores provided the only barrier holding back the silence. It was no barrier against my thoughts, however, and I couldn't stop them running in all directions. Mostly, I thought about the myriad things that could go wrong tonight.

I waited a little longer until I thought it was time. Then I slowly pulled out my watch but could not see the face. With my blanket and lamp clutched against my chest, I picked my way between the rows of beds to the shelf of bedpans and checked the time in the light. I was early by fifteen minutes. That's what anxious waiting does to a person—it throws out her usually very accurate sense of time.

I took down one of the pans and went through the motions of relieving myself into it without doing so. Without letting go of my coat and its cargo it was awkward, but at least that helped pass the time. If anyone watched me from their dark bed, they would hopefully grow bored and close their eyes.

When I guessed the fifteen minutes to be almost up, I returned the bedpan to the shelf and drew in a fortifying breath. With a shaking hand, I opened the nearest door and slipped through. The corridor was unlit. I kept the door open to allow the wan light from the dormitory to filter through long enough for me to see that I was alone and that four doors led off the corridor.

I closed the door and was engulfed in the dark and a silence so profound I could hear my own heartbeat. When I remembered to breathe, it sounded loud. Hopefully Matt would join me soon, but I couldn't hear any approaching foot-steps and I couldn't see how he would know where to find me if he didn't know his way around or have a light.

I set my bundle on the floor and fumbled for the lamp wrapped in my coat. I fished out the box of matches from the pocket and struck one to light the lamp. I returned the matches to the pocket and picked up both the coat and lamp.

The small circle of light illuminated a figure a few feet away. I stifled a gasp.

"How did you find me in the dark?" I asked Matt.

He put his finger to his lips and winked. I passed him the lamp and allowed him to lead the way. He opened doors quietly and peered inside, moving methodically from door to door down the corridor. He closed each of them before I could see what room lay beyond. The last one he left open and entered. A staircase led down into the depths of the building.

He held out his hand for me and, after a hesitation, I took it. The staircase was just wide enough to fit us side by side. I worried that the echo of our footsteps on the stones would alert someone but no one came. The corridor above had been quiet, with most of the staff leaving after lights out. We ought to be safe.

The stairs opened up to a cold room filled with filing cabinets, crates and logs of wood. The low vaulted ceiling didn't fit with the more modern building above us and I wondered about its original use. Matt and his lamp moved off. I followed quickly, wanting to be as near as possible to the light and him. I'd never thought of myself as fearful, but there was something nightmarish about a dark cellar full of shadows.

"Here," Matt said, reading the labels on a set of cabinet drawers. "These are from the first half of the sixties." He opened a drawer labeled SIXTY-THREE. The scrape of wood against wood sent a nearby creature scurrying. Matt didn't seem to notice. He was too busy flicking through the files.

I helped him sift through the section marked W. Twice. There was no one by the name of Wilson listed.

"Damn," he muttered.

"I'll check again," I said.

"Don't bother. The odds of finding the vagrant were long anyway." He slid the drawer closed. "We'll leave. There's no point staying all night."

"Won't it look suspicious if we walk out now? Will they even let us?"

"We're not prisoners, India." There was a laugh in his voice and I was glad that he wasn't too upset about not finding Mr. Wilson's name. He was right and it had been a slim chance anyway.

The door at the top of the stairs opened and light filtered down to us. I went still, my blood ran cold. Matt pressed a finger to his lips then extinguished the lamp.

The light from the top of the stairs brightened as it came closer. Footsteps echoed, tapping on the stone steps with an ominous rhythm. "Who's there?" boomed a deep male voice.

"I saw her come in," said a woman.

My body sagged. Someone had seen me. I thought I'd been so clever and quiet too.

"And I saw him," came a second man's voice. A voice I recognized as Mr. Woolley's, the man in charge of the shelter. If he recognized us, we'd be in awful trouble.

"Come out of there," said the first man again. Trouser-clad legs appeared on the stairs, taking each step with caution. "This is Constable Lalor. Come out of your own accord or you'll be arrested."

CHAPTER 9

"*H*ide," I whispered, pushing Matt toward a stack of crates.

He wouldn't go. He caught me and trapped me against his chest. He must have put the lamp down because he held me with both hands. "I have a different plan," he whispered back. "We ain't done nothing!" he called out to the constable. "Don't arrest us, sir!"

So he planned on talking his way out of it. Knowing Matt, he could do it.

His fingers touched my throat, feeling their way in the dark to my collar. He undid a button on my dress, then another and another, and followed suit with my chemise.

So *that* was his plan. I helped him with my outer clothing until my corset was exposed. His fingers left me and I heard fabric rustle as he saw to his own attire. I decided to go a step further and tug my corset down to expose the swell of my breasts.

The constable's lamplight fell on us. I blinked and lifted a hand to shield my eyes, knowing the movement would draw attention to my state of undress. From the woman's gasp, I knew I'd succeeded. The light was too bright to tell if the constable and Mr. Woolley were shocked.

Matt noticed me too. He hastily buttoned up my dress, his gaze averted. Whether he meant to skim his knuckles across my bare flesh was impossible to tell. Thank goodness the light wasn't strong enough to see my reddening face.

The policeman lowered his lamp. "It's just two lovers, not thieves."

"Even so!" It was the pinch-lipped matron from the front door. "Fraternizing is against the shelter's policy! It's strictly forbidden."

Mr. Woolley came into view alongside her. He stretched his neck forward, peering into the dimness at us. I lowered my face, but Matt did not.

"We ain't frat'nizing," Matt snapped. "We're married."

"Married or not, it is still fraternizing!" Matron's clipped words bounced off the walls.

"It ain't illegal," Matt declared. "Ain't that right, Constable?"

"He's right," the constable said. "This is not a public place, and if they are married…"

"This is outrageous." Matron turned to Mr. Woolley and jerked her head at us. "Well? What say you about this…this immorality, sir?"

Mr. Woolley stepped down and approached us. He ignored me but strode straight up to Matt. I watched them through my lowered lids, eyeing one another. Was Matt mad? He ought to look away before Woolley recognized him. My heart hammered wildly, willing Matt to back down. Finally he did. I hazarded a glance at Mr. Woolley. He looked pleased to have won the contest of wills, but there was no recognition in his eyes, thank God.

"We're sorry, sir," Matt mumbled into his chest. "Anne frets without me, see, so I told her to meet me down here. It's quiet with just the mice for company. Cold, mind, but we got each other for warmth."

"Frets?" Mr. Woolley asked with a tilt of his head.

"Aye, sir. She gets all shaky and whimpery like a puppy without her master."

A puppy without her master! I refrained from rolling my eyes, just.

"I see," Mr. Woolley said.

"She's a good wife," Matt went on. I was beginning to think he was enjoying this. "Agreeable and eager to please." He was definitely enjoying this. "I don't like that in a wife so much, though. Prefer me a fiery girl to a meek one, but I can't cast my Anne out for being what she is, and what she is is silly in love with me. Ain't that right, Anne?" His beard twitched with his smirk.

Well. Since he wasn't afraid of being recognized, I wouldn't be either, although I kept my face averted. "I didn't know you liked your women-folk fiery, William," I said, matching Matt's accent as best as I could. "Now that I do, things'll change." I took his hand and led him up the stairs past the others. "First up, you're going to take that job in the sewers what you turned down, then you're visiting the barber with your first wages and shaving off that ugly beard."

We marched down the corridor and out through the women's dormitory then the men's. We left Mr. Woolley and the constable behind, but Matron kept up. Perhaps she wanted to make sure we well and truly departed. We'd left our lamp behind in the cellar but it didn't matter. All that mattered was our freedom.

"Good riddance," Matron said as we descended the front steps to the street. The door slammed behind us.

Matt circled his arm around me and drew me into his side. He chuckled softly and kissed the top of my head. "Well done, Mrs. McTavish. That was quite the performance."

I should have pulled away but did not. It felt warm

against his body, and safe. "My accent was awful. I'm sure they'll realize and come after us at any moment."

His arm tightened and his quiet laugh echoed in the foggy air. "With a name like McTavish, we should have tried a Scottish accent. Next time."

"My acting talents do not stretch to Scots. I'll have to pretend to be mute."

"Then I won't get the pleasure of your biting wit. You managed to put me in my place with a few choice words."

"I'm not sure Matron appreciated my outburst. I swear her lips pinched so hard they almost disappeared."

"Matron has very odd ideas about men and women. She'd probably faint if she interrupted us actually fraternizing."

"I don't know if anything would make Matron faint. She seemed rather stoic. I wonder if she blushes."

"Her cheeks wouldn't dare."

I laughed and he squeezed me again. His pace slowed, and I glanced up at him only to see him turned toward me. It was too dark to make out his expression, thankfully. I didn't want to see his desire. I'd made my mind up to dissuade him from liking me in *that* way, but so far I was doing a terrible job of it. Indeed, how could I dissuade him when I enjoyed being with him? That mountain seemed too high to climb right now with my blood thrumming from the excitement of the night and our closeness.

"India," he said, all seriousness. Too serious. He touched my jaw and angled my face just so. Then he brushed his lips against mine.

I pulled away. I needed to fill the silence but I couldn't think of anything to say. I wasn't sure I could speak anyway. My body trembled and my voice would too, betraying me. I could not let him know my true thoughts on the matter of us being together. Not yet. Not until he was well enough to walk away from me and from England.

Thank god Cyclops moved out of the shadows and

opened the coach door. Both he and Matt sat with me inside. I did not try to talk to either man and avoided looking at Matt the entire journey.

He spoke quietly with Cyclops, telling him how we'd fared at the shelter. There was no laughter in his voice now, no sense of fun or adventure.

Duke drove directly to the mews. I waited as Matt and Cyclops helped him and the sleepy stable boy unhitch the horse in the coach house and settle it in the stables.

"Well?" Duke asked as we trudged back to the house. "Did you find Wilson's name in the records?"

"No," Matt said.

Cyclops lifted the lamp to see our faces. "Want to try another shelter?"

"I don't see the point. Finding out about Wilson isn't going to help us find the killer or the diary."

"Unless the killer murdered Dr. Millroy in retaliation for experimenting on Mr. Wilson," I said. "And Wilson's records point us in the direction of his previous address, and any family he may have had."

"He had no family or friends," Matt said. "So Chronos believed."

"Ain't that a sad state," Duke murmured.

"Chronos could have been mistaken," I said.

"I doubt he was." Matt kicked the cobblestones. "It was a pointless exercise. I wish we hadn't bothered."

Cyclops and Duke exchanged glances then looked to me with brows raised in question. I merely forged ahead.

We entered the house via the basement service entrance. Duke was about to shut the door when a man carrying a lamp descended the steps from the street level.

"Wait for me." It was Willie, not a man. She grinned at us and slapped Duke on the shoulder in a friendly greeting.

He stepped aside to let her through. "You're only getting home now?"

"Aye, and that ain't your business, Duke." She pushed past him and hooked my arm with hers. "How'd your investigation go?"

"We learned nothing about the vagrant," I said. "Where have you been?"

"Here and there."

"Playing poker?" Matt asked.

"Didn't I just say it were none of your business?" she said hotly. "That goes for all of you."

"It is Matt's business if he has to get you out of trouble again," Duke shot back.

"I ain't gambling." She strode ahead, her lamp swaying with her steps. "Christ, can't a woman do nothing around here without everyone poking their goddamned noses in?"

Duke made to go after her but stopped. "She's right," he said to me. "It ain't my business if she's got herself a man."

I walked slowly with Duke as Matt and Cyclops said their goodnights and headed off with Willie. "Are you sure it's not your business?" I asked him gently.

He merely shrugged. "It ain't like that between us."

"It could be if you told her how you feel."

He shook his head. "I can't. I don't even know how I feel."

"Try to explain it to me then. It might help you work out how to approach her."

"Let's see." He blew out a breath. "She's frustrating and irritating. She says and does foolish things that make me want to yell at her one second and kiss her the next."

I smiled. "So you desire her."

"I s'pose. But what would happen if I did kiss her? Everything would change between us, that's what. I don't know if I want it to change. I like the way we've always been."

"You're just afraid of being rejected. Or perhaps you're afraid of change."

"Could be. I didn't want to leave America because I was

worried about being out of place here. And now I'm here, I don't know if I want to return."

That was quite a statement, and not one I expected to hear from any of Matt's party. They always seemed so determined to return home as soon as Matt's watch was fixed.

"I don't like the thought of her seeing another man," he added. "I hate that she's sharing secrets and jokes with someone else. It's always been me, see. We've been friends forever." He sighed. "Guess I always thought I was the most important man in her life, aside from Matt. Now…now I may not be, no more."

Poor Duke. I tucked my arm through his and rested my head on his shoulder. "You should tell her this."

"She'll laugh at me or tell me I'm being a sop." He did have a point. "India…will you find out if she's got a man? She might talk to you."

"I'll try, but if she confides in me and asks me not to tell you, I have to abide by her wishes." I patted his arm. "Anyway, anything's possible with Willie. For all we know, she could have been anywhere from watching a prize fight to a play."

"Then why the secrets?"

* * *

I ASKED Willie the following morning after a late breakfast but she refused to tell me a single thing about her nocturnal excursion.

"Tell Duke to mind his own business," she said. She also blushed. I took that as confirmation that she had indeed had a liaison with a man. I did not inform Duke.

I offered to stay with Miss Glass and not visit Mrs. Millroy with Matt, but he would have none of it. "I know you want to come," he said.

"Yes but I ought to spend time with your aunt. She seems lonely. And what if she wanders off again?"

"She won't, because she's not going out with my Aunt Beatrice again. I've asked Willie and Duke to take turns sitting with her. They also need to interview a new coachman. There's a man coming today. Cyclops will drive us."

Dr. Millroy's widow lived only a few minutes away by carriage. We could have walked but Matt used the excuse of the incessant drizzling rain to drive. I did wonder if he simply wanted to spend as little time with me as possible after the awkwardness of last night's journey home. Conversation was stilted between us, and it ground to a complete halt before we arrived.

I found it difficult to even look at him. It was hard seeing him still so tired, even after sleeping for several hours, but it was even harder facing him knowing that he had feelings for me.

Me!

I'd lain in bed, tossing and turning as I tried not to picture myself walking down the aisle toward him. Tried and failed. It was impossible not to dream about a life with him and impossible not to be thrilled that he might want it too. Impossible not to be sad that it would never happen.

"We can do this without feeling awkward around one another," Matt said, interrupting my self-pitying.

I nodded and smiled. "Of course we can. We have an important task at hand. Will you try to charm her or will I try to comfort her?"

"We'll see how she reacts when we mention the mistress."

I wasn't looking forward to that part.

Fortunately, Mrs. Millroy lived in the same house she'd lived in during her marriage to Dr. Millroy. Chronos had given us the address but he'd not checked to see if she still lived there. Her house was located in an area known for high rents and within easy walking distance to her deceased husband's surgery on Savile Row. I was pleased to know she hadn't been forced out due to reduced circumstances following his death.

"Are you Mrs. Millroy?" Matt asked the slender, well-dressed, gray-haired woman who opened the door upon his knock.

"Yes. And who are *you*?" Her rounded vowels reminded me of Miss Glass and her ilk. She dressed like Miss Glass too, in a well-cut tailored day dress that showed off her cinched waist and narrow chest. She made me feel plump by comparison.

"My name is Matthew Glass and this is my partner, Miss Steele. We're private inquiry agents assisting the police in the matter of your late husband's murder."

A pronouncement of that magnitude, made so many years after the event, would have sent me reeling if I were in her position. But she merely lifted one thin, patchy eyebrow. "I see."

Matt smiled but it wasn't convincing. He already knew his charms wouldn't work on her. "May we come in, Mrs. Millroy? This isn't a matter for the front porch."

She responded to his more business-like approach by opening the door wider. Inside, it wasn't much warmer than out. No rug covered the blue and white tiles in the entrance hall and the fireplace in the sitting room was clean of ashes. Someone had sat in here very recently, however, if the dirty teacup on the table and blanket tossed over the chair arm were an indication.

Mrs. Millroy folded the blanket and invited us to sit on the faded sofa. Like the entrance hall, the sitting room was rather bare. Aside from a lovely Wedgewood vase, the few other knick knacks looked like the sort one could buy from a barrow in Petticoat Lane. "I would offer you tea," she said stiffly, "but my housekeeper has the day off."

She'd given her the day off mid-week? How generous.

"Mrs. Millroy, we know these questions will be difficult for you," I said, "but we have to ask them."

"Why? Why do the police want to find out who killed my husband now? He died years ago."

"It's something they do from time to time."

"Nonsense. I am not a fool, Miss Steele." She may look thin and old but she had a sturdy mind and spirit. It would take more than two people asking questions about her husband's death to knock her off balance.

"Someone has come forward with new evidence," Matt lied.

"What evidence?"

"We're not at liberty to say, but Commissioner Munro doesn't have the staff to send a detective so he asked us. We've assisted him on other investigations with some success."

Her nostrils flared. "So that's how much significance he lends to my husband's murder, is it? Not enough to send his detective, but just enough to pass the problem on to someone else. I assume he hopes you'll find nothing and James's death will once again be confined to the archives where it gathers dust with the hundreds of other crimes that go unsolved in this city." She clicked her tongue. "Typical."

"We can see that it upsets you," I said gently. "And rightly so. It must have been an awful time and the lack of resolution means you've not been able to grieve properly for him."

She barked out a bitter laugh. "Is that a joke?"

"Er, no."

"Miss Steele." She angled her knees toward me and clasped her hands in her lap. "You are correct in that it was an awful time, but not because of my husband's murder. That almost came as a relief."

I leaned forward, as intrigued as I was appalled. "Go on."

"I know you already know, so there is no need to pretend ignorance. The police found out all the sordid facts. They even suspected *she* did it at one point, but they told me they had no proof. Perhaps I was even a suspect. I ought to have been, but they did not tell me so."

I did not tell her that she was one of *our* suspects still.

"You're referring to your husband's mistress," Matt said. Thank goodness he took over the conversation because I felt quite unable to confront her about it now that the time had come.

She gave a stiff nod.

"You were questioned at the time of his murder," Matt went on. "Indeed, it was you who mentioned he had a mistress and son, but you didn't say how long you'd known about them."

"I suspected for some time but only knew for certain a month before his death."

"How?"

"He told me." She smoothed her hands over her knees. "Well, I confronted him and he told me. He often came home late from his rooms. That was nothing new. Then he started coming home smelling of expensive perfume. Not every night, but enough to cause suspicion. I didn't confront him immediately. I assumed it would stop of its own accord. It was not the first time I suspected him of having liaisons with trollops, but this time...well, the perfume was always the same."

"How long did you wait before confronting him?" I asked.

"More than a year. When he began denying me certain things, that's when I decided enough was enough."

"Denying you?" Matt prompted.

"New curtains, a holiday at the seaside, the best cuts of meat, that sort of thing. All of a sudden, we seemed not to have enough money. So I asked him outright if he kept another woman. He told me he did, and that she had recently given birth to a son." Her shoulders sagged, but just for a moment then she quickly recovered her erectness.

"You have no children of your own," I said gently.

"That is neither here nor there. The fact is, my husband kept another house and another family."

"Do you know their names?" Matt asked.

"He took that information to his grave. Not even his lawyer knew."

"The child was not provided for in his will?"

She thrust out her chin. "Why should he be? He was not James's legitimate child. He has no claims to anything. I do." She once again smoothed her hands along her skirt. "Anyway, James didn't leave much in his will. It's my assumption that he spent a lot on the woman before his death. So perhaps you ought to look there for his murderer, Mr. Glass."

"I would, but I don't know where *there* is."

"As a private inquiry agent, that is your job to find out."

"Why would she kill him if he was giving her money?" I asked. "It doesn't make sense."

She lifted one shoulder. "Perhaps he was going to leave her. Perhaps he was seeing someone else, or she was. Or perhaps they argued about any number of other things. There are many reasons, Miss Steele. If you put your mind to it, you might come up with some all on your own."

I bristled. Well there was no need for rudeness.

"What else can you tell us about the night of his murder?" Matt asked.

"Nothing. I was here, as I told the police."

"Dr. Millroy was found in Bright Court, Whitechapel. Do you know why he was there?"

"No. He had no clients in Whitechapel, no friends or acquaintances that I knew of. I can only speculate that he was visiting his mistress and child. Either that or he kept another secret from me. Perhaps you ought to ask the residents if any remember him."

"We have."

She raised her brow. "And?"

"And our inquiries continue."

Her gaze narrowed. "I would like to be kept informed of anything you learn."

I was inclined to tell her no, but Matt got in first. "We'll be sure to inform you of anything that you need to know."

Her lips flattened. It wasn't quite what she'd asked for, but he'd worded it so that she could not argue.

"Does the name Nell Sweet mean anything to you?" Matt asked.

Her eyes flashed. "Is that her name?"

"What about Chronos?"

Mrs. Millroy stiffened.

"The name is familiar to you," Matt went on.

"Yes," she said. "Of course it's not his real name. I only knew him as Chronos. He was a watchmaker and an acquaintance of my husband's. Do you think…" She shifted her weight in the chair. "Do you think he had something to do with James's murder?"

"No," I said at the same time Matt said, "Possibly."

I glared at him but he ignored me. He looked directly at Mrs. Millroy, and she looked straight back as if his gaze mesmerized her.

"Your husband was a magician," Matt went on. He was like a steam engine, gathering speed as he stormed down the hill, smashing through any barriers in his wake. I would not want to be a barrier on the tracks right now. Mrs. Millroy had better answer him truthfully because he would not stop until he was satisfied.

She gave a small nod. "He was. As was the watchmaker Chronos, but I suspect you already know that."

"Did your husband have any family?" Matt pressed.

"A cousin, but I don't know much about him except that he's dead now and had no children. He was also a doctor and lived for some time in America. Whether he was a magician or not, I couldn't tell you."

Dr. Parsons was the cousin, but neither Matt nor I offered up the information.

"And you already know we had no children together," she went on. "Of course, James's bastard might be magical but I don't know where to begin looking for him. Is that the real reason you're here? To find a doctor magician?" Her lips twisted as if the notion disgusted her. "You're all the same. You don't really want to find his killer, do you? So are you sick? Is one of you dying?"

"Scotland Yard sent us," I told her. "Ask Commissioner Munro or Detective Inspector Brockwell if you want verification."

"The Surgeon's Guild knew your husband was magical," Matt pushed on. "They found out just before his death and confronted him. Perhaps they killed him."

Her lips parted in a silent gasp. Her gaze searched his then fell to her hands. Those hands suddenly became very busy, wringing in her lap. "They wouldn't do such a thing. They're *doctors*. They don't murder people."

"You told them he was a magician, didn't you?" Matt asked.

Her eyes gave her away before she closed them and gave the slightest nod. "It wasn't anyone from the guild. It can't have been. Dr. Ritter is head of the London Hospital now, a very respectable man."

"How did he react when you told him?"

She frowned then rubbed her forehead with her left hand. She wore no wedding ring. "It was odd. He wasn't shocked. He seemed relieved. I think he was jealous of James's skill, and magic explained that skill. Doctors value their education above anything else, you see. It matters to them where a physician or surgeon studied and who he studied under. Learning that James's skill was innate, not learned, made Dr. Ritter feel more like his equal when before he had not."

"Did you tell anyone else about your husband's magic?" Matt asked.

She shook her head. "Only the guild." She looked pleased with herself, and I knew she'd done it as retribution for her husband's infidelities. Part of me forgave her for it.

"And the Watchmaker's Guild?" I asked. "Did you tell them about Chronos's magic?"

She studied her linked hands. "Dr. Ritter informed the Watchmaker's Guild. When I explained about the experiment performed on the vagrant, Dr. Ritter asked for the name of the second magician so I told him about Chronos. Since I didn't know his real name, I described his appearance. He said he was obliged to inform the Watchmaker's Guild's master. It was nothing to do with me."

"You got him into awful trouble!" I cried. "How could you do that to someone you hardly knew simply because you wanted revenge on your husband?"

"Chronos had a hand in a man's death, Miss Steele. That's why I did it. He didn't deserve to get away with it. Although he did, in a way, by dying." She was all blotchy red cheeks, white lips and flared nostrils, like a raging bull. "I heard Chronos died shortly after James, so neither of them paid for the crime they committed on that poor man. His family never received justice."

"He had no family," Matt said.

"Are you sure?"

Matt and I exchanged glances. "We were informed that he was a homeless man named Mr. Wilson with no friends or family. He was dying with no hope of recovery."

"Some of that may be true, but unlike you, I don't trust my source." Mrs. Millroy looked as if she was about to lay down a winning poker hand. "My husband was a liar, and a self-centered, boastful man with loose morals. He came home every evening from his rooms and lied to my face for more than a year when I asked if he'd worked late. That is not the act of a trustworthy man."

"Do you have any proof that the vagrant had a family?" Matt asked.

"I spoke to the man myself. I was visiting James at his Savile Row rooms one evening, hoping to catch him not there so I could confront him. He was there, however, with Chronos. That was the first and only time I met the watchmaker. I guessed what they were up to, since James had talked of such an experiment for years, but had never met a watchmaker magician before. When I saw the ill man lying on the bed, I knew what they were going to do that night." She shook her head but did not look too upset by the memory. It was more of a narration from a distant observer than participant. "I spoke to the man very briefly before James ordered me away. He said his name was Wilson and that he had a child and a wife but had lost them. I supposed that to mean they died, but I could have been mistaken. He was very confused, his words difficult to understand, but I think he had spent time in a doss house and planned to return there later that night." Another shake of her head. "He believed Chronos and James would cure him."

"But they did not," I said heavily.

"Apparently the magic was imperfect. But that's by the by, Miss Steele. The point you appear not to grasp is they ended that man's life sooner than God intended."

"You don't know that."

"And you don't know otherwise."

She had me there.

"Why are you interested in whether the man had a family now anyway?" she asked Matt. "He is irrelevant to my husband's murder."

"His family may have sought revenge against your husband," Matt said.

"James was murdered by his mistress or someone associ-

ated with her. Another lover, an avenging family member...
Look for her and you'll find the killer."

"You seem convinced. Why?"

"It's not sour grapes, if that's what you're thinking."

Matt held up his hands in surrender.

"It's common sense, that's all," she said. "If not her, then an opportunistic thief who went too far."

"So you don't know anything about her?" I said. "Did he ever let her name slip, or that of his son?"

"No."

"Did he ever go somewhere he should not have been?"

"Bright Court on the night of his death," she offered with an arched look that implied I was stupid.

"You think his mistress lived in one of London's vilest slums?" I wanted to give her an equally arched look but managed to keep my features schooled.

She shrugged. "It's unlikely. He valued cleanliness above all things. Cleanliness and good teeth."

Old Nell's teeth may have been better years ago, but Whitechapel had filth oozing from every crumbling brick. That hadn't changed in twenty-seven years, despite attempts to clean up the slums by the authorities.

"What about his patients?" Matt said thoughtfully. "Did he ever discuss them with you?"

"He used to, in the beginning," she said quietly. "In later years, we grew apart and he stopped confiding in me unless I asked a direct question. He was always something of a charming man with women. Coupled with his magic, it meant he had patients queuing to see him."

"What about employees?" Matt asked. "Did he have someone to take appointments, type letters *et cetera*?"

"Of course. I did it in the beginning, but as he grew more successful I decided my time was better spent in the home. He employed two women over the course of the remainder of his life. One married and left his employment, and Miss

Chilton, the second one, was with him until the end. And no, she was not his mistress. She was a spinster of about thirty years. I lost contact with her after James's death. She did not have a child, to him or anyone else, during that time. I would have noticed."

Matt pulled out a notepad and pencil from his jacket pocket. "May I have her full name and last known address, please."

"Miss Abigail Chilton." She retrieved a portable writing desk from a shelf in the corner and set it down on the table. She plucked a small book from it and flipped the pages until she found the one she wanted. "She lived at number twenty-three Theberton Street, Islington. Whether she lives there still, I cannot be certain."

Matt wrote the address in his notebook. "What of the patient records?" he asked without looking up. "Did you keep them?"

She slammed the writing desk shut. "I destroyed them. Why would I keep them?"

Damnation. They could have been useful if the mistress was a patient of Dr. Millroy's.

"What about his diary?" Matt asked.

She paused mid-step, the writing desk in hand, before continuing on. She carefully deposited the desk on the shelf again, taking her time. "So you do want his magic. And I thought you were telling me the truth and wanted to bring that woman to justice."

"The diary wasn't found on his body," Matt persisted. "If he had it with him, his killer must have taken it. But you already knew that, Mrs. Millroy. Is it possible he didn't have his diary with him that night? Did he leave it here by any chance, or in his Savile Row rooms?"

"It wasn't here, and I did not find it among the paperwork at his rooms when Miss Chilton and I cleaned them out. He always kept it on his person. I told the police that much, but I did not tell them what secrets he kept in it. You seem to have guessed, however, that he wrote his spells in it, among other things."

"Spells? Plural?" I asked in wonder. Chronos knew of only one.

"I don't know how many. He couldn't get most to work."

"Why not?"

"I'm not a magician, Miss Steele, but I believe it had something to do with not knowing the right way of saying the words. They were complex, foreign."

"The spells in that diary were passed down from his ancestors," I said. "Correct?"

"Are you implying that James was killed for the diary and the spells in it?" she asked, not answering me.

"It's a possibility."

"I disagree."

"Why?"

"Because very few people knew about the importance of the diary. Only me and probably Chronos. My husband was careful. He did not discuss magic with many people and certainly none in his profession. The guilds are powerful and dangerous, and they do not like magicians. He would never take such a risk except with someone he trusted completely."

"He trusted *you* and you betrayed him, Mrs. Millroy," Matt said, the thread of steel in his voice clear as day. "You told the Surgeon's Guild about the experiment and his magic."

"He killed a man! He had to be stopped."

Matt closed his hands into fists on his knees then spread out his fingers, as if he were releasing his frustrations.

"The question is," she said to him, "how do *you* know about the diary? Who told you?"

Someone coughed and footsteps sounded on the steps leading upstairs. Mrs. Millroy suddenly stood and stalked to the sitting room door.

"Morning Mrs. Millroy," came a man's voice, followed by another cough. "I heard voices."

"I have callers," she told him.

He came into view, peering over her head at us. He was a young man with blond hair in need of a comb and clothes that looked as if he'd slept in them. He waved cheerfully at us then stifled a yawn.

"Any breakfast?" he said to Mrs. Millroy.

"I told you, breakfast is served before nine. You'll find porridge in the kitchen but it will be cold."

He groaned. "Porridge again? And cold? You do recall that I'm paying you for bed *and* breakfast." He stormed away, expressing his dislike of a cold breakfast with every thumping step.

"My lodger," she told us.

Now I knew why she claimed her maid was off mid-week. It was likely she kept no maid anymore and had taken in lodgers to help her financial situation. It also explained the threadbare nature of the furnishings. Despite her haughty manner, she was struggling like thousands of other widows in the city.

"Thank you for your assistance, Mrs. Millroy," Matt said, extending his hand to her. "I know it hasn't been easy for you to talk to us, but I assure you we are determined to find your husband's killer."

She shook his hand and even looked pleased to do so. "And bring her to justice," she added.

She saw us out and Matt gave Cyclops the address for Miss Chilton.

"Clearly Mrs. Millroy thinks the mistress is guilty," I said.

Matt smiled. "What gave you that idea?"

"I'm excellent at reading the signs." He laughed. "I found it difficult to like her," I added. "Sympathize, yes, but not like. Does that make me an awful person? As a woman, shouldn't I be on her side? Her husband did wrong her terribly."

"You're the best person I know, India," he said, that smile never wavering. "Mrs. Millroy doesn't deserve to be liked because her husband treated her terribly. Pitied, but not liked. So what do you think about what she said?"

"She was honest, perhaps brutally so."

"She could be an excellent liar."

"True, but why lie?"

"To point the finger at the mistress."

I nodded, slowly. "Do you think the vagrant had a family, as she claimed? Why would she lie about that?"

"I can't think of a reason. It seems Wilson's wife and child died before him, though."

"Poor man. No wonder he lost his way. Probably his will to live too."

Matt sucked in a breath and wagged a finger at me. "If that's so, why did he agree to participate in the magicians' scheme? That speaks of desperation to *live*, not to die."

"Yes," I said, nodding. "I see your point. Perhaps he didn't mean his family died when he told Mrs. Millroy they were lost. Perhaps he meant…what?"

Matt shrugged. "That is a good question."

* * *

Miss Chilton no longer resided on Theberton Street. The new lodgers had never heard of her but they'd only lived there five years. One of the near neighbors had lived in the street longer and recalled Miss Chilton married and moved away.

I felt deflated when I climbed back into the carriage, but Matt was a little more hopeful.

"We can check the marriage register at the local parish churches," he said. "It's likely she got married in one of them."

"The General Register Office will have the records," I told him.

"Then I'll put my lawyer onto it while we continue our

investigation elsewhere. We're on the right path, India. I sense it."

I sensed nothing, but I smiled along with him so as not to dampen his good mood.

Cyclops drove us home but we didn't reach the door before it burst open and Willie ran down the stairs, Duke on her heels. He wasn't running after her to stop her, however. He was eager to get to us too.

Willie shoved a newspaper at Matt. It was a copy of *The Weekly Gazette*, opened to an inside page. Her breaths were so ragged that she couldn't speak, only stab her finger at an article headed MAGIC: PROOF IT EXISTS.

Written by Oscar Barratt.

"India," Duke muttered, "what have you done?"

CHAPTER 10

I pressed a hand to my chest but my heart continued to rampage. I had to read the article twice to take it in, but even then I couldn't quite fathom it. I understood the words but not the betrayal. How could Oscar do this? We'd decided against writing such an article. Hadn't we? Or had I decided and assumed he agreed?

"Matt," I began. I shook my head and continued to stare at the newspaper in his hands, my mind numb.

What did it mean? What would happen now?

I read the article a third time. I concentrated hard, but still failed to grasp why Oscar would do this to me, to other magicians, and even to himself and his family. He'd invited suspicion to the door of every craftsman or woman with superior skill.

His article spoke about magic being kept hidden to keep the magicians safe from jealous guild members. He wrote about the way it was inherited, like blue eyes or black hair. He described what magicians do with their spells, using examples of carpenters, boat builders, jewelers, paper manufacturers and countless others. He wrote about mapmakers, goldsmiths and watchmakers but did not mention names. There was no mention of ink magicians or doctors.

My legs wobbled. My vision blurred. My heart raced too fast, too hard. I went to sit down on the step, but found Matt's arm around me, supporting me. He walked me inside, Duke and Willie in his wake.

"India?" Miss Glass's voice had never sounded so clear and strong. "India, what's happened? Are you ill?"

I sat on the sofa in the drawing room. Miss Glass fussed around me, plumping cushions, giving orders. I couldn't see past her. I couldn't see Matt. I needed to see him. Needed him to know I did not sanction that article.

"Matt." My voice rasped. "Matt." Miss Glass tried to get me to lie down but I shooed her away.

She frowned. "Lie there until the doctor comes, India."

"I don't need a doctor."

"You had a turn."

"My corset is too tight."

Her eyes widened. "You are not undressing here in the drawing room!"

"Aunt," Matt's firm voice chided. "India simply needs air."

I needed to read that article again and catalogue everything Oscar had written. And then I would march to his office and demand he print a retraction.

How could he do this?

"Matt," I said again. "Can we speak alone?"

"No," Miss Glass said before he could answer. She moved out of the way, allowing me to see him.

He stood in the center of the room, arms crossed over his chest, every muscle taut. His gaze raked down my length. Then he turned and walked out.

I refrained from calling after him. I closed my eyes to block out the vision of Willie and Duke, glaring at me as if my name was in the byline, not Oscar's. I sank back into the sofa and groaned.

"How could you?" Willie whined. "Is there something loose in your brain, India?"

"What are you talking about?" Miss Glass asked.

No one answered.

"Duke, give me that newspaper," she said.

He sighed and handed it to her. She skimmed the newspaper, pausing on the article in question. She quickly read it and lowered the paper. "Oscar Barratt is your friend, India."

"Acquaintance," I said into my chest. "How could he do this to me? We agreed not to publish anything."

"But you discussed it," Duke said with a shake of his head.

"You dang fool," Willie snapped. "Do you know what'll happen now?"

"Every member of every guild will turn against those who are better, more skillful than they are," I said. "Yes, Willie, I am well aware of what will happen now. That's why Oscar and I agreed not to do anything about it."

"Seems he didn't agree," Duke said.

Miss Glass scoffed. "Come now. No one will believe this."

"Let's hope not."

I pushed up from the sofa. "I have to see Matt. I have to explain."

"Explain what?" Willie growled. "That you and Oscar conspired to do this behind his back?"

"You're being ridiculous, Willie. Nobody conspired. We discussed the pros and cons, that's all, then decided it would be a bad idea to bring magic into the open."

She snatched the newspaper from Miss Glass. "If you didn't talk to Barratt about it, he wouldn't have written this!" She slapped the paper down on the table.

"Miss Glass is right," I said. "No one will believe it."

"Those who suspect something will! Those who've seen things they can't explain will! Those who've ever lost business to a craftsman better than themselves will!"

"What if this is just the beginning?" Duke said. "What if

this leads to more investigations? More vendettas and vigilante attacks? Christ, India, watchmakers are mentioned in here."

That was the worst part. I thought Oscar was my friend. I thought he'd liked me for me. Apparently he only liked me for what I could tell him about magic. Yet another man I got very, very wrong.

I lowered my head into my hands and closed my eyes against the well of tears. I was such a fool. Such an utter, pathetic fool.

"That's why Matt's angry," Duke said, gentler. "He's worried someone will link you to being—"

I looked up to see why he'd stopped mid-sentence. He and Willie stared at Miss Glass, their mouths tightly shut. Miss Glass, however, stared at me, her eyes like saucers.

"You're a…a magician, India?" she whispered.

Oh hell. Not now.

But it was too late. We'd forgotten she didn't know about magic, and now I had to tell her the truth. I couldn't back away from it. "Yes, I am."

"Oh." Her eyes lost focus, her features slackened. "I do like the seaside, don't you? Perhaps Harry will take me when he comes home. Do you know when he'll come home, Veronica?"

I sighed, suddenly wanting to take her to her room and hide there with her. "Duke, fetch Polly."

"Who's Polly?" Miss Glass asked in a thin voice.

"Your maid."

"No." She shook her head. "You are my maid, Veronica. Silly girl."

Polly arrived with Mrs. Bristow in tow. Miss Glass went meekly with them. Her exit left me even more deflated, yet more determined to speak to Matt.

With a fortifying breath, I stood, only to see Chronos enter. "The house is in some sort of commotion," he said, glancing over his shoulder. "What happened?"

Duke tossed him the newspaper. I thought it a good time to leave.

I got no further than the entrance hall. Matt stood there, accepting his hat from Bristow. Peter rushed in from the back of the house. "Mr. Cyclops is returning now with the conveyance, sir."

"I'm coming with you," I told Matt.

He shot me a flinty glare. "You don't know where I'm going."

"Of course I do. Believe me, I have as much to say to Oscar Barratt as you do. Perhaps more."

His frown only deepened.

Bristow opened the front door just as Cyclops stopped the coach by the steps. Matt had a quick word with him and Cyclops's gaze met mine over Matt's head. I didn't wait to be assisted into the cabin.

"I know you don't believe me," I said to Matt when he sat opposite, "but I did not ask Oscar to write that article. We discussed it but came to the conclusion that the risks were too great to reveal magic to the world. At least, I thought we both came to the same conclusion."

"I believe you, India."

"You do? Then why the scowl?"

"Can I not scowl and still believe you?"

"No! Save it for Oscar. I want only your smiles, clear eyes and charms." I sniffed, aware of how silly I sounded and how unfair I was being but unable to stave off the melancholia. "You are angry with me, Matt. I know you are."

"Not angry," he said, his clipped tone implying otherwise.

He turned to stare out one window and I looked through the other. The minutes passed in excruciating silence. Instead of focusing on Matt, I considered what I'd say to Oscar instead. It was much easier to come up with words to berate him, although they also brought tears to my eyes. He'd betrayed me. I'd given him information in confidence and he'd splashed it across his newspaper without a care. He'd tricked me into liking him so he could get what he needed. I'd been such a fool.

The coach slowed as the traffic increased near Fleet Street. When it stopped altogether at the Ludgate intersection, Matt moved to sit beside me. He placed his hand over mine, resting on my thigh. Despite both of us wearing gloves, the gesture was as intimate as any of our kisses had been. My tears welled again and I couldn't look at him.

"Don't," he said simply.

"Don't what?"

"You're blaming yourself. You shouldn't. I know you well enough to know you wouldn't sanction that article. This is all Barratt's fault."

"We did discuss it together."

He removed his hand from mine. "You're defending him."

"If I hadn't gone there with the purpose of discussing such an article, he wouldn't have gone ahead and written it. It's only fair that I take part of the blame."

He didn't answer immediately, forcing me to look up at him. He blinked back at me. "You went there to discuss the idea of an article?"

I cringed. It had been such a foolish notion. "Yes."

"No other reason?"

"I did think it polite to see how his recovery progressed, but that wasn't foremost on my mind at the time." It sounded so heartless now that I said it out loud.

"I see," he said.

"See what?"

He studied his hands, fanned out on each thigh. "I see now that my idea for you two to become...more than acquaintances won't work."

I managed a laugh. "That was never going to work." I did not tell him why and he didn't ask. The topic was forgotten and we arrived a few minutes later at the office of *The Weekly Gazette*.

We did not wait in the front reception room for a staff member to attend us but barged through into the larger room where three men stood around a long table, studying the papers laid out there. They all looked up. I recognized the elderly editor, Mr. Baggley, who'd been present when Mr. Pitt had shot at Oscar a mere few days ago.

"May I help you?" he asked.

"Where's Barratt?" Matt demanded.

Mr. Baggley came around the table to greet us. "Not here."

But Oscar was already filling the doorway to his office. "It's all right," he told his editor. "I've been expecting them." He stood aside and invited us in.

Matt squared up to him. For a moment, I thought he'd thump Oscar, but his gaze shifted to his arm in the sling. Matt would not hit an injured man who couldn't fight back. He huffed out a frustrated grunt.

Oscar shut the office door and invited us to sit. Neither of us did. "How dare you!" I spat at him. "We agreed not to publish an article revealing magic."

He moved to the other side of his desk, perhaps to remain out of Matt's reach. Matt did look very fierce. "I had to do it, India."

"Don't call me India. You have no right to anymore, Mr. Barratt. We are no longer friends."

He gave me a sad smile. "So you won't go to the theater with me now?"

I didn't even bother answering him. I merely sat in one of the chairs and rubbed my forehead. How could he joke at a time like this?

"You fool, Barratt," Matt said in that quiet steely voice of his. "You didn't think it through."

"Of course I did." Oscar sat too and cradled his injured arm. "I know you're both concerned about the repercussions the article will cause, but I strongly believe any of the repercussions we discussed, Miss Steele, will be short-lived."

"A lot of harm can be done in a short time," Matt growled. "Do you honestly think magicians won't be hurt by this exposure?"

Oscar bristled. "I did not name anyone."

"It doesn't matter. Anyone who has ever been the subject of jealousy from his fellow guild members will become the focus of suspicion. It's only a small step from there to outright resentment and hatred. For God's sake, India has already suffered at the hands of the Watchmaker's Guild."

"Not just me," I reminded him. "Or that guild." But Matt didn't seem to hear me. He remained standing, using his full height to best advantage as he leaned his knuckles on the desk and glared at Oscar.

Oscar didn't flinch. "Miss Steele is not a member of the guild. She doesn't have a shop, create timepieces or practice her magic. She's no threat to anyone and will be quite safe."

"You're naive if you believe that."

"What about your own family, Mr. Barratt?" I said. "They are involved in the ink making industry and by your own admission, your brother's company makes the finest ink in the country because he's a magician. Your article will expose him most of all since *you* wrote it."

He held up his hand. "I've already had a telegram from my brother. Let him fight his own battles with me. He doesn't need you to fight them on his behalf."

I sat back. Was this an elaborate way to anger his brother? Was there a rivalry there that I'd not been privy to? "Have our investigations taught you nothing?" I said. "I know you are aware of the details. A young mapmaker was kidnapped and killed because of his magical ability. Because of *jealousy*, Mr. Barratt."

"And Mr. Pitt killed Dr. Hale," he shot back, "yet *both* were magicians. You're coming down very strongly against me and yet I know you liked the idea to a certain degree. You must have or you wouldn't have come here to discuss it. Just because *you* changed your mind—"

Matt slammed his hand on the desk, making me jump. It earned Oscar's silence and undivided attention. "Do not blame India. She came to her senses. You did not."

The office door opened and Mr. Baggley poked his head through. "You have another visitor, Oscar. He's refusing to leave."

"Show him in."

The door wrenched open wider to reveal the newcomer. "Mr. Gibbons!" I said, rising. I hadn't seen the grandfather of the mapmaker's apprentice since his grandson's death at the hands of his rival. The elderly cartography magician had taught me some valuable lessons about my own magic, but he ultimately believed as Matt did—that the artless should not be made aware of our magic. With valid reason, as it turned out—his grandson had lost his life because the artless became jealous of his prodigious talent.

"You?" Mr. Gibbons pointed a finger first at me then Matt. "You are behind this?"

"No," Matt said. "Barratt wrote that all on his own. We're here for the same reason I think you are. To tell him what an utter fool he is."

The snowy haired Mr. Gibbons looked ancient as he stood in the middle of the office, the extra lines on his face a record of his recent suffering. I took his arm and directed him to the other chair and sat again myself.

"This is madness," he said, his voice frail. "Do you know what you've started by writing that article, Mr. Barratt?"

Oscar's lips stretched into a hard, satisfied smile. "I have started a revolution."

Perhaps Mr. Gibbons was right and Oscar was mad. He certainly looked it in that moment, with his angry smile and the fierce gleam in his eyes.

"People die in revolutions," Matt said.

"Oppressors are overthrown," Oscar countered.

"And the innocent on both sides become victims."

"This is absurd," I said. "You haven't started a revolution, Mr. Barratt, you've planted the seeds of suspicion and jealousy at the least, and retaliation at the worst. We are not oppressed by the guilds, for goodness' sake!"

He spluttered a laugh. "You said yourself they've persecuted you. I've heard of dozens of cases where magicians had to hide their talent from their guilds because they worried they'd be thrown out. Indeed, being banished from the guild was the least of their worries in some cases. I spoke to you, Mr. Gibbons, after your grandson's death, and you told me how you had to hide your magic for your entire life. You even made deliberate errors in your maps so that the guild wouldn't suspect."

"I told you that in confidence," Mr. Gibbons said through a clenched jaw.

"And your name does not appear in my article. Indeed, no names do. The world is not ready for that, but when it is, I'll be the first one on the list of magicians." Oscar stabbed his finger on his desk. "I'll be at the very top. I'll show them that they can't bully me."

"You'll risk your life," Matt said with a shake of his head.

"It's a risk I'm prepared to take."

"You might change your mind after you see the hatred and fear your article spawns."

"I have no fear for myself, Mr. Glass."

"No fear for your family either, or for India, or Mr. Gibbons." Matt tapped the side of his head. "You are not thinking, Mr. Barratt."

"My head is clearer than it has been in years. Your recent investigations helped me see how important this is to future generations of magicians. I wrote glowingly about all the good magic can do—all the possibilities. The artless will flock to us and praise us, and the guilds wouldn't dare retaliate. If they do, it'll be seen for what it is—jealousy. People will no longer believe the guild members are the best craftsmen because they'll know the best have been locked out for generations. The guilds will lose their power and then the system will fall by the wayside altogether. It's an archaic system anyway. They deserve to be eradicated."

"If you think the guilds will disappear quietly, you're even more naive than I thought," Matt said with a shake of his head. "They'll fight with every weapon they have."

"They have no weapons against public opinion, Mr. Glass. And it's public opinion that matters in the end, nothing else. That's what changes behavior and opinions, and ultimately changes laws."

He really was talking about a revolution. Could this indeed be the beginning of one? Could he be doing the right thing?

Even if he was, I couldn't see the future he described without a lot of people getting caught in the middle. My friends the Masons would be forced to choose sides, and since they were artless, it was easy to know which side they'd choose. Mr. Abercrombie and others had also proved how unscrupulous the guilds could be to save themselves. The cost wasn't worth a revolution. Was it?

"You won't get many supporters," Mr. Gibbons said. "Not from magicians."

Oscar picked up a pile of papers from his desk. There must have been at least ten sheets. "These are messages of support that were slipped under the *Gazette's* door since the article appeared in this morning's edition. Each one of them *thanks* me for bringing magic into the open."

"Are they anonymous?" Matt asked.

Oscar put the papers down but did not answer.

"A revolution requires its army to come out of the

shadows to fight, Mr. Barratt. You'll need more than anonymous supporters."

"They will come. They'll grow in confidence once I print more articles. I plan on creating a conversation about magic through my pieces, and when that conversation gathers momentum, that's when magicians will declare themselves. They just need to see that a movement exists. When they do, they'll join it. I hope *you* will join me, Mr. Gibbons. And you, India." His voice gentled, and his gaze softened, drawing me in. He'd used my first name again, a tactic that wasn't lost on me. And yet, part of me hoped he was right, and that he had started a revolution. But dear lord, I prayed it would be a bloodless one.

"Leave India out of this," Matt snapped. "She's much too clever to fall for your propaganda. So is Mr. Gibbons."

"Quite right," Mr. Gibbons said.

"Perhaps Miss Gibbons will be more amenable. She certainly seemed keen to discuss her son's—"

Mr. Gibbons lunged across the desk but Oscar leaned out of the way. "Leave my daughter out of this. She's vulnerable since Daniel died, and she's not a magician anyway."

Oscar held up his hand in surrender. "If you don't mind, I have another article to write for next week's edition. My editor is pleased with the response of the first one and wants me to write a quarter page piece outlining specific cases of the wonderful work magicians have done, and the way their guilds have stifled them. Don't fear, it won't mention names."

"But it will mention events I've shared with you," I said. "How can you betray me like this, Oscar? I thought we were friends."

"I still consider you my friend, India. I always will. But on this, we will have to disagree. I *must* see it through."

I shook my head and sighed. There would be no convincing him. "Be careful. You've just become a very big target."

He indicated his sling. "I'm used to it."

Mr. Baggley peered around the door again. "There are two gentlemen here to see you, Oscar." He smirked. "One is Mr. Force, a reporter from *The City Review*."

"*The Review*!" Oscar gave a gruff laugh. "What does he want with me?"

Mr. Baggley shrugged but Matt said, "Your article impacts businesses and guilds. No doubt he wants to find out what you know about magic, who your sources are, and whether you believe what you wrote or are just trying to stir up trouble."

The City Review was a newspaper that came out every morning Monday to Friday and concentrated wholly on business matters. It was read by bankers, lawyers and others in the financial and government sectors on their commute to work. The editorial staff would find Oscar's article very relevant as it impacted the guilds enormously, and that in turn impacted the country's finances. Businesses large and small were tied together in countless ways, not all of them clear to an outsider. As Matt said, a reporter from the *The City Review* would want to know if Oscar knew something in particular or was simply being sensationalist to sell newspapers.

"And the other gentleman?" Oscar asked, ignoring Matt's points.

"A Mr. Abercrombie, master of the Watchmaker's Guild."

CHAPTER 11

I groaned. Matt placed a hand on my shoulder and shot Oscar an accusatory glare.

Oscar looked smug. "Good. Let's have it out with Abercrombie. Will you stay, India?"

"No," Matt said before I could decide whether I wanted to or not.

"He'll see us leaving," I said to Matt. "We might as well hear what he says and reassure him I had nothing to do with the article."

His jaw hardened. He didn't look at all pleased with my suggestion but he didn't urge me to go.

Mr. Gibbons, however, wished us well. "I may not be involved in the Mapmaker's Guild anymore," he said to Oscar, "but neither I nor my daughter want a part in this. Do not mention my family's name. Is that understood?"

Oscar nodded. "Of course. Thank you for stopping by."

Mr. Gibbons pushed past Mr. Abercrombie and left. The second gentleman, the reporter named Mr. Force, entered behind Abercrombie but remained near the door and allowed Abercrombie to say his piece first.

Abercrombie only had eyes for me. They were hard and

filled with disgust. "I knew you would be behind this, Miss Steele."

"You're mistaken," I said. "I came here to tell Mr. Barratt that I do not approve of his article."

Abercrombie's oiled mustache twitched in glistening outrage. "I am not a fool, Miss Steele. Your words were all through that article."

"Are you calling me a liar?"

"India had nothing to do with this," Matt snarled. "We're here for the same reason you are—to warn Barratt against writing anything further." He glanced past Abercrombie to the other journalist and nodded a greeting. I suspected Matt wanted to say more but didn't trust the stranger.

"You are mistaken, Mr. Glass," Mr Abercrombie said. The pinched lips beneath the mustache contorted into an odd smile. "I don't want to warn Mr. Barratt against writing further articles about magic. I want to encourage him to write more.

"More?" I prompted, knowing I was taking the bait he dangled in front of me.

"He's a laughing stock, Miss Steele. This newspaper is already seen as a second rate sensationalist rag, and Barratt's article plunges new depths."

"I say!" Mr. Baggley protested.

"So write more, Mr. Barratt," Mr. Abercrombie said. "Write more of the same and bring your paper into even further disrepute. I dare you."

Was his plan to simply hope the public would dismiss Oscar's claims as ridiculous? It didn't seem like a good plan to me. Londoners believed all sorts of outrageous claims newspapers made purely because they thought if someone published it, it must be true. A recent report of a mermaid sighting in the Thames being a case in point. Many Londoners still swore they could hear mermaids singing on a clear evening down by the river.

"My paper is neither second rate nor sensationalist," Mr. Baggley said, crossing his arms. "Oscar can back up every claim he made in that article. Can't you, Oscar?"

"Indeed," Oscar said.

Mr. Force from *The City Review* stepped into the room. He was slender and not much taller than me, with an air of confidence and smugness about him that reminded me of Oscar, although they looked nothing alike. Where Oscar had brown hair and eyes, Mr. Force was all fair hair and freckles. "Prove it," he said. "Publish the names of your sources."

"I will not," Oscar shot back.

"Then your story about magic will be seen as a hoax."

"By who? You?"

"By me and every other journalist and member of the public who suspects you made it up to sell more papers."

Mr. Baggley smirked. "We *are* selling more papers. We've already run out of copies, a *Gazette* record for this time of day. There'll be more copies of this edition available tomorrow, and in next week's edition, I'll print more copies with Oscar's latest article, and I'll wager we'll sell out of those too. Oscar has hit on something. Londoners saw the truth in his words. They believe it because they've long suspected the guilds were hiding something to make themselves more powerful. So many have suspected, and some even guessed the truth." He picked up a copy of the latest edition from the corner of the desk and waved it in front of Mr. Force's face. "I should have let Oscar print this when he first mentioned the idea to me, but I asked him to wait until he had proof. Well, he has the proof now."

"Then print that proof!" Mr. Abercrombie shouted. "Print the names of your sources!"

Oscar shook his head, unfazed by the man spitting over his desk. "I won't be publishing anything of an identifying nature. My sources asked for anonymity and I'll give it to them. If any are happy for me to print their names then I will gladly do so."

He did not look to me but it didn't matter. Abercrombie knew I was the main source. He just wanted the world to know it and that was why he'd come here—to shame Oscar into revealing it.

"Coward," Abercrombie sneered.

"Any journalist would do the same," Oscar said with a speaking glance at Mr. Force.

Mr. Force merely grunted. "Your cockiness will be your downfall, Barratt."

"And choosing the wrong side will be yours, Mr. Force, and that of your newspaper."

Mr. Force snorted. "*The City Review* is bigger than this silly story, Barratt."

"Then why are you here? Because you and your investors," he nodded at Abercrombie, "are worried. Aren't you? Otherwise, why bother with my silly little story in the silly little weekly?" I had never seen Oscar so supercilious, so righteous. He believed utterly in his greater cause, his revolution as he called it. There would be no swaying him against it.

Mr. Abercrombie must have realized too. "You sniveling little prick! You're going to cause enormous upset and harm to families and you don't even care."

It was, perhaps, the only time he'd said something that I agreed with.

"Come, Abercrombie," Mr. Force said. "You and I have work to do." Unlike Abercrombie, he didn't look at all worried. He and Oscar had their cocky attitudes in common.

"They're going to write a counter-argument," Mr. Baggley said, watching them leave.

"Let them," Oscar said. "It'll give weight to my story. Those who buy their paper and not ours will now be curious and seek out a copy of the *Gazette*, and give my article a thorough read."

Mr. Baggley rubbed his hands together. "I'm glad I didn't listen to the naysayers who thought you were a crackpot." He chuckled. "You two," he said to Matt and me, "it's time you left. My best reporter has work to do."

While I wanted to try to talk sense into Oscar again, I knew it was a futile exercise. Matt must have realized too because he took me by the elbow and steered me out.

"India," Oscar called.

"Don't listen to him," Matt said, not stopping.

"I don't hold grudges," Oscar said from the doorway of his office. "When you see that writing the article was the right thing to do, I'd like to talk. My door will always be open to you."

Matt halted in the outer office and rounded on him. "Don't come near India again. Is that understood?"

Oscar saluted him, earning another fierce scowl from Matt. His forehead seemed permanently fixed in that position today.

I withdrew my elbow from Matt's hand and exited the *Gazette's* building ahead of him. He ordered Cyclops to return home then climbed into the coach behind me. He removed his hat and dragged his hand through his hair. His skin sported the waxy pallor of illness and his eyes the signs of an aching head. It was past time to use his watch.

Should I tell him to use it now or withhold my opinion? Despite his illness weakening him, he still seemed ready to snap my head off. Perhaps I wasn't being fair and it was Oscar's head he'd rather snap off, but I decided to hold my tongue until the situation became desperate.

He ended up retrieving his watch from his pocket without me prompting. He closed the curtains, opened the watchcase, and welcomed the magic into his body.

A minute later, he shut the case. His skin returned to normal and the muscles in his face no longer looked as if they were trying to keep the pain at bay.

"You could not have stopped Oscar from writing that article," he said as he returned the watch to his pocket. "He'd made his mind up before he even met you."

"But I gave him the proof he needed."

He sighed. "India, no. Don't blame yourself."

I didn't respond. I wasn't the only one blaming me. He may be saying all the right things, things I needed to hear, but I knew he blamed me, at least a little.

I turned to the window and, after a moment, opened the curtain again. I no longer wanted to discuss Oscar and the article, or the implications. What happened next was out of our control. We couldn't stop Oscar from writing a second article any more than we could stop Mr. Force from *The City Review* writing a counter-article. It only remained to be seen which side the public took, or if they even cared at all.

But the main reason I didn't want to talk about it anymore was because I didn't want Matt to realize I agreed with Oscar's idea of a revolution. That didn't mean I wasn't worried. I was. Even more so now after seeing how angry Abercrombie had become when Oscar couldn't be forced into publicly revealing his sources. But the notion of magic being out in the open appealed to me. To walk into a watchmaker's shop and not feel like I carried a contagious disease would be wonderful, liberating. I had grave doubts that we would ever reach that point, yet I had to hope.

Matt would not agree, and I didn't have the heart to argue with him anymore.

* * *

I INFORMED CHRONOS, Willie, Duke and Cyclops of our encounters at the *Gazette* office while Matt rested in his rooms. They did not take it well.

"I'll march down there and point my Colt at that low down pig swill until he agrees to stop writing more articles."

Willie spoke her piece while pacing the library floor. Fortunately her gun wasn't on her person or she might have marched out of the house.

I kept a close eye on her while the others debated the merits, or not, of Oscar's article. Only Chronos thought it could turn out well, if people kept their heads.

"That's the problem," Duke said. "People don't keep their heads. They can't see the other side, only their own."

"You have more faith in people than I do," Cyclops said to Chronos. "Where common sense gets thrown out and emotions rule, trouble follows."

"Aye," Duke and Willie agreed.

"Abercrombie's worried or he wouldn't have gone to see Barratt in person," Chronos added with a twisted smile. "I wish I'd seen his face when Barratt told him he was writing another article."

"Revenge ain't a good reason to support Barratt," Duke said. "Specially when good people will suffer alongside the bad."

"The Masons will lose business," Cyclops said with a shake of his head. "They're your friends."

"Not mine, Elliot's," Chronos said.

"And mine," I added, once again unsure which side I fell on. I couldn't bear it if the Masons suffered. There was no doubt they'd lose business to magicians if the public believed Oscar. On the other hand, there were no horology magicians in London except Chronos and myself, and neither of us had a shop.

Duke nudged Cyclops with his elbow and winked. "You'll take care of Miss Mason, if it came to that."

"Shut it," Cyclops mumbled.

Duke and Willie both chuckled.

We heard Bristow greet someone out in the entrance hall beyond the closed door but could not hear the responding voice.

"A word of warning," I said quietly to Chronos while the others were distracted by the possibility of a visitor. "Matt is against Barratt's plan. If you want to remain here you'd better not say anything to support it."

"Thanks for the warning," he said. "But you're the one with more to lose by speaking up, so you're wise to stay silent. You could have all this for the rest of your life if you play your cards right, but my presence here is only fleeting. I'll move on again soon."

"Stop it," I hissed. "I work for Matt, that is all. Stop implying otherwise."

He shook his head. "Clearly your parents instilled too much sanctimonious nonsense into you. If I'd brought you up—"

The door opened and Bristow slipped through a gap barely wide enough to fit his frame. "Miss Steele, Mr. Hardacre is here to see you. He says he knows you're here and refuses to leave until you speak with him." His gaze slipped to Chronos. "What shall I tell him?"

"How does he know she's here?" Cyclops asked.

Bristow didn't have an answer for that.

"I'll get rid of him," Willie said, already halfway across the room.

I rose. "I'll go. If he wants to see me, he won't be satisfied until he does."

"Question is, why does your ex-fiancé want to see you?"

"Hardacre?" Chronos asked, understanding dawning. "That's the fellow who stole my shop."

His shop? Well, *honestly.* "Bristow, please show Mr. Hardacre to the drawing room. Close the door and wait with him until I arrive."

He slipped out again. I could not see Eddie through the gap which meant Eddie could not see in here. Good. If he saw Chronos, it would bring more trouble to our door than we already had.

I turned to Chronos, hands clamped firmly on my hips. "It was not *your* shop. You gave up the right to it when you left and falsified your own death. It should have been *my* shop, inherited from my father. Now, stay in here and don't come out until I return. Is that clear?"

He sniffed. "I am your elder. You'll speak to me with some respect."

"I'll give you respect when you prove you've earned it. Until then, I'll treat you like the man who left his wife and family behind to save his own skin."

"They were fine without me. Better off, in fact."

"Stay out of sight," I snapped.

"I am many things, but a fool is not one of them. Of course I'll wait here."

I checked the coast was clear before I emerged from the library. I crossed the hall to the drawing room, glancing up the staircase as I passed it. There was no sign of Matt. Hopefully I could send Eddie on his way before he awoke. Matt had enough on his plate without the irritating presence of Eddie to contend with.

My former fiancé did not look at me when I entered, but over my head. I glanced behind me, expecting to see Matt but the hall was empty.

"Thank you, Bristow, that will be all."

The butler took my hint and bowed out. I shut the door.

"No tea?" Eddie asked. "No cake from the lady of the house?"

"You're not staying long enough for tea and cake," I said.

He smiled that oh-so-charming smile that I used to think was dashing but now knew to be false. It made him even more handsome if one liked fine, delicate features topped with wavy blond hair. Coupled with his blue eyes, I could well remember why I once thought myself in love with him. His good looks had blinded me to his ugly heart. Now I could barely even look at him without my stomach churning.

I wished it hadn't taken me until my father's funeral to see that ugliness. In my defense, Eddie had been very persuasive. His smiles seemed genuine, his concern for me real. I'd desperately wanted to believe he would keep his promise to take care of me. Now, I knew I could take care of myself, but then, I lacked the confidence as well as the means. How things changed in a mere few months.

He sat on an armchair by the fireplace and indicated I should sit on the sofa. I remained standing.

"Where's your master?" he asked.

"Assuming you're referring to my employer, Mr. Glass is not here."

"Is he at home? The butler wouldn't say."

"Why do you ask?"

"Why do you not answer?"

"Eddie, I don't have time for games, and I doubt you can afford to keep the shop closed for any length of time. Get to the point."

His fingers tightened around the chair arm, but that was the only sign that my words had any effect. "How do you know I haven't employed an assistant?"

"I doubt you can afford to. Profits weren't very large when my father operated the shop and he was a better watchmaker than you and a better salesman too."

"What rot! Who is spreading lies about my business? Is it that stupid Mason girl?" He snorted. "Ridiculous creature, batting her eyelashes at every man in her path. She's a hopeless flirt, do you know that?"

"You're mistaking friendliness for flirtation."

"You would defend her."

"Yes, because she's my friend and has been good to me when I needed her. But you wouldn't recognize kindness in others since you don't possess the capacity for it yourself. State your business then leave. I have better things to do with my time than talk to you."

"Like getting into bed with newspaper reporters?" He crossed his legs and clasped his hands in front of him.

My fingers twitched, wanting to wipe that smug smile off his face. "The article in the *Gazette* had nothing to do with me."

"Don't play me for a fool, India."

"Why not? You are one. You are also Abercrombie's puppet. Did he tell you to come here?"

His smile tightened. "I'm far too clever to be anyone's puppet."

"You? Clever? Hardly." It was a horrid thing to say, but it felt good to say it to him. The sour look on his face was satisfying to see. It would seem his intelligence was a soft spot for him.

He uncrossed his legs and leaned forward. "You're an unnatural woman, India. It's no wonder you're not married yet. Who would want a vicious wasp for a wife?"

I slapped him across the cheek.

His head jerked to the side and a red patch in the shape of my palm bloomed on his face. "You bitch!" He wiped his face and checked his hand as if he expected to see blood. "I should thrash you for that."

I stumbled backward but he did not come after me. Even so, I moved closer to the clock on the mantel. If he tried to harm me, I'd throw it at him and hope that it would swerve to hit him as the clock at the gambling den had once changed course to hit my assailant.

"But you won't because you know Matt and his friends would make you pay." Somehow I kept my voice steady when my heart thundered ferociously. Showing weakness to Eddie now would be humiliating. "You ought to be careful or this wasp will sting you." I stepped forward again and smiled. He sat back slowly. "The thing is, Eddie, you fail to grasp the notion that most women would rather not marry at all if men like you are the only option."

"It seems you also fail to grasp something, India." He tugged on his cuffs and straightened his tie. "A woman like you cannot afford to be without a man forever. Oh, I know you have a little money set aside thanks to the reward, but it won't keep you forever. You have no family and no means to support yourself. We both know you can't rely on Mr. Glass marrying you. A man like that can have any woman he desires—why would he have plain, plump India Steele? A little dalliance, yes, but marriage?" He snorted. "So I'd be careful of that sting, India, or you might find yourself cast out sooner than you think."

"Don't worry about me, Eddie," I said sweetly. "I only reserve my sting for the deserving. Speaking of which, it's time you tell me why you're here."

"Ah, yes, time. It always comes back to that with you. Well, let's see. Why am I here?" He glanced at the door. "I met with Abercrombie this morning. It was quite a long meeting, in fact, as he's taken to sharing the burdens of leadership with me since I joined the guild."

"You met with Abercrombie this morning?" Did he mean before or after Abercrombie came to the office of the *Gazette*?

"About an hour and a half ago," he said, checking the clock.

An hour and a half ago was the exact time Abercrombie came to Oscar's office. He left with the intention of providing Mr. Force with information for his article. Eddie could not have had a long meeting with the guild master then. Was he lying just so he could make himself look important? Pathetic.

He glanced at the door again. He must be afraid Matt would enter and interrupt us. So that was why he wanted to know where Matt was and whether he had time to talk to me alone.

"I'll ask again," I said. "What do you want, Eddie?"

He sat on the edge of the chair, not deep into it or with his legs crossed as he did before. It was as if he were preparing for another attack from me—preparing to flee. "Mr. Abercrombie has learned of your investigation into Dr. Millroy's death."

"How did he learn of it?" I asked, even though I was quite sure Mrs. Millroy was the culprit.

He merely smiled. "I'm sure you don't expect me to answer that."

I shrugged. "Our investigation is not a secret. The police have asked us to look into Dr. Millroy's murder."

"Why?"

"To find the killer, of course. We're proving to be quite good at detecting." I smiled.

He frowned. "But why now? It was twenty-seven years ago."

"You would have to ask Commissioner Munro for his reasons. I am not privy to them."

"Nonsense," he spat.

My smile widened. It was extremely satisfying to see him riled. "Why do you care about our investigation, Eddie?"

"We're not fools, India. Mr. Abercrombie knows your grandfather and Dr. Millroy experimented with combining their magic and subsequently killed a man when their experiment failed."

"That doesn't explain your reason for being interested. My grandfather is dead and cannot be brought to justice over it. It is not a Watchmaker's Guild matter, anymore."

He lifted his gaze to the ceiling and heaved in a breath. "Let me explain it to you. It's likely the murder of Dr. Millroy is linked to the murder of the man they experimented on. That makes it a matter for both guilds."

"Both men are dead! Anyway what makes you think the two events are linked?"

"Even you must be able to see that they are."

I wouldn't be baited into telling him what evidence we did and did not have. I wanted nothing more than to keep Abercrombie in the dark. Besides, I still couldn't fathom why it mattered so much to him.

"It's not murder if the victim knew the risks and agreed to be their subject," I said.

"How do you know he agreed? Were you there? Has your grandfather's ghost told you?"

"Don't try to be funny, Eddie. You're not very good at jokes. I could ask you the same question—how do you know Mr. Wilson *wasn't* willing? Even Mrs. Millroy claims the man wanted to be involved and she briefly met him."

He blinked. "Mr. Wilson?"

"The vagrant's name."

"Is it? What's his first name?"

"I don't know. Are you finished now?"

He sat deeper into the chair, tipping his head back. His hands gripped both chair arms and his foot jiggled just enough to be annoying.

"Eddie?"

He suddenly stood and buttoned up his jacket. "You have been warned, India."

"Have I? Remind me, what are you warning me about specifically? To stop speaking with Oscar Barratt or stop our investigation?"

"Both."

"And if I don't?"

He strode to the door and jerked it open. Bristow stood there with Duke and Cyclops hovering nearby. Chronos was nowhere to be seen, thankfully.

"That's up to Mr. Abercrombie to decide," Eddie said.

I grunted a laugh. "You are a pathetic sycophant and coward. I'm sure Mr. Abercrombie is glad to have you shovel dirt for him."

Bristow's eyes widened ever so slightly. Cyclops and Duke moved forward as if to grab Eddie if he lunged at me, but Eddie was too busy spluttering in indignation.

"I'm an important member of the guild now." He tapped his chest and lowered his face so that it was near mine. His breath smelled of the fish he must have eaten at lunch. "You couldn't even get membership, despite your family connections."

"Thanks to the guild's prejudice against magicians and women. Don't pretend otherwise, Eddie, when you know that's the truth. Now go away. I don't like being threatened in my own house."

His hollow laugh bounced off the paneled walls and tiled floor. I bit my tongue, wishing I hadn't used those words and given him ammunition. "*Your* house? My, my, you are getting ahead of yourself. Be careful, India, it's a big fall from these heights. And believe me, you *will* fall when he finds himself a lady worthy of marrying."

"You are far too predictable, Eddie," I said with more poise than I felt. My body shook and my heart hammered, but I would not let him see how his words affected me. "Bristow, please see that Mr. Hardacre leaves. I'm sure Cyclops and Duke will help, if necessary."

Matt's sudden appearance at the top of the stairs caught Eddie's attention. He straightened, tugged on his hat brim and let himself out before Bristow could even step forward.

"India?" Matt called to me as he trotted down the stairs. "Was that Hardacre?"

I blew out a ragged breath and exchanged a glance with Cyclops. "Yes," I said.

"What the bloody hell did he want?"

The door to the library cracked open. "Is he gone?" Chronos asked.

"He's gone," I said. "He wanted us to stop investigating Dr. Millroy's murder and also to stop speaking to Oscar Barratt."

"Millroy's murder?" Matt said, placing a hand at my back. Somehow he'd guessed I needed his steadying presence. "Why?"

"Apparently Abercrombie asked him to come here. I think they're scared we'll blacken the guild's name if we delve too deeply into Dr. Millroy's experiment with Chronos."

"Which implies the guild is guilty of something."

"Like the murder of Dr. Millroy, perhaps."

Matt smiled. "Good work, India. Well managed." He rubbed my back and his smile faded. He touched my chin. "You look pale. Did he threaten you?"

"In a way, but not specifically."

"Come and sit down. Bristow, send for tea and see if Cook has something sweet for her. She likes confections."

I had to laugh at that. "Blame my maternal grandparents."

Matt's smile returned but it wasn't convincing.

He led me back into the drawing room, along with the others, and questioned me a little more. I repeated what Eddie had said, omitting the insults we'd both slung, and the slap. By the time I finished, Bristow returned with a tray of tea things and bonbons. Matt made sure I put two on my plate.

"How could you have agreed to marry that fellow?" Chronos asked, studying a bonbon from all angles. "He sounds like a sniveling little weed."

I sighed. "Believe me, I wonder the same thing."

"He wasn't always like that," Matt told him.

"You met him when he and India were engaged?"

"No."

"Then how can you know?"

"Because India is no fool. He played a part when he met her, like an actor at the theater. A part he knew a woman like India would appreciate. He hid his true nature until later."

Chronos bit into his bonbon. "If he managed to do that for months," he said, his mouth full, "then he's cleverer than you all give him credit for."

* * *

I SPENT what remained of the afternoon with Miss Glass. While she didn't insist on my company, she did hint several times that she'd like to go for a walk and browse the shops on Piccadilly.

The sky was overcast but the clouds not too thick, and we risked leaving the house without umbrellas. We took the long way to Piccadilly, via Hyde Park. Miss Glass maintained a slow walking pace, which I matched, and a rapid pace of conversation. She moved from topic to topic at speed. Just when I was about to interject with an opinion, she moved on to the next. When it came to discussing her nieces, however, I was happy to remain silent.

"Hope will not be a suitable bride for Matthew," she declared. "My sister-in-law is backing the wrong horse if she thinks Patience's wedding will force them together. Beatrice thinks having Matthew staying at Rycroft House will make it easier to throw Hope into his path, but she is forgetting about me. I will not let that little nitwit get her claws into him. They'll try to trick him, you know. Hope and Beatrice. They'll put him in the bedroom nearest hers and somehow manipulate it so that she is caught *in flagrante* with him. With so many guests, word will quickly spread and Matthew will be forced to propose." She clicked her tongue. "But I'll stop it before it happens. Indeed, Matthew may already have a sweetheart by then. It's very likely, given how handsome and charming he is."

Not to mention his wealth and station. I sighed as I watched two children of about eight years old riding their ponies with a groom seated on a large gray between them. While the ponies looked docile, I eyed them closely in case something startled them. Neither child looked to be in complete control and the groom couldn't manage three horses if it came to it. "Perhaps Matt should stay elsewhere," I said, my mind only half on the conversation now as we drew closer to the riders.

"Nonsense! Rycroft is his house."

"Not yet."

"It will be. He has more of a right to be there than those girls."

I didn't agree with her logic but she'd made her mind up about it; there'd be no swaying her. The children rode by without any cause for alarm and I relaxed a little, until I heard one of them tell the other that magic exists. Her papa said so.

Two brisk walkers overtook us, their heads tilted toward the other so that their hat brims touched. "What a sensation it caused in my household when my son read out the *Gazette's* article over breakfast," the taller lady said to the other. "He thinks magic's real, but I told him he was being a fool." She laughed. "Can you imagine?"

"Don't be so quick to dismiss it, Frederica," the other woman said. "My George believes magic is not only possible but it explains why our set of crystal Baccarat sherry glasses didn't break when the delivery man dropped the box. Not a single one shattered. He declared it a miracle at the time, but now…"

"One of them did break last summer," the tall woman said. "I recall it quite clearly."

"True," the companion said thoughtfully.

Oscar had not written the fact that magic didn't last forever into his article. I wondered if the omission was deliberate.

Beside me, Miss Glass took my arm in hers. "What a lovely day," she said dreamily. No doubt she too had heard the exchange, but in her addled wisdom decided to pretend she hadn't.

It became harder and harder to ignore, however. Nearly half the people we passed were discussing the article with their friends. Many hadn't read it themselves, since they couldn't get a copy, but that didn't stop them speculating, sometimes wildly. I even overheard one woman say that she assumed the reporter who wrote the article had first hand knowledge of magic and was perhaps a magician himself.

Miss Glass's fingers tightened around my arm. "Do you require anything, India?" she asked.

Her question was quite unexpected and I took a moment to gather her meaning. "I have everything I need," I assured her.

"But I must buy you something."

We exited the park near Hyde Park Corner and waited for a break in traffic. "Please, Miss Glass, there's no need to buy me gifts."

"There is no *need*, but you've been working so hard lately and had an unfortunate run of luck that I'd like to buy you something you *want*."

"Is this why you insisted on coming to Piccadilly? I did wonder."

"What about a new hat?"

"I already have three perfectly good ones."

"One can never have enough hats or gloves. Shoes, too, and shawls."

"You bought me a shawl quite recently." I steered her across the road between carriages and carts. She did not look where she was going but at her feet to avoid stepping in muddy puddles.

A newspaper boy stood on the corner, announcing more copies of *The Weekly Gazette* becoming available. Five passersby stopped to buy a copy and another three back-tracked to him.

"It's all nonsense!" shouted the burly shoemaker standing in the doorway to his shop. "*The Gazette* is making you look like fools." Some shoppers nodded in agreement but the pronouncement did not stop the newspaper boy from being swamped.

"People will believe anything if its in the papers," said a woman passing us.

"*The Weekly Gazette's* always been sensationalist," said her male companion. "This was orchestrated by its editor to sell more papers, mark my words."

"Gullible fools," muttered a butcher who'd come out of his shop to see what caused the flurry of activity.

"I wonder what a butcher magician's magic achieves." Miss Glass's statement, said quietly enough that only I could hear, had me suppressing a smile.

"I don't think there is any magic in butchery."

She pulled a face. "Probably not."

She picked up her pace and directed me to a haberdasher. "A new reticule! We'll purchase some beads and whatever else you like to make a new one. We'll design the pattern together." She paused before entering the shop. "Do you think it rude if we ask if he's a haberdashery magician?" she whispered.

"Yes!" I cried. "Do not mention the word magic inside the shop. Is that understood, Miss Glass?"

She sighed. "Spoilsport." It would seem she had come to accept the existence of magic in our world faster than I expected. Thank goodness. There was now one less reason for her to have a turn.

* * *

"Talk of it is everywhere," I told Matt when we arrived home with our purchases. Along with beads and ribbon, Miss Glass had bought a hat and hatpin for herself and ordered a new walking dress with three quarter sleeves that I overheard her telling the dressmaker was for me.

"I noticed it too," he said.

"You've been out?" We sat in the library alone. Rather, I sat and he stood by the sideboard, his hands clasped behind him, contemplating the decanter. I hoped talking would distract him from the lure of brandy.

"I also went shopping." He withdrew a paper bag from his inside jacket pocket. "I went out with Chronos, as a matter of fact, but he wanted to go his own way after a while."

"You didn't think he'd run off this time?"

"I trust he'll return."

"He does like it here."

He passed me the bag. "These are for you."

I looked inside and took out a sugar plum. "Thank you, but I'm going to get fat if you keep buying me sweets."

"What if I promise to buy them only on rare occasions?" He watched as I popped the sugar coated comfit into my mouth. "Like when I have something to apologize for."

Unable to speak with any dignity, I arched my brows at him instead.

He hiked up his trousers at the knees and sat on the winged chair by the fireplace. "I am aware of how over-bearing I sounded in Barratt's office earlier today, when I ordered him to stay away from you. I had no right to do so. You're free to see whomever you want to see, of course. I should have kept my mouth shut."

"Don't trouble yourself over that remark. It was said in the heat of the moment, and I don't blame you for it. I don't wish to see Oscar again right now, anyway."

"You may change your mind when all this settles down."

"Will it settle down?"

Someone knocked and opened the door without waiting for Matt's order. Peter stood there, looking panicked. "Mr. Glass, sir, there's a constable here. He wants to see you."

Matt and I exchanged glances. The presence of constables at number sixteen Park Street never resulted in anything good. "Is he alone?" Matt asked, rising.

"Yes, sir."

I followed Matt out and greeted the constable too.

"You'd better come with me, sir," the constable said gravely.

"What are you arresting him for?" I demanded. "Who has made an accusation against him this time?"

The constable frowned. "I'm not arresting anyone, ma'am. A patient at the London Hospital asked for him."

"Who?" Matt and I said at the same time.

"I took an injured man to the hospital not long ago. He wouldn't give me his name or the name of his assailant, but he said to come here and fetch Mr. Glass."

"What does he look like?" Matt asked. But I already knew the answer.

"Old, white hair and beard," the constable said.

Chronos.

"He's in a bad way, sir. You better come quick before it's too late."

CHAPTER 12

*M*att seemed to think I needed comforting. He asked me several times if I was all right on the way to the hospital. "Of course I am," I said. "While I do hope Chronos isn't badly injured, I'm not going to be as upset over his death as I was over my father's or mother's. I hardly know him. And anyway, I'm sure he won't die now that he is receiving medical attention."

He looked down at our linked hands and said nothing. I realized a moment later that I'd been holding on tightly and forced my fingers to release him. We shouldn't be holding hands anyway. It was inappropriate; we'd both sworn to ourselves not to be intimate with the other, albeit for different reasons.

"I'm more worried about you, Matt." It was dusk, and some hours since he'd last used his watch. I tried to see his face but it was in shadow. "We'll close the curtains so you can use your watch before we arrive at the hospital," I told him, reaching for the curtain.

"I'm fine, India." His hand closed over mine and he once again held onto it. "I used it just before you arrived home."

"Right. Good. Do you think I should speak the spell into it

again? Last time I made it work a little longer. Would you like me to do it now?"

"No."

"Later then."

"If you wish."

We fell into silence despite my efforts to think of something to say. Since I could think of nothing and no one except Chronos, I decided I might as well speak about him. "He's an old fool."

"Yes."

"He should not have left the house at all."

"No."

"It serves him right."

"It does."

"He should have stayed in the house where it's safe." I sniffed. "Boredom is no excuse to put one's life in danger." I sniffed again. "He's a selfish, arrogant old man who only cares about one thing."

"What's that?"

"Combining his magic with a doctor's, of course."

"Of course."

I looked up at him. He was a little blurry. "You disagree?"

"We've arrived." He opened the door before the coach came to a complete stop and folded down the step. "Wait for us," he told Duke and Cyclops, both on the driver's seat.

He assisted me down the step and escorted me into the London Hospital. It was the first time we'd come to the Whitechapel Road institution to see a patient and not question a staff member.

The nurse on the desk in the reception room refused us entry to the men's ward at first as it was outside visiting hours, however when Matt explained the situation, she made sure we were escorted directly to Chronos's bed.

His eyes were closed and his skin pale but not dangerously so. A patch of blood stained the bandage wrapped around his head and a bruise darkened his swollen jaw. His knuckles sported cuts from fighting back. He did not look to be at death's door, as the constable reported. Still, the unexpected sight of a fragile man in the place of Chronos brought a lump to my throat.

"He's asleep," whispered the nurse who'd escorted us. "Thank the lord. He's a difficult one."

"In what way?" Matt whispered back.

"Wanting to leave and not giving his name. He walked out before we could get him cleaned up, and it took two orderlies to bring him back."

I smiled, but I wasn't sure why.

"He can walk?" Matt asked.

The nurse nodded. "You can take him with you, if you like."

"Let him sleep a little longer. Is Dr. Ritter on duty?"

"I believe he's doing his rounds in the women's ward. If you wait in reception, you'll see him soon."

Matt touched my arm. "Do you want to remain here?"

"I'll come with you," I whispered.

We followed the nurse back to the front reception room. "If you wouldn't mind giving the aide at the desk the patient's name for our records," she said.

She returned to the ward, leaving Matt and me standing there. The nurse at the desk looked up and smiled. "His name?" she prompted.

"Will Wordsworth," Matt said. "He's a relative from America staying with me."

"William Wordsworth?" I whispered, walking with him away from the desk. "You couldn't think of someone who's not a famous poet?"

"I was put on the spot."

The door at the opposite side of the reception room opened and Dr. Ritter walked out, a clipboard wedged under his arm. He stopped when he saw us and groaned.

"We're seeing a patient," Matt assured him. "But we thought we'd ask you a few more questions since we're here."

"I don't have time." Dr. Ritter brushed past him and headed to the men's ward.

Matt and I followed. "Then we'll talk as you walk," Matt said.

"I'll call the orderlies to escort you out."

"And create a scene? That won't be a good sight, Dr. Ritter. Come now, it's just a few questions. Do you know a woman named Nell Sweet of Bright Court, Whitechapel?"

"I don't remember the names of patients."

I picked up my skirts and raced after them, back into the men's ward. I looked along the row of beds to Chronos's at the end. He still slept.

"Dr. Millroy was murdered outside her home," Matt whispered.

Dr. Ritter paused to check the chart hanging from a hook at the end of a patient's bed.

"Do you think she was his mistress?" Matt asked.

"A Whitechapel whore?"

"I didn't say she was a whore."

"All women in Whitechapel are in my experience working here."

"We spoke to Mrs. Millroy, and she confirmed that she was the one who informed you about her husband's experiment with a watchmaker."

"So?"

"So you know the name of his co-magician?"

Dr. Ritter glanced at the nearest patient. Matt had whispered so it was doubtful anyone else would have heard. "He called himself Chronos. Ridiculous name." His gaze flicked to me. Did he know, or guess, that Chronos was my grandfather?

"You informed the Watchmaker's Guild of his involvement in the experiment and described his appearance to them based on what Mrs. Millroy told you. Did they know him from your description?"

"You'd have to ask them."

"What about the man they experimented on? What can you tell us about him?"

"Is any of this necessary? I'm very busy." He moved on to the next patient. After checking the chart he asked the patient some questions about his level of pain as he pressed his stomach. Going by the man's cries and the way he curled into himself with each poke of Dr. Ritter's fingers, I'd say his pain was considerable.

Dr. Ritter signaled for a nurse to administer a dose of morphine before moving on to another patient, closer to Chronos. Had he already seen Chronos? Surely he wouldn't have met him all those years ago, nor recognize him now if he had.

"The vagrant that Dr. Millroy experimented on," Matt prompted, dogging Dr. Ritter. "Our investigations suggest he had a family after all. Do you know anything about that?"

Dr. Ritter didn't so much as blink at Matt's question. "Since you've spoken to Mrs. Millroy, who is a very direct, no-nonsense woman in my experience, I would say you already know that I know. Whatever she told me she probably told you. Now, do you mind? My patients need me."

He moved on to another bed, read the chart, then spoke quietly to a nurse. He was four beds away from Chronos. Matt seemed unconcerned. I was not. Even if Dr. Ritter had never met Chronos all those years ago, would he not think it strange that we were collecting a patient from the hospital? He might guess the connection.

"Have you been in contact with Mr. Abercrombie lately?" Matt asked when Dr. Ritter moved on to the next bed.

The doctor wrote something on the chart and took his time studying it. "We've met to discuss your investigation into Dr. Millroy's murder, along with the present Surgeon's Guild master. That is not a sign of guilt, Mr. Glass. We simply wanted to discuss what it might mean for our respective guilds since you've been quite secretive about your reasons for re-opening the case."

"I haven't been secretive," Matt said. "The case was re-opened by the police."

Dr. Ritter grunted and moved on again. He was now two beds from Chronos.

Chronos cracked open his eyes. He looked drowsy and confused as he took in his surroundings. He noticed his bruised knuckles then touched his bandaged head. A nurse approached him, smiling and talking softly.

I remained where I stood, unsure whether to go to him or not. In his muddled state, he might say too much in front of Dr. Ritter.

"What time did you get to the hospital today?" Matt asked.

Dr. Ritter frowned. "Mid-morning. Why?"

"Have you been out?"

"You have no right to ask me these absurd questions. They have nothing to do with Dr. Millroy's murder."

"Did you ever meet the horology magician known as Chronos?"

I sucked in a breath. The question was far too audacious considering Chronos was lying mere feet away.

"No," Dr. Ritter said. "He died before I was able to question him about his involvement in the vagrant's murder."

"It wasn't murder," I said. "The vagrant agreed to participate and knew the risks."

Dr. Ritter peered down his nose at me. "You would say that, Miss Steele. I believe he was your grandfather, wasn't he?"

So he did know. Oh hell. I didn't dare look in Chronos's direction.

"Excuse me, Dr. Ritter, sir," said the nurse leaning over

Chronos. "Will you take a look at this patient before he's discharged?"

My heart stopped dead in my chest as Dr. Ritter read Chronos's chart. Chronos looked first to me then Matt, a question in his eyes. Matt offered him a small smile.

"This is my uncle by marriage," Matt said, holding out a hand to Chronos.

Chronos took it and allowed Matt to assist him to sit up. Dr. Ritter came closer and frowned into Chronos's face. He'd already admitted he'd never met Chronos but did he see a family resemblance to me behind his white whiskers? If he did, and he informed Abercrombie, Abercrombie would come directly to our house in search of him.

"His name is Will Wordsworth," Matt added.

"Like the poet," Dr. Ritter said, nodding.

"He's staying with us but went wandering today. It seems he found himself in a spot of bother."

"Matt's uncle is quite the bumbling fool," I said.

Chronos's gaze narrowed.

"It appears he wandered into a bad area." Matt sounded cavalier, but he watched Dr. Ritter's reaction closely.

Dr. Ritter's gaze flicked to me then back to Chronos. It was a good time to study my boots.

"Can I take him home now?" Matt asked. He went to assist Chronos to stand, but Dr. Ritter put his arm across Chronos's chest, forcing him to remain in the bed.

"One moment." Dr. Ritter asked the nurse to pass him the chart from the end of the bed. He pulled out a pencil from his top pocket and held it poised over the chart. "What's your name?"

"Will Wordsworth," Chronos said in an American accent.

The nurse frowned but said nothing as Dr. Ritter wrote.

"Where do you live?" Dr. Ritter asked.

"California, but I'm visiting my nephew. He's got a big house in Mayfair, thanks to his English relatives."

"How long have you been in London?"

Chronos's gaze flicked to Matt. Dr. Ritter's gaze followed it. Matt stood utterly still and I made sure not to give anything away either. "A week," Chronos said. "Maybe more." He touched his head and winced.

"What ship did you arrive on?"

Matt scoffed. "That information isn't necessary to make his head feel better."

"But it does help me to ascertain whether he injured his brain."

"My brain is working perfectly," Chronos said, shoving the bedcovers off. "Pass me my trousers. I want to leave. I hate hospitals."

"See?" Matt said cheerfully. "He's fine. He's always like this, isn't he, India?"

"Usually worse," I said, turning my back as Chronos dressed.

Dr. Ritter dictated instructions for tending to Chronos's head wound, telling us to fetch a physician if he became unwell or dizzy. Then he walked off without so much as a goodbye.

Matt offered his hand to Chronos, but Chronos batted it away.

"I can walk," he growled.

"Remarkable," the nurse said as she led us back to the reception room. "You didn't speak with an accent before."

"The blow to my head must have affected my speech," Chronos said without missing a beat.

"How curious. I ought to report it to Dr. Ritter. He'll be interested—"

"No," both Matt and I said together. "That will lead to questions, and my uncle doesn't want to be bothered," Matt added. He turned a bright smile on her. "You do a remarkable job here, Sister...?"

She blushed. "Lorelei Kenner, sir. Thank you, sir. It's not often we get praised."

He fell back to walk alongside her. "Have you had a long day today?"

"Quite long. I started at midday and have a few more hours to go before the nightshift take over."

"Has it been busy?" What was Matt getting at?

"Not overly. Weekends usually are, but not mid-week."

"So you probably had time to sneak out to dine at a chop house," Matt said with a secretive smile that had the nurse blushing more.

Ah, now I caught on. I smiled to myself. He was good at getting information this way. Far too good.

"Not me, sir," the nurse said. "I've been here all afternoon. Some of the other nurses go out when they can, and the doctors come and go."

Matt gave a knowing nod. "Dr. Ritter said he went out about an hour or two ago."

The nurse did not show any sign that she detected his lie. If I hadn't known Dr. Ritter refused to answer that question, I would have thought Matt spoke the truth. "I believe he dined at a chophouse," she said.

"Come, Uncle Will," Matt said, taking Chronos's arm. "Allow me to assist you to my conveyance."

Matt signed a form at the front desk and we made to leave.

"Matt!" cried a voice I knew. "India! What are you doing here?" We turned to see Willie descending the staircase that led up to the doctors' offices and other staff rooms.

"Willie?" I said, and repeated the question she'd just asked us.

She approached, smiling, then caught sight of Chronos. "This ain't a wise place to bring him, considering...you know." She glanced up the stairs.

"Dr. Ritter thinks he's my uncle from America," Matt said,

directing us to the front door. "He was in a fight and got brought here."

"That explains the bandage." Willie shook her head. "What you doing fighting at your age?"

"I was attacked," Chronos said as we headed down the front steps to our coach, waiting by a streetlamp. "I didn't see him."

"Willie?" Duke stood up on the driver's platform and squinted into the gloom. "What the blazes are you doing here?"

"She hasn't yet explained," I told him, wildly curious myself.

"Ain't none of your business, Duke," she called up. "That goes for the rest of you, too."

Duke sat down again with a *humph*. Cyclops chuckled, earning him an elbow in the ribs. "Get in," Duke growled. "I'm cold and it's dinnertime."

"Let's go before Ritter gets suspicious," Chronos said. He rested his palm flat against the door for balance. He allowed Matt to assist him into the coach and sat heavily on the seat.

"If he's suspicious," Matt said, "he'll pay us a visit. My guess is he'll discuss it with Abercrombie and decide if there is anything to be suspicious about, first."

"Abercrombie will be more skeptical about the sudden appearance of an uncle," I said, sitting alongside Chronos. He'd closed his eyes and tipped his head back. I touched his arm. "Are you all right?"

"I have a headache."

"Mrs. Bristow will have something for it."

"I need Dr. Millroy." He cracked open an eyelid when no one answered him. "I'm aware he's dead. My memory's fine. But a magician doctor can cure some headaches since they're only temporary ailments anyway." He gingerly touched his bandage. "If I ever catch the person who did this…"

"Any clues as to who it was?" Matt asked.

"No," Chronos growled. "He came at me from behind. I tried to fight him off but he got the better of me. I fell and hit my head on the pavement." He fingered the swelling on his jaw. "I think my tooth is loose."

"You're lucky," Willie told him. "I've seen men die after hitting their heads."

We took a corner a little quickly, causing Chronos to slide against the side of the cabin. He winced and thumped the ceiling. "Slow down!"

"Duke's driving," Willie said. "He's mad at me for not telling him why I was at the hospital."

"Why were you at the hospital?" Matt asked.

"Ain't no one's business but mine."

That seemed to satisfy him but it certainly didn't satisfy me. Why was she being so secretive? Was she ill or injured? If so, why had she been smiling when we first saw her? Perhaps a doctor had just informed her she was cured of her mystery ailment.

"What were you talking to Dr. Ritter about?" Chronos asked Matt. "I couldn't quite hear."

"I wanted to know if he was aware that Mr. Wilson had a family," Matt said.

"I told you, he didn't. Why else would he be living on the streets?" Chronos closed his eyes again and didn't open them until we stopped outside Matt's house.

Peter helped Chronos up the stairs and acted as valet, but I insisted on taking a tray into him with a light supper. He lay in bed but sat up when I entered. I moved Mrs. Bristow's headache tonic aside and set the tray down on the bedside table.

I perched on the edge of the bed. "How do you feel?"

"Like I hit my head on the pavement." He inspected the contents of the tray and plucked off a carrot stick. He took one bite and put it back. "I'm not hungry."

"I'll leave it here if you change your mind." I rearranged

the pillows so he could sit up better and caught him giving me an odd look. I frowned back at him. "What is it?"

"It's been a long time since a pretty girl took care of me."

"I'm your granddaughter."

"You're still a pretty girl. There's nothing wrong with saying something that's true." He settled back with a sigh. "I forgot how nice it is to be taken care of."

"You're lucky you're still walking and talking. At your age, a blow like that could have been fatal."

"I'm feeling my age, India." His usually steady voice sounded reedy, brittle. "Sometimes I wonder how I got this old. Time slipped past while I was doing other things." He smiled weakly. "Ironic for a horology magician."

"You should have slowed down more. Smelled the roses, as they say."

"Smelling roses wasn't for me."

"Nor was keeping shop or raising a family."

He sighed. "Will you always be angry with me for leaving?"

"Probably." I picked at a thread of embroidery on my cuff that I hadn't stitched well. "Perhaps I shouldn't be. Your absence didn't have a great effect on me. It did on my father and grandmother, I'm sure, but I was well loved by both my parents and never lacked for affection."

"So why did you go searching for it with Hardacre?"

I plucked at the thread, loosening it. "I'm twenty-seven and never had a paramour. I've been told I can be prickly and am too clever for most men. That didn't seem to bother Eddie. I was…grateful for his attention."

"Matthew Glass isn't like most men."

"Don't." The thread needed to come out. It looked terrible, all loose and dangly. I plucked faster.

"He sees your unique character as attractive, not as a fault." He lifted a hand and touched my hair near my ear. "I've been searching for similarities between you and me, and you and your grandmother, but it's not easy to see them. You are your own person, and that's a good thing, India. A very good thing."

I stood and turned away. When I was sure my tears wouldn't spill, I faced him again. "You'll be safe here. Matt won't allow Abercrombie or Ritter inside."

He sank further into the pillows, sighing deeply. "What about the police? He can't stop them arresting me. I wouldn't put it past Abercrombie or Ritter to tell them I'm here if they work it out."

"Matt has some influence with the police commissioner. He might be able to convince them that Mr. Wilson's death was the result of his pre-existing condition."

His eyes slowly lowered, as if they were too heavy to open. "Goodnight, India."

"Goodnight—" I almost said 'Chronos', but it somehow didn't seem right tonight. Calling him Grandfather didn't either. "Sleep well."

I closed the door and saw Willie heading into her room across the hallway. "Willie, wait."

She stopped, half way into her room. "I ain't telling you why I was there, India, so don't ask."

"We need to talk." I ushered her into her room and shut the door, somewhat surprised she'd acquiesced. "I know you don't want to talk about it, but you should."

She screwed up her face. "Why?"

"You're a woman and I'm a woman, and we're friends. I thought you might need a female friend to talk to, that's all."

"Have you gone do-lally?"

I steeled myself. How did one approach this delicately? I was hardly the most experienced woman in matters of an intimate nature. "Are you with child?"

Her eyes bulged. Then she threw her head back and laughed. "Did Duke put that into your head?"

"Are you?"

"No!"

Well. That was one difficult item off my list. Now for an even more difficult question. "Have you caught something of a...of an itchy nature? Down there?"

"No! Christ, India, can't a woman go to a hospital without people thinking she's there because of a man?"

"I just thought...well, you've been spending some time in gambling dens surrounded by men, I thought you might have..." I shrugged, not quite sure how to end it without making her seem like a whore.

"You thought I wagered my body and lost." She crossed her arms over her chest and forked her brow.

I laughed nervously. "You did once. Almost."

She swore under her breath. "I ain't been gambling much lately. I ain't got nothing to wager. Money, that is."

"Oh? But you've been absent quite often. Where are you going?"

She reached past me for the door.

I clicked my fingers. "To the hospital? Yes? But why?"

"Seems we're back where we started, don't it?" She opened the door but it hit my bustle. She gave me a little shove out of the way.

"Were you at the hospital for medical reasons at all?" I pressed. "Or something else?"

"Goodnight, India." She made a shooing motion.

"This is going to torture me until I find out. You know that, don't you?"

She grinned. "Tell Duke everything I just told you so he don't bother me with the same questions." She gave me another little shove, pushing me into the corridor, and shut the door in my face.

The chuckle from along the hallway had me spinning on my heel toward Matt. "Why don't *you* ask her?" I said. "She'll probably tell you everything."

He approached, his smile not wavering. "I doubt it. Besides, I like a little mystery."

"Well I don't." I crossed my arms.

"She'll tell us when she's ready."

"I suppose you're right."

"How is he?"

I lowered my arms and glanced at Chronos's door. "He didn't want to eat and his head aches terribly. He's not quite back to his usual annoying self yet. I suppose we should be grateful for that."

He rested his hands on my shoulders and dipped his head to see my face properly. It was gloomy in the corridor, despite the lit lamps on the two hall tables, but he could probably still see the shine in my eyes. "Are *you* all right?" he asked gently.

I closed my fists at my sides. "Of course."

His thumbs rubbed, easing some of my tension. "He's a survivor."

I swallowed. It wasn't easy with the ball of tears in my throat. "He's old."

"I'm not sure he'd agree with you."

"And anyway, I thought he was dead all my life so I'm hardly going to miss him when he...when he leaves."

His hands moved to cup my jaw and his thumbs continued their caress. "I don't know if your act is fooling him, India." He pressed his lips to my forehead in a warm, lingering kiss. "But it's not fooling me."

I buried my face in his shoulder and let my silent tears flow into his shirt. The rhythmic beat of his heart felt so strong, vital, and alive. I closed my eyes and breathed deeply, drawing in the scent of him.

Then I pulled away and accepted the handkerchief he offered. I wiped my cheeks and patted his damp chest. "You need to change your shirt."

One corner of his mouth twitched in a smile. "Will you join us for a drink in the library?"

"I think I'll retire." I handed back his handkerchief and he took it, along with my hand.

"I'll see that he doesn't leave again."

Did he mean the house or London? It didn't really matter, because he couldn't stop Chronos going anywhere.

* * *

THE FOLLOWING MORNING, Matt, Cyclops, Duke, Willie and I sat in the library, pondering how to proceed with the investigation, when a message arrived for Matt from Hope Glass. He read it in silence, his face impassive, then passed it to me.

"What do you make of this?" he asked.

I read it and passed it on to Willie. "I wonder what she needs to tell you." According to the brief note, Hope wanted to meet Matt by the south eastern end of the Serpentine in Hyde Park to tell him something important. She'd given a precise time of eleven o'clock.

"She's going to tell you what Payne is up to," Cyclops said, reading the note with Duke looking over his shoulder. "I reckon she's been duping him all along just to learn his plan so she could confide it in you."

"And thereby win your gratitude," Duke finished.

Cyclops passed the note back to Matt. "And your friendship. Or more."

"Then I have to go," Matt said.

"There's no question of whether you go or not." I checked the clock on the mantel. "You have forty-seven minutes."

"I ain't so sure it's a good idea," Willie said.

"You getting all cautious on us, Willie?" Duke regarded her levelly. "That ain't like you. The doc give you some medicine in that hospital to change your character?"

Willie rolled her eyes. "I'm just saying, Matt needs to be careful. I don't trust Hope. She might try to trap him into a liaison he can't get out of."

"We'll be in a public place." Matt sounded amused. Amused! Clearly he wasn't taking Hope and her desperation seriously.

"That's the whole idea," Willie said before I could. "For someone who reads a lot of books, you can be mighty dim witted sometimes, Matt. Do I need to spell it out to you or do you know how girls like that operate?"

Matt stood and tugged on his cuffs. "I know Hope isn't as nice as she makes out to be, but she's clever. She must realize what a hopeless case I am by now, and that trickery won't work."

"That kind of fool talk gets gentlemen of means into trouble all the time."

"I won't be put into any compromising positions. India will come along and make sure of it."

"Me?" I shook my head. "She expressly asked you to go alone or she wouldn't say a word."

"That doesn't include you. You're my assistant. "

"I think she was referring quite specifically to me."

His lips flattened. "Very well. Hide behind a tree and watch."

I laughed.

"Wear a big hat," he said, heading out, "and a plain dress. Something that won't get noticed."

He was gone before I could protest. "He's mad," I said to the others.

"He needs a witness on his side," Willie said. "Just in case that little snake gets her claws into him."

"Snakes don't have claws," Duke told her.

"That one does."

* * *

THE BLUSTERY BREEZE drew intricate patterns on the surface of the Serpentine and tossed the newly sprouted spring leaves into each other. Few people were out, and those that had come to the park preferred to walk on the paths. No one hired the boats or paddled in the water.

Matt leaned against the broad trunk of an oak, looking casually handsome as he waited for Hope. I sat on a bench seat, book in hand, my hat brim pulled low. We did not acknowledge one another.

At precisely eleven o'clock, he shifted his stance as she approached, wrapped in a black cloak. What he didn't notice as he greeted her were two more figures approaching from the opposite direction. The ladies walked arm in arm, their pace slow, their heads bent in discussion. I recognized neither of them yet I couldn't help thinking they were out of place.

Matt greeted Hope with a bow. Without a word, she took his arm and led him to a nearby weeping tree. Its long, elegant branches swept the ground, providing a good hiding spot for lovers' trysts. I wasn't surprised when Hope directed Matt through the veil into the naturally formed room beyond.

On cue, the women quickened their pace and headed for the same tree. Determined steps and triumphant gleams in their eyes told me what they expected, perhaps hoped, to discover—a young woman of their acquaintance in a compromising position with a gentleman. It was beautifully orchestrated and timed.

I tucked the book under my arm, clamped a hand to my hat, and ran.

I was too late. The women were ahead of me, their strides long and determined. Shedding all pretense of being idle passersby, they thrust aside the weeping branches and barged through.

And Matt, in his willful disbelief of her deviousness, was caught in Hope Glass's web.

CHAPTER 13

I reached the tree moments behind the women. The leaves and twigs whipped at my face and brushed my hat and skirts. I didn't care, just kept pushing through.

I bumped into the back of one of the women standing at the edge of the clearing. She lurched forward with a yelp but regained her balance without falling. The other lady went to her friend's aid.

The clearing was empty.

"Excuse me," I muttered. "I didn't realize anyone was in here. It looked like an interesting tree…" It sounded ridiculous, but I had to say something. Both women frowned at me, their lips pinched. They knew why I was really there.

"Come along, Sarah," one of the women snipped. "We might as well leave."

They exited through the tree's branches on the other side of the clearing. I followed them and spotted Matt and Hope walking side by side toward a footpath. They were in the open and several other pedestrians passed them. No one could accuse them of anything untoward.

Hope glanced over her shoulder at the two women. She saw me and her lips parted in a gasp.

Matt said something that drew her attention. I smiled at the two ladies and tugged on the brim of my hat. Let them report my sudden appearance to Lady Rycroft. I didn't care. I was only too pleased that Matt had not been duped by Hope.

She hooked Matt's arm with both hands and sidled very close to him. So close, that when she rolled her ankle in a slight dip, he easily caught her before she fell. She blinked up at him, smiling gratefully.

And all the while, her fingers undid his jacket buttons. Her brazenness was shocking. She would be seen here! Within the seclusion of the weeping tree, and with her mother's friends as witnesses, she could blame a seduction entirely on Matt. But out here, with Matt behaving like the perfect gentleman, *she* would be blamed.

A lady did not recover from that sort of scandal easily. Was that her intention? Limit her prospects so that Matt felt sorry for her and married her out of a sense of responsibility? I didn't know whether it was a stupid plan or diabolically clever.

It might have worked on another man, but not Matt. Although her fingers were swift and agile, he caught her hand as it plunged inside his jacket.

Fury turned his features rock hard. He let her go and said something under his breath that leached the color from her cheeks.

I picked up my skirts and strode toward them. The game had come to a crashing end and there was no point pretending anymore.

"Why, Hope?" I heard Matt growl at her.

"I don't know what you mean." Her voice quavered and she shrank away from him. He had never directed such anger at her before. From her reaction, she probably thought he never would.

"You were trying to steal my watch."

My step faltered. Of course. *Of course* she was. Unbuttoning his jacket, reaching inside… Matt wasn't the fool; I was.

"I just wanted to feel—

"No. No more lies." He turned his head a little toward me and acknowledged me with a nod. "Good timing, India. Hope is just about to tell me every detail of her conversations with Sheriff Payne."

In that moment, Hope had never looked more like her oldest sister. Where Patience was afraid of everything and everyone, Hope had always been bold. But now she was the fearful one as she cowered before Matt.

"I…I don't know who you're talking about," she whispered.

Matt slapped his hands together behind him. The *thwack* of glove against glove made her jump. "No more lies, Hope. Do you understand? I know far more than you think. For example, I know your mother set this up." He jerked his head at the weeping tree. "But I know your father would not approve. He would be furious if he learned of your behavior."

If it was a guess, it was a good one. Hope swallowed heavily. Her lips trembled. "Don't tell him. He'll send me away."

"Perhaps *away* is the best place for you."

"Sheriff Payne came to me," she blurted out. "I didn't seek him."

"I know that too."

"*How* do you know?"

"What did Payne talk to you about?"

She pulled the edges of her cloak together at her throat. "Your watch. It's magical, isn't it?"

Matt didn't answer and I hoped my face gave nothing away. I tried to keep my features as passive as possible. She wasn't looking at me anyway. She only had eyes for Matt.

"The sheriff told me the watch is special to you and he asked me to get it so he could see why. Naturally, I refused.

At first," she added when Matt raised an eyebrow. "But after reading the article in *The Weekly Gazette*, I started wondering if it could be powered by magic. I saw your watch glow once, and he's seen it glow too. And Miss Steele has—" She gave me a sideways glance.

"Miss Steele has what?" Matt prompted.

"She is important to you and yet you haven't known her long. You invited her to live with you after such short acquaintance. I knew there had to be a reason."

"There is a reason," he said.

"She's a watch magician, isn't she?"

"No."

She scoffed. "I'm not stupid, Matt. Your watch has magical properties thanks to Miss Steele. Why else would she be living with you?"

"You have a brain and eyes. Use them to work it out."

She bristled. "Sheriff Payne thinks the watch's magic somehow makes you strong and healthy. Based on my own observations, I have to agree, but I admit that I don't understand it. Before the article in the paper, I dismissed the sheriff's theory. But afterward…it all began to make sense. Particularly the presence of Miss Steele.

"I already told you, she's in my home because I want her there."

Matt was rising to her bait. He needed to be careful before he said something he regretted in the heat of the moment.

"So the sheriff told you to steal Matt's watch and you decided to set up this elaborate scheme to do so," I said. "Or did you only decide *after* Matt foiled your attempt to trap him into marriage?"

That took the wind out of her sails. "The rendezvous in the tree, the witnesses…it was all my mother's idea."

"Which you decided to go along with," Matt said, regaining his composure.

Hope's face crumpled and her lips twitched and twisted as

she struggled not to cry. "I'm sorry. I'm so sorry. The sheriff forced me, Matt. I had no choice."

He drew in a breath and another. I couldn't work out if he believed her or not.

"Sheriff Payne accosted me outside my house when I came home from a walk alone one day," she said.

Well, that was a lie. She hadn't been alone, her sisters had been with her.

"He told me what he guessed your watch did, and he ordered me to steal it from you. After I refused, he said he'd tell the police everything he knew about you." She blinked damp lashes up at him. Somehow she looked small and child-like. How did she manage to do that? "Did you do the things he's accusing you of?"

"Most likely," Matt said, "but without hearing his list, it's impossible to compare it to mine. Don't fret. The authorities on both continents know the truth. Sheriff Payne can try to make me the villain all he likes. No one will believe him." He handed her his handkerchief. "So you were trying to protect me?"

Did he really believe that? Surely he wasn't that gullible in the face of big, sad eyes and a pouting mouth.

"It's not only that," she said, dabbing at her eyes. "He has information about Patience that could ruin her if it gets out. Lord Cox won't have anything to do with her if he knew."

This I wanted to hear. "Knew what?"

"She had an indiscretion with a gentleman last year."

I barked out a harsh laugh.

"It's true, Miss Steele," she said in a small voice. "Patience was seduced by a fortune hunter. My father discovered the plot before it was too late, and paid the gentleman to stay away from her and keep quiet. If Lord Cox heard, he'd call off the wedding. He's an extremely upstanding man and values his reputation above all else. Above his affection for Patience. Indeed, I'm sure he only has affection for her *because* he believes she has an equally good reputation. Somehow Sheriff Payne found out about her indiscretion. I wouldn't put it past him to follow through on his threat and send an anonymous letter to Lord Cox. It would not only ruin my sister, it would devastate her. She would never recover if he rejected her."

Matt's brow creased as he stared at his cousin. She blinked big eyes back at him. Well, if he wasn't going to confront her, I would.

"You do have an active imagination, Miss Glass," I said. "What an excellent story."

"You don't believe me?" she said.

"Why would we? You've hardly shown yourself to be trustworthy."

She cringed. "I'm not lying about this. Patience really did have an indiscretion, and Sheriff Payne does know about it. I don't know how, but he does. He seems to know an awful lot about our family."

"When he sets his mind to something, he gets what he wants," Matt said quietly. "It's what makes him so dangerous."

Hope handed the handkerchief back to Matt. When he went to take it, she clasped his hand in both of hers. "Please, Matt. You must believe me on this. I'm not lying."

He opened his mouth then closed it again. He gave a slight nod.

I almost stormed off, but I didn't dare leave him in her clutches. How could he believe shy, fearful Patience had a liaison? It was unfathomable.

"What do you expect Matt to do?" I said to Hope. "Hand over his watch to you so you can give it to the sheriff and save your sister's reputation?"

"No, Miss Steele, I only want Matt to understand why I did what I did today. I don't want anything from him. Not now." She let him go and flattened a hand to her stomach.

"Pray for my sister, Miss Steele. She's going to need all the prayers she can get."

I watched her walk off, my hands on my hips. "The nerve of her! It's one thing to try to steal your watch, Matt, but it's quite another to say such awful things about her own sister."

"You'd better write to Patience as soon as we get home and warn her," he said.

"You believe her? Matt! I never expected you to be so gullible."

"I need to make sure." He indicated I should walk alongside him.

"But...why? What will you do if it is true? Not that I think it is, mind."

"I don't know. I'm not sure there's anything that can be done. If Payne wants to ruin a member of my family, I can't stop him. I don't even know where to find him."

I clutched my book to my chest and bent my head into the breeze. "I don't believe for a second that Patience did anything wrong, but I can see you've fallen for Hope's story."

"I haven't fallen for anything. I'm far too cynical."

I sighed.

"But you're forgetting one thing," he said, taking my hand and placing it on his arm. "You can easily verify Hope's story."

"Very well. I'll write to Patience as soon as we get home and put your mind at ease."

"I hope you do."

We followed the path toward Park Lane. Matt seemed preoccupied with grim thoughts, and I couldn't blame him. To think that Sheriff Payne had tried to enlist a member of Matt's own family to betray him. To think that Hope had attempted to steal his watch! And then there was her attempt to trap him in the tree.

"Did you know those two ladies were Hope's witnesses?" I asked him. "Is that why you left the clearing?"

"I suspected, but that's not why. I didn't want to be beneath a tree alone with Hope." He pressed a hand to his heart in mock indignation. "I felt like she was taking advantage of my naivety."

"You're not the only one. I thought she had you fooled. When I saw those two biddies make a beeline for the tree, I expected them to catch Hope in your arms."

"Even if she'd thrown herself at me, I wouldn't have caught her."

Despite everything, I laughed.

WE DIDN'T HURRY HOME, but took our time strolling through the park listening to conversations. Some were about Oscar's article in the *Gazette*, but not many. It seemed the initial excitement had faded. Neither of us spoke about it to the other, however. It was something of a sore point, and I, for one, didn't want to argue with Matt.

When we got home, I immediately dashed off a letter to Patience and had Peter send it. I was about to go in search of Miss Glass when Catherine Mason arrived, all aflutter. At first I thought her red face and nervous demeanor had something to do with Cyclops emerging from the library as soon as he heard her voice in the entrance hall, but I quickly realized she had something important to say. I led her into the library, a room Miss Glass rarely entered. She might know about magic, but I didn't think her mind was strong enough to endure another frank discussion about it.

Matt shut the door and invited Catherine to sit. Willie was once again out, and Duke was in the coach house showing the new coachman around. Cyclops took up a seat not too far from Catherine.

"Are you all right?" he asked her, frowning. "You look unwell."

She touched the back of her hand to her cheek. "I'm a little warm. The omnibus deposited me at Hyde Park Corner and I walked quickly from there."

"Can I get you tea?"

"No, thank you, Nate. That's very kind, but I'm all right. I wanted to see you. All of you," she quickly added, blushing. "I read the article in the *Gazette*."

Matt sat back and steepled his hands. "I think most of London has read the article."

"Have your parents?" I asked.

She nodded and winced. "We had rather a fierce discussion about it. And about you, India."

I'd expected Catherine to mention my magic to her parents, but I hoped the conversation would be civil. "Was it very bad?" I asked.

"A little. They both already knew, of course, so I didn't feel like I was betraying your confidence by mentioning that I knew too."

"They were angry that you knew?"

She sheepishly shrugged one shoulder.

"Angry with me," I said heavily. "They think I've drawn you into a dark and dangerous world by keeping you informed."

"Don't worry about them, India. They're just concerned for me. But a discussion followed about the future of our shop. They're not worried for themselves, you see, but for my brothers. They'll take over the shop one day, but if they lose business...well, it can hardly support one family now let alone two."

I didn't mention the notion of expanding their business, or setting up a factory to produce watches on a mass scale at a cheaper price. Catherine didn't have a good business head and I knew Mr. Mason liked keeping his shop small and offering personable service to his customers. It was also what his customers liked. But even without magic, a small business would lose against the factories and mass-produced watches and clocks eventually. It was the way of the world.

"Please reassure them that there are no known watch-maker magicians in the city except my grandfather and me," I said. "Neither of us intend to set up a shop again. We're not a threat to anyone's business. On second thoughts, don't mention Chronos. It would serve no purpose worrying them and the fewer people who know about him the better."

"I haven't as yet, but...you want me to continue to lie to my parents?"

"Only by omission." Now if only I could get my conscience to believe it was not quite lying. The look of disappointment Cyclops gave me was almost enough to convince me other-wise. "The important point is, we have no interest in running a shop or making timepieces."

"That's what I told them—about you, I mean." Catherine's hands clasped and unclasped in her lap. "My father put it differently, however. He said you don't want a shop now, but you will. He believes magicians are called to their magical craft. You will feel compelled to work with watches and clocks. India, is...is that true?"

"One can work with timepieces without selling them," Matt said.

"I tinker with them as a sort of hobby," I added. "Rather like painting or embroidery."

Her teeth nipped her lower lip. "I suppose. And if you say you are the only watch magician then perhaps we're worrying over nothing."

"I'm glad you agree. I don't want us to be at odds with one another, Catherine."

"We won't be. You're my closest friend." She lowered her face but she could not hide her blush. "Indeed, I hoped we could talk privately for a few minutes."

Matt and Cyclops both stood and bid her good day before exiting. Catherine pretended not to watch them leave but did a terrible job. She couldn't take her gaze off Cyclops. He cast a winsome smile in her direction before closing the door.

"I think I know what this is about," I said.

She got to her feet and strode to the window. She stared at the street for a moment before striding back. Her cheeks still sported a flush but more from agitation than embarrassment. "I wrote to him asking him to meet me."

"Cyclops? And he refused?"

She nodded. "Why, India? What's wrong with me?"

"Nothing." I took her hand and bade her to sit next to me. "You need some patience with Cyclops—and a little persistence. You know why he has reservations, and they're nothing to do with you. He does like you. I can see it in the way he looks at you."

She sighed and slumped deeper into the sofa. "Here we are, two hopelessly romantic spinsters."

I laughed. "For one thing, you're not old enough to be called a spinster, and second, there is nothing hopeless about either of us. We're two fine women with independent thoughts."

"Independent thoughts are only of value when you can act on them. It's all well and good for you, India. You have means now, and gainful employment. I'm at my father's mercy until I marry then I'll be at my husband's."

"All the more reason to choose wisely. Thank God I never married Eddie. What a disaster that would have been."

"Of monumental proportions."

"I wonder if he would have gone through with the marriage. If my father hadn't died, or hadn't willed the shop to Eddie…would we be married now?" I pulled a face at the distasteful thought. For the hundredth time, I wondered how I could have been so blind to his true nature.

"He could certainly use a clever wife like you, one with knowledge of shop keeping in general and watches in particular. My father says Eddie is struggling to make ends meet. It's as if he lacks the will to make a real go of it."

"Lacks the will? But he went to so much trouble to get the shop. Why does your father think he hasn't the interest in it now?"

"He's late with orders, for one thing, and his repairs take far too long. He's often absent and since he employs no staff, the shop must close when he goes out. It's not every day but often enough that customers go elsewhere. It's all right for Mr. Abercrombie to leave; he has so many assistants that his absence isn't noticeable. But it's different for Eddie."

"Yes," I murmured. "It is. He's going to run that place into the ground and my grandmother's and father's efforts will be for nothing." My family's name may not be above the front door anymore, but our history existed in those walls, so to speak. If that shop no longer belonged to a watchmaker, another chapter of the Steele family would close.

"It was your grandfather's shop too," Catherine said. "He was excellent at his craft, by all accounts."

"I think my grandmother had more to do with its success." At her raised brows, I added, "I have reason to believe my grandfather was somewhat like Eddie—not as interested in keeping shop as a shopkeeper ought to be."

Catherine glanced at the clock on the mantel and gathered her reticule. "That's a story for another day. I have to get home or they'll grow suspicious."

I saw her out. She seemed disappointed that Cyclops wasn't hovering nearby to see her off. I found him with Matt and Duke in Matt's study after she left. It wasn't the best time to admonish him for his rejection of Catherine, however it was telling that he did not meet my gaze.

"You've told them what Hope said?" I asked Matt as I sat on the chair Duke vacated for me.

He picked up the letter laid out in front of him. "In detail."

"I knew she was a bad apple," Duke said with a shake of his head.

"She was desperate," Cyclops told him. "Desperate to secure her future. Sometimes people make bad choices when their future don't look too bright."

"You're defending her?" Duke grunted. "Willie would be on my side. Where is she, anyway?"

No one had an answer, and I wasn't sure Duke wanted to hear my suspicions. I was about to change the topic when Matt did it first.

He handed me the letter. "This is from my lawyer. He tracked down Miss Chilton. She's married and still lives in Islington but on a different street. Shall we visit today?"

"An excellent idea."

I looked in on Chronos before leaving. He still sported dark bruises and he sat gingerly in bed, but he had his wits about him and was in good spirits. Until Miss Glass arrived, that was. He groaned when she held up a deck of cards in one hand a book in the other.

"I can either read to you or play Old Maid," she said, sitting on the chair by the bed. "Which will it be?"

"Neither," he muttered.

"Don't be difficult. You must do something."

"Do you know any other card games?"

"Willemina has been teaching me poker."

He rubbed his hands together. "Right-oh. What'll the stakes be?"

* * *

MRS. RANDLEY, nee Chilton, lived with her husband in a modest house on a modest street in Islington. Mr. Randley worked for a bank in the city, and their two children were grown up and married. She was alone in the house when we called upon her in the late afternoon.

After telling her we worked for the police and were investigating Dr. Millroy's death, she readily agreed to talk to us once she got over her shock, expressed in the form of a small squeal.

"I am sorry for my outburst," she said as we sat in the parlor decorated with floral wallpaper, upholstery and curtains. Even her dress had flowers embroidered over the bodice. "But I'm so surprised that you're investigating it after all this time. I am pleased, however. Very pleased."

"You want to see justice served," Matt said with a friendly nod. "We understand. Dr. Millroy's death wasn't investigated thoroughly enough, and we want to right that wrong too."

"It may not end in a good result," I warned before she got her hopes up. "The guilty party may have also passed on and justice won't be served after all."

"It was an awfully long time ago." She peered at us over her spectacles with gray eyes that were both kind and quick. "The police made up their minds very early," she went on. "Do you mean to tell me it may not have been a thug from the slum after all?"

"We want to investigate all angles," Matt said. "It still seems likely it was someone from the area Dr. Millroy wandered into. Did you think it odd he was found in Whitechapel?"

"Lord, yes. Why would he want to go there? It didn't make sense."

"Could he have simply been lost?"

"A Londoner from birth? Unlikely."

"What about his mistress?" Matt asked bluntly.

Mrs. Randley pressed her lips together and fidgeted with her cuff.

"Mrs. Millroy told us about her," I said.

"She did?" She pushed her glasses up her nose. "Then I suppose it's all right if I tell you what I know, if it will help."

I gave her an encouraging smile. "Mrs. Millroy didn't

know her name but suspected you might, since you met all his patients and maintained their records. Was the mistress one of his patients?"

She nodded. "You know she bore Dr. Millroy a child?"

"We do. What sort of woman was she? The sort that comes from Whitechapel?"

"Lord, no. She was a proper lady."

"Her name?" Matt prompted. "Do you remember it?"

She bit her lip.

"Please, Mrs. Randley, it's very important. It's likely she's linked to Dr. Millroy's death."

She acquiesced with a nod. "Very well. I'm not a tattler, mind, but you're right and it's necessary. Her name was Lady Buckland. She was a young widow who came to see him for a sore throat. After that, she made regular weekly appointments. It became...obvious what they were up to."

Matt looked to me but I shook my head. I didn't know the nobility, and Lady Buckland in particular, any more than he did.

"What about their son?" I asked. "What was his name?"

"I never did learn it," she said, somewhat dreamily. "He'd be twenty-seven now. Imagine that."

"My age," I said, for no particular reason.

"Where was she living at the time?" Matt asked.

"I can't recall, Mr. Glass. I am sorry."

"Do you still have the patient records?"

She laughed. "Of course not. They were destroyed soon after Dr. Millroy's death."

"Never mind." Matt's words sounded amiable enough, but I detected the tiredness behind them. He'd been hoping for an address that we could visit immediately. Now he had to task his lawyer with finding another address, and that meant waiting.

"We'll find them," I assured him.

"Not *them*," Mrs. Randley said. "Even if you find Lady

Buckland alive and well, you'll not find her son with her. She gave him away."

I blinked at her even as my heart sank. "Before or after Dr. Millroy's death?"

"Before. You know how it is for a woman, Miss Steele. I suspect it's even more difficult for a lady of her standing to keep a baby she bore out of wedlock. She gave birth to him in secret, feigning illness, then gave the boy up. Dr. Millroy and I were the only ones who knew."

"Yes, of course." I nodded, somewhat numb. So even if we did find Lady Buckland, she would not know where to find her son. "She'll know which orphanage took him in," I said hopefully, once again for Matt's benefit. "They'll have records."

"Why would you want to find him?" Mrs. Randley gave me an arched look. "He can't help you discover the identity of Dr. Millroy's murderer."

"I...I...that is..." I couldn't think of an excuse quickly enough and ended up shrugging.

"There's another line of inquiry we want to follow," Matt chimed in before she grew suspicious. If he was disappointed that the son would be harder to find, he didn't show it. "What do you know about the experiment Dr. Millroy conducted just before his death?"

Mrs. Randley focused intently on him, as if she knew we had another motive for questioning her but couldn't quite put the pieces together yet. "What experiment?"

"Come, now, Mrs. Randley. We know you know about it. You were an excellent assistant to Dr. Millroy. His right hand, I believe."

"I was very good at my job."

"Then you'll know what happened that night with the vagrant," he said.

"I wasn't there."

"Nevertheless, Dr. Millroy probably spoke to you about it."

Her shifting gaze told me Matt was right. Under the pressure only a charged silence can bring, she sighed and her spine lost some of its stiffness. "I suppose it may be important. The thing is, Mr. Glass, Dr. Millroy didn't conduct the experiment alone. Did Mrs. Millroy tell you that?"

"She did," Matt said.

"A man named Chronos helped him."

"That's an odd name."

"I suspect it's a false one. I also suspect he forced Dr. Millroy to try his new treatment before it was ready."

"You don't know that," I said tightly. "You said yourself you weren't there."

"He can't have been up to good if he felt compelled to use a false name." She pushed her glasses up her nose again and settled her gaze on me. "He disappeared from the scene entirely as soon as the vagrant died, too. Coward. He left Dr. Millroy to face the Suregeon's Guild alone."

"You think Chronos was another doctor?" I asked cautiously.

"What else would he be?"

"Quite."

"Tell us about the experiment," Matt pressed. "How did Dr. Millroy feel about it?"

"He regretted his actions, so he told me the next day. He was in an awfully agitated state, worrying about his wife finding out about his mistress and telling the guild all sorts of things." The memory of it agitated her now. Her fingers alternately worried her cuff or flattened against her stomach, as if warding off a wave of nausea. "As it turns out, his fears were justified. If not for Mrs. Millroy, the vagrant's death would have gone unnoticed and the guild would have left him alone. But she told them and they questioned him mercilessly over it. I could hear them through his office door. They threatened to see him hang for murder! It was awful."

"What about the victim, Mr. Wilson?" Matt asked. "Mrs.

Millroy thought he had a family but suspects they died and he lost his way. Does that fit with how Dr. Millroy described him to you?"

"The doctor did allude to that, yes," she said carefully. "But that name…it's not quite right but I can't put my finger on the reason why."

"He wasn't named Wilson?"

She frowned. "It was so long ago. I can't remember now, but it has an odd ring to it. Does that make sense?"

"Yes," Matt said before I could tell her no.

"I believe he wasn't a vagrant either, in the strict sense of the word," she said.

"He had a home?"

Her frown deepened. "Again, I can't remember what Dr. Millroy told me precisely, but the man apparently rambled on about having a home he could not return to. We thought it was because his family had died there and he was unwilling to face it after their deaths. I suppose that makes him homeless after all, doesn't it? It did trouble Dr. Millroy the next day. So much so that he regretted his haste in performing the experiment without learning more. I blame that Chronos fellow for rushing him."

"According to Mrs. Millroy," I said, "Mr. Wilson *wanted* them to perform the experiment on him. He was eager to be cured."

"That's all well and good, except he wasn't cured."

It was impossible to argue with that.

"Apparently the fellow slept some nights in a doss house," Mrs. Randley went on. "Did Mrs. Millroy tell you that? Dr. Millroy said the man mentioned retrieving his things from the Bethnal Green doss house."

Bethnal Green! I very much wanted to look at Matt but kept my gaze fixed firmly forward.

Mrs. Randley sighed heavily. "The whole thing is upsetting. I wish Dr. Millroy had never met Chronos. And now, to think, his murder may have been linked to the experiment."

"We don't know that for certain," Matt said quickly. "It's simply another line of inquiry."

"We're far more interested in Lady Buckland," I told her.

Matt's gaze slid sideways to me, and I got the feeling I'd said too much.

"And Mrs. Millroy too, of course," I added. "She has quite the motive for murdering her husband."

"She certainly does, and she has the cold-heartedness that a murderer requires too," Mrs. Randley said. "But I don't think it was her. For one thing, her husband was a good provider, and killing him would cause her financial difficulty. For another, I don't think she cared enough about him to kill him. I think she was glad that he found himself a mistress. She rather liked playing the poor wife overlooked by her dishonest husband. She never made a secret of it. If you ask me," Mrs. Randley went on, "Chronos killed Dr. Millroy."

"Why do you say that?" I snipped.

"To keep Dr. Millroy quiet so he wouldn't get into trouble with the guild too."

"That's—"

"One last question," Matt cut in. "Do you know anything about a diary Dr. Millroy kept?"

She smiled. "His little book of magic, he called it."

I sucked in air between my teeth. She knew about magic?

"Pardon?" Matt said.

"It's just a silly name for the notebook. He was often jotting things down in it or looking through it, but I never saw its contents. It contained information pertaining to his medical experiments, I believe."

"Do you know what happened to it after his death?"

"I assume it was on his person, like always. So unless his killer took it, the police would have given it to Mrs. Millroy. Why?"

Matt smiled. "Thank you, Mrs. Randley. You've been most helpful."

Outside, Matt assisted me into the coach waiting by the curb, our new coachman on the driver's seat.

"The nerve of her," I said, throwing myself onto the seat. "Blaming Chronos for coercing Dr. Millroy when she has no evidence that he did."

"It's a logical conclusion," he said. At my glare, he cleared his throat. "Of course we know Chronos didn't kill Millroy."

I had cooled down by the time we reached Mayfair and was able to see it from Mrs. Randley's point of view. "It's a little hard to think of my own grandfather being a cold-hearted killer," I said quietly. It was rather overwhelming to think I had a killer's blood flowing through my veins alongside the magic. He may not be guilty of Dr. Millroy's death but he was responsible for Mr. Wilson's, at least in part.

Matt leaned forward and took my hand. "India," he said smoothly. "Chronos believed he was doing the right thing. He's not cold-hearted or a killer. He wanted the vagrant to live, not die. You could say he wanted it badly enough that he overlooked things that should have mattered, like the fact Mr. Wilson may not have been homeless or without a family."

I closed my fingers around his. "Thank you, Matt, but don't defend Chronos too much. I'm not convinced he deserves it." I wanted Matt to know how I felt. It seemed important he not think I blindly trusted my grandfather simply because he was my kin. "I won't be taken in, this time. I've fallen victim to men who've tried to pull the wool over my eyes lately, and I no longer want to be that victim. In Chronos's case, I'll weigh up the evidence and make a decision based on what my head tells me, not my heart."

He stared down at our hands for a long time before letting go and sitting back. "You make it sound so simple."

We both knew it was not.

Matt suddenly sat forward again; something through the

window caught his attention. "Damn it. What's he doing here?"

"Who?" I nudged him aside and saw Mr. Abercrombie standing alongside his conveyance parked near the steps to number sixteen.

He was not alone. Another man climbed out of the coach. He pushed his hat brim up and followed Abercrombie's gaze toward the front door. Then he turned at the sound of our arrival.

I gasped. "Eddie! What the bloody hell does he want now?"

CHAPTER 14

"*What* do you want?" Matt asked Abercrombie on the steps to his house. The front door stood open, and Peter waited to greet us. But Matt was in no mood to invite our visitors in.

Abercrombie's moustache twitched with the pursing of his lips. "Good afternoon, Mr. Glass, Miss Steele. I hoped we could have a civil conversation in private." He glanced at the window of the neighboring house. The curtain fluttered and the elderly man who'd been watching us retreated from view.

"Say your piece out here," Matt snapped. "Then leave."

"I say!" Eddie thrust out his chest and chin. He reminded me of a rooster strutting around his territory. "We only want to talk. Your uncivil manner may be how Americans are with one another, but you're in England now."

"Just get on with it, Eddie," I said before Matt's temper frayed altogether.

"But it's growing dark," Eddie said, as if I were a fool for not noticing. "The lamplighter will come by soon."

"Then you'd best talk quickly if you want privacy." Matt took a step toward him and Eddie shuffled backward. He kept a wary eye on Matt. "Is this about Barratt's article?

Because we had nothing to do with it, and I'm not going to discuss it with you. Is that clear?"

"It's not about that." Abercrombie rocked back on his heels, pleased with himself. "Our rebuttal will come soon enough."

"Then get to the point."

"We have reason to suspect you're harboring a criminal."

My heart ground to a halt. Beside me, Matt had gone utterly still. "Pardon?" he said icily.

"We have reason to suspect a man known as Chronos is living here."

How the devil did he know? From Dr. Ritter? If not him then who? Was it the same person who'd attacked Chronos? "That's an odd name," I said, trying hard to look unconcerned.

Abercrombie glanced at Peter who hadn't moved from the doorway. "His real name is Gideon Steele."

I gasped so loudly that even Peter reacted. Perhaps I over-played it a little. "Your information is incorrect, sir. My grand-father is dead."

"Is he?" he asked idly. "Everyone was told he died, yes, but there's no proof, no record of his death."

It seemed he'd investigated and knew more than we suspected. "I assure you, he's dead. Perhaps the records have been lost. Don't you think I would know if he were alive? Don't you think he would have come to my father's funeral or tried to make contact with me? I can assure you, he has not sought me out." That, at least, was not a lie.

"He wasn't much of a family man, as I recall."

"Come now, India," Eddie soothed. "Admit that he's here. We know he is."

I pressed my hands to my hips. "I'll admit no such thing since it's not true!"

"Why are you making such absurd accusations?" Matt asked. "Why do you think he's alive and here after all this time?"

"He has been sighted," Abercrombie said.

"Sighted where and by whom?"

"I'm not at liberty to divulge that information."

I placed a hand on Matt's arm. The muscle was taut with coiled tension. "Your source is mistaken," I told Abercrombie. "If my grandfather is alive, which I doubt, he is not here."

"You would say that," Eddie said with a smile that was as ugly as his heart. "You're his bloody granddaughter."

"Go away," Matt growled, steering me to the steps.

"You know he was involved in a murder before his apparent death," Eddie said softly, as if he knew his words alone were explosive enough.

"You have a nerve accusing my grandfather of such a thing," I said as levelly as possible.

"Stop pretending, India. I am not a fool. You've been investigating the death of Dr. Millroy and that will naturally lead to his association with Gideon Steele. How far along is your investigation, anyway? Perhaps if we share information, we can both achieve our aims. You find out who killed Dr. Millroy, and we get our hands on your grandfather."

"You're mad," I said. The nerve of him to think we'd tell him anything!

Eddie opened his mouth to speak, but Abercrombie put up his hand. Eddie snapped his mouth shut but he didn't look happy to be silenced.

"Who is accusing India's grandfather of murder?" Matt asked.

"That is none of your concern," Abercrombie said.

"It is if someone is making up accusations. It is when you come here and upset India like this."

Abercrombie gave me an oily smile. "She doesn't look terribly upset."

Matt grabbed Abercrombie's jacket front, twisting his fist into it. Something inside the pocket cracked.

"My pince nez!" Abercrombie cried. "You broke it."

"That's not all I'll break if you don't get away from here this instant." Matt pushed Abercrombie away.

He stumbled but the railing stopped him from tumbling into the stairwell leading down to the service area. He straightened his tie and tugged on his jacket, all the while glaring at Matt.

Matt took my hand and placed it on his elbow. He escorted me upstairs and inside. I heard Abercrombie's coach roll away before Peter closed the front door.

"Tea for Miss Steele, please," Matt ordered Bristow as Peter took our hats and coats.

"Not tea," I said. "I need something stronger. It's been an eventful day."

"I'll bring sherry," Bristow said.

Matt led me to the library and directed me to sit.

"I'm all right," I told him before he could ask. "We need to warn Chronos and the others."

He stood by the unlit fireplace and stared into the grate. "The question is, how did they find out Chronos is your grandfather and that he is staying here? Did *they* attack him?"

"If not them, they are probably communicating with the party who orchestrated the attack," I said. "The chances of Chronos being seen by two separate people who knew him back then and recognized him now are slim."

"Dr. Ritter?" he said with a shrug.

"Should we confront him about it?"

"He'll deny it."

"Follow him then?" I suggested. "If he comes here and watches this house, hoping to catch Chronos coming and going, we'll know for certain."

"I'll send Cyclops and Duke out."

"Not Willie?"

"I don't even know where she is."

Bristow entered carrying a tray with two glasses. Matt

plucked them off and handed one to me. "Is Willie here?" he asked the butler.

"Yes, sir."

"Ask her, Duke and Cyclops to join us."

Matt sat in the armchair, looking relaxed after the ferocious display outside. He even managed a small smile for me, but the effect was somewhat spoiled by the tiredness in his eyes. "Are you sure you're all right?" he said.

"Of course. Neither man upsets me now, particularly when you're present. A lot of the wind seems to have gone out of their sails in recent weeks, anyway. Now that I am aware of what Abercrombie knows about me, and he is aware that I know, it's as if he has no more hold over me."

"His power was knowing your secret, even before you knew it yourself, and the potential to use that secret to hurt you. Ever since you gave up on obtaining guild membership, his power receded."

I didn't dare raise the idea that the secret also had less effect now that the entire world was discussing magic and magicians thanks to Oscar Barratt's article. It lessened the unspoken threats of exposure that Abercrombie directed my way. But Matt wouldn't want to hear it.

"What I want to know is," Matt said, "why was Hardacre with him?"

It was a good question and not one I'd considered. Abercrombie treated Eddie as if he were an irritation he had to endure rather than an equal. He'd occasionally made himself useful, chiefly when it came to telling Abercrombie about my magic, something Eddie had learned from my father. I could think of only one reason Abercrombie would allow Eddie to join him in confronting me. "Perhaps the information about Chronos came from him and as a condition of passing on the information, Eddie demanded he be here when Abercrombie confronted me."

"Precisely. But why does Hardacre care?"

"To see me hurt? To see the effect his accusation has on me so he can rub my nose in it?" Even as I said it, I knew it didn't ring true. Eddie didn't care enough about me to want to hurt me. That had never been his aim. "Because if my grandfather is alive," I said, warming to my theory, "then my shop—*his* shop—actually still belongs to my grandfather. It was not my father's to give away in his will. And with Chronos still alive, the shop becomes mine upon his death."

Matt lifted his glass in salute. "I think so too."

Willie barged in, Duke and Cyclops on her heels. "Drinks before dinner again? This is becoming quite the habit. What will Miss Glass say?"

"I see your frequent outings have not blunted your tongue, Willie," Matt said with a smirk.

"More's the pity," Duke muttered. "She went back to the hospital."

"I learned something too," she said, throwing herself into a chair with such force it slid backward. "Dr. Ritter had a visit from Abercrombie."

"Did Ritter summon him or did Abercrombie go of his own accord?" Duke asked.

She threw her hands in the air. "Well I don't know, do I?"

"Then it ain't all that useful, is it?"

"Thank you anyway," Matt said, rubbing his jaw in thought. "It's intriguing news."

She beamed at Duke. His face darkened even further. It was as if the happier Willie became, the less happy it made Duke.

"Who told you?" Cyclops asked with a wicked smile. "Your new doctor friend?"

She stretched out her legs and crossed them at the ankles. "It ain't your business who told me." Now she looked unhappy too, but Duke's mood did not improve. It was a dangerous path to navigate around those two and I gave my head a small shake to silence Cyclops.

He sighed. "There ain't no fun to be had here no more."

Bristow entered with three glasses and the mail that he handed to Matt.

Matt opened the top letter. "It's an invitation to Patience's wedding."

"Are we invited?" Willie asked, trying to peer at the invitation without getting out of her chair.

"Just myself and Aunt Letitia."

"What do you care?" Duke asked her. "You hate weddings on account of you're supposed to wear a dress."

"That's not the only reason I hate weddings," Willie shot back. "But I want to see Rycroft, Matt's estate."

"Not mine," Matt said.

"Not yet."

"Anything interesting in the other letters?" Cyclops asked. "Anything from back home?"

"Or from Patience?" I asked.

"Just one from Commissioner Munro." He opened it. His face remained impassive as he read. "He's summoning me to his office tomorrow morning."

"Should we be concerned?" I asked.

"It's likely he simply wants an update. I'll write a brief report this evening and we'll take it to Scotland Yard before we visit Lady Buckland."

"But we don't know where she lives."

"Who is she?" Willie asked.

"Millroy's mistress. India will fill you in," Matt said, rising. "I'm going to ask my aunt if she knows anything about the mysterious merry widow."

Ten minutes later, Matt returned looking rejuvenated. He must have used his watch in his absence.

"You're smiling," I said, smiling back. "So Miss Glass knows her?"

"She does. She is still styled Lady Buckland, having never remarried. Apparently she's rich and lives not far from here, preferring the city to her country estate. According to my aunt, Lady Buckland had quite the reputation and still manages to have the odd dalliance with younger men."

"But she must be old now," Willie said.

"Old ain't dead," Duke said.

"She was very much the subject of gossip twenty-seven years ago," Matt went on, "but is now simply considered an eccentric and largely ignored."

I leaned back and contemplated my sherry. "I find that a little sad. To be talked about in a poor light is not particularly nice, but to be completely ignored is perhaps even more upsetting."

"To some," Cyclops agreed. "To others, going unnoticed would be a blessing."

Matt picked up his glass and held it to his smiling lips. "I'm looking forward to meeting her."

I grinned. "That's because you're a handsome younger man. I will definitely leave the interrogation of Lady Buckland to you."

* * *

COMMISSIONER MUNRO WAS NOT ALONE in his office when his assistant led us through. Detective Inspector Brockwell stood by the window, his oversized jacket open at the front, revealing a stained waistcoat. The two men could not be more dissimilar. The older, gentlemanly Munro was all distinguished authority, in his smart uniform, whereas Brockwell looked like he'd slept in his suit and forgotten to comb his hair. Their twin gruff expressions matched, however.

"We've been receiving complaints about you," Munro began.

"Good," Matt said, not bothering to take a seat. "Upset people means we're closing in. Who has complained?"

Munro clasped his hands on the desk in front of him. "That's not something I'm at liberty to divulge."

"Tell me how your investigation fares," Brockwell said, punching out the consonants.

"It fares well," Matt said.

"I'd like more detail."

Matt handed his report to Munro. "It's all in there."

I knew it wasn't *all* in there. He'd left out the parts pertaining to magic and Chronos's involvement in the experiment twenty-seven years ago.

Munro signaled to Brockwell to read with him. "Remain here," Munro said to us.

"We can't," Matt said. "We have an appointment."

"Unless it's with the queen or prime minister, I don't care. Sit."

Matt pulled out a chair for me. I sat but he did not. Five minutes felt like an hour. I could no longer stand it after three so pulled out my watch. The smooth silver case warmed to my touch, just a little, but it was enough to soothe my nerves.

Finally, Brockwell straightened and Munro set the report down on his desk. He removed his spectacles and regarded Matt. "You seem to be following a number of lines of inquiry."

"Yes," Matt said. "I won't speculate on which is the more likely outcome, if that's what you're asking."

"Not at all. I don't like my detectives to have an opinion until they're in possession of all the facts."

"In that case, India and I have to go now." He held out his hand to me and I took it.

"Just a moment." Munro tapped the report with the glasses. "There's no mention of the man named Chronos in here."

Matt's fingers tightened. I dared not look at him for fear of giving anything away. "Chronos?" Matt asked.

"Don't play the commissioner for a fool," Brockwell said. "We know you are aware of him."

"It seems you've been talking to Abercrombie. Since you know about the difficulties we've had with him in the past, you won't be surprised to learn that he's trying to upset India. Let me assure you, gentlemen, we have not met the fellow named Chronos. He is linked to this investigation through the experiment he conducted with Millroy years ago. I don't know his real name and so can't attempt to trace him."

"What of the suggestion that he is Miss Steele's grandfather?"

If they knew that then they certainly must have spoken to Abercrombie or someone from the guild. Mrs. Millroy didn't know Chronos was my grandfather, and I doubted Dr. Ritter knew. He'd told the Watchmaker's Guild that Chronos was Dr. Millroy's co-magician in the experiment and had given them Mrs. Millroy's description of him, but we weren't yet sure if the guild had told him the description matched that of Gideon Steele.

"Speculation only," Matt said. "As I said, Abercrombie is trying to cause upset. As far as Miss Steele is aware, her grandfather is dead."

I stood and let go of Matt's hand. "I'll tell you what I told Mr. Abercrombie and Mr. Hardacre," I said to both men. "If my grandfather were alive, he would have come to my father's funeral. He would have tried to contact me, but most of all, he would not have allowed a fool like Eddie Hardacre to take the shop from the Steele family. If he were alive, he would have come forward so the shop would be in his hands again."

"Unless he's guilty of murder twenty-seven years ago, and does not want us to find him," Brockwell countered.

"If that's the case," Matt said, "then he's hardly going to move in with India, is he? He might as well lead his enemies directly to him."

"We are not the enemy," Munro said.

"Unless he's guilty," Brockwell added.

"Good day, gentlemen." I spun round and marched out of the office. "I no longer like Inspector Brockwell," I said to Matt as we exited the building.

"He's doing his job. Unfortunately for us, he's doing it a little too well." He held the coach door open for me. "You think Abercrombie complained about us?"

"Of course it was him, with Eddie following behind like a dog."

"Don't disparage dogs, India." He climbed in behind me, his eyes sparkling with humor. How could he be in such a good mood after that meeting? "I rather like them. If I didn't live in the city, I'd own several, all of them very large and very friendly."

I clicked my tongue. "You're impossible, Matt. I don't know how you could dismiss that meeting so easily."

"All will be well. Unless they search the house, they won't find Chronos. That attack has frightened him into hiding. And now we're about to be one step closer to finding the doctor magician we need to fix this." He tapped his chest where his magic watch hid beneath his waistcoat. "We're not far from finding Millroy's killer, either. All in all, things are looking positive."

I conjured up a smile from the depths of my frustration. "I am looking forward to meeting the merry widow."

It took us longer than it ought to have done to reach Lady Buckland's townhouse. She didn't live far from Matt, but he made the coachman take a circuitous route, and fast, to insure no one followed us. While Matt claimed he couldn't see anyone, I suspected he had an inkling Payne was tracking his movements.

Lady Buckland was indeed merry, but from sherry not natural good humor. I could smell it on her breath when she greeted us in her dusky rose dressing gown in a parlor that was also wallpapered in the same shade of pink. She sat on the sofa with a small white dog in her lap and a tall blonde footman standing to attention at her side. She wasn't at all the dignified lady I expected, based on Mrs. Randley's answers to our questions, but I supposed people changed over time.

"I am sorry for my appearance," she said, slurring her words a little. "I'm not usually ready for callers this early in the morning, but my butler said you insisted."

It was eleven o'clock, according to the marble and gold clock on the mantel. We'd deliberately waited so as not to disturb her morning routine.

"We're very sorry," Matt said, "but your butler was right to insist. This is very important. You're the key to our investigation." He sat forward a little, and spoke directly to her without letting his gaze drop. His undivided attention, along with his insistence that *she* was important, certainly got the desired result. She was riveted to his every word.

"I am? How thrilling. Now, tell me, what are you investigating?"

This was the part I worried about most. A woman who'd had a scandalous liaison with a married man would not like talk of that affair to resurface, even years later. If we didn't handle it deftly, she could close up entirely and refuse to answer any of our other questions.

"My name is Parsons," Matt said. "Matthew Parsons."

Parsons! I managed to contain my surprise to a sharp look in his direction. My quick movement startled Lady Buckland, however. She squeezed her dog so tightly it yelped and leapt out of her hands. The footman chased it, but it retreated beneath another sofa, out of his reach.

Lady Buckland touched the fur collar of her dressing gown at her throat. "Go on, Mr. Parsons. What do you want from me?"

Matt offered her a gentle smile. "Just the answers to a few questions about my cousin."

"Cousin?"

"My father's cousin, to be precise. Dr. James Millroy and

my father were first cousins, but my father moved to America and they lost touch. I wanted to connect with him on my visit here, but discovered he died, alas."

Lady Buckland seemed a little lost without her dog to hold on to. Her thumb rubbed the back of her hand, pushing at the loose skin over her knuckles. "And what has that got to do with me?"

Matt eyed the footman, now on his hands and knees trying to reach the dog. The dog was having none of it, crouched at the back corner, its dark eyes on the footman. "Cousin James told my father all about the two of you," Matt whispered.

The rubbing suddenly stopped. "Milo, come here."

I thought she was calling the dog but it was the footman who answered. "Yes, m'lady?"

"Please leave us. Shut the door."

He bowed and dutifully left but not before he shot the dog a warning glare.

"Dr. Millroy was my physician years ago," Lady Buckland told us. "Why would you come *here* to learn more about him? You ought to speak to his wife, if the dried up old prune still lives."

"She does and I have," Matt said easily. "But you are the one I really wanted to speak to, ma'am. You're the one who knew him best. You're the one he loved."

I almost choked, but Lady Buckland looked pleased with Matt's flattery. Her face brightened like a flower blooming beneath the sun.

"You know," she said simply.

"I know," Matt said. "Cousin James mentioned you frequently in his letters to my father. He wrote glowing words about you. Positively wonderful things."

"Tell me some of them."

The dog emerged from beneath the other sofa but did not approach. Matt bent down and clicked his fingers. "Here."

The dog trotted happily to him. It must be female.

"He wrote about your glorious hair and fine eyes." Fine eyes? I bit back my smile. Mr. Darcy couldn't have said it as smoothly.

A flush infused Lady Buckland's cheeks and her gaze became distant. "My dearest James. How I miss him."

Matt picked up the dog and passed it to her. "Tell me what you remember. I'd like to know everything about my cousin."

She stroked the dog's fur as it settled in her lap, her attention on the task as she watched the fur slide through her fingers. The dog closed its eyes and rested its chin on Lady Buckland's other hand in perfect contentment.

"James was clever and amusing. We had marvelous conversations and would stay up until all hours talking. He was generous too, and I'm not merely referring to the gifts he bought me. Generous of spirit, was my dear James. He was always complimenting me on this or that." She touched the gray curl at the nape of her neck. The rest of her hair was tucked beneath a lace cap. "He always had time for me too, and never asked for anything in return." She sighed. "Until... Well, until the end."

"You mean just before his death?" Matt asked. She nodded. "Did he change toward you?"

Tears pooled in her eyes. "I don't want to talk about it."

Matt waited until the silence became uncomfortable, then said, "His wife told me he was murdered and his killer never caught. What a terrible time that must have been for you."

"It was awful, particularly considering how things were between us in the days leading up to his death. If I could go back and make things right between us, I would. Not that I would have made a different decision, but I would have tried to smooth things over rather than argue."

Was she referring to giving up their child? Had Dr. Millroy not known until it was too late? I waited for Matt to ask her, but he did not. It was most frustrating, but I knew by now he often came to his point in a round about way to get the other person to trust him.

"Do you think an opportunistic thief attacked and killed him as the police assumed?" he asked.

"It seems the most likely answer, but..." She buried her hand in the dog's fur. "Let's just say there is another person with a reason to kill him."

"Who?" I blurted out. It was the first time I'd spoken, and Lady Buckland looked surprised to hear me speak at all. I'd been introduced as Matt's fiancée, the one who'd urged him to seek out information about his father's cousin, but she'd largely ignored me until now.

"Mrs. Millroy of course." She screwed up her nose and stroked the dog vigorously. "Cold, barren woman, and I don't mean in the sense she couldn't have children. Barren of heart was Mrs. Millroy. I wouldn't put it past her to have killed him, not from jealousy, but simply because I made him happy."

"Do you have any evidence that she did it?" Matt asked.

"You've met her. What did you think?"

"Her character is not evidence."

"It ought to be," she muttered.

"She told me the Surgeon's Guild had a heated argument with him over an experiment he conducted on a homeless man. Do you think that event could have triggered Dr. Millroy's murder?"

Her gaze narrowed. "Why do you want to know?"

"I don't like thinking of his death being in vain, or of his murderer going unpunished. Cousin James's wife said the police gave up looking for his killer. I thought perhaps I could find some answers. It seems right, somehow."

"You are a good man. A very good man. He would have been proud to call you family."

Matt offered her a gentle smile. "Thank you. So do you know about the experiment I'm referring to?"

"A little," she hedged. "He told me the Surgeon's Guild were hounding him over something. But, to be honest, we were not on good terms ourselves at that point, due to…a certain matter, so I know little about it."

"I am sorry to hear that. I know how much he adored you, and I'm sure he would have tried to make things up to you if he'd lived. Nothing would have come between you forever."

"Perhaps," she said on a deep sigh. "We'll never know now."

Again, I waited for Matt to press her about the child but he did not. "Perhaps the Surgeons Guild's master had him killed," he said.

"Good lord, do you think so?" She patted her chest as if trying to settle a racing heartbeat. "That's rather extreme punishment. Why not simply expel him from the guild if they were unhappy with his experimenting?"

"Why not indeed? Or perhaps the man he experimented on had a family who sought revenge."

"That's entirely possible too. I recall James wanted to find out for certain if the man was indeed alone in the world. Perhaps he located a relative and they…" She swallowed. "Considering his plans for the evening of his death, it's a strong possibility he found someone."

"Go on."

"He sent me a letter asking me to receive him the following day. But he died that night." She lowered her head and sniffed. "In the letter, he briefly mentioned his search for more information about the man."

Matt handed her his handkerchief. "Do you recall what he wrote?"

"Not the exact words. He said he wanted to meet me to discuss…our disagreement, but he couldn't until his conscience was clear. The experiment had played on his mind and even distracted him from what I'd done."

"What did he do to clear his conscience?" Matt asked.

"He wrote that he had to visit a doss house. That was all."

"The man had been staying in a doss house?" Matt asked.

"It would seem so. I suppose James hoped to find out more about him from the staff."

"What did he hope to achieve if he found the man's relatives?" I asked. "Compensate them for their loss?"

She lifted one shoulder then let it sag along with the other. She looked very much her age, all signs of youthful beauty gone beneath the weight of time and sorrow. "I think he just wanted to know for certain if the man had a family or not. It would ease his conscience greatly to know there wasn't one. At the time, he assumed there wasn't, but later, he began to have doubts. If you ask me, Mrs. Millroy planted the seeds of doubt. She was cruel like that, always saying little things to unsettle him."

"Do you think that's why Dr. Millroy was in Whitechapel on the night of his death? Because he'd gone to a doss house there to learn more about Wilson?"

"No. If he'd died in Bethnal Green I would have a different answer, but why he was in Whitechapel is a mystery to me. He only mentioned going to a Bethnal Green doss house in his note, you see."

"Bethnal Green?" I echoed.

"Yes. Why do you ask?"

"I wonder what he learned about Mr. Wilson at the doss house that sent him into Whitechapel," Matt said quickly.

"Mr. Wilson?" She shook her head. "That wasn't his name."

The news surprised Matt into silence for several seconds. "Do you know his name?" he eventually asked.

"It escapes me but…Wilson is not quite right."

"Perhaps it will come to you." He smiled.

She smiled back. "Perhaps it will. I am so glad you've come. You've brightened my day. I don't get out as much as I used to, and my friends do not call on me with any regularity." She lifted the little dog to her chest and cradled it. The dog seemed content enough to be woken up and adored. "Without Bliss here, my day would be unending boredom. Milo is pleasing to look at but not as much of a companion as I'd hoped he would be."

Milo was a companion, not a footman? Merry widow indeed.

"Does the name Chronos mean anything to you?" Matt asked, clearly not ready to leave.

She frowned. "An acquaintance of James's had an odd name like that," she said, once again settling Bliss in her lap. "I think that's the name of the man who assisted him with the experiment."

"Do you know his real name or profession? Anything about him?"

"We never met, and James merely mentioned him in passing. I assumed they were working on a new medical technique or device together."

"What about a woman named Nell Sweet?"

Her spine stiffened. "Was James seeing another woman?"

"No. You were the only love mentioned in his letters to my father."

She relaxed a little but her features remained strained, and her vigorous stroking of Bliss continued, much to Bliss's happiness. "I did wonder if I'd driven James away, if my action led him to fall out of love with me and into the arms of another. He was so *angry* with me, you see. So very angry."

Matt glanced at me, the first sign that he wasn't sure of himself. I gave him a small nod of encouragement. As sensitive as the topic was, we *had* to broach it.

"Ma'am, forgive me," Matt said gently, "but you've mentioned an argument between you and my cousin a few times now. I think I know what you're referring to." He paused. The silence felt weighty, oppressive. "I don't want to seem impertinent, but was the argument over your son?"

She did not seem surprised that he brought it up. Indeed, I

wondered if her constant mentioning of the argument was a way of introducing it into the conversation. I suspected Lady Buckland wanted to talk about it after all this time.

"He was born in this house." She blinked up at the chandelier hanging from the ceiling rose. "I initially told James I'd keep him and raise him, telling people I'd taken in a ward in need of a home. Whether anyone believed that, I don't know. I'm sure the gossips enjoyed themselves at my expense. But that's not why I gave him up. I didn't care about anyone's opinion of me. I still don't."

"Good for you," I felt compelled to say. "Why did you give him up?"

She smiled wanly. "I quickly learned that motherhood is a difficult business and doesn't come naturally to every woman. Maternal instincts are not a thing, Miss Steele. At least in my case they are not."

"So you gave him away for adoption," Matt prompted.

She nodded. "I knew James wouldn't allow it, so I organized it in secret. When he found out, I didn't tell him where I sent Phineas, no matter how relentlessly he questioned me."

"He must have been furious," Matt said quietly.

"Oh yes. And I understand why. I do. James wanted a child so desperately but seed can't take root in barren earth. And Mrs. Millroy was a desert. He finally got a son from me then I sent him away. I don't regret it. Phineas could not be raised as James's own child, or even as mine. He would not be afforded privileges or James's name. At least by giving him up he had the chance of a good life." Her entire body sagged into the sofa, momentarily disturbing the dog before she resettled. "Phineas is much loved in his new home. I'm sure of it. Much, much loved with a normal family and lots of siblings."

"You know who adopted him?" Matt asked, rather incredulously. Or perhaps it was hopefully.

"Only in my heart."

Matt gave her an understanding smile, but I knew it wasn't genuine.

"I tried telling James that Phineas would be loved, but he wanted to hear none of it. He railed at me, demanding to know which orphanage I sent Phineas to. But I wouldn't tell him. I couldn't have him undoing all my hard work, all the hopes I had for our child. He would ruin everything by bringing Phineas back here. What did he think would happen? We could not live as a family, and I could not raise a boy alone. What did I know about children or mothering? I did the right thing," she said with certainty.

"But Cousin James didn't give up trying to find out where you took him," Matt went on. "Hence the letter he sent you on the day of his death asking you to meet him."

She nodded. "He sounded more reasonable in his letter, not as angry. I suspected he was going to try to coax the answer out of me instead of force it. He talked about how special Phineas was, how I didn't understand the gravity of my actions because I didn't know what his child was capable of becoming. *His* child, not mine." She rolled her eyes. "As if I had nothing to do with his conception."

Special. Dr. Millroy expected, and perhaps hoped, his son would be a magician. A rare doctor magician, at that.

"Do you know why he thought his child would be special?" Matt pressed.

She waved her hand. Bliss opened her eyes at the loss of her mistress's touch. "Doesn't every father think his son is special?"

I detected no lie, no understanding of magic and how it passed from one generation to the next. If she knew about magic at all, she had not once given an indication during the interview.

"Ma'am, thank you for your honesty," Matt said. "I knew from Cousin James's letters to my father that he had a son, and I'm glad you confirmed it. You've given me something to hope for."

"Hope for?"

Matt looked at her guilelessly. "Your son is my only surviving blood relative. I want to meet him."

She blanched.

"Will you tell me which orphanage you sent him to so I can trace him? They'll have records and—"

"No! Definitely not!" She pushed the dog off her lap. Bliss landed on the floor with a whimper then scurried under the other sofa as her mistress stood. "Good day, sir. I'd like you to leave now."

Matt stood so I followed suit. "Please, ma'am. If I could meet my cousin, it would mean the world to me. To us." He put his arm around me. It was hard as a rock, at odds with his soft plea. "I won't tell Phineas anything about you, if that's what you want."

She gave the bell pull a fierce tug. "No. I cannot risk him learning who I am. I cannot risk him coming here, expecting me to acknowledge him."

Milo entered and bowed but did not speak.

Lady Buckland barked a laugh. "Can you imagine it? He would be older than Milo. Isn't that absurd?" She went to Milo, arms outstretched. He took both her hands in his and kissed her flushed cheek. "What would he think of me?" she said, casting a dreamy look at her footman.

"Lady Buckland," Matt pressed. "Please, this is important."

She spun sharply. "Stop it," she hissed, her eyes flashing. "Stop it! You're just like James, demanding answers I cannot give. Get out of my house! Go!"

Matt took a step toward her but Milo blocked his path.

The footman cracked his knuckles and smiled. It was all crooked teeth. "You heard her ladyship," he said in a broad Cockney accent. "Get out."

Matt stared down at the floor, as if the roses woven into the carpet could help him. The room suddenly seemed too close, too cloying with its abundance of pink. I had to get Matt out before he got so frustrated that he shed his disguise and did something he would regret. Milo looked as strong as he was handsome.

I took Matt's hand and urged him toward the door, my mind searching for something to say to dissolve the tension. I spied a newspaper on a table and picked it up to idly discuss the news.

Only it was the latest edition of *The Weekly Gazette*, opened to Oscar Barratt's article. I forged on anyway. "What a sensation this article caused."

"Has it?" Lady Buckland said with disinterest.

Matt eyed Milo as if he wanted to punch him, and Milo continued to smile back at Matt. I'd seen that look before. It was the sort of smile a guilty man has when he knows the police can't catch him. He could do anything in this house to us and Lady Buckland would protect him with her money and status.

I pulled hard on Matt's hand and dragged him out before he buried us in a hole we could not climb out of.

CHAPTER 15

*M*att gave our coachman directions to the Bethnal Green shelter and assisted me into the carriage.

"Are you all right?" I asked, trying to look at his face without making it obvious. He stared out the window, however. Was he thinking over what had happened in Lady Buckland's house? Wishing he could strike Milo? Or looking for Payne?

"I'm fine," he said, turning to me and offering a smile that didn't quite meet his eyes. "She gave us the information we need to continue. We now know Dr. Millroy went to the Bethnal Green doss house that night. I suspect he learned that Wilson had a family in Bright Court. All we have to do is find his records and we'll discover which of the Bright Court residents is related to Wilson, just as Millroy did twenty-seven years ago."

"But we already looked and there were no records for Mr. Wilson at the Bethnal Green shelter. There could have been another doss house in Bethnal Green at that time."

He scrubbed his hand over his jaw and chin. "We'll return to the same one and look again. Maybe his details were misfiled. If we have no luck, we'll ask some locals if there used to be another doss house in the area."

"What if his details weren't misfiled?" I asked as an idea grew on me. "What if they were filed under another name? Not everyone is convinced that Wilson is the real name of the vagrant. 'Not quite right' is how everyone seems to put it."

He nodded slowly. I waited for him to say something, to mention the very obvious problem facing us now, but he did not. It would seem I had to bring it up.

"Lady Buckland did not tell us how to find Phineas."

"No," he said flatly.

"Perhaps we'll ask her again in a day or two. She might soften her stance if we wear her down."

"Or we could just break in and search through her house."

"Matt!"

"She's bound to have information somewhere relating to her son. Some paperwork from the orphanage, a letter. A mother wouldn't throw that sort of thing out."

"Matthew Glass! It's one thing to break in to a shop when no one is inside, but this is the home of an elderly lady who doesn't leave her house. Not to mention she has servants who'll protect their mistress."

"Don't worry about Milo."

"I am worried, as you ought to be. He doesn't look like someone you should cross, particularly not in her house. I'd say he has her wrapped around his little finger, and she no doubt pays him handsomely for…services."

"You're blushing, India."

"I am not!"

He shot me a sly smile. "Don't worry, India. I won't ask you to join me in the search."

"This is not a joke!"

His smile faded into a frown. "No one will get hurt, either her or me. I can't make any promises about Milo, but I'll be careful. I've done this before."

"Yes," I said hotly. "Back in America, where you just happened to get shot by your own grandfather!" I crossed my arms over my chest. "Didn't that teach you not to do anything rash?"

"I can't back away from this, India. You know why I can't."

"We can wear her down," I said lamely. " One day at a time, one question at a time. She'll give in, Matt."

"I can't wait for that."

"I'll befriend her or...or you'll charm her. She liked you. She'll do anything you ask of her if you play your cards right. You're an excellent card player."

His sad, crooked smile twisted my heart. He leaned forward and touched my hands. "I don't have the time. My watch is slowing down."

"But I extended the magic."

He lowered his head and his hair fell across his eyes. "A little."

"But not enough," I said heavily.

I took his face in my hands, forcing him to look up. The exhaustion had come over him suddenly. It was as if stepping into the carriage meant he could remove the mask of healthfulness he presented to the world. I ought to be pleased that he allowed me to see him as he was but it only made me feel sad to my bones.

I stroked his cheeks with my thumbs. His eyes glazed over then closed, and his breathing became unsteady. It took all my strength of will not to kiss him.

"India," he purred in a rich, modular tone.

I withdrew my hands and focused on drawing the curtains, not looking at him. Not until I heard his sigh and his watch case open. His glowing veins lit up the cabin in an ethereal light that grew brighter as the magic spread through his entire body. When it reached his hairline, he closed the case and returned the watch to his pocket.

"Better," he announced.

We both knew he needed to rest as well, but that would have to wait. We were not far from the Bethnal Green shelter.

"Do you think she regrets giving up her son?" I asked, reopening the curtains and banishing the lingering effects of the glow.

"Sometimes, perhaps, when she allows herself to dwell on it. She certainly wishes it hadn't ruined her relationship with Millroy. Hardly surprising that it did, though. Not only did he finally have a child, but that child has a strong possibility of inheriting his magic."

"I wonder what Phineas is doing now that he's grown."

"If he did inherit his father's power, it's likely he's in the medical profession in one form or other. He'll be drawn to healing."

"He probably isn't aware of his magic," I said. "Without his father to inform him, who will know?"

"He'll get a shock when we tell him."

He sounded so sure that we'd find him that I had to smile and agree. I couldn't bear to see him lose hope entirely. At least we had something to go on, a task to perform next. While I didn't like the idea of breaking into Lady Buckland's house, it did seem like the only course available to us. It was better than sitting idle. While we waited for nightfall, we at least had something to go on with—finding Dr. Millroy's killer. We still needed the diary.

The Bethnal Green shelter was so quiet that we initially thought it closed. Our knock was answered by the bespectacled volunteer we'd met on our first visit. She remembered us —or rather she remembered Matt, if her shy smile and blush were any indication. Thankfully she hadn't been present the night we'd lied our way into the cellar.

"Mr. Woolley is in his office," she said, stepping aside.

"We don't wish to speak to Mr. Woolley," Matt said. "We need to see your records. It's imperative, Miss...?"

"Garnet."

"It's important we check them, Miss Garnet."

"Actually my first name is Garnet."

"I am sorry," Matt said.

"It's an easy mistake to make."

My heart tripped over itself. My God, it was so simple I couldn't believe we hadn't realized we'd made a similar mistake! The vagrant's name wasn't *Mr.* Wilson. His *first* name was Wilson. We'd assumed it was his surname.

"We must see those records, Garnet," Matt went on. His urgency made his voice hard, his eyes harder.

I touched his arm to calm him a little. "Garnet," I said sweetly, "Mr. Woolley has refused us access before, and we don't wish to try that route again. It's much too frustrating, and I know he won't budge. He doesn't care, you see." I thinned my voice and dabbed at the corner of my eyes with my little finger. "He doesn't understand that this is my only way of finding out more about my grandfather. He died a tragic death but we know he spent nights here. He was such a lost, unhappy soul, but he wasn't without family who loved him. It's that family I've been attempting to trace for years. My own branch has lived comfortably, but I know I have cousins who have not, and I'd like to find them and help them if I can. Please, Garnet. Please let me do this for my poor departed grandfather." I thought I acted rather well. I even managed to conjure up real tears. In a way, it wasn't far from the truth—Wilson *had* died tragically and we *were* searching for his family.

Garnet chewed on her lip and glanced toward the door behind her that led to the men's ward. The rectangle of afternoon sunshine fell across the spotless floor tiles, probably scrubbed by Garnet's own hands. Volunteers like her were a marvel, true angels on Earth, helping the helpless and hopeless. I felt a little guilty for lying to her.

I wasn't sure which way she would fall, for or against my plea, and I never got the chance to find out. Matt fished some coins out of his pocket and opened his palm. They were all sovereigns and half sovereigns.

Garnet blinked wide eyes at him.

"A donation," he said.

"Such a generous sum." Garnet hesitated briefly then held out both her hands.

Matt tipped the coins into them. "There's no need to trouble Mr. Woolley."

"I should come with you to make sure…"

"Of course. Shall we?"

She dropped the coins into her apron pocket and led the way. The men's ward was clean and the beds ready for the homeless who would come seeking shelter at nightfall. The door to Mr. Woolley's office was shut, and there were no other volunteers in sight, although a woman's voice came from the adjoining female ward. We exited a door at the back of the vast space and I found myself in the dimly lit corridor that led to the kitchen and cellar.

Garnet opened the door to the cellar and lit the lamp hanging from a hook using the box of matches on the nearby ledge. Closer inspection revealed it to be the lamp we'd left behind in our haste to escape last time.

"His *first* name is Wilson," I whispered to Matt as we followed Garnet down the stairs.

He paused before resuming his pace again. He nodded once and headed directly for the row of filing cabinets. He made a show of reading the labels.

"Sixty-three," he announced for Garnet's benefit.

There were far too many records to search every single one for a man whose first name was Wilson. It would take an hour at least. Garnet would grow suspicious after five minutes. A granddaughter ought to know her grandfather's name. I had to think of something.

"Garnet?" The voice of Mr. Woolley boomed down the

stairwell. "What are you doing? I saw you entering with two people. Who are they? Garnet?"

I froze. Matt, however, worked faster, flicking through the cards.

"The game is up, I'm afraid," Garnet said. "We have to tell him after all. I'm sure he won't mind when he sees your donation." She jiggled the pocket with the coins.

"Just a few minutes," Matt said, his fingers flying through the records.

But a few minutes would not be enough. I touched his arm. "We'll attempt to convince him," I said gently.

"Down here, Mr. Woolley," Garnet called. "I'm helping a young lady find information about her grandfather."

"You're doing *what*?" He trotted down the steps and emerged into our circle of light. He glanced at me then Matt, still rifling through the cards. "You again!"

"I know it's not your policy to allow members of the public down here, Mr. Woolley." Garnet dug some of the coins out of her pocket. "But they offered a generous donation."

"Why didn't you come to see me first before letting them in?" He grabbed Matt's shoulder. "Stop that at once! You can't go through those. It's private information."

"She only wants to find out about her grandfather," Garnet said, no longer sounding sure.

"A likely story." Mr. Woolley grabbed Matt's shoulder again and attempted to wrench him away from the filing cabinet. Matt didn't budge. "Get out before I summon a constable!"

Garnet gasped. I felt sorry for her. We'd put her in an awkward position. But we'd come this far and, like Matt, I didn't want to walk away without answers. We were just too close. Wilson *must* have spent nights here when it was a doss house. It was too unlikely that there'd been another in Bethnal Green.

Desperate times called for desperate actions. I leaned toward Matt. "Get ready to grab and run," I whispered.

His gaze slipped to me. He inclined his head and gathered up a stack of records while blocking Woolley's view with his body.

I placed my hand to my forehead. "Oh dear, I feel faint. All this excitement…" I lurched in Mr. Woolley's direction.

He would have easily caught a slight woman, but my fuller figure worked in my favor for once and he could not hold up against the full force of my weight. He stumbled backward, losing his balance. I would have fallen with him if not for Matt's arm circling my waist. He steadied me and we ran off together, past a flustered Garnet and up the stairs.

"Stop!" Mr. Woolley cried. "They have the records!"

"What does it matter?" Garnet whined. "They're old ones."

We didn't hear if Mr. Woolley answered her. I doubt he told her the real reason he was so protective of the old records —they could prove the shelter and its sponsors were cheating the government out of funds by lying about the number of homeless that came through the doors.

We ran through the men's ward and outside. The day seemed so bright after the dimness of the cellar.

"Home," Matt barked at the coachman. "Drive fast and take an indirect route. Look out for anyone following." He clambered into the carriage after me and thumped on the ceiling before I had the door closed. The coachman took off just as Mr. Woolley emerged from the shelter, shaking his fist.

Matt deposited the armful of cards on the seat beside him and tried to keep them in a neat stack as we turned corners and he peered out the back window.

"Is he following us?" I asked.

"No, nor is Payne that I can see."

I'd forgotten about him. Fortunately Matt had not.

A few blocks later, Matt turned to me. "We're safe." He grinned, banishing the worry and tiredness and making him look so very handsome. "That was your plan, India? To throw yourself at Woolley?"

"To knock him off balance. It worked, didn't it?"

"The margin for error was large."

"As am I. The odds were in my favor."

"You are not large by any stretch of the imagination. You're generous in all the right places." His gaze dipped to one of those places but quickly returned to my face—my *hot* face. He didn't blush at all, merely grinned wider. The devil.

"Did you get them all?" I asked, nodding at the records. There must have been hundreds of the palm-sized cards, yellowed with age, beneath his hand.

"I checked a good number before we were rudely interrupted. These are the remaining ones. At least it'll give us something to do this afternoon while we wait for nightfall."

"I'm still not convinced you should break into Lady Buckland's house."

"I'll go while you're asleep. You won't even be aware of my absence."

"Sleep won't come easily to me tonight, I can assure you. If you had any care for my nerves, you would abandon your scheme."

"Your nerves are stronger than you let on. If they weren't, I wouldn't have told you my plans. Shall I refrain from sharing the details next time?"

He had me there. I'd rather be aware of his activities and worry than be kept in the dark. "Take Duke and Cyclops with you. If Willie goes too, tell her to leave her gun behind."

"There's a good chance she may not be home anyway. She seems to spend much of the time elsewhere lately. Do you think she has a paramour?"

"What other explanation is there?"

"But it's so unlike her to..." He shrugged and did not go on.

"Fall in love?" I offered. "Have tender feelings? It does

seem unlikely, but I do think there's a soft heart beating beneath the prickles. I'm just sorry it's not soft on Duke. He'll be crushed if she casts him aside in favor of her secret lover."

"I'm not sure Duke ever had much of a chance with her."

"Oh? Why not?"

Another shrug. "Just a feeling."

* * *

I EXPECTED a letter from Patience to be waiting for me when we arrived home, but there was no word. I wasn't sure if that was a good thing or bad. Was Patience upset with me for mentioning her past? Was it already too late and Payne had told Lord Cox about her indiscretion? Or did silence mean all was in hand and steps were being taken to protect her reputation? I was wildly curious but could only wait.

Matt and I stacked the records on the large table in the library and then I sent him to his room to rest. Chronos joined me instead, bringing in a plate of sandwiches for the two of us to share.

"Shouldn't you be convalescing?" I asked, plucking the first card off the pile. A name, date of birth, last known address and a list of dates were written in a tight scrawl. The information from the nightly register had been transferred to these cards to monitor the number of times the residents used the shelter, so Mr. Woolley told us. He and his predecessors didn't want the "undeserving" to take advantage.

"I feel well enough to be up and about." Chronos lowered himself onto a chair with a sharp intake of breath. "Besides, Miss Glass doesn't come in here much."

"I thought you enjoyed her company."

He tapped his temple. "She's not all there."

"Only sometimes. At others, she's perfectly normal, if a little snobby. I thought you liked playing poker with her."

"She's too bloody good."

I laughed. "She fleeced you?"

"It's not amusing."

"It is from where I'm sitting." I handed him a card. "Be of use and help me go through these while we eat. You're looking for a man with the first name of Wilson, not last."

He arched a brow. "I hadn't considered that."

"Nor did we until today."

With an egg and cucumber sandwich in one hand, Chronos picked up cards in the other and read each one before setting it aside. I followed suit and we got through most of the pile and all of the sandwiches in twenty minutes. It felt like longer, however, since we did not talk.

"You did a good job with the clocks in the house," he finally said. "They're all working perfectly."

"Thank you. It was nothing."

"Of course I expect them to work well after a powerful magician tinkers with them."

I narrowed my gaze at him. "Is this leading somewhere?"

He smirked. "Clever as well as powerful. Pity you're not a man."

"That's insulting."

He held up his hands. "It's merely an observation. A clever and powerful man can get ahead in the world. He is admired and highly sought after in both his professional and private life. A clever and powerful woman is seen as unnatural by both men and other women."

"Thank you for pointing that out to me. I wasn't aware I was a freak until now."

"There's no need for sarcasm. I didn't say *I* saw you as unnatural."

"I don't care if you do—or if anyone else does, either. I don't see myself that way and nor do my friends."

He nodded slowly, emphatically. "I admire you for that, India. You get that from me. I never cared what others thought either."

"The difference is, you didn't care about others at all. I don't care for opinions, but I don't neglect anyone."

"We're revisiting that argument again, are we?"

I lowered the card I'd been reading. "Why shouldn't we? It's important."

"That's the problem with young people these days. Always blaming the parents for your problems. Grandparents, in this case."

"I'm not blaming you for how my life turned out. I'm blaming you for how poorly you treated my grandmother, your wife. You abandoned her. It's not easy for a woman alone."

"She wasn't alone, she had your parents. And I already told you, she was better off without me. If she were here now, she'd say the same thing. She'd be shooing me out the door, injuries and all, without a care for who waited outside."

I checked the card and set it aside. I reached for the next one at the same time as Chronos and our fingers touched. I quickly withdrew my hand and he plucked off the next card with a sigh.

"Speaking of people waiting for you," I said, "you have to be careful. Don't leave the house at all. Don't even poke your head out the door. Matt has ordered the staff not to mention you to anyone and told them to come to him immediately if someone asks questions about the patient we're harboring."

"Bloody Abercrombie," he growled. "And that fool you almost married."

"It's not just them. The police asked us whether you were still alive and if I'd been in touch with you. Abercrombie must have tipped them off."

He lowered the card. "You won't tell them, will you?"

"Of course not."

"If I go to jail, I'll die there."

"Actually you're more likely to die on the scaffold as a

murderer." I immediately regretted my quip when he paled. "Don't throw up on the cards."

He set down the card and laid his hand over mine. I glanced up at him but regretted making eye contact. He looked too serious, too heartfelt. I preferred the niggling banter. "I want you to know I've made a will and had the butler sign it as my witness. You're named as my heir."

My jaw went slack. "I…I…"

"It's all right." He smiled and patted my hand. "You can continue to scold me, it won't change anything."

"I see."

"Do you?" He sat back, wincing at the pain, and regarded me. "The thing is, I am not dead, which means I still own the shop."

"Everyone thinks you're dead so that is a moot point."

"Several people know I am alive."

"You just told me you have no plans of getting caught and going to jail, which means you have to remain dead, for all intents and purposes."

"Or I could be known to be alive yet escape the authorities and leave the country."

"Impossible," I said, my tone snippy. "It's too much of a risk. You'll continue to be dead as far as the authorities are concerned. It doesn't matter about the shop. I can't sell time-pieces anyway, without guild membership, and the guild are hardly going to allow me in now. Besides, I'm gainfully employed here."

"Until Glass returns to America."

"I'll remain his aunt's companion."

"She's old, India. She won't last forever. You could marry Glass, you know."

I snatched two cards off the dwindling pile and concentrated very hard on the words and numbers.

He sighed. "Very well, be missish about it. The truth is, you might find you need the income a shop will provide." He held up a finger, halting my protest. "The guild may not oppose you forever. Bear that in mind. Even if they do, you don't need guild membership to lease the space to a shop-keeper. It doesn't even have to be someone in the clock trade. The space could serve a variety of retailers, and I own the premises."

"I'm not sure if your will would be accepted by the courts, considering you're supposed to be dead. Eddie will contest it and I don't know if I have the inclination to fight it, or the money for a lawyer."

He tossed the cards he was holding away. "So you won't even try? I thought you better than that, India. I thought you had a sense of justice and a spine for battle. I see I'm wrong."

"What I have is common sense. I know when to back away from something that could drag through the courts for years. Haven't you read *Bleak House*?"

"That was written years ago, and Dickens exaggerated for the sake of a good story." He took another card from the stack. "My will is written, and I'll have Glass lodge it with his lawyer. When the time comes, you can do what you want with the information. I'm not going to care, am I?" he bit off.

Duke, Cyclops and Willie entered, and I greeted them weakly. Perhaps I shouldn't have been so hard with Chronos. He was trying to make things right with me, in his own way. He didn't have to make a will in my favor.

"What have you got there?" Cyclops asked, nodding at the cards now spread across the table.

"We're looking for a man with a first name of Wilson." I eyed the thin pile of remaining cards. There were only a dozen or so. "This is our last chance of locating the man Chronos and Millroy experimented on. If this yields no result, we may have to give up on finding out more about him and any family he may have left behind."

"There are still other avenues," Duke said with a questioning look at me. "Still other things we can do to find the killer. Right?"

"We'll think of something." I didn't sound convincing and he didn't look convinced.

Cyclops and Willie inspected the pile of cards. Then they both dove for the topmost one at the same time.

"Here!" Willie cried, doing a tug of war with Cyclops. "This is him! Wilson! Give it to me, Cyclops."

He let go and peered over her shoulder.

"God damn," Willie muttered. She stared at me, her mouth open and her eyes wide.

"What is it?" I said, springing up and grabbing it from her. "What does it say?"

"It says 'Mr. Wilson Sweet,'" she said at the same time as I read the words. "'Last known address: Bright Court, Whitechapel.'"

CHAPTER 16

"What do you think the chances are that he was Nell Sweet's brother?" I asked Matt as he read over the card. Willie had insisted on waking him, despite my protests. He'd napped for half an hour—hopefully it was enough. He did look refreshed, but the brightness in his eyes could have been due to our breakthrough.

"Very high." He slapped the card against his palm. "Very high indeed."

The others agreed. Chronos even thumped his fist on the table in victory. But I was beginning to have doubts. Nell Sweet hadn't struck me as a murderess. On the other hand, twenty-seven years was a long time. Perhaps she'd changed, as Lady Buckland had changed.

"She killed Dr. Millroy in revenge and stole his belongings to make it look like he'd been murdered for his possessions," Matt said.

"Except the pencil," Willie said.

Matt strode to the door. "Come on, India, let's pay her another visit."

I rushed after him and caught up to him in the entrance hall. "Nell told us her brother was gone, not dead."

Matt sent Peter to inform the coachman that we were in need of the carriage again. "She was lying," he then said to me.

"I agree." Willie plucked her hat off the hat stand and slapped it on her head. "She must be lying. Don't feel bad that you're wrong, India. You know you ain't good at understanding people."

I thrust my hand on my hip but Duke came to my rescue before I could think of a retort.

"She understands that *you're* rude, Willemina Johnson."

Cyclops held up a hand to each of them to keep them apart. "Let's not judge until we speak to her."

Matt accepted his coat from Bristow. "Agreed. I take it you're all coming with us."

"Aye," chimed three voices.

Chronos merely sighed. "Think I'll go back to the library and read."

"Bristow, ask Miss Glass to keep Chronos company in the library," I said. "Tell her he'd like to play poker."

Chronos shot me a withering glare over his shoulder as he retreated.

* * *

MARY, the partially deaf maid, answered Matt's fierce knocks eventually and after three shouts from Nell to "Get the door!" She took one look at the five of us and attempted to shut it again. Matt thrust out his arm and muscled his way in.

"Stop, sir!" Mary cried. "I been told not to let you in!"

Matt ignored her and led the way to Nell's bedroom. The others followed but I felt compelled to comfort the poor maid. "We just want to talk to your mistress. No one will get hurt."

Matt's angry roar did nothing to support my promise. I left Mary and followed the noise.

"Keep it down," I hushed Matt. "You're scaring Mary and probably alarming the neighbors."

"I don't think the neighbors round here are unused to shouts," Willie said. "Nor murder, neither."

Nell whimpered in the bed and pulled the blanket to her chin. "I ain't done nothing, Mrs. Wright."

"My name is in fact India Steele," I said. "We used false names last time. This is Mr. Glass, my employer."

"I don't care who you are. Just keep him away from me. Keep him away!" She screwed up her eyes tight.

"No one will be hurt," I repeated. "But you must answer some questions we have about...about your brother's murder," I said at the last moment. Perhaps steering the discussion away from Dr. Millroy would get her to trust us if she was indeed guilty.

Matt closed his fists at his sides and lowered his head. He was frustrated, no doubt wanting answers immediately, now that we were so close to finding the diary. He would have to wait. He couldn't beat answers out of an old lady, even if she were a murderess. It was a pity his charm seemed to have deserted him. I would have to try instead.

Nell opened one eye, saw that Matt wasn't standing over her anymore, and sat up. "My brother left me. You telling me he's dead?"

"You know he is," Duke said.

I shook my head at Duke and he clamped his lips shut. "We know Wilson was the subject of a medical experiment that went wrong," I said. Nell did not look surprised or try to refute my claim. "He died in Dr. Millroy's surgery," I forged on. "A few days later, Dr. Millroy decided to find out if the man he thought was homeless and alone in fact had a family. That led him here, to you." I went to sit on the edge of the bed but Matt pulled me roughly back, out of her reach. Did he think she would attack me? She was bedridden, for goodness' sake.

"You couldn't quite believe what Dr. Millroy told you, could you?" I went on. "You'd finally had word about your missing brother, after he walked out on you, only to be informed of his death, which came at the hand of the man who brought the news. Did Dr. Millroy offer his sincerest apologies and perhaps money to compensate for your loss? Is that what happened, Mrs. Sweet?"

"It's *Miss* Sweet." She sniffed and wiped her nose on her shoulder. "The doctor came here, that much is true. All sorrowful about what he'd done, like you say. He gave me all the money he had on him. It weren't much, what with my baby starving and me not able to find the good customers like Wilson could. He had a knack for finding 'em, he did. I couldn't, not when I had to stay here and take care of my Jack."

"So you killed the doctor when he left," Willie said. "Out of revenge for killing your brother."

Nell pushed herself forward and stabbed a shaky finger at Willie. "A *man* killed him! You ask around. There was a witness, a boy. He'll tell you. A man was seen leaving Bright Court, not a woman. Go on. Go ask him."

"He's dead," Matt said.

"His sister ain't. Ask her. Them two were thick as thieves, the little beggars. He would have told her everything he saw that night. She lives here still. Go on, ask!"

Maisie had already told us the same thing. Her brother had seen a man walk away from the scene. So if it wasn't Nell, then the police must have been right all along, and it was just an opportunistic theft that ended up in murder. No belongings had been found on Millroy's person, so theft was a certainty. It was disheartening. We'd taken several small steps forward only to be shoved back to the starting line. Matt, however, had a curious look in his eyes.

"Women can dress as men," Willie said, indicating her own attire.

Nell wrinkled her nose. "Thought you were a pretty boy."

"Boys don't have Colts." Willie opened her coat to reveal the gun strapped to her hip.

I groaned. We'd forgotten to check her for weapons in our rush to leave.

Nell sank into the pillow, pulling the covers up. "He was tall," she said quickly. "Go ask Maisie, she'll tell you what her brother saw. The man leaving here was tall. I ain't tall. If one of you helps me up, I can show you."

Matt took my hand. "India, come with me. The three of you stay here. Willie, don't shoot anyone."

"Damn it," Willie muttered.

Matt and I almost bumped into Mary standing in the hall, wringing her hands in her apron. She shied away from us and lifted the apron to her mouth to cover her gasp.

"It's all right, Mary," I said, patting her shoulder. "No one will come to harm." I hoped I sounded convincing. I wasn't entirely sure of anyone's safety now that I'd seen Willie's gun.

Outside, Matt nodded in the direction of the copper sitting idle over a brazier. The last time we'd come to Bright Court, a woman had stood there doing laundry. She'd told us that Maisie couldn't be believed.

I clutched Matt's arms, turning him to face me. "I know what you're going to tell me," I said, unable to keep the excitement out of my voice. "Maisie's a liar."

That quirk of a smile appeared again, I was pleased to see. I thought his hope had vanished entirely. "Let's find out, shall we?"

We'd seen Maisie's children when we entered Bright Court, and the squabbling siblings could now be heard through the thin walls of their tenement. Matt knocked but it was some time before Maisie answered the door. Tired eyes flared momentarily upon seeing us but quickly faded again.

She folded her arms over her chest. "What do you want?"

"I want the truth this time," Matt said. "What did your brother really see the night Dr. Millroy died?"

"I ain't got nothing more to add to what I already told you." She went to shut the door but Matt wedged his foot in the gap.

He pulled coins out of his pocket. "The truth, Maisie."

She eyed the coins and licked her lips, as if she could taste the food they could buy. Then she glanced past him to Nell's door and shook her head. No one living in a miserable Whitechapel tenement with hungry mouths to feed refused money unless they were scared.

"Nell paid your brother to lie to the police, didn't she?" Matt pressed. "He witnessed her kill Dr. Millroy so she paid him to make up the story about seeing a tall man leave. She threatened him too, didn't she?"

She pushed against the door but Matt still held it open.

"There's no need to fear Nell now," I told her. "She's an old woman. She can't harm you."

"It's not Nell what worries me," she said, some of the wind knocked out of her sails. "It's her son."

"Has he threatened you lately?" Matt asked.

She hesitated then nodded.

"Do you know where he lives or works?"

She shook her head. "He comes here sometimes to visit her. He brings money and sweets. He's good to her but he hates visiting. He thinks he's above us because he left here and got all respectable. But he ain't better than us. He's the lowest of the low." Her mouth attempted a grin but she must have been out of practice because it was twisted, strained. "He might look like an angel but he's an abomination."

"Abomination?" I prompted.

Her lips flattened. "I've said too much. Leave me be." She put out her palm and Matt paid her, despite not receiving direct answers to his questions.

He stepped back and she slammed the door in his face.

"It's as much of an answer as we needed," he said. "The boy lied. Nell lied."

We trudged back across the court to Nell's house and let ourselves in. Mary still stood in the hall outside Nell's room, and she still looked scared out of her wits. I couldn't blame her. Fury darkened Matt's face. If I didn't know him, I'd be scared too.

He marched into the bedroom. "I know you killed Dr. Millroy," he said, his voice pitched low. Beside me, Mary leaned forward, straining to hear. "I don't care that you killed him, Nell. I just want his diary."

I could not see Nell's reaction from where I stood and all I could hear was silence.

"Where is it?" Matt growled.

"I don't have it," Nell shot back.

"Did you throw it out? Burn it?"

"I don't have it," Nell said, louder. "I can't remember what I did with it."

"Duke, Cyclops, help me turn the place inside out. Willie, don't let Nell out of that bed."

Mary blinked teary eyes at me. "What's happening? What are they doing?"

I linked my arm with hers. "Come with me to the kitchen and we'll make tea."

"Oi!" Nell cried. "What're you doing? Leave my things alone, you bloody pirate!"

We left the sounds of the search behind and entered the kitchen. It appeared to serve a dual purpose as Mary's bedroom. A small bed, which didn't look big enough for her, was tucked into the corner, a carpet bag at its foot probably housing the maid's meager possessions. The bed was made neatly, and every surface of the kitchen had been scrubbed clean. The beginnings of a meal were being assembled on the table.

She put the kettle on the stove with shaking hands and

produced cups made from good china, better than I expected to see in a Whitechapel kitchen. But each one had a chip or crack and there were only three. It didn't matter. The others would not be having tea.

"Tell me about Nell," I said. She didn't hear me at first, so I laid my hand on her arm and repeated myself when she looked at me. She was young, probably not even twenty, and her hearing difficulty must be an impediment to finding better work.

"She's not so bad, now she don't get out of bed much," Mary said with a glance toward the door. "I take care of her, do the washing, help her in and out of bed, cook and clean. She don't eat much so there ain't a lot to do. I just got to be company for her."

"Does she have many visitors?"

"Just Mr. Sweet, her son. She ain't got no friends and the neighbors don't call."

"Tell me about Mr. Sweet."

"He ain't so bad. He don't take his liberties with me like my last employer, and he don't beat me. He's nice to look at too." She smiled. "Miss Sweet tells me he gets his looks from his father, but I hear she were pretty in her day too, all fair hair and good bones."

"Where is it?" Matt's shout echoed down the corridor to us.

Mary shrank into herself, and no amount of comforting brought her out again. Not when sounds of the search came closer. When Cyclops reached us, Mary whimpered at the sight of him.

"Let's take the tea into Miss Sweet's room," I said cheerfully. I helped her assemble the tea things on a tray and carried it to the bedroom.

She stuck closely to my heels and jumped at the slamming of a drawer.

"This ain't right," Nell protested as we entered. "It's a cruel way to treat an old lady. You get your man to stop this instant, Miss, or I'll scream the place down until the constables get here."

"I'm sure the police will be happy to hear that you killed Dr. Millroy twenty-seven years ago," I said.

Mary gasped. Fortunately she had not been holding the tray or she probably would have dropped it. "Killed?"

"Be quiet, you stupid girl," Nell spat. "Pour the tea. Where's my flask? For God's sake, Mary, my flask!"

Mary went to leave again but Matt blocked her exit. "No one leaves this room until we've finished our search." He looked to Willie. She gave him a nod and then he left.

"Sit on the bed, Mary," I said, patting the mattress near Nell's feet. "It'll be all right. It's almost over."

They'd finished searching the bedroom, leaving only us four women. They'd left the room as neat and tidy as when we'd entered, although the rumpled bedcovers were an indication of their thoroughness.

"Have you ever seen a diary here?" I asked Mary.

She shook her head. Nell had not threatened or prompted her. If the maid hadn't seen it then it was very well hidden or it was no longer here.

My heart sank. The possibility that it had been destroyed was high.

"All this trouble," Nell grumbled into her teacup. "My bloody useless brother is dead and he's still causing me grief."

Useless. She'd used that word to describe her son's father too. Perhaps it was a coincidence, and she'd had two useless men in her life back then, but I wasn't one to put much stock in coincidence. But if not a coincidence, then her brother and the father of her son were one and the same.

They'd committed incest and the result had been the child, Jack.

I pressed a hand to my stomach, feeling somewhat ill at the thought. I pushed the nausea aside and tried to think.

Maisie had called Jack an abomination. Because she knew, or suspected, he was the result of incest?

Nell told Mary her son was fair and handsome like his father, and yet she'd been fair and handsome herself. Perhaps brother and sister looked alike so naturally their child inherited those traits.

Could that be why Wilson Sweet left? Could he have felt guilt, or disgust, at his own actions? The birth of their child could have brought on all manner of emotions, driving him to lose his mind and walk away. That's why there was some confusion about whether he still had a family or not. He did, but he'd chosen to distance himself from them.

"Miss?" Mary said, peering closely at me. "You all right? You look white as a sheet."

"We need that diary," I said weakly to Nell. "If we don't get it, someone close to me will die. The secret formula for a medicine is in there, one that Dr. Millroy perfected and wrote down. If we can't make that medicine..." I choked on the clog of tears in my throat. "Please. Did you destroy the diary?"

Something in my voice or words must have got through the hard shell Nell had built around herself. Her face softened, her gaze lowered. Her hands trembled so much the cup and saucer were in danger of developing another chip.

"It's not destroyed but it's not here," she said.

I almost cried in relief. "Where is it?"

She shook her head and tried to sip but spilled the tea over the sides of the cup.

Willie pulled out her gun. Mary screamed, and I quickly wrapped my arm around her shoulders and shushed her until she quieted.

Matt came running. "Willie! Lower your weapon!"

"She says it's not here," Willie said, not putting the gun away or taking her eyes off Nell. "So where is it? Where's the diary?"

"I won't say." Nell thrust out her chin. "So shoot me. Go on."

Willie cocked the gun. "Why do you care so much about the goddamned diary?"

"She doesn't," I said. "It's not the diary she's protecting."

"It's her son," Matt said, entering the room.

Nell wasn't very good at hiding her reactions and she gave her answer away with a twitch of her shoulders and a sharp intake of breath. She was protecting Jack. "I ain't," she said, not convincing me.

"Where is he?" Matt pressed. "Where can we find him?"

Nell made a great show of setting her teacup in the saucer. "Like I said, I ain't telling you nothing."

Matt slammed the wall, punching a hole through the plaster. "Where the hell is he?"

Nell just smiled.

I circled the whimpering maid in my arm. "Mary, you must tell us where to find Jack Sweet. You will be protected. Mr. Glass will give you gainful employment in his Mayfair house if you help us."

"I don't know where he is, miss," she wailed, tears streaming down her plump cheeks. "He lives at his shop, but it could be anywhere in the city."

"Mary," Nell snapped. "Don't tell them nothing."

If Nell needed to warn Mary to stop, what more did the maid know? I glanced at Matt, but he was in no state to think clearly. He was a tower of fury, his eyes cold, the planes of his face hard as rock. I had to do the thinking for him.

"What sort of shop does Mr. Sweet have?" I asked the maid.

She looked to her mistress but I caught the maid's face and forced her to look only at me. Her entire body trembled and the tears continued. She was terrified. Of Nell? Jack? Or us?

"Listen to me, Mary. When we leave here, you will come with us and bring your things. Mr. Glass will employ you and you never have to see these people again. Is that understood? Your wages will be better, the conditions better, and you'll share a room with our other maid. You can make friends there. Do you understand? You'll be safe and have a chance of a better life than you have here. Now, tell me what else you know about Mr. Sweet's whereabouts. We *have* to find him and that diary or my friend will die."

Nell threw the teacup and saucer at me. Tea splashed over my dress and the saucer smacked my shoulder. The cup fell in my lap. I calmly picked them up and handed them to Matt, who'd rushed to my side. He looked in utter turmoil. If a man had thrown something at me, he would have punched him. But he could do nothing to Nell.

I wasn't so sure Willie's morals were as strong. She pointed her gun at Nell. "Don't move again."

"Don't listen to the bitch," Nell spat at Mary. "You stay here. I saved you, girl. Remember that. I saved you and gave you a job here when no one else would."

"You don't pay me," Mary whispered.

"What?" Nell shook her head, confused.

"You don't pay me," Mary said, louder. "Mr. Sweet did, at first, but then he stopped. He told me I got a roof over my head and food, and I should be lucky I had that much."

Nell stared at her, her jaw slack. "I have money. Take it! Take it! Tell them nothing."

Mary accepted the handkerchief from Matt and dried her cheeks. "All I know about where Mr. Sweet lives is that he has some rooms above his shop."

"We already know that," Willie ground out.

I glared at her and she pressed her lips together. "Anything else?" I asked Mary gently. "Do you know if he needs to get an omnibus here from the shop or can he walk?"

She shook her head.

Willie huffed out a breath. Matt rubbed his jaw with his closed fist.

"Miss Sweet says her son likes to fix things," I said. "Is that what he does in his shop? Fix things?"

She nodded. "And sell them too."

"What sort of things?"

"Watches and clocks."

My arms fell away from her. I reeled back and blinked hard.

And then I got the oddest sensation in the pit of my stomach. It was part horror, part disbelief, but also a curious sense of triumph. The more I thought through the facts we knew about Nell's son, the more the pieces fitted together.

"You know who it is, India." Matt was at my side, his hand on the back of my neck. It was then that I noticed my rapid breathing, my hot skin.

"When did Mr. Sweet begin to give his mother money, sweets and trinkets?" I asked Mary.

"About two months ago, at the start of spring. When he went from being an apprentice to owning the shop."

Guessing was one thing, but having my suspicions confirmed was entirely another. My chest constricted. I couldn't breathe. I reached out for balance and found Matt, solid and comforting with a look of pure shock on his face.

He'd realized too.

"Well?" Willie prompted. "Who is he? *Where* is he?"

"They don't know." Nell snorted. "They don't know a bloody thing." But the slump of her shoulders told another story. She knew we'd guessed, but she couldn't possibly know how we knew her son. I'd used my real name and it had meant nothing to her. Eddie hadn't told his mother he'd been engaged to an India Steele and inherited his shop from my father. He hadn't told his mother that he'd changed his name, lied, cheated and tricked us.

And it was only just dawning on me why he had done all those things.

I shivered.

The front door opened and a voice I knew too well called, "Ma?"

"Run, Jack!" Nell shouted. "Run away now!"

Matt sprinted out of the bedroom but the front door had already slammed. The lock tumbled.

"Damn it!" Matt roared, thumping on the door. "Damn it to hell."

CHAPTER 17

$\mathcal{B}$y the time Mary fetched another key and opened the front door, Jack Sweet—also known as Eddie Hardacre—was gone. Even so, Matt, Willie, Cyclops and Duke ran out of Bright Court after him.

Mary and I carried her carpet bag to the conveyance and the coachman had just finished strapping it to the back when the others returned.

"St. Martin's Lane near Covent Garden," Matt barked at the coachman. "And quickly. Everyone, get in and hold on. Not you, Mary." Matt placed some money in her palm. "Take a hack to number sixteen Park Street, Mayfair. Tell Mrs. Bristow the housekeeper that I sent you. We'll bring your bag with us when we return."

I only had time to squeeze her hand before Matt hoisted me into the carriage without bothering to lower the step.

"I don't goddamned believe it," Willie declared with a shake of her head. She'd joined us inside, along with Duke, while Cyclops rode with the coachman up front. "That low down pig swill."

"I don't know how you worked it out," Duke said to us.

"There were small clues," Matt said, "but it wasn't until Mary mentioned watches and clocks."

"So let me see if I got it right," Duke said slowly. "Eddie Hardacre—Jack—knew that Chronos was your grandfather, India, and that he had a hand in killing his father all them years ago?"

"His father *and* his uncle," Willie said, incredulous.

"Huh?" It took Duke a moment to digest her meaning. When he reached the right conclusion his face distorted into a grimace. "Goddamn. The Sweets make you Johnsons look normal."

I turned to look out the window and didn't see Willie's reaction.

"So Jack Sweet planned his revenge on Chronos by getting the shop," Duke went on. "But if he thought Chronos was dead, why bother? It ain't like he could rub it in his face."

"Perhaps he knew he wasn't dead," Matt said. "Or perhaps he didn't care if he had an audience, it was enough that *he* felt he'd got revenge."

"He must be behind the recent attack on Chronos. But how did he know Chronos was alive and back in London, or that he was staying with you, India? How'd he even know what Chronos looked like if he's never met him?"

"All questions we'll ask when we catch him," Matt said darkly. "If I don't kill him first."

My eyes burned with unshed tears. It seemed implausible, fantastical even, that Eddie had planned his revenge over such a long time, particularly when my grandfather might never learn about it. He'd been my father's apprentice for years. He'd taken his time to win my father's trust, to woo me and ingratiate himself with Abercrombie. Why not just kill my father or me and be done with it? Chronos caused the death of his father, why not then kill one of Chronos's family in return?

"I underestimated him badly," I muttered. "I should have

guessed. Even Chronos said that Eddie must be clever to dupe Father and convince me to marry him."

"You wanted to believe he loved you and cared for you." Willie's sympathetic tone was almost my undoing.

But it was Matt's arm around my shoulders and his warm lips against my temple that sent the tears trickling down my cheeks. I swiped them away with the back of my gloved hand. I'd stopped crying over Eddie months ago. I refused to start again now.

"Let's hope we get to the shop before he does," I said. "We have to find that diary before he destroys it."

"He doesn't know we want it." Matt didn't sound entirely convinced, however. He fell into silence, perhaps thinking over every recent encounter we'd had with Eddie and his mother.

"We didn't mention it to Nell until today," I said. "He knows we want to find Dr. Millroy's killer, but he can't know why."

"He might have guessed," Duke suggested.

That was entirely possible if Jack Sweet was as smart as I now knew him to be.

The familiar sights and sounds in St. Martin's Lane did nothing to soothe my nerves. Mr. Finlay, the draper, stood outside his shop, hawking a discounted bolt of cotton, while Mr. Macklefield the tailor held a conversation with a gentleman. He saw me and his jaw dropped. He did not wave back when I lifted my hand in greeting.

Jimmy the errand boy appeared from behind the chop house's sign board where he'd probably been lounging in the sun. He trotted over to me upon my signal.

"Miss Steele," he said, tugging on his cap brim. "Been some time since we saw you."

"I'm glad to see you looking well, Jimmy. Can you tell me, have you seen Mr. Hardacre these past few minutes? Is he inside? The shop looks closed."

"Aye, it is. Ain't seen him for an hour, I reckon. He ain't been here much, lately. That sign says closed more than it says open. Mr. Finlay reckons he'll shut it up, soon enough. Real shame that would be, Miss Steele. Real shame."

I gave him a coin from my reticule. "Thank you, Jimmy."

I rejoined Matt and the others and told them Eddie wasn't in. "We can enter from the back," I said.

"You've got a key?" Duke asked.

Willie and Cyclops looked at him like he was a fool.

"Right," Duke said. "We're breaking in."

"Everyone will see." Willie eyed Mr. Finlay and Mr. Macklefield. "They'll put the law onto us."

Matt glanced at the coach, the lane, then back at the coach. "Not if they think we've left." He spoke to the coachman then rejoined us. "India, you'll ride up front. We four will get inside."

"Why?" I hedged.

"Because having one of us leave with the coach will make it look more authentic, and I'd prefer it if you weren't performing a criminal act."

"You're forgetting two things." I held up a finger. "It will look odd for me to be banished to the driver's seat." I held up a second finger. "And I know the best way inside that doesn't involve breaking windows or doors."

Matt turned to Willie.

"Why me?" She threw up her hands. "Duke, you go."

"No!" he snapped.

"Duke, go," Matt ordered.

"But why?" he whined.

"Because if I make Willie, I'll never hear the end of it."

Duke sighed and climbed up beside the coachman. Matt gave his final instructions then stepped into the coach with Cyclops, Willie and me. He closed the curtains and we drove forward ten feet, only to stop at the entrance to the laneway.

The coach sank on one side as the driver got down from his perch.

"We'll be off in a minute, sir," he called out, loud enough for Mr. Finlay and Mr. Macklefield on the other side of the road to hear. "One of the horses seems to be limping."

Matt opened the door a fraction, peered out, then opened it fully. He jumped down and assisted me, his hands on my waist. There was no time to enjoy the sensation of his firm hold as we raced off up the lane, shielded from view by the coach. Willie and Cyclops followed close behind.

We didn't see anyone as we unlatched the gate that led to the small courtyard behind the shop. Matt, the last to go through the gate, signaled to Duke, still on the driver's seat. A moment later, the gate closed and I heard the coach drive off.

Little had changed in the yard. There was only one empty delivery crate instead of three, and a pile of soggy newspapers rotting in the corner. In his later years, as my father's eyesight deteriorated, I took over the fine work of repairs inside while he swept the yard each morning. It didn't look like it had been swept since Eddie moved in.

"The latch on that window is loose," I said, pointing. If Eddie neglected the cleaning, perhaps he'd neglected to do repairs too. "If you can reach it, you only need to jiggle it a little to open it."

"I'll try," Willie said with glee. "Been a long time since I climbed through a window. I need the practice."

Cyclops lifted her up, and she had the window open in seconds. She wriggled inside and unlocked the door moments later. She stood there, beaming.

"That weren't much of a challenge, India," she said.

I patted her shoulder as I slipped past. "Then next time you can climb through a window on the second level."

I led the way through to the workshop and drew the smell of metal and polished wood into my lungs. The scent almost undid me. It was the scent of my childhood. It was the scent that enveloped me when my father drew me into his arms. It was the scent of safety and home.

But this was no longer my home. Not this messy workshop with the tools left out and a clock's innards spread over the bench. I scooped the scattered pieces together and went to return a pair of pliers to the toolbox, but caught Willie's narrowed gaze and put it down again.

"You ain't here to tidy up," she hissed. "You and Matt look upstairs. Me and Cyclops will search down here."

"Don't go into the shop unless necessary," Matt ordered. "You might be seen from the street."

I led the way up the stairs to the apartment I'd lived in my entire life. It seemed so small after Matt's house, with its one bedroom, a sitting room that we'd used as a second bedroom, and kitchen. We hadn't felt the need for more space since my father and I spent most of our day downstairs.

Eddie had returned the sitting room to its former use but furnished it with only a faded green leather armchair and a small table. He'd left my framed embroidery sampler on the wall and my mother's two vases stood at either end of the mantel, empty of flowers. I also recognized the rug, but it was somewhat filthy with crumbs scattered over it. A dirty plate and cup occupied the table, but there was no other sign that Eddie had made this a home. Even the clock on the mantel was one that we used to display in the window downstairs. It was the loveliest twin fusee skeleton clock, one of the most expensive pieces in the shop, and he'd brought it up here where no one but him could admire it.

"Are you all right?" Matt asked, touching my elbow.

I nodded. "We need to hurry."

We searched the kitchen quickly then Matt moved on to the bedroom while I looked through the sitting room. I skimmed my hand over the spines of the books in the narrow bookcase and tried not to let the emotions overwhelm me.

"Where are you going?" I asked as Matt walked out of the bedroom.

"The kitchen for a knife to cut open the mattress."

I resumed my search of the bookshelves, reading each of the spines with my head tilted. I recognized every book —except one.

It sat on the lowest shelf, out of place between a volume of poetry and a weighty tome on the history of clocks. I slid it out, my heart racing, and traced the gold initials embossed in the soft black leather cover.

J.M.—James Millroy. Eddie had hidden the book in plain sight.

"Matt! Matt! I found it."

He suddenly appeared at my side. I waved the diary at him and could not stop my smile.

He flipped through the pages, his face lifting in relief. Then he snapped it closed and clutched the book to his chest. "Let's go home."

We returned to the workshop and gathered the others on our way out. No one saw us leave the courtyard or run down the lane in the opposite direction to which we'd entered it. Duke and the coachman waited at the other end.

"Home," Matt ordered, opening the door for me. He showed Duke the diary.

Duke looked like he would cry before sucking in a deep breath and directing his gaze forward.

Once ensconced inside and on our way, Matt opened the diary on his lap. We all leaned closer. "It's mostly medical notes," he said, turning the yellowing pages.

"His thoughts on new treatments and medical break-throughs," I added, pointing to a detailed diagram of the inner workings of an arm.

"Some of it's not in English," Cyclops said. "Could they be spells?"

Matt shook his head. "They're Latin terms used in the medical profession."

"Go to the last pages," Willie said. "He died soon after the experiment so the spell might be there."

Matt flipped to the final pages. The last several in the diary were blank, but those beforehand were packed with a tight scrawl to make efficient use of the remaining pages.

"Here." Matt's hand flattened out the spine. "He mentions Wilson Sweet."

I leaned closer again, my shoulder against his, and read the text.

"What's it say?" Cyclops asked, turning to read better.

"That Wilson Sweet was ill with no hope of a medical cure," Matt read. "And that he told Dr. Millroy he had a son by his sister. He felt so ashamed of his actions that he left them to do penance."

"Do penance?" Willie echoed.

"He must mean participating in the experiment," I said.

"Wilson Sweet believed he was doing something for the greater good," Matt said. "Something that would absolve him of his sin." Matt pointed to where Dr. Millroy had written those exact words.

"He told Dr. Millroy that he would contact his family again if he lived," I said, reading over Matt's shoulder.

"That it?" Willie asked after a pause. "Does it say Millroy planned to visit Nell after the death?"

"No." Matt turned the previous page, working backward through the diary. He pointed out Chronos's name. It was the first time the two men had met and Millroy wrote in excited terms about the possibilities of collaboration. The word magic was not mentioned, nor that they hoped to extend life through their experiment. It was vague enough so that it could not implicate him if read by the guilds.

Matt turned the page backward again and his finger stabbed on a few lines half way down a page. "This…" His fingers skimmed over the lines. "This isn't in any language I recognize."

Cyclops and Willie both got off their seat and twisted to read the words. Willie let out a *whoop*. "That must be it! That's the spell, Matt!" She clamped a hand on Cyclops's shoulder. Cyclops hugged her.

The coach turned a corner and they both sat heavily on the seat again, laughing.

"Now all we need is a doctor magician to speak it while you recite your spell, India." There was no elation in Matt's voice. He would not whoop or hug or allow himself to get excited. Nor would I. Not when the job was only half done. Besides, it wasn't just a matter of speaking the spell but speaking it correctly. Dr. Parsons had got the pronunciation right, but Dr. Millroy had not. The difference between living and dying came down to mere syllables.

"What do we do about Nell?" Cyclops asked. "Tell Munro and Brockwell she murdered Millroy?"

"I'm inclined to say no," Matt said. "She poses no threat to the community now, and explaining the motive would only raise questions we're not prepared to answer."

"It would also drag Chronos into it," I said. "At the moment, they don't have evidence that Chronos is alive, or that he's in fact my grandfather, merely accusations from Abercrombie. But confronting Nell and Eddie will bring the truth out."

"Speaking of Hardacre," Willie said with a loaded glance at me.

I sighed. "Go on. Out with it. I know you want to tell me how foolish I've been, how naive. You might as well get it off your chest."

"That ain't what I'm thinking. What I want to know is if Eddie didn't go to the shop, where is he?"

"Running away?" Cyclops said with a shrug.

Matt suddenly swore then threw down the window sash. "Faster!" he shouted at the driver.

My heart tumbled over itself. I knew where Eddie had gone too.

"You think he's gone to our house to get Chronos," Cyclops said, half statement, half question.

Matt nodded. "It's likely he's behind the attack on Chronos, and he knows he's living with us."

"And he's been bent on revenge for some time," I added weakly. "Now that we know the lengths he has gone to, there's no reason for him to hold back. He'll go after Chronos and...and kill him, this time."

And thanks to our stop at the shop, we would be some way behind.

It wasn't just Chronos at home, however. There was Miss Glass and the servants too.

Matt sandwiched my hand between both of his. "He won't hurt anyone. He wouldn't dare."

I did not agree. Eddie was beyond caring what happened to him. He knew the game was over. Diabolically clever men like Eddie tended to resort to desperate measures when they were backed into a corner. I'd witnessed it too many times to assume otherwise.

Dusk made visibility low, but I recognized the Wellington Arch easily enough through the hazy evening light. I thumped on the ceiling and the coach immediately slowed in response.

"What're you doing?" Willie cried. "We got to get home!"

"Tell the driver to stop," I told Matt. "We can't return unprepared."

He lowered the window and called out to the driver to find a place to pull over. "Willie, is your gun loaded?" he asked.

"Course," she said. "Ain't no use if it ain't."

"Good. It's the only firearm we have."

"I've got knives here," Cyclops tapped his forearm, "and here." He lifted his trouser leg to show us the blade strapped there.

My eyes widened. "You walk around wearing those?"

"I'd be a fool not to."

I looked to Matt. He pulled up his jacket sleeve and showed me the small knife. "There have been too many dangers, of late. I prefer to be armed and ready for any eventuality."

"Hence my Colt." Willie patted the gun strapped to her hip.

If I ever doubted that I associated with Wild West outlaws, those doubts were banished now.

The coach stopped and Duke opened the door. "What's all this then?"

"We think Hardacre might have gone to our house to find Chronos," Matt told him. "We need to approach him carefully and with a plan of attack."

"Jesus," he muttered. "What if Chronos is already dead? What then?"

I bit the inside of my cheek until I tasted blood. No one spoke but I guessed Matt must have glared at him because Duke winced and apologized.

"It's a distinct possibility," I said. "And that's why we need to have a plan for multiple eventualities. I propose that only Matt and I return to the house openly. The rest of you return in secret."

Ten minutes later, we had more than one plan in place. Which one we followed depended on what scenario presented upon our arrival.

Matt and I drove off, leaving the other three to walk. We'd agreed on most points of the plan, but the one thing we'd disagreed on was the possession of Willie's gun. I thought Matt ought to have it, but no one else supported me. Willie's opposition was most vocal of all.

The coach stopped in its usual position at the front steps of the townhouse. I clutched my watch and Matt tucked the diary into his jacket pocket. We both preferred to have our most valued possessions on our person.

"It's not too late to change your mind," Matt said. "You know I'd prefer it if you did."

"I have my watch at hand," I said. "I'll be fine. It's you who are unarmed except for that little knife."

He smirked. "You mean my charming character won't be enough?"

"Not on Eddie."

He got out first and lowered the step for me then assisted me out. The front door to the townhouse remained shut, a telling sign. Usually Bristow or Peter greeted us.

"My guess is he's here," Matt murmured. He signaled for the coachman to drive on then offered me his arm.

We walked up the steps together. My watch chimed once in warning. My heart raced but I didn't pause. Matt pushed open the door and angled his body to shield me before I could squeeze past him. I'd planned to enter ahead of him since the watch was a good weapon. Clearly he decided to ignore that plan. I refrained from digging my elbow into his ribs as a reminder. We could not afford the distraction.

"Bristow?" Matt called out. "Peter?"

"In here, sir," came Bristow's strained voice from the drawing room. "Don't come near! He's got a—" His warning ended with a groan.

A woman screamed.

Matt thrust me behind him and marched to the drawing room door. My watch chimed again, louder. I clutched it tighter and peered past Matt. Miss Glass sat on the sofa, her hands in her lap, her feet together, the pose as prim and proper as always. Except this time she had a gun pointed at her temple.

Eddie cocked the gun. "Come no closer, Glass, or your dear aunt will pay."

Miss Glass made no sound, not even a whimper. She stared straight ahead, her eyes unfocused and distant. Her mind had folded in the face of danger. It was something of a relief that she was not fully aware of the situation.

Bristow touched his cheek where a bruise bloomed. He stood near Eddie, close enough to be struck by the gun handle. Eddie now ordered him and the rest of the servants back, out of reach.

"All of you, back, back, back! No one comes near me or Miss Glass."

The servants obliged. They were all there, Peter the footman, Mr. and Mrs. Bristow, their daughter, Mrs. Potter the cook, Polly Picket, and even Mary, who must have arrived moments before Eddie. Mrs. Bristow drew the young maids with her, and Mrs. Potter blocked them from Eddie's view with her ample frame. I silently willed Mrs. Bristow to grab a heavy object while she could do so without being seen, but she did not. Perhaps it was for the best. If she attempted to throw something at Eddie but missed, she would become a target. At the moment, he had not killed anyone, but I wasn't convinced he would refrain if he felt threatened.

The only person missing from the scene was Chronos himself. Perhaps he was in hiding.

The presence of the rest of the household rendered our plans inadequate. Matt couldn't overpower Eddie with so many people present. If the gun accidentally went off, the chances of someone getting shot were high. Willie couldn't shoot at Eddie through an open window for the same reason. And using my watch in full view of so many artless would reveal the strength of my magic. Still, it was a risk I would take if necessary.

"You're a coward, Hardacre," Matt growled. "Let the women go and we'll discuss this man to man."

"Where are your friends?" Eddie asked.

"Informing the police that your mother killed Dr. Millroy."

"What!" Eddie exploded. "She's an old woman! Leave her be."

"My aunt is an old woman too." Matt nodded at Miss Glass. "Release her—release everyone—and I'll see what I can do to keep the police away from your mother."

Eddie adjusted his grip on the gun. He shook his head. "I can't set anyone free. Not until I have Chronos."

"She's your mother!" I said. "You have a chance to save her—"

"Be quiet, India. It's too late for my mother. You've seen to that."

Yet another part of our plan shriveled and died. We could not use Nell's safety as leverage. He cared for no one and nothing, only his revenge.

"I won't release anyone until I have Chronos." Eddie pointed his chin at Matt. "Where is he?"

"I told you," Bristow said. "He's gone."

"Glass?" Eddie snapped.

"If Bristow says he's gone, then he's gone," Matt said. "He's not going to lie to you when lives are at stake."

Eddie looked to me. I stared back, not really seeing him as I tried to think. Would Bristow lie in the hope Eddie would merely give up and walk away? Or had Chronos indeed left? If so, where had he gone?

"Where is he, India?" he ground out between gritted teeth.

"I don't know," I said. "I've been out all day."

"You're his granddaughter. He would have told you his plans."

"He did not. He is only my grandfather in the literal sense. It's a mistake to think that a man who walked out on me as a baby would care enough to remain now when his enemies are closing in."

"Enemies." He snorted. "You make it sound as if he is the

victim. *I* am the victim. My mother, my father...both victims. Not Chronos. He killed my father as surely as Millroy did."

"Your father volunteered to participate in their experiment. He knew the risks."

He swung the gun toward me. "He did *not* know the risks!"

My watch chimed loudly but did not jump out of my hand in an attempt to strangle or shock him. Matt shoved me behind him and I could no longer see Eddie.

"Your family had their revenge for the crime committed against your father," Matt said. "Your mother killed Millroy and you've humiliated Chronos's granddaughter. You took India's shop, her livelihood, and you destroyed her trust. What more do you want?"

"I want Chronos dead now that I know he's not."

"If Bristow says he's gone then he's gone. You have to settle for the revenge you've already wreaked on India."

"It's not enough!" Eddie screeched. "I thought it would be, I thought I wanted the shop, but when I learned Chronos still lived... I have to punish him directly. I can't think, can't sleep or work knowing he's out there, free."

"Let the police catch him," Matt said. "I know for a fact they're searching for him."

Eddie snorted, a wet, slimy sound. "The police won't bother. They're in your pocket."

"Let Chronos go then, and your mother will not be arrested. That's fair."

"It is *not* fair! My father's death sent her mad, then after Millroy... She went even madder. She was never the same. She couldn't get work, and with no one to protect her...men took advantage. I spent most of my childhood hungry and in fear, hiding from her latest so-called protector. She thought they'd save her, but she only ended up beaten half to death. Tell me how it's fair that Chronos's granddaughter lived in comfort while his victim's son lived in poverty. Well? Tell me that!"

"How do you know your father's death sent her mad?" Matt asked. "You were too young when it happened. Perhaps she was already mad." He lifted one shoulder. "Considering she had no remorse in committing incest with her brother, she must have already been a little crazed at least."

One of the servants gasped.

"Matt," I whispered. "Don't provoke him."

"Listen to India." I heard the smile in Eddie's voice, even though I couldn't see him past Matt. "She knows me well enough to know I'm capable of taking revenge for a slight against my family."

I tried to muscle my way through to the room, but Matt was having none of it. He continued to block me. "I don't know you very well at all, Eddie." I said. "I never did. But I do know this. You care about your mother enough to send her money and sweets. You still visit her. You don't want her arrested for murdering Dr. Millroy. So end this now or the police *will* be informed."

"Nicely put, India, but I won't leave here until Chronos gives himself up to me. Do you hear that?" he shouted. "Come out, Chronos! I can stay here all night!"

"Please, sir," Mrs. Bristow begged. "Let the girls go. They're frightened."

"Let them all go," Matt said. "I'll stay as long as you like."

"No one leaves," Eddie growled.

I slipped in beside Matt, still standing in the doorway. Eddie focused on the servant women, backed into a corner behind Mrs. Potter. Miss Glass hadn't moved and didn't so much as blink. Bristow and Peter could do nothing, kept at a distance as they were.

"It appears we're at a stalemate," Matt said. "Shall we settle in for the evening?" He put his hands in the air and walked slowly into the room.

Eddie let him take a few steps then ordered him to stop. "Keep your hands where I can see them."

"Do you really think you can outlast all of us? Do you think the police won't storm in here?"

"I can kill a number of you before they get me, or before I tire. India first, of course." He turned the gun on me and my heart plunged. "If I can't have Chronos, then I'll kill his one remaining family member."

I barked out a laugh. "You think he cares about me? A man who has been absent my entire life? A man who let me think he was dead? Hardly."

He frowned. "You truly thought he was dead?"

"Yes. Did you?"

"I recently heard rumors of sightings from other watchmakers. An old fellow swore black and blue he'd seen Gideon Steele. So I began a little investigation and you can probably guess what I discovered. Or rather, what I didn't discover. There was no death recorded for Gideon Steele. I wondered how much you knew and if he'd contacted you, so I watched this house. I saw an old man fitting Chronos's description leave here one day. I called out his name and he didn't turn around but he picked up his pace. It was as good a signal as any that he was, in fact, your grandfather."

Chronos hadn't mentioned that someone recognized him that day. What else hadn't he told us?

"Did *you* attack him the second time he left?" Matt asked.

Eddie simply smiled, all wet lips and gleaming eyes.

"You were looking for him that day you called on me here," I said. "What would you have done if you'd seen him? Chased him and killed him right here in the house?"

Eddie's smile turned hard. "You accuse me of entering your house with false intentions, yet that's precisely what you did to my mother!"

"She was not harmed," I snapped. "Nor was it anyone's intention to hurt her."

"You terrified her. You searched through her belongings and upset her."

"She told you about her American caller, didn't she?" I said. "After we first visited her, she described us to you and you realized Matt and I were investigating Dr. Millroy's death. *That's* how you knew what we were doing. That's why you came here, to encourage us to stop. No wonder you had an odd look on your face when I mentioned the vagrant's name was *Mr.* Wilson. You hoped we'd never learn Wilson was his first name and that he was connected to Nell and you."

"Congratulations for finally working it out. It's not surprising that it took you so long—you are something of a dim wit."

I caught Matt's arm but he had not taken a step forward, as I expected him to. He stood rigid, the muscles in his jaw working. I hoped he was forming a plan because I didn't know how we would get out, short of simply waiting until Eddie fell asleep. Of course, there was a good chance that Eddie would grow tired of waiting for Chronos and shoot me anyway.

I swallowed the bile burning my throat.

"May we open the window for air?" Matt asked. "It's warm in here."

"So one of your gunmen can take a shot at me? Ha! I only *played* the fool, Glass. No windows will be opened, but curtains will be shut. The housekeeper may light one lamp first and the rest after she closes the curtains."

Damnation. What would Willie, Duke and Cyclops do now? What could they do except wait, like us? The drawing room didn't have a hidden passage to the service area, so even if they got into the house via the servants' door, they would not be able to make their way in here and catch Eddie unawares.

Waiting was our only option.

I glanced at Miss Glass and thanked God she was still unaware of our predicament. "May I sit with her?" I asked Eddie.

"No. You may sit where you are, on the floor."

"India will not sit on the floor," Matt growled.

"I prefer to remain standing for now," I said.

Eddie snorted. "You always were stubborn."

I bit my tongue. Throwing out retorts would not help our situation. I watched as Mrs. Bristow closed the curtains and lit two more lamps. She then returned to the girls, clutching them to her in matronly support. I was glad to see she had already accepted Mary into the fold. It was a bright moment in the otherwise dark situation.

"What's in your hand?" Eddie's voice cut rudely through my thoughts.

I uncurled my fingers to show him. "Just my watch. I find it a comfort to hold."

"A watch? A comfort? God, India, I knew you were sentimental, but that's absurd. It's just metal parts even if you have put your magic into it."

One of the servants drew in a sharp breath. I felt several gazes fall on me.

"Speaking of watches." A slow smile crept across Eddie's lips. "Glass, your watch please."

Matt pulled out his regular timepiece, not the magical one. He tossed it to Eddie. Eddie dropped it onto the rug and ground it beneath his heel.

"That cost me a pretty fortune," Matt said.

"I know how much it's worth. I sell others just like it in *my* shop." Eddie shot me a slick smile.

Biting my tongue almost wasn't enough to hold me back from reminding him that the shop belonged to my grandfather. I swallowed the drop of blood that filled my mouth and managed to keep my silence.

Eddie waved his hand at Matt. "Your other watch, please,

Mr. Glass. Your magic one." He laughed. "You ought to see the looks on both your faces. Yes, I know about the second watch. Hand it to me."

"There is no other watch," I said quickly. Perhaps too quickly, too vehemently.

"Don't try to talk your way out of this one. I know you have a second watch and that it's special to you. Your friend, a particular sheriff, called upon me one day, asking questions about the two of you. He told me all about it."

"So you know it brings me luck?" Matt said. "At cards, the horses…"

"Don't lie to me. I know it keeps you alive, Glass. I also know it must be slowing down. Why else are you looking for Dr. Millroy's killer? I admit it took us both a little time and much discussion, but we worked it out. I see you found the doctor's diary." He nodded at the book protruding from Matt's jacket pocket. "All the trouble you went to yet it won't help you. That spell doesn't work, remember? It killed my father. Whatever spell Millroy, or some other doctor magician used on your watch, is lost. Yes, I've read the pertinent parts of the diary and know what he and Chronos tried to achieve. It doesn't say it in so many words, but it wasn't too hard to guess once you put the pieces I knew together with the pieces Payne had witnessed with his own eyes. What makes you think you can succeed with *that* spell where it failed for Millroy? And anyway, you don't know a doctor magician. It could take years to find one."

So he did not know about Millroy's son or that the spell in the diary was correct; it just needed to be spoken with the proper accent and inflection to make it work. Thank God or he would have destroyed the diary, or hidden it better.

"Hand the watch over," Eddie said. "I want to see it."

Matt stretched his arms wide. "Come and take it."

"Nice try, Glass. Throw the watch to me or I shoot India."

"You're going to shoot her anyway, because Chronos isn't

here. If he was, he would have shown himself by now. You shoot India and I'll kill you."

"Not before I turn the gun on you. You're not fast enough."

"Oh, I'm fast enough." That calmly angry tone that was never far from Matt's voice lately was back, darker than ever. "The question is, are you?"

Eddie's smile vanished. "Throw me the bloody watch."

Matt slowly opened his jacket then his waistcoat and unbuttoned the secret pocket where he hid his magic watch. Surely he wouldn't let Eddie have it. He would crush it too!

"Don't, Matt," I said.

He responded by throwing the watch. It sailed through the air in an arc and Eddie took his eyes off us long enough to catch it. The instant of his distraction wasn't enough for Matt or anyone else to tackle him. He was simply too far away.

"Thank you." Eddie dropped the watch onto the carpet with a triumphant smirk. "Say goodbye to your loved ones, Glass. Then let's see how long it takes for you to die."

He lifted his foot over the watch and brought his heel down.

CHAPTER 18

"*S*top!" The command was hardly out of my mouth when I lunged at Eddie.

Matt, however, was faster. He threw himself forward and reached Eddie before me.

The gun went off, the deafening boom filling the room, a nightmarish sound that seemed to go on forever. It filled my head and vibrated through my body. It completely drowned out the rapid chimes of my watch but not the screams.

So many screams and shouts.

None came from Matt. His body went limp, crushing Eddie beneath him. One of the screams came from Eddie.

I did not waste a single moment. Matt's momentum had sent Eddie backward, removing his foot from its dangerous position above the watch. It nestled in the rug, whole and untouched. Letting my own watch go, I snatched his up, too afraid to lose precious time in being thankful for its unbroken state. I removed Matt's glove from his right hand, opened the watch case, and tucked it into his palm.

And that's when I noticed the blood. It seeped through his clothing, covering Eddie beneath him. Eddie tried to shove

Matt off, pushing at me as he did so and knocking Matt's watch out from between our joined hands.

"If you move again, I'll kill you," I snarled at Eddie. I plucked up the watch and once again pressed it to Matt's hand. *Please, don't die.*

He'd told me after the coach accident in which he'd been brought back to full health by his watch that it couldn't save him if he stopped breathing altogether or if he lost too much blood. The danger of that happening now was high. There was so much of it…

The magic began its work. The veins in his hand glowed, and I watched as the glow disappeared beneath his sleeve.

"God's balls, what the bleeding hell is that?" Eddie's high pitched shout had a strong Cockney accent that I'd never heard from his lips before. He'd finally shed the last layer of his mask, but it had taken a shock on a monumental scale to do it. "Jesus, get him off me! Get him off!" He tried to wriggle out from beneath Matt, and I struggled to keep the magic watch in place. If he didn't lie still, I would lose my grip.

I balled my free hand into a fist and smashed it into Eddie's jaw. His head hit the floor. His eyes rolled up and closed. The room fell blessedly silent, allowing me to listen.

I leaned closer to Matt, my ear to his lips. He breathed. Thank God, he still breathed, albeit shallowly. But his blood was everywhere, pooling on the carpet, over Eddie…

It seemed to take an interminably long time for the magic to reach Matt's face. Time in which I became acutely aware of the others watching us.

"Is he…" It was Willie, kneeling beside me. She, Duke and Cyclops must have rushed inside when they heard the gunshot.

Behind her, Miss Glass watched, her hand clasping her throat, her eyes huge. She did not speak, but she was aware of her surroundings now, of that I was sure. I became even more sure when she ordered the servants out.

They exited the room just as Matt's fingers twitched. He opened his eyes and his gaze fell on me. I tried not to cry. I really did try very hard. But it was hopeless. The tears ran down my cheeks unchecked.

Willie was the first to hug me, followed by Duke and Cyclops who then helped Matt to sit up.

Willie pointed her gun at Eddie, also regaining consciousness. "Shall I shoot him?" she said. "He shot you, so it's only right."

"Yes," Miss Glass said. "I, for one, would be happy if you shot him. I'll even tell the police I did it in self-defense. They won't arrest me."

I lay a hand on Willie's arm, just in case she thought Miss Glass's assurance gave her free rein to do as she pleased. She snatched up Eddie's gun and stepped back. She did not holster her weapon.

"Wh—what happened?" Eddie sat up unassisted, rubbing his jaw.

"India punched you," Miss Glass said, crossing her arms. "And you thoroughly deserved it."

Matt smiled weakly. "Good for you, India."

Willie patted my shoulder. "Feel better?"

"Somewhat," I said.

"You know what'll make you feel better?"

"Tea? Sherry?"

"Shooting him." She flipped her gun around and held it handle-out to me. "Go on. Miss Glass'll take the blame."

Eddie put his hands in the air. They were covered in Matt's blood. "Blimey, India, you won't, will you? You and me got too much history."

"We have no history," I said. "You're a different person to the one I thought I knew." I turned my back on him. There was nothing more to say, no words that could express how much I loathed him.

Matt offered up a small smile and touched his fingers to

mine. He still sat on the floor, his face deathly pale except for the dark smudges beneath heavy-lidded eyes. He needed to rest.

He clasped Cyclops's offered hand and stood. Blood smeared down the front of his clothes, obscuring the hole the bullet made. I dearly wanted to inspect the wound, just so that I could see for myself that the watch had indeed worked its magic, but there were too many people in the room.

"Gawd almighty," Eddie murmured shakily. "You're... you're immortal."

"Take him to Scotland Yard," Matt said, tucking his magic watch back inside his waistcoat. "Tell Inspector Brockwell how Jack Sweet, also known as Eddie Hardacre, duped India and her father then tried to win India back. Having none of it, India refused him."

Eddie snorted. "They won't believe *that*."

"Upset at the rejection, Eddie took the household hostage in the hope that would force her to change her mind."

Cyclops grabbed one of Eddie's arms and Duke the other. They marched him out of the room, his feet hardly touching the floor.

"Put me down, you lumps of shite!" he growled.

"I'll go too and keep him in line," Willie said with glee. "I ain't going to let him speak to my friends like that."

"Be sure to hit him if he becomes too crass," Miss Glass said.

Willie patted the older woman's shoulder as she passed. "I like you more and more, Letty."

"It's Miss Glass to you."

Once they were gone, Matt took his aunt's hand. "Are you all right?" he asked.

She drew in a deep breath and let it out slowly. It was remarkably steady considering her ordeal. "I am now. I, I don't seem to recall very much before you got..." She went to touch his chest but pulled back.

"There's not much to tell," Matt said. "He wanted Chronos and was prepared to keep us all hostage until he got him. By the way, is he really gone?"

She nodded. "He left a note for India."

I blinked owlishly back at her, trying to take it in. Chronos gone? But I'd only just met him.

"India?" Matt frowned at me.

"I'm all right." It was the truth, and I smiled to reassure him. It wobbled a little, which was odd because I was completely unconcerned by the news. I'd never had a grandfather so his leaving didn't matter.

"I'll check on the servants," Matt said. "When I come back, we'll talk."

"Certainly not." Miss Glass patted his cheek. "I'll speak to the servants while you bathe and change. Do not sit on anything until you're clean. Is that understood?"

Matt sketched a small bow. "Yes, ma'am."

"Don't mock me." He lightly kissed her forehead and she smiled up at him. "You are all right, aren't you, Matthew?"

He nodded. "Completely unharmed."

"Then go and clean up before dinner."

I went to follow her out but Matt caught my arm. "Don't run off yet."

"I'm not running off." It was precisely what I was doing. Being alone with Matt at such an emotional time would play havoc on my nerves. We'd been alone all of three seconds already and my heart flipped wildly in my chest.

"You're avoiding me," he murmured in my ear. "And I know why."

He couldn't possibly read my mind that well. On the other hand, he often knew what I was thinking. I gulped, not ready for this discussion now.

"You don't want me to admonish you," he said.

Oh. Er... "Admonish me? For what?"

"You were about to tackle Hardacre on your own when he

went to crush my watch. What did you plan to do? He had a gun, for Christ's sake."

"I...I don't know. I wasn't thinking, just reacting."

"He would have shot you before you could reach him."

"My watch would have saved me."

"Against a bullet?" He drew in an unsteady breath and shook his head. "Don't do anything so foolish again."

"You did something equally foolish, Matt. You may have been counting on your watch saving your life, but how could you know you wouldn't bleed out before the magic worked?"

"There was no other option."

He was right, of course. My shattered nerves simply needed to get it off my chest.

"You're going to cry, aren't you?" he said gently.

"No."

But his lopsided smile and warm eyes made a liar of me. Fresh tears welled. Happy tears. He was alive. We all were. Nothing else mattered.

He went to wipe away my tears with his thumb but noticed the blood on his fingers. "I would offer you my handkerchief but it's not in a fit state for a lady."

"*You* are not in a fit state for anyone," I said, attempting lightness.

He opened his jacket and waistcoat, and undid his shirt. I ought to look away but if he didn't mind revealing himself to me, then surely it was perfectly all right for me to look. After all, I'd seen his chest before so I wouldn't be overwhelmed by the sight.

Overwhelmed I was not. But mesmerized, yes. I couldn't take my gaze off the smoothness of his skin stretched over strapping muscle, the smattering of hair only enhancing his masculine physique. My gaze dipped lower to the drying blood and the wound inflicted by the bullet at his stomach. It had already closed over, leaving only a small scar.

"It will vanish almost entirely in time," he said.

"Yes." My voice was thick with wonder and emotions I couldn't express for fear of opening the flood gates. "The bullet?" I said, concentrating on practical matters.

"It'll remain in me, I suppose. Dr. Parsons took out the last one, but it wasn't necessary."

I nodded and folded my arms lest I reach out and touch the scar. "You'd better do as your aunt suggests and bathe." I turned to go but he once again stopped me.

"India," he purred.

I blinked at him when he did not go on. Should I encourage him to say what he wanted to say? Or would that also open the floodgates?

"I want you to know that Eddie is wrong," he said. "Don't listen to him."

"I don't."

"You're clever and kind and beyond lovely."

"Thank you, Matt," I managed to say despite my welling emotions.

"I'm not just saying that to make you feel better. Ask any man. Christ, ask Barratt, if you like." He shook his head. "Eddie doesn't see you for your worth because there's something wrong with him. At first I thought him a misogynist, but I don't think that's the entire explanation. There is a fundamental flaw in him as a human, something that stops him having empathy for others. You cannot put any stock in what someone like that says."

My eyes burned, and once again my tears hovered on the brink. I could only manage a nod to show him I agreed with everything he said. Eddie's words did not affect me. How could I believe I was any of the things he called me when Matt believed the opposite?

"Go and read your letter from Chronos in private, and I'll see you soon." He kissed my cheek, somewhat shyly. "And thank you for saving my life. Again. I'm beginning to think I cannot live without you."

I watched him leave the drawing room, his shoulders a little rounded from exhaustion but his head up. He didn't look back and so did not see my tears flowing silently and freely.

* * *

"HE LEFT LONDON ALTOGETHER," I said as we sat at the dining table the following morning. We were all there except for Miss Glass, who chose to breakfast in her rooms. With the door shut, and Bristow told to keep the servants away, we could talk without being overheard.

"But not the country?" Matt asked.

"Just London. He did not mention where he was going or what he was doing. He might be looking for Dr. Millroy's illegitimate son or he might have given up."

"What else did his letter say?" Willie asked from the sideboard where she was collecting more bacon.

"You don't need to answer her, India," Duke said with a glare for Willie.

"She does if it's relevant," Willie shot back.

"It's her private letter!"

"Ain't nothing private 'round here."

"Is that so?" Duke pointed a butter knife at her. "Then why you being all secretive? Why are you always at the hospital lately when you ain't sick?"

"We ain't discussing me." She sat at the table directly opposite him. I didn't think it a safe place to sit, considering they were within kicking distance of each other. "We're discussing Chronos."

"He told me he taught me everything about my magic that he could," I said before they continued their argument. "He suspects that the spell in Dr. Millroy's diary, combined with the one he taught me, will fix Matt's watch when spoken by a doctor and timepiece magician at the same moment." Chronos had mentioned the problem of the medical spell's pronunciation—how Dr. Millroy had got it wrong but Dr. Parsons got it right. I didn't remind them that an untrained medical magician wouldn't know the right way when reading it.

"We're half way there," Cyclops said, stabbing at a sausage with his fork. "And we know where to start looking for Millroy's son."

"Not yet," Matt said. "After tonight, hopefully."

After yesterday's events, he'd decided to postpone breaking into Lady Buckland's house, but only by one night.

Chronos had written more in his parting letter to me. Aside from mentioning his fear of being caught by the guild or the police, he went on to apologize for abandoning my family when I was a baby. It was impossible to tell whether it was sincere but I appreciated it nevertheless. He added that he regretted leaving again now, and wished he'd had more time to get to know me, although he could tell from our short time together that I was "smart, capable and fierce." Glowing praise indeed, which he then spoiled by telling me that my morals were too strong and would get in the way of my happiness. In case there was any doubt what he was referring to, he told me not to leave it too late to secure Matt in marriage "or any other manner possible." If I did, there was a very real danger that he would give up and another woman would catch his eye, and my prospects for a comfortable life would diminish. My principles would not keep me warm and fed, Chronos wrote.

I received another letter after breakfast, this one from Patience Glass. It was more than an answer to the question I'd asked about her indiscretion. Not only did she admit it, but she went on to beg me to find Sheriff Payne and silence him. It took me several re-reads and a full five minutes to get over the shock. Patience was not the innocent I believed her to be. Of the three Glass sisters, she wasn't the one I expected to have had a secret dalliance.

"That is the exact phrase she used," I said to Matt when I showed him the letter in his study. "'Silence him.'"

"Her definition of silencing someone is unlikely to be the same as mine," he said as he read. "She must have spoken to Hope."

"And it seems Hope has told her everything, or at least the part about Payne blackmailing her. Poor Patience."

"Poor Patience indeed. I'd happily silence Payne if I knew where to find him."

I sat heavily on the chair and rubbed my aching forehead. "I'll write to her and encourage her to talk to Lord Cox. It would be better coming from her than a stranger or via the gossips."

"You know Englishmen better than I," he said. "Do you think Cox would end their engagement over this?"

"He might, particularly if he's marrying her because her reputation is faultless."

"And I thought love mattered above all else in a marriage," he muttered.

"Love doesn't come into the equation with the nobility."

"Then couples only have themselves to blame when they come to despise one another." Clearly he didn't count himself among the nobility.

He skirted the desk and perched on the edge near me. "India," he began. "A letter from my lawyer arrived today asking for your instructions about the Willesden cottage. A newlywed couple have expressed interest in leasing it."

"Oh." I'd almost forgotten about the cottage and the papers waiting for me to sign. I was no longer sure if moving into it and commuting to Mayfair was a good idea. Imagine if I hadn't been present to place the watch in Matt's hand? And then there was the extra time it would take for me to travel to and fro. Some days we couldn't afford to waste precious minutes.

"What would you like to do?" he asked, his voice bland,

not giving away his thoughts. "Stay here and lease it, or move there?" He gripped the desk on either side of him, and tapped the underside of the surface with one twitchy finger.

"I don't want to move until I know your watch is fixed. When Dr. Millroy's son is found, and we've infused our magic into the watch, I'll move out."

His finger stopped tapping. His gaze narrowed. "There'll be no need to move then. I plan on giving you every reason to stay…as my wife."

My heart stopped dead in my chest. *No, not now.* I wasn't ready for this conversation or the argument that would follow when I explained that I cared too deeply about him and his aunt to bring him down to my level. I looked away because the confusion in his eyes clawed at my heart.

"India?"

I shook my head and stood. He caught my wrist and when I still wouldn't look at him, he repeated my name, only gruffer.

"Something is bothering you, and I want to know what," he said. "Is it because you don't think I'll get better?" When I didn't respond, he went on. "Are you worried I'll want to return to America? Because I don't care where I live."

"Let me go, Matt."

"Is it the Johnson side of my family? I know they're a little frightening, but they won't bother to come here." He paused. "India, look at me. Talk to me."

Bristow cleared his throat from the doorway. I'd left the door open upon my entry to stop Matt broaching topics of a personal nature. I should have known the risk of being overheard wouldn't bother him.

"Yes, Bristow?" I said before Matt could dismiss him.

"Detective Inspector Brockwell is here to see you both," the butler said. "He's waiting in the drawing room."

"Thank you." I pulled free of Matt's grip and walked quickly to join Bristow.

"I took the liberty of asking Peter to bring in tea," the butler said.

"Thank you. Is he all right after yesterday's excitement?"

"I think he rather enjoyed it, miss."

I attempted a smile. "And the other servants?"

"Mr. Glass has promised to increase our wages to compensate for our trouble." He glanced behind us, but Matt had not followed. "Mrs. Bristow is anxious on account of our daughter."

"I'm sure she is. And if anyone wishes to leave, Mr. Glass will understand."

"Thank you, miss."

I reached the drawing room well before Matt and discussed the weather with the inspector until he arrived. He showed no signs that our conversation played on his mind. He was all smiles for Brockwell.

Peter brought in the tea then silently retreated, closing the door behind him.

"What can we do for you, Inspector?" Matt asked as I poured.

Brockwell accepted the teacup and sipped then sipped again. The delaying tactic was one he employed well and agitated me beyond measure. But Matt remained calm, a benign smile plastered on his lips. He let the silence stretch.

"Two things," Brockwell finally said. "I want to know what happened here yesterday evening that led to the arrest of Eddie Hardacre, also known as Jack Sweet."

"I believe my cousin and friends already informed you," Matt said. "I have nothing more to add."

"The thing is, Mr. Hardacre is saying it's all a lie and he was in fact here looking for a man who killed his father, Wilson Sweet."

"His father or his uncle?" I said, rather devilishly.

Brockwell raised his brows. "Father, I believe. What does his uncle have to do with anything?"

I handed him a teacup and saucer. "You ought to ask him that. Or his mother."

"So you deny that Gideon Steele, also known as Chronos and perhaps William Wordsworth, lives here?"

"He did," Matt said, "but we did not know his connection to any murder until Mr. Hardacre accused him last night. I wouldn't believe him if I were you, sir. He's a liar."

"It's not just him. Mr. Abercrombie accuses Miss Steele's grandfather of murder too. Are you saying a pillar of the community is also lying?"

"The only thing Abercrombie is a pillar of is his own over-inflated self-worth. Whether Mr. Steele is guilty of any crime is open for debate, but the point is, he's not here and we don't know where he is."

Brockwell looked to me. "Did he leave you a departing message?"

"Yes."

"May I see it?"

"No, you may not."

He sipped. Naturally it took longer than an ordinary sip. Naturally it made my blood boil listening to him slurp.

"Matt is correct," I said crisply. "We don't know where my grandfather went and I say good riddance. He brought nothing but trouble to our door. We've had enough excitement. We only wish to live quiet lives now."

Brockwell considered this with a tilt of his head to the side. "Why did you lie at the hospital and say the man you collected was named William Wordsworth?"

"Because Abercrombie and Hardacre would have hounded Mr. Steele if they learned he was here," Matt said. "It was easier to lie than to face them. The thing is, Inspector, both those men want revenge upon India and her family. They cannot be trusted. They'll accuse Mr. Steele of anything if it means upsetting her."

Brockwell set his teacup and saucer on the table. "Thank you for the tea."

He was leaving already? He believed us? I glanced at Matt but he did not look my way.

Brockwell got to his feet and looked around. "Where is your rug?"

"Pardon?" I blurted out.

"Last time I was here there was a carpet on the floor. It's gone."

"I spilled tea on it," Matt said. "The housekeeper took it away to clean it."

"And the bullet?"

Oh hell. He *knew*. Eddie must have told him he'd fired his weapon. But had he told Brockwell that the bullet hit Matt? I stared into my teacup, not daring to look at Brockwell for fear of giving myself away.

"What bullet?" Matt asked.

"Hardacre claims he shot you."

Matt stood and stretched his arms out. "As you can see, I haven't been shot. Hardacre is madder than we thought if he says that."

"He says the bullet injured you but you recovered thanks to your magic watch."

Matt chuckled. "He's been reading that article. It seems everyone in London is obsessed with the notion of magic lately. I can assure you, Inspector, no magic was performed here last night. Don't you think if magic could cure bullet wounds the world would have known about it before now?"

"I would have thought so." Brockwell didn't so much as smile. He didn't find the thought amusing or absurd.

"Do you believe in magic, Inspector?" I asked, genuinely curious.

"No, Miss Steele, I do not."

"I didn't think so. I may not be all that good at judging character but I had you pegged as a very practical minded man who needed solid evidence presented before he believed the fantastic."

Of all things, that coaxed a smile from him. "Thank you, Miss Steele. That is one of the nicest things anyone has ever said to me. Now, if you'll excuse me, I'll be on my way."

"Certainly," Matt said, indicating Brockwell should walk ahead of him. "What will happen to Hardacre now?"

"He'll go to trial but his crime is not a capital offence. He'll serve time in jail. It's likely you'll be called as witnesses."

"Of course."

Brockwell accepted his hat from Peter at the door. "Mind you, be careful now, sir, miss. You two seem to attract more than your fair share of dangerous activity." He nodded in farewell and headed out the door into the rain.

I quickly turned to go, determined to avoid Matt. I did not succeed.

"India!" he called.

"I have to see to Miss Glass," I said from the staircase. "She requested I go for a walk with her."

"It's raining."

"Then we'll play cards."

I suddenly found him alongside me on the staircase. "You can't avoid me forever," he said quietly. When I didn't respond, he added, "I *will* find out why you won't accept me. I can read you like a book. It's only a matter of time before I reach the last page and all is revealed."

I lifted my skirts and ran up the stairs. I dared to glance back when I reached the landing, only to see him still standing where I left him, his hand on the balustrade, his gaze fixed on me. He opened his mouth to say something but closed it again. Without another word, he turned and trotted back down the steps.

THE END

Now Available:
THE CONVENT'S SECRET
The 5th Glass and Steele novel by C.J. Archer.

FREE Glass and Steele short story
Sign up to C.J.'s newsletter through her website to be notified when she releases the next Glass and Steele novel. Subscribers also receive a FREE Glass and Steele short story.

GET A FREE SHORT STORY

I wrote a short story for the Glass and Steele series that is set before THE WATCHMAKER'S DAUGHTER. Titled THE TRAITOR'S GAMBLE it features Matt and his friends in the Wild West town of Broken Creek. It contains spoilers from THE WATCHMAKER'S DAUGHTER, so you must read that first. The best part is, the short story is FREE, but only to my newsletter subscribers. So subscribe now via my website if you haven't already.

A MESSAGE FROM THE AUTHOR

I hope you enjoyed reading THE MAGICIAN'S DIARY as much as I enjoyed writing it. As an independent author, getting the word out about my book is vital to its success, so if you liked this book please consider telling your friends and writing a review at the store where you purchased it. If you would like to be contacted when I release a new book, subscribe to my newsletter at http://cjarcher.com/contact-cj/newsletter/. You will only be contacted when I have a new book out.

ALSO BY C.J. ARCHER

SERIES WITH 2 OR MORE BOOKS

After The Rift

Glass and Steele

The Ministry of Curiosities Series

The Emily Chambers Spirit Medium Trilogy

The 1st Freak House Trilogy

The 2nd Freak House Trilogy

The 3rd Freak House Trilogy

The Assassins Guild Series

Lord Hawkesbury's Players Series

Witch Born

SINGLE TITLES NOT IN A SERIES

Courting His Countess

Surrender

Redemption

The Mercenary's Price

ABOUT THE AUTHOR

C.J. Archer has loved history and books for as long as she can remember and feels fortunate that she found a way to combine the two. She spent her early childhood in the dramatic beauty of outback Queensland, Australia, but now lives in suburban Melbourne with her husband, two children and a mischievous black & white cat named Coco.

Subscribe to C.J.'s newsletter through her website to be notified when she releases a new book, as well as get access to exclusive content and subscriber-only giveaways. Her website also contains up to date details on all her books: http://cjarcher.com She loves to hear from readers. You can contact her through email cj@cjarcher.com or follow her on social media to get the latest updates on her books:

Made in the USA
Monee, IL
03 March 2020

22649847R00189